PASSION'S TOUCH

"I must go," he whispered hoarsely.

"Why?" she purred in protest, rubbing her cheek against his shoulder, loving the feel, the aroma of him, all around her.

"Because, dear lady, I fear you have made a gentleman of me."

"Why must you be a gentleman tonight?" she murmured in weak protest.

"Because, my love," he said, his voice husky with bridled desire. "I"—he paused, kissing her temple and her eyes and her earlobes—"I don't remember why."

He gave up finally, finding her lips again. His mouth was a wellspring of new and fanciful pleasures, and the small sound that issued from his throat played upon the strings of her heart, which he had so finely tuned.

Her hands found his hips, and she wanted to reach around to his buttocks to pull him closer again, but she dared not. It was too bold, too deliciously forbidden....

D1472402

Touched By Moonlight

Carole Howey

LEISURE BOOKS **NEW YORK CITY**

For Slavica and Anjelo—Thanks, Mom and Dad

A LEISURE BOOK®

August 1995

Published by

Dorchester Publishing Co., Inc.
276 Fifth Avenue
New York, NY 10001

Printed in the United States of America.

Acknowledgments

This book was inspired by our family's favorite seashore resort, Ocean City, New Jersey, and by a book titled *Peck's Beach: A Pictorial History Of Ocean City, New Jersey* by Tom Cain, published by Down The Shore Publishing, Harvey Cedars, New Jersey (ISBN 0-945582-04-8).

I would also like to send a virtual magnum of Moet in the direction of Cynthia King, who graciously handed me a dustpan.

Touched By Moonlight

Chapter One

"Be my wife." The Count's sapphire eyes seemed to pierce Celeste's very soul. "I don't care that it means the end of a dynasty! I must have you, Celeste. I adore you!"

Celeste trembled, the flesh of her hand burning where he held it in his own.

"Yes, my darling," she answered swiftly, before her sense could protest. She loved him. She knew that, now. She loved him in the face of the myriad reasons why she should not. "Yes, Hugo," she murmured again, the peace of her accession filling the void in her heart. "I will marry you."

Philipa Braedon typed the last punctuation mark and leaned back in the swivel armchair until its joints creaked, rubbing her eyes with her balled fists. Drivel, she thought, drying her cheeks with her Irish lace handkerchief. Utter drivel. And I love it so! Satisfied by the happy denouement of her latest opus, she surveyed the last sentences with the paper still in the platen. Count Hugo, the rogue, had been redeemed by his pure love for the innocent Celeste, but not before enjoying a series of scandalous escapades with a variety of women whose life-styles would not bear close inspection by a critical Victorian society. But that very society would devour Emma Hunt's *The Calumnious Count* with the same rapacious enthusiasm as it had his predecessors, now too numerous for Philipa to recall.

A quiet knock retrieved her fertile imagination from the courts of seventeenth-century France to the Braedon study of twentieth-century New Jersey. She felt the chignon of her nut-brown hair to be sure it was still in place. It required but another moment for her to gather her wits and to reply to the intrusion in a collected manner.

"Mrs. Tavistock is here for tea, Miss Braedon," Arliss, the new maid, informed her in her anemic and timid voice.

Philipa sighed, stretching her arms over her head to work out the crick that had magically formed in her neck. Was the sudden feeling of tension caused by Arliss? Esmaralda Tavistock? No, probably just the result of two hours of laboring over her typewriter. Arliss was trying, at times, and Lord only knew that Esmaralda could be wearying, as well, but this was an honest crick, brought about by the honest labor of an artist at work, over which she need feel no excessive guilt.

"I hope you haven't left her standing in the foyer, Arliss." Philipa tried not to sound too scolding. The day before, the pretty, fragile-looking thing had left Mrs. Waverly waiting on the porch without offering her so much as a glass of lemonade and then had forgotten to call Philipa from the study. Mrs. Waverly had not been pleased, as it was warm and her lumbago was acting up.

"She has, Philly, but I followed her back here. I simply couldn't wait to tell you—"

Esmaralda Tavistock, in her typical dramatic fashion, flung open both doors of Philipa's heretofore sacrosanct study. Philipa was on her feet, both stunned by her friend's bold entrance and vexed by her own forgetfulness in having neglected to lock herself in.

"Essie! Whatever in the world—"

In haste, Philipa gathered her papers and stacked them haphazardly upon the desk, hoping to conceal both evidence of her scandalous writing and of her discomfiture at this unexpected intrusion. Of all people, it would not do for Esmaralda Tavistock to discover her shameful, secret avocation.

But Essie was not looking at Philipa. Not in a measuring way, in any case. Blessedly, Essie was not a measuring individual, except in the most traditional sense; that is, Essie's measurements were limited to determining the effect of external events upon her own sphere. Her pretty, if ordinary, features were rapt with excitement, as they usually were when she had news to impart. Her large brown eyes were made even larger by the expression.

"I have just come from luncheon with Charles," she puffed, referring to her banker husband of some four years. "And guess what he has told me!"

Philipa pretended to be interested, although she knew from experience that Charles Tavistock was as dull as his ledgers and accounts and seldom had anything to say which was of the remotest interest to anyone except his devoted young wife. She stuffed the last sheaf of papers into the top drawer of her desk. They crinkled in protest as she slammed the drawer closed with her bustle.

"What?" she asked, breathless with relief at having concealed the evidence of her literary transgression.

"Terence Gavilan is coming to Braedon's Beach!"

Philipa stared hard at her friend, pondering the meaning of the news that Essie found so intriguing. The name meant nothing to her, although, judging by Essie's flushed and beaming smile, it seemed that it should.

"Terence Gavilan," Philipa repeated, hoping that utterance of the name would kindle some recognition within her. It did not.

Essie was not deceived.

"Oh, Philly! You can't mean that you don't know the name of Terence Gavilan!"

Philipa shrugged and sank her tall figure into the easy chair across from her desk.

"No, I don't," she admitted, aware that she really didn't

care, either. "But judging by your delight, Terence Gavilan at least is not a dreaded epidemic of some sort, which would be an improvement over Charles's last revelation."

Charles Tavistock had predicted, with distressing accuracy, the devastation wrought by a hurricane two seasons before, which had left much of the island in rubble.

Essie laughed, that bell-like, girlish giggle that had not changed since their childhood.

"Philipa Braedon, can you be so steeped in your scholarly pursuits that you don't recognize the name of Terence Gavilan?" Essie chided her, lowering herself into Philipa's swivel chair before her desk, turning it to face the center of the room.

Essie, like all of Philipa's friends and acquaintances, believed that her writing was an esoteric analysis of obscure works of classical literature, of interest to no one except other academics such as herself.

"You are too sheltered, that's certain," Essie was going on. Essie's formal education had ended, like that of most other genteel ladies of her station, with two years at a finishing school, culminating in a prosperous marriage. "I've said so, many times, to Charles. In fact, I insist that you come this Saturday. You and Elliot. I'll have a garden party, and—"

"Essie?" Philipa politely interrupted her rambling friend, crossing her right knee over her left and clutching it with both hands.

Essie was startled.

"What?"

"Terence Gavilan?" Philipa prodded, hoping to reroute Essie's runaway train of thought.

"Oh! Of course. How could I have forgotten? Well." She settled in, adjusting the bustle of the pale pink chintz afternoon confection she was wearing. She leaned her elbow on the desk behind her, in front of the typewriter. Philipa looked up and realized at once, to her mortification, that Count Hugo and his darling Celeste were still trysting there for all the world, or at least for Essie Tavistock, which was the same thing, to see.

"Terence Gavilan," Essie was going on, unaware of the lovers carrying on behind her, "is an empire builder, on the scale of J. Pierpont Morgan and John Jacob Astor. Some even say that he was the genius behind Coney Island and that he made Atlantic City what it is today.''

Even in her distressed state, Philipa managed a small, lady-like sound of disgust.

''And what is Atlantic City today but a cheap, tawdry little tourist town where day excursionists crowd the jitneys and expectorate on the promenade?'' she exclaimed, watching her friend for any sign that she might turn around and find the page in the typewriter. All she could hope was to keep Essie's mind on another topic, and Terence Gavilan was as good as any.

Essie sent her a reproving look, trying, Philipa was sure, to look mature, and succeeding, despite her twenty-two years, only in looking like a small, impish child dressed up in her mother's finery.

''Philipa, you are quite wrong. Charles took me to Atlantic City only last month, where we dined at the Marlborough-Blenheim, and I assure you that it was a gentrified establishment. Except...''

She paused, fidgeting in her seat. Philipa held her breath, wondering how she would explain the paragraphs in the typewriter should Essie turn her head and notice them.

''Except what?'' Philipa prompted, keeping her features composed, despite her agitation over Essie's proximity to the lovers in her typewriter platen.

Essie's thin lips, enlarged by the cunning application of a pale rouge, pursed together, and her eyes stared downward at the fading Aubusson carpet at her feet.

''There are arcades on the Promenade now,'' she allowed thoughtfully, ''where there are Nickelodeons and penny-pitches. And a carousel with a real calliope on Steel Pier, right near the diving horses. There is a funny old man who will guess your weight for a penny. And fortune tellers, and even a hall of mirrors... I so wanted to try it, but Charles can be such a stick when he chooses. They say that people are getting rich in Atlantic City, thanks to Terence Gavilan. Of course, he is getting richer than anyone.''

Philipa uncrossed her legs and sat up again, waving her hand in annoyance.

"I wish you would not talk of money as though it gave credibility to the basest rogue, Essie," she snapped, her impatience largely due, she knew, to the page she had so carelessly left in view. "You were not reared that way, any more than I was. Essie, let's go into the parlor for our tea. I'm sure it's much cooler there."

Esmaralda looked hurt at her friend's assessment of her character and apparently was in no hurry to change the subject.

"I don't admire the money so much as I admire the way a man goes about getting it," she sniffed, puffing out her full bosom like a pouter pigeon. "And one has to admire the way Mr. Gavilan has built his empire from the ruins left by his father."

"Does one, indeed?" Philipa interjected, monitoring Essie's continued proximity to her manuscript. "Is it admirable to destroy established family communities for the sake of Mammon?"

Arliss entered the room, struggling with the baroque tea service which had been Great-Grandmother Braedon's wedding gift to Philipa's mother. The girl, perhaps seventeen, sidled into the room with the heavy tray and no particular grace. Philipa bit her lip to prevent herself from castigating her for bringing the tea into the study. Now she would be forced to entertain Essie where they were. Arliss did put the tray down on the tea table near the window, however. She withdrew at once, glad, it seemed, to have escaped from Philipa's presence without rebuke.

Philipa masked her relief as she conducted her friend away from the desk to the divan in the shady window.

"Oh, lemon cakes! How I adore them! Philipa, you must persuade Mrs. Grant to share her recipe with me." Thus was Esmaralda distracted from all other matters. Philipa generously conceded the lemon cakes to her friend, as she preferred the chocolate ones. There was no further mention of Terence Gavilan and destroyed communities until all traces of both cakes had been completely demolished. Thankfully, Philipa reflected, wiping the last remaining crumb from her lips with the corner of her napkin, that was another characteristic which had remained untouched during her lifelong relationship with Essie: They could unabashedly make gluttons of themselves in one another's company.

"Charles says that Mr. Gavilan means to add Braedon's Beach to his conquests," Esmaralda remarked, eyeing the empty tray with regret. "In fact, he's going to present his preliminary plans to a meeting of the Town Council tonight. Oh!"

Essie's petite, gloved hand covered her mouth and her brown eyes were as wide as a Kewpie doll's. Philipa grimaced at her friend.

"And you were not supposed to tell me that, were you, Essie?" Philipa sighed, not sure whether to be amused or annoyed at her friend's compromised loyalties. "Only on a tray of lemon cakes. Your allegiances are easily purchased, I see."

"Please, Philly, you won't go, will you? I promised Charles that I wouldn't tell—"

Philipa was impatient. "Save your tears," she advised the distraught younger woman. "They may work on Charles, but they have no effect on me whatever. Of course I'm going to the council meeting, Essie. I knew about it weeks ago, and you had nothing to do with my decision to attend and upset the proceedings. Have no fear. I shall not jeopardize your marital relationship by revealing your indiscretion."

She stopped herself from going on, realizing that she was beginning to sound like a severe duenna from one of Mrs. Emma Hunt's outrageous novels. In fact, it seemed to her that she must have used those exact words in one of her books not too very long ago.

Chapter Two

The Town Hall was in the northern part of Braedon's Beach, where the island narrowed to but a few hundred yards of sand between the ocean and the bay. This portion of the strip of land had been entirely submerged for several days after the hurricane that Charles Tavistock had prophesied, and for weeks afterward the basement of the hall had played host to a variety of displaced sea life while the flooded structure served as an unwitting aquarium. The prevalent joke, at the time, was that civic decisions made in the lower reaches rivaled any which may have been made above.

Philipa Braedon was inclined to agree with the sentiment. She never failed to appear at town meetings and to let her opinion, as the sole surviving great-grandchild of the town's founder, for whom she was named, be heard. She even voted, although she was certain the aldermen disregarded her strong alto among the thin fabric of timid tenors and baritones. Her outspoken behavior had earned her few friends among the Town Council. She enjoyed the support of residents, however, many of whom had known her since birth. Even if she had gone away to college, an excess of which many of her family's friends had disapproved, she was still a Braedon. And the Braedon name, even if it was no longer coupled with the wealth of previous generations, remained respected on the island.

Philipa walked the distance from her home to the Town Hall, a commute requiring some twenty minutes on neat, trim sidewalks paved in red brick and grouted with white sand. It was a fine evening for a walk. It had been an unseasonably warm May, but the evening ocean breezes were a welcome relief from the heat. The sun would not set until after eight o'clock. A brisk walk after a long day at the typewriter would do her good. If she needed a ride home after the meeting, she was certain she could count on Roger Waverly or his son, Elliot, if that young man was in attendance.

She called polite greetings to her neighbors along the way and was acknowledged in kind. It was a nice feeling, knowing that all of these people knew her and had known all of her family before her. It gave her a feeling of permanence and of belonging. It enhanced her sense of responsibility to the community in which she was raised, and reminded her that the well-being of that community belonged not only to the few aldermen who came and went with each election, but also to the men, women, and children who lived out their lives on the island.

She aimed herself for the cluster of men who stood upon the broad steps of the Town Hall in their suits of various shades of gray gabardine and broadcloth, and their derbies and bowlers. It was warm enough for seersucker and skimmers, although none of them, she realized with some amusement, would have dared to flaunt such attire until after Decoration Day. It would not have been considered proper. She recognized tall Dr. Waverly among them, whose aged, ascetic features smiled at her approach, and short Charles Tavistock, whose soft, somewhat babyish features frowned.

"Philly!" Roger Waverly beckoned to her with a wave. "Delightful to see you, as always. Come to give us all a talking-to tonight?"

"Naturally." Philipa took both of Dr. Waverly's gloved hands in her own and kissed him lightly upon each cheek. "I am as a voice crying in the wilderness, as usual.''

"More like the voice of a plague of locusts," grumbled Charles Tavistock, not quite concealing his annoyance with a reluctant grin that did nothing for his boiled oatmeal features. Charles, Philipa noticed, remained true to his habit of mixing biblical metaphors.

"Good evening, Charles." Philipa greeted Essie's middle-aged husband archly. "It's nice to see you, too." She returned her attention to Dr. Waverly, a far more agreeable companion. "How is Mrs. Waverly this evening? I suppose she told you that she was kept waiting at my door yesterday."

Roger Waverly chuckled, taking Philipa's round chin between his thumb and forefinger. He was the only man on earth, save possibly his own son, if he would ever dare, who could take such a liberty with her. Or with any other woman in Braedon's Beach, having delivered most of them.

"She did," he acknowledged, nodding. His silver hair shimmered beneath the silk top hat on his head. "She's none the worse for the experience, although she did have some harsh words for your new serving girl—"

"Arliss Flaherty," Philipa supplied, her features tightening into a grimace before she mastered herself again. "She's a sweet girl and she means well. But . . ." She trailed off, allowing the doctor to draw his own conclusions. His hand squeezed hers.

"Bless you, Philly," he whispered to her, his blue-gray eyes earnest. "It's good of you to take her on. They need the money. Her mother is not well, poor woman. She may not last the summer. And her sister's gone bad . . . I shouldn't say, of course. Forgive me. But you always did have a kind heart, just like your dear mother. I don't know why my son doesn't—"

Dr. Waverly stopped himself. Philipa neither moved nor responded. She had known for a very long time that Roger Waverly had courted her mother many years ago, before Henry Braedon had stolen her heart. She did not know, however, if Dr. Waverly was aware of her knowledge. And the doctor was widely known to be encouraging his son, Elliot, two years her junior, in his courtship of Julia Wilson Braedon's only child. There followed an awkward moment during which Philipa longed to say something to comfort the man before her, but realized that such comfort was beyond her capability to impart. The older man continued to hold her hand, and Philly felt herself slowly begin to blush.

She was rescued from the uncomfortable situation by a loud noise, like the humming of that plague of locusts Charles Tavistock had mentioned. Roger Waverly released her hand, turning his regal head, as did everyone else present, in the direction of the increasing racket.

The rumbling grew louder still, silencing the small gathering in front of the Town Hall. Dr. Waverly, Charles Tavistock and every other man—and there were only men present, except for Philly—turned their stiff-collared necks in its direction. Their collective curiosities were rewarded by the sight of a black horseless carriage whipping around the corner, its fat, spoked wheels giving it the appearance of a monstrous spider descending mercilessly upon its trapped prey.

But it was not the spectacle of the vehicle that commanded Philly's attention.

Behind the wheel of this outrageous and clamorous conveyance sat a man in a mustard-yellow suit with a brown shirt and a golden four-in-hand tie. Atop his head of overlong dark hair, the color of chestnuts, was a crisp new skimmer with a brown band. The man's shoulders seemed to span the vehicle, almost crowding out the beautiful young woman, much younger than Philipa, who sat flushed and breathless, her hand upon her stunning red hat, on the seat beside him. The man's smile was wider than any Philly had ever seen and she realized that it was because he had an excessively generous mouth. Excessively generous, but attractive nonetheless. With his merry, dark eyes, puckish nose and sharply angular face, he was, she decided at once, the most handsome man she had ever seen. She could not tear her gaze from him.

"Welcome to Braedon's Beach, Mr. Gavilan."

That was Charles Tavistock, his tenor gushing and obsequious. Philipa watched, immobilized by her fascination, as the man climbed down from the automobile with a grace astonishing in so tall a man. Or perhaps he was not as tall as his grace made him appear. He turned to help his companion down, and Philipa realized at once, stunned, that the woman in red was none other than Jessamyn Flaherty, Arliss's older sister, who was perhaps twenty. The realization shocked her. She returned her stare to Terence Gavilan and found, to her embarrassment, that his dark eyes were looking into her own from some twenty feet away. Her cheeks blazed with sudden heat.

He is thinking that I might be pretty were my face not quite so round, she found herself thinking, and her blush renewed itself.

He did not look away, and so she was obliged to do so, angered by his boldness and flustered by her unexpected response to it. She turned and ran up the steps of the Town Hall to escape his gaze, running squarely into the mayor, John Brewster, as she did so.

"What's your hurry, Miss Braedon?" The robust Brewster laughed, his stentorian announcement alerting all within range as he took hold of her arms. "The meeting's not started. Come down and let me introduce you to Mr. Terence Gavilan."

She would rather have perished in a flame than meet Mr. Terence Gavilan at that moment, but John Brewster was a forceful and persistent man. She could not even protest as he guided her by the elbow back down the steps and into the very thick of the men clustered about the newcomer as boys might crowd around a playmate boasting a new bicycle. The crowd parted at their arrival, and she found herself staring at a pair of polished brown boots of an extraordinary imported quality.

"Miss Philipa Braedon," John Brewster proclaimed through the roaring in her ears. "Allow me to introduce Mr. Terence Gavilan. It's fitting that you should meet here at the Town Hall this evening, as one of you represents our past and the other our future."

Philipa had no choice but to look up at the man, extending her gloved hand weakly as she did so.

"It is indeed a pleasure, Miss Braedon," she heard him say, even as she met his gaze. The amused glimmer in his dark eyes, now but inches from hers, was amplified by his rich, expressive baritone.

He was tall. Her first assessment had been correct. It was as if she were watching the whole tableau from some distance outside her own body. He took her hand, and she knew he was going to kiss it. She swallowed hard and willed herself not to blush any further at the act. There was only the warm pressure of his mouth against the back of her fingers, buffered by her cotton gloves. It was actually a little disappointing, although she could not fathom why.

"How do you do, Mr. Gavilan?" She remembered, under the spell of his magnetic eyes, to speak.

"Remember those words, Gavilan," a voice from the crowd advised him. "They're likely to be the kindest you'll ever hear from Miss Braedon."

The jest was met by a round of laughter from the gathering, and Philipa drew herself up under the scrutiny of the dandified Terence Gavilan, even managing to smile at him.

"It appears our reputations precede us both, Mr. Gavilan." She contrived to keep her voice low and cordial in spite of her hammering heart.

She was rewarded by another of his wide, winning smiles.

"I find that reputations count for little in life or in business, Miss Braedon," he said, and it was as though he were addressing her alone—as though the others had, in fact, ceased to exist. And indeed, with her fingers in Gavilan's protective custody, Philipa wished that they had. "Each new meeting is a fresh beginning," he went on. "Uncluttered by what may have come before."

"Your philosophy would explain your choice of clothing and accessories, would it not?"

She had not intended for that to come out as an insult, but somehow she perceived that it had. Terence Gavilan's smile faded and nervous laughter was heard nearby, reminding her that there were, indeed, other ears and eyes present. She wanted to apologize, but the words stuck in her throat and would probably have made matters worse anyway.

"See what I mean?" the unnamed, faceless voice called again. The laughter resumed.

Philipa withdrew her hand from Gavilan's and turned away, unable to sustain his gaze. She was shaking. She was mortified by her own behavior and began to wish she had not come to the meeting, after all. For now, she had to stay. It would not do to let these men, all of whom were acquainted with her outspoken ways, believe she had been scared off by Terence Gavilan. You are wrong, Mr. Gavilan, she thought, climbing the steps to the Town Hall as though she were mounting the gallows even as she held her head high. A reputation counts for far too much in Braedon's Beach. Especially in one's own estimation.

The meeting was called to order by Mayor Brewster, and the three aldermen exercised parliamentary procedure to address concerns of those present. Dr. Waverly, ever an advocate for education and the general welfare, petitioned for a branch library in the poorer section of town. Father Pierce of St. Gabriel's reported a family of Irish immigrants establishing a trophy fishing business, and he inquired on their behalf as to proper licensing procedure. Zoning matters were tabled pending Mr. Gavilan's presentation. He and his companion, the flamboyant if not beautiful Jessamyn Flaherty, were seated two rows behind Philipa, who dared not turn around lest she find herself staring at the man once again, this time without the excuse of ignorance.

After a brief discussion of old tax matters, Terence Gavilan was asked to come forward with his proposal. Philipa felt his hand brush her shoulder as he walked past her, his gait an assured swagger which, she was sure, was envied by every man in the room.

"Gentlemen," he began, standing at the podium, surveying the gathering of some 25 members, looking like a poised and polished political candidate, "and ladies."

He directed his penetrating dark eyes at her, his expression one of amusement. Her face grew warm again.

"I'll be brief," he said, looking about the room, apparently not having noticed the discomfiture which he had thrust upon her. "My secretary, Mr. Parrish, will be distributing copies of my plans for the properties my company has recently purchased. The plan very clearly outlines the financial advantages to Braedon's Beach, as well as increased employment opportunities for our disadvantaged.''

" 'Our' disadvantaged?'' That was Roger Waverly. His tone was skeptical. "Do you mean to say that you plan to settle in Braedon's Beach, Mr. Gavilan?''

The suavely handsome Terence Gavilan nodded, his engaging grin broadening. "I have purchased the Somers estate.''

Dear God, he was actually going to live there, not three blocks from her own house! A thin sheaf of papers dropped into her lap. She looked up to see Mr. Parrish, a short, balding man of perhaps 35, whose suit aped Mr. Gavilan's own, except that he wore it with none of the elan of the younger man. His small, piercing eyes assessed her rapidly, and she shivered, feeling as if the man had just taken something of value from her.

"It says here that you plan to build a bathhouse on Ninth Street,'' Horace Finch, owner of the local hotel on Tenth Street, grumbled. He wouldn't like that, Philipa observed. Bathhouses catered to day tourists, and day tourists did not rent hotel rooms.

"And an arcade on the promenade.'' The Reverend Michaels of Holy Innocents Episcopalian Church sounded unhappy. "We are a religious community, Mr. Gavilan. A family community. We have no desire to become another Long Branch.''

Father Michaels referred to the notorious gaming hell north of Atlantic City, a town established, its many critics insisted, for the various carnal pleasures of the New York newly rich. Philipa had never been there, of course. Her travels had been limited to Bryn Mawr College outside of Philadelphia and the cultural and society bastions connected thereto. Oh, and a daring excursion to the Willow Grove Amusement Park once with a girlfriend and her beau, where she had enjoyed the pleasure of hearing Mr. Sousa's famous band.

"I am deeply sensitive to your concerns, Father Michaels.'' Did the man know everyone already? "And you have my assurances that they will be addressed. After all, this will be my community, as well.''

"It's been rumored that you've had a carousel built in the warehouse on Fourth Street," another voice volunteered, and more grumbling ensued. Philipa found herself, against her will, wanting to defend Mr. Gavilan, who had so far demonstrated nothing but patience and conciliation with his would-be detractors. Terence Gavilan, however, needed no champion. He appeared to be more than capable of managing this crowd. She was on her feet suddenly without knowing how she had gotten there.

"Braedon's Beach has an advisory committee," she said in a light but strong voice, "of which I am president pro-tem. We have no voting power, as you gentlemen are aware, except among ourselves. Yet we do have a commendable record of helping our town maintain a high moral and social standard. May I suggest that the Council table Mr. Gavilan's zoning requests until the committee has had the opportunity to review them?"

She had addressed the entire gathering, but her gaze rested upon the imposing Mr. Gavilan, whose dark eyes were no longer smiling.

"I make a motion," Roger Waverly, whose wife was corresponding secretary of the committee, exclaimed in a loud, almost triumphant voice, "to accept Miss Braedon's kind offer of help from our auxiliary in this matter."

"I second the motion."

Philipa tore her gaze from Mr. Gavilan. The second voice belonged to Elliot Waverly, and she tried, and failed, to find his face in the small crowd.

Some commotion ensued. John Brewster banged his gavel, and after some minutes of discussion, the motion was narrowly passed. The meeting was adjourned. Philipa watched as Terence Gavilan drew his assistant aside and whispered into his ear, but soon she was swarmed by the men who had supported her, including Fathers Pierce and Michaels, Roger Waverly and others. But not Elliot. He was an exasperating beau at times. In the confusion, her hand was taken up and she was led aside as the others continued their debate. She found that it was Mr. Gavilan's secretary who had arrested her hand and spirited her to the side of the dais.

"Wait here," he told her in a thin and reedy voice before disappearing again.

Her impulse was to run, but before she could obey it, she felt a firm but gentle hand upon her arm.

"Miss Braedon." She recognized at once the cordial baritone of Terence Gavilan at her elbow. "May I have the pleasure of escorting you home? There is something I would like to show you."

She turned to him, intending to decline. Elliot was here somewhere, and she wanted to talk with him. She thought, in fact, that he might walk her home. Meeting Terence Gavilan's penetrating gaze, however, she found that her refusal stuck in her throat, much as her apology had an hour earlier. Before a word passed her lips, the tall, confident man was leading her out the back way to the street, where Mr. Parrish waited beside Mr. Gavilan's automobile.

"What about Miss Flaherty?" Philipa found her voice as she looked around for the woman, who was nowhere in evidence.

"Her mother is ailing. She was called away. Mr. Parrish has seen to her," Gavilan assured her. His hand was on her waist as he helped her in to her seat.

The sun had all but disappeared, leaving only a faint rosy glow in the west over the bay. The breeze had faltered and the cry of gulls could be heard in the distance as they scavenged for their low-tide snacks. The evening air was full of the clean, cool smell of the ocean. Philipa gripped the edge of the black leather seat as Mr. Gavilan climbed in beside her. She watched as Mr. Parrish cranked the engine. Terence Gavilan's broad, hard shoulder pressed firmly against her narrow one as he settled in behind the steering wheel.

There was a loud rumble and a small explosion, and Philipa could not help but cover her ears at the deafening sounds. She had ridden in horseless carriages on a few other occasions, but could not become accustomed to their unholy commotion. Through the din, she heard Mr. Gavilan laugh, as though her reaction delighted him. The vehicle jolted forward, and Mr. Parrish darted out of its way like a startled animal. They were off.

"Where are you taking me?" Philipa shouted to be heard above the din as they careened along Ashbury Avenue. She was holding on to her broad-brimmed picture-frame hat with her gloved left hand while gripping the edge of the seat with her right, praying that Mr. Gavilan would not stop suddenly. Her eyes were on the road before them, but she could feel his brief gaze upon her when he uttered the words, "You'll see."

In minutes, he had slowed to an easy halt before a large gray clapboard building that Philipa knew to be the Fourth Street warehouse which had been referred to in the meeting. Gavilan applied the brake, cut the engine and alighted from the vehicle with the agility of an athlete. She was still surveying the large building by the light of the dim street lamps when she realized he was waiting on the sidewalk for her, his arms outstretched to help her down. She remained in her seat.

"I have seen carousels before, Mr. Gavilan," she told him, aware that she sounded prim and prosy.

He smiled indulgently, and against her will, her heart quivered.

"It would astonish me to discover that anyone who had been to college had not, Miss Braedon." His amused baritone was teasing.

She could not hide her chagrin, acceding to his wishes. It was apparent that Terence Gavilan knew far more about her than she him, and she felt, for a brief, panicky moment as she accepted his help down, that she might have blithely strayed into waters far beyond her depth.

Mr. Gavilan removed a ring of keys from the pocket of his summery jacket and worked the padlock on the huge sliding door of the building. In no time he solved it and, with a small grunt which hinted at the strength camouflaged by his fine, if unseasonable, attire, he pushed back the door until it gave way to a large, dark space.

"Wait here," he advised, and he disappeared into the dark facility.

She waited, pondering the folly of her precipitous decision to accompany a strange man, unchaperoned, to this remote and deserted location. Terence Gavilan, she had begun to believe, represented danger. Not to the population at large, or even to the population of small, conservative Braedon's Beach, but certainly to her. To her sense of well-being, if not to her very person. Yet she could not deny that there was something extraordinarily thrilling about that notion.

Suddenly the space before her was flooded with a warm, golden light. In its very midst, like a huge wedding cake, was a pink, white and gold carousel.

Philipa was standing beside the ornate spectacle without knowing how she had gotten there from the doorway of the warehouse. The tall, prancing horses, frozen in motion, were brightly painted and ornamented with huge, glittering paste jewels. The scored brass poles upon which they were impaled shined golden in the light. Above her head, enameled panels bordered by tiny, gleaming mirrors depicted exotic scenes and scandalous women with alluring smiles. Above that, beyond the spokes of the frame, was a high tented dome of white and pink striped canvas. And in the center, in the very heart of the gaudy and magnificent machine, was a multi-piped calliope, complete with drums and cymbals. She touched one of the white horses on its glistening nose.

"Isn't it a beauty?"

Terence Gavilan was beside her, the very warmth of his breath teasing her ear. For a fleeting moment she felt exactly like a heroine in one of her own—that is, Mrs. Emma Hunt's—novels. She very nearly fainted at the thought, and at the fact of the attractive man's proximity.

"It's—it's lovely," she conceded, after a false start. "But"—she drew herself in once again—"I still don't understand why you wanted to show me this. Do you imagine I will be swayed to influence the committee merely on account of a charming, if somewhat excessively ornate, children's amusement? Or have you some other persuasion in mind?"

She almost could not believe she had spoken those words. Mr. Gavilan, too, seemed surprised. His dark eyes widened, and his eyebrows, like two lines of black lightning bolting straight across the ridge of his forehead, arched in wonder. Then his expression changed mercurially to a rueful smile that made him appear engaging and boyish.

"I like you, Miss Braedon. I really do. You're smarter than most women I know. Probably a lot of men, as well. No, Miss Braedon, I can see you're going to take a lot more persuading than just a pleasant spin on a carousel and a ride in a Hurricane. But I've never shied away from a challenge, and I don't intend to start now. Since we're here anyway, suppose I crank her up?"

Mr. Gavilan did not wait for her protest. He climbed through the maze of waiting horses to the calliope, calling out "Get on!" just before he disappeared into the works. Philipa found herself smiling as she tried to recall when she had encountered as perplexing and exasperating a man as Terence Gavilan. She mounted the step up to the platform even as the sounds of a hissing steam engine emanated from the confusion of machinery into which he had vanished.

It took several minutes for the engine to build up steam. Philipa selected a pink horse on the outside and climbed, with some difficulty, owing to the bustle on her navy blue poplin dress, to a sidesaddle position. She waited, feeling a little foolish, hoping that no neighbor or acquaintance would happen by and find her perched like a schoolgirl on the back of a carousel horse. Presently the carousel swayed and jerked forward, and she grabbed the brass pole which had begun to rise, lifting the horse and her into the air. The ride picked up momentum and soon was rotating like a great wheel of light.

The calliope coughed and sputtered and finally tooted out a magnificently garish version of Sousa's "El Capitan" march. Philipa laughed, giddy with the motion of the ride as well as the ludicrous sound of the mechanical instrument.

"It is fun, isn't it?" Terence Gavilan was beside her again on the carousel. He had taken off his jacket and rolled up his shirt sleeves, revealing dark hair on his muscular forearms as he steadied himself by holding on to the support pole beside her. He was regarding her with an expression of such joy and wonder that she felt much younger than her 25 years.

"I'm sorry about that remark I made earlier, about your manner of dress," she said suddenly. Impulsively. What was it about Terence Gavilan that made her want to give in to her impulses? "It was unforgivably rude of me."

He laughed, and her face grew warm again as she watched the absurd drum beat furiously in time to the march.

"It was," he agreed. "It was the last thing I expected to hear coming out of your tidy and proper little mouth. But that's why I like you. Look, Miss Braedon! Here comes the brass ring. Do you think you can grab hold of it?"

She could not help but stare at him, with the odd sensation that he was not really referring to the circle of brass that glistened and beckoned from the feeding arm of the nearby device. His handsome features, smiling and frank, gave her no clue.

"Here. Look. It's easy. All you have to do is . . ." He took hold of her right wrist and pulled it gently until their hands were stretched into space.

The carousel spun and the arm came into view. Instinctively Philipa leaned out toward it, then lost her balance even as the ring slid from its place and onto her finger. Terence Gavilan's strong arms were about her waist and he skillfully lifted her back onto her saddle before she could even blush. He disappeared again, and in moments the calliope racket had ceased and the carousel slowed. Philipa felt the hard metal of the brass ring in her hand, and Gavilan was before her again.

"Well, Miss Braedon?" He breathed, placing one strong hand on the horse's neck and the other upon its flank. "What do you think?"

His dark eyes reflected the bright light of the carousel like the hundreds of tiny mirrors bordering the decorative panels. Philipa glanced about her at the confectionery amusement again, more to try to ignore the nearness of Terence Gavilan than to inspect the ride.

"I think I'd better be getting home."

Was that her voice? It sounded so small, so remote. She felt, oddly, as though she might faint. Suddenly she slipped from her perch and found Gavilan's arms around her. In surprise she looked up and found him regarding her with concern, and no hint of amusement.

"Are you all right?" he asked.

No, she thought, meeting his intense gaze because she was not equal to the task of breaking away from it, or from him.

I am in danger. I am in terrible, terrible danger of losing my heart, which I have so carefully protected for all of these years . . .

"I—" She could not manage more than a whisper and so abandoned all attempts at speech.

His mouth on hers was strong, but his lips were surprisingly soft, evoking a tremor along her spine and into her legs. She would have fallen, she realized, had he not been holding her up. A small cry issued from her throat—of protest, or desire? Before she knew it, she was kissing him back, seeking his mouth with her own, welcoming his tongue as it softly traced the outline of her upper lip.

What was happening to her?

She pushed him back with just enough strength to sever the current of their brief and unexpected passion. She would, she knew, staring at his gold-colored silk tie, be perfectly justified in slapping his face. But inasmuch as she had actually enjoyed their enterprise, she could not bring herself to perform such a symbolic hypocrisy.

"Mr. Gavilan," she said, unable, thanks to her own shame, to manage more than a breathless whisper. "You are not a gentleman."

To her surprise and further humiliation, he chuckled at the end of a brief sigh.

"That's true," he conceded. "And you, Miss Braedon," he added with an unmistakable hint of regret, "are a lady. But sometimes, I think"—he held her chin captive between his thumb and forefinger as he lifted her face inevitably toward his, until she unwillingly met his thoughtful dark-eyed gaze—"you wonder what it would be like—not to be a lady?"

A small shudder rocked her. How could this man, who had known her for but a few hours, have in that short time perceived her so clearly, when Elliot Waverly, whom she had known all of their lives, seemed to know her not at all?

"I—I must go," she said, breaking away from his hold.

"Let me take you home," he offered, as though nothing at all were amiss between them.

"No, you have already done quite enough," she retorted,

gaining strength and resolve as she placed more and more distance between them, but not quite enough to return his bold gaze. ''Good evening, Mr. Gavilan.''

She could not begin to comprehend, as she fled the warehouse in what she hoped was a sedate and dignified manner, why she experienced the sudden urge to cry.

Chapter Three

"Philly, what on earth happened to you after the meeting?" Elliot Waverly descended the four steps from her porch as she approached in the darkness. Elliot was tall and lean, even moreso than his father, but without his father's commanding, if austere, features. His smooth, white cheeks were as round as a young boy's, and his pale blue eyes radiated earnest innocence. He was dressed in charcoal gray pinstripe gabardine despite the heat. Philipa, unable to avoid comparing him to the debonair Mr. Gavilan, thought for a fleeting instant that he looked ridiculous.

"One moment you were there in the thick of things, as usual, and the next, you had vanished!" The younger Waverly sounded more agitated than Philipa had ever heard him before. Agitated, but by no means angry. Elliot Waverly was never angry. She doubted he had ever been angry in his life.

"I—had an appointment," she murmured, glad of the darkness around them. The walk from the warehouse had taken but fifteen minutes and she still felt the resulting blush of her unsettling encounter with Mr. Terence Gavilan keenly. She was sure that evidence of their actions was etched upon her face, as a mortal sin might appear on one's soul in the eyes of God. She prayed that Elliot would not question her further about her disappearance, for she would not lie, but neither did she have any compelling desire to tell him the whole truth.

Fortunately, he did not.

"I'm sorry not to have called upon you this week." He seemed satisfied by her guarded response. He was, she reflected as she stared at him in the darkness, a trusting soul. "I was in Philadelphia on an important matter."

She grasped his hands, forgetting about Terence Gavilan and his heavenly carousel for the moment.

"Oh, Elliot, do you mean to tell me that you are going back to medical school, after all?"

He did not answer her right away, and she felt a curious stab of disappointment. Elliot's mother and father had been crushed when he'd announced his intention, some weeks before, of not returning to the University of Pennsylvania for the autumn semester of medical training. Philipa had not offered judgment at the time, secretly believing that Elliot lacked the necessary determination and desire for the profession. She had hoped, however, that the thoughtful and serious young man would decide once and for all just what it was that he wanted to do with his life, so they could get on with the business that was expected of them: to marry and have children.

Elliot's expression, even in the dim light from the porch, was somber; indeed, almost grim.

"I'd rather discuss this inside, Philipa, if you don't mind."

Philipa released his hands, regretting that she had taken hold of them.

"Of course, Elliot."

She led him into the house. It was dark inside, Arliss having the evening off and Mrs. Grant, the housekeeper, apparently having retired for the night. Philipa lit the small lamp on the table in the foyer and its dim and flickering amber glow revealed the sliding doors to the parlor. Elliot obligingly opened them. Philipa illuminated the floor lamp beside the Steinway. She faced her young man expectantly. Elliot stood in the center of the room on the medallion of the Persian rug which

Mrs. Grant had not yet had taken up, looking very much like a truant lad awaiting punishment from his schoolmaster.

"Sit down, please, Elliot." Her voice, for some reason, sounded very formal and remote in her ears.

"I think I'd rather stand," he replied, regarding her with a steady and serious gaze.

His tone filled her with foreboding. She felt a pressure inside her chest which made breathing difficult. Did he mean to propose to her at last? Now, when his life was in more of a turmoil than ever? Or had he some other grim news to impart? She sat down upon the striped Queen Anne loveseat and folded her hands in her lap so Elliot could not perceive their trembling. She waited for his next words, wondering how she would answer them.

He appeared to have lost his resolve. He held his black derby in his gloved hands and pressed his thin lips together. Elliot was not handsome in the classical sense, but his serious nature lent a certain distinction to his appearance. That distinction was overwhelming, at present.

"I've enrolled in St. Charles' Theological Seminary in Philadelphia, Philipa," he announced in a quiet but sure voice. "I want—I hope to become a minister, if it please God."

Philipa was at once disappointed and relieved. He hadn't had second thoughts about their unspoken betrothal. At least, not yet. Neither had he seen fit to officially ask her to be his wife. She considered him in the dim light. Was this latest venture merely another in his efforts to find, as it were, the meaning of his life? He had, since their adolescence together, exhibited a brooding and often discontented nature, an almost perpetual air of melancholy, which he'd cultivated throughout his academic career. At first Philipa had thought it a noble badge of his sensitivity, but in recent months she had begun to believe that Elliot Waverly simply did not know why he had been placed on earth, and that he was content to flit like a moth from whimsy to whimsy until he found out, even though it might take a lifetime.

"Well?" His question jarred her from her contemplation. "Aren't you going to say anything?"

Philipa considered him. If he were a hero in one of Mrs.
Emma Hunt's books—and with his brooding looks, he very
well could have been—and she a heroine, she would, no
doubt, have gone to him, thrown her soft, white arms about
his neck and declared that she would follow him to the gates
of Perdition and beyond just to be by his side. But she was
merely Philipa Braedon, academic and spinner of tales.
Somewhat erotic tales of lust and desire and the ultimate triumph of pure, true love.

Could Mrs. Elliot Waverly, wife of an Episcopalian minister, connect herself, however surreptitiously, to so shameful
an occupation?

Philipa swallowed a hard, bitter mass in her throat.

"I'm glad for you, Elliot," she said in a remarkably firm
voice. "I know you have not arrived at this decision lightly,
and I want you to know that I will support your decision in
every way I can."

There, she thought. It was a fine, solid speech, and she was
proud of it. She watched him grimace and expel a hard breath.

"Very safe and sensible words, Philipa," he said, his tone
heavy with disappointment. "I know you expected to be the
wife of a doctor. But I also know you're an intelligent and
pious woman with a generous heart and a pure soul. I pray
that you will come to do more than merely support me in this.
I want your wholehearted approval, and your encouragement.
I need for you to share my mission, Philipa. I won't ask you
to make your decision right now. I know I've given you much
to think about. But I'm starting my studies at the end of June,
and I hope—I pray—that you'll know your mind by then.
I . . ." He paused, clearing his throat. "I love you, Philipa. I
want you by my side in this life I have chosen. But you must
be sure as well, Philipa. It's too much of a sacrifice, too much
of a commitment, to enter into lightly. I'll leave you now.
I've given you a lot to think about. I'll speak with you again
tomorrow. My mother and father expect you for dinner. May
I come for you at seven?"

*Sacrifice. Commitment. I'll speak with you tomorrow. I love
you, Philipa.* Suddenly she felt as though she were bound to
her chair by silken chains labeled with those very words.

"Of course, Elliot," she replied, marveling at her even tone as she rose from her seat.

She escorted him to the door, where he paused and turned to her.

"I do love you, Philipa," he whispered, his earnest gray eyes searching her face. "I want to make you happy."

Unexpectedly, he touched his lips to hers. They were warm and gentle. They were pleasant.

But she did not sob, or cry out. Her legs remained firm and sturdy. After her recent experience with Terence Gavilan, it was almost a relief.

"I love you too, Elliot," she whispered in return. "Good night."

"Good night, Philipa." He kissed her again, this time upon her forehead. Then he was gone.

She closed the door behind him and slipped the bolt. She leaned her head upon the doorjamb, exactly on the spot to which Elliot had pressed his lips. She'd had no intention of crying, but she discovered presently that her face was wet.

> *The silver moonlight shimmered in a broad band on the darkened sea like a silken sleeve. Arianna lifted her face, a druid priestess in worship to a pagan god, longing to feel the cool, salty water bathe the pain from her soul. With a languid slowness, she undressed herself, peeling the layers of the day's cares away until she stood naked, alone on the dark, rocky beach, with only the moonlight as her witness.*
>
> *Or so she thought.*
>
> *Philip had followed her after the ball, compelled by her profound sadness, and now he stood in the shadow of the rocks, spellbound by the sight of his Venus, returning to the sea from whence she had sprung . . .*

Terence Gavilan placed the book on the bed, open facedown, and closed his eyes. The book, he knew, would have remained open to that page, even had he not preserved its place. It was Emma Hunt's most recently published work, *Fire Beach*, and he had read that particular chapter so many times that it was embedded upon his memory. The images it evoked had consumed him since he'd first read it several weeks before. He envisioned that he was Philip, and that Emma Hunt, a faceless, formless woman, bathed for him in the moonlight of that steamy and exotic place.

He was breathing hard, and perspiration beaded down his temple. Emma Hunt! He cursed her name. He had read every one of her books since they had first appeared several years before, quickly becoming addicted to their sensuality. But this one . . . this one. Its all too vivid imagery haunted his dreams, day and night. The very idea that a lady—all of Mrs. Hunt's heroines were ladies of unquestionable virtue, if inordinately sensuous—would strip naked on a beach for a moonlight swim had shocked him the very first time that he'd read it. It had shocked him and titillated him at the same time. And her description of the scene, and of the sensations experienced by the bather, had convinced him that Emma Hunt, whoever and whatever she was, most certainly had firsthand knowledge of the experience.

> *Arianna felt the warm, salty waves lap teasingly at her very femininity, like the naughty tongue of a secret lover . . .*

He shivered, seeing the words as clearly as if he held the page before his eyes, and the image they evoked as if it were a portrait. Damn Emma Hunt twice!

Emma Hunt, he tried to tell himself time and again, was in all likelihood a dried-up old spinster, at least 50 years old. No doubt the woman lived in a decrepit tenement in New York, surrounded by mewing cats and lace antimacassars, and had probably never been nearer to a beach than her own bathtub. And yet . . .

He was doing it again. He shook his head. He rubbed his eyes with his fists, then opened them wide to the pale light afforded by his reading lamp. He stretched in the brass bed, enjoying the feel of the soft, cool cotton sheets against the bare skin of his back and chest. He reached across the pillow, his hand finding the warm, voluptuous mass that was Jess

Flaherty in the bed beside him.

"You finally finish that old book?" she murmured like a whining kitten waiting impatiently for its bowl of sweet cream.

"I won't ever finish this book, sweetheart," he told her, knowing full well, with sadness, that Jessamyn Flaherty would never understand what he meant, any more than any other woman would. Emma Hunt held his reason in thrall, and as long as she did, he could never truly be satisfied with anyone else. But he would take them. Oh, yes, he would take them. He would take what was offered, and there were plenty of offers, and he would envision them all to be Emma Hunt. And he would, he realized with a familiar pang of regret, continue to wake up in the morning robbed of his illusions.

Caressing the very caressable Miss Flaherty, he thought once again of Miss Philipa Braedon, and he smiled. She was not old, but she was by no means young, either. And while she was probably a virgin, it was likely she'd had some experience with men. After all, the woman was not unattractive. Not a raving beauty, mind you, but certainly pleasing enough to the eye, even if her face was a bit round, and her variable hazel eyes a bit too direct. Her mouth had been pleasingly astonished and surprisingly willing when he'd kissed her on the carousel. And he could only guess at the conformation of her womanly parts, obscured as they were by proscribed layers of proper dress, but he assumed them to be acceptable, at the very least.

He pulled Jessamyn close to him, cupping a firm, round breast in each hand as her bare back rested, warm and smooth, against his chest.

"I'm mad at you for packing me off with that awful old Owen Parrish," she whined petulantly, and he could tell that she really didn't mean it. In fact, knowing Jessamyn, it was altogether likely that she shared her favors with his dour and cynical secretary, as well. He didn't mind.

He laughed at her. His hardening manhood pressed into the soft crevice of the young woman's buttocks as she rubbed herself against him. For an instant, to his surprise, he envisioned Philipa Braedon there, her hair loose upon his pillow—

what color had it been? It had been difficult to tell in the darkness, and with that enormous hat she'd worn. But it was probably brown, like her shapely, articulated eyebrows.

What, he wondered, idly tracing circles on Jess's hardened nipples with the tips of his fingers, would it take to discover the passions simmering within the intriguing, if somewhat prickly, Miss Braedon?

In his arms, Jessamyn issued a broken sigh of desire awakened. He was happy to oblige her, having aroused himself with the combined thoughts of the mysterious Emma Hunt and his new project, Miss Philipa Braedon. A huntsman, he recalled an old expression from his college days, hunts wisest when he is not hungry. He intended to hunt on a full stomach, and let Miss Braedon beware.

Philipa could not sleep. It was late, and it was warm. The three-quarter moon was high in the May night sky. Sighing, she slipped from between the muslin sheets on her sleigh bed, finding her old slippers on the polished pine floor beneath with her toes. She took the robe from the footboard and slipped her arms into its sleeves as she padded from the room.

The Braedon house backed on to the beach, several blocks to the north of the promenade. It was a private beach, but never more private than during these moonlit nights before the summer residents moved in. The sound of the ocean in the darkness, perpetually crashing upon the shore like a sporadic and arrhythmic orchestra of cymbals, was at once soothing and invigorating. The dark water, it being May, would be cold.

She stretched, lifting her nightclothing above her head easily as she did so. She kicked off her cotton tick slippers and kneaded the cool sand with her toes. Unceremoniously she dropped her nightgown and robe in a heap upon the sand and reached her arms wide, allowing her chest to expand freely without the restraints of the corseting that held her prisoner by day.

A trickle of a wave washed against her ankles. It was like ice. She shivered, sending her loosened hair down her back. It was like a warm, soft blanket about her shoulders. She wanted to feel the chill of the ocean all around her. To swim in the strong, cold currents of the North Atlantic and strive against their deadly whims. Good, strenuous exercise would clear her turbulent thoughts.

It was much easier to swim without the restrictions of a cumbersome bathing garment, but the tide was powerful. Philipa was pleasantly exhausted by the time she trudged back on to the beach. She longed, after her exercise, to lie down in the sand, which felt much warmer since her emergence from the cold Atlantic, but she dared not. It was altogether possible that she would fall asleep right there. Some dawn beachcomber might find her and believe that Hans Christian Andersen's mermaid fable had come to life, some ten years too late.

She giggled at the silly, romantic notion, scouting the dark beach for the clothing she had left behind. It took her a moment to get her bearings by the pattern of lights from the distant houses on the beach, but she spotted her own house quickly, and soon after, the pile of nightclothes, now sprinkled with sand. She shook them out and put them back on, aware of a sense of deep contentment. She had purged herself, for a time, of the troubling events of that day, and would find the release she so desperately sought in sleep.

Chapter Four

The residents of Braedon's Beach, both seasonal and permanent, practiced the sociable habit of sitting out on their porches on fine spring and summer evenings, reclining in wicker rockers and swings and calling polite greetings to neighbors and acquaintances who passed by on the sidewalks. When protocol or friendship demanded, they would exchange conversation with the same, lasting in length from a few sentences to a few hours. The purpose for this tradition, as far as Philipa, an avid student of human nature, could discern, was to allow those living within close proximity to one another as much access to their neighbors' business as possible without giving the appearance, however deserved, that they were busybodies. When Philipa strolled along Ocean Avenue with her gloved hand tucked in the crook of Elliot Waverly's arm, heads bobbed and neighbors smiled and waved. Philipa felt rather like a specimen in a fishbowl, and she mentioned as much to her escort, who was in lighter spirits than the previous evening.

"I'm sure they mean no harm, Philly," he chided her gently, giving her hand a squeeze. He smiled at her from under

his crisp black derby, his blue-gray eyes expressing a fondness that caught her off guard. Elliot was not a demonstrative
person. "These people have known both of us all of our
lives," he reminded her..

"I know that, Elliot," she grumbled at him, somewhat ex-
asperated by his failure to appreciate the larger implications
of her comment. Elliot never suspected a deeper meaning behind anything. Certainly, he never seemed to look for one.
"But it never ceases to amaze me that a stroll upon a spring
evening in Braedon's Beach can be escalated, by the following morning, into another matter entirely."

"Oh." He nodded, as if understanding her inference at last.
He doffed his hat to the Moss family across the way, whose
five children, like gamboling puppies, played noisily in their
front yard. Emily Hanford Moss, Philipa recalled, had been a
year behind her at school, and had married, at eighteen, a man
fifteen years her senior.

"I suppose I see what you mean," Elliot went on. "But
what is the harm, after all? The whole island knows we're
practically engaged, and that you are merely waiting for me
to find my place. Won't it surprise everyone when they learn
I'm going off to St. Charles?"

Elliot, Philipa knew, did not mean to be insensitive, but she
could not quench the spark of annoyance his presumption
ignited within her. The whole island might indeed be privy
to his intentions, but that did not alter the fact that Elliot
Waverly had never really bothered to spell them out to her.
Their betrothal, like so much else in their relationship, had
never been more than implied. That, perhaps, was due in part
to the fact that Philipa had no surviving relatives to whom
Elliot could petition his courtship. But more likely, she knew,
it was just another assumption, like so many others upon
which Roger Waverly's son built his trust.

Of course, she reflected dismally, remaining silent at his
side as they continued on their way to the Waverly home, she
was as much to blame for the state of their relationship as he.
She could certainly, as Essie and other friends often encouraged her, have pressed him for a token of their engagement,
if not to an actual date. But she never had, preferring to im-

merse herself in her work, both academic and secret, and to allow Elliot to come to himself in his own time. Apparently he had come to himself, at least where she was concerned, but it would have been nice if he had taken the trouble to inform her of the fact.

She was angry with him again, she realized, wanting to pull her hand from his arm, but not caring to cause a scene. And she was frustrated by the feeling, as she always was. Her anger toward Elliot, no matter what its cause, was always amorphous and indefinable. Master of the language though she was, she never seemed able to articulate her feelings to this man at her side. The situation was, to say the least, disturbing.

It might have been easier if Elliot Waverly were cruel, or even overtly insensitive. But part of the problem, she knew, was that he was so very, very considerate.

In most ways.

Her impotent anger blinded her to the approach of another stroller from the opposite direction, with the result that all three reached the Waverly gate at the same moment.

"Good evening, Miss Braedon."

The horrifyingly familiar baritone, faintly mocking in its courtesy, caused her to look up. Terence Gavilan wore a tan seersucker suit this evening, and a skimmer, this one with a cream-colored band. He sported an insolent grin on his wide, sensuous mouth and in his sparkling brown eyes. Philipa was suddenly flooded by the memory of the previous night, their kiss, and all of the accompanying emotions. She was hard put to form a civilized, if not a sane, salutation.

"Mr. Gavilan," she stammered after only one false start. A warm blush crept into her cheeks, maddeningly. "What are you—I mean, what a surprise!"

"Dr. Waverly invited me this afternoon when I stopped by his office to pay him a call," he informed her smoothly, removing his hat with a slight bow. She suspected at once that the handsome and enigmatic Mr. Gavilan had gone to Roger's office for the purpose of extracting just such an invitation. "He mentioned you would be in attendance, as well. And this gentleman is . . . ?"

Philipa continued staring at Gavilan for nearly a full minute before realizing that Elliot, too, was standing patiently by, waiting for an introduction. She performed the courtesy, surprised by the calm sound of her voice. She thought the boulder in her throat would have rendered her incapable of speech. She watched in detached wonder as the two men shook hands: the one to whom she was unofficially engaged, and the one whom she had permitted to kiss her in a most indecent fashion only the night before.

"Oh, yes. My father mentioned you had dropped by, Mr. Gavilan. Welcome!" she heard Elliot say through the rushing in her ears, and his voice sounded strangely callow and raw to her.

He knows that Elliot is younger than I, she thought, wondering why that would suddenly bother her.

Elliot opened the gate for her, and insisted that the dapper, if perpetually unseasonable, Mr. Gavilan precede him through the gate as well. Quite as though it were the most natural thing in the world, Terence Gavilan took up her arm, enfolding it to his own in the manner of a doting uncle. If she were not so full of a tumult of emotions, Philipa might have thought the gesture very funny indeed.

"How delightful," Gavilan, beside her, commented. "I had no idea that Miss Philipa Braedon and Mr. Elliot Waverly were 'an item,' as the saying goes."

Was there really derision veiled in his remark, or did she only imagine it? She dared not look at his face to try to gain a clue.

Elliot, uncharacteristically, laughed.

"Philly and I have been 'an item' since we were children, Mr. Gavilan," the younger Waverly informed him blithely.

Philipa desperately wished that Elliot would not speak again as they made their way, with no particular haste, thanks to Terence Gavilan's lead, up the flagstone walk to the Waverly home.

" 'Philly?' " Gavilan dared to chuckle. Then she did meet his gaze, glaring murderously. "A very charming pet name, Mr. Waverly. Your baptism?"

He addressed Elliot, but he was staring at Philipa in a bold manner which the younger man, behind them, could not possibly have marked. Philipa was abruptly reminded, riveted to Mr. Gavilan's dark-eyed gaze, of his overwhelming and perilous appeal.

"Her mother's, Mr. Gavilan," Roger Waverly, on the porch before them, answered for his son. Philipa was able to look away, as if the older man's interjection had shattered a wicked spell. The doctor was regarding Gavilan with an almost stern expression which caused Philipa to wonder why he had invited the man to join them in the first place.

If Terence Gavilan was caught off guard by Roger Waverly's intervention, he gave no sign of it. He released Philipa from his custody to shake hands with his host, uttering all of the appropriate salutations in a surprisingly sincere and respectful tone. Roger Waverly responded in kind, holding Philipa back with a discreet hand while ushering Gavilan and Elliot inside. After they had gone in, Roger turned to her with a look of concern that made her blush anew.

"Are you all right, my dear? You look quite flushed."

Philipa swallowed, still trying to eliminate the obstruction in her throat. Roger Waverly knew her as well as, or better than, any other living person. She might have known he would sense some tension between her and Terence Gavilan. She disliked having to keep anything from him.

"I am fine," she managed, not looking at him. "I would like something to drink. The walk has winded me, I think."

Roger Waverly issued a small grunt. "You are the fittest young woman I know, Philipa Braedon," he scolded her. "If having Gavilan here has upset you in any way, I apologize."

Philipa drew herself up. The idea that any man could throw her into a mire of confusion did not sit well with her.

"Whyever should his presence upset me?" she replied, ignoring the hammering of her heart as she met her host's probing gaze. "I barely know the man."

That, of course, was perfectly true. But it was also true that she had allowed him to kiss her, and that she was therefore guilty on several counts of omission to all parties present this evening. Oh, what a lovely mess she had gotten herself into with one sweet, unguarded moment!

Roger Waverly continued to monitor her, and she knew he suspected her of withholding something. But she also knew he would not pry, and that her painful secret was safe, for now.

Not allowing, of course, for anything the unpredictable Terence Gavilan might let slip, intentionally or otherwise . . .

Mrs. Waverly was already serving lemonade in the parlor by the time Philipa entered with the doctor. Philipa noticed that Roger Waverly was eying the newcomer with veiled suspicion. There was no doubt that Terence Gavilan, whether he knew it or not, had gotten himself off on the wrong footing with Dr. Waverly, who was very protective, not to say possessive, of Philipa. But Gavilan already appeared to be working his charm on Mrs. Waverly, admittedly no easy task.

Beatrice Waverly, although nearly a head shorter than Philipa, imparted an air of power not unlike that of her husband. She was one of the most maternal women in Philipa's experience, but there was a ruthless side to the diminutive but solid lady, as well. She was fiercely protective, Philipa had learned early: of her family, her dearest friends and her standing in the community. Once when they were children, Philipa had dared Elliot, then but five, to walk the top of the garden fence, some four feet above the ground and a few inches in width. Elliot had, of course, fallen, spraining his wrist as well as ruining his mother's herb garden. Dr. Waverly, as she recalled, had dismissed the event as a child's romp, but Beatrice Waverly had dragged her home for punishment to her shocked mother. She had not been allowed to play at the Waverly home for a month. Elliot's mother had long since forgiven her, of course, but Philipa hadn't forgotten the event, and she doubted, even as the older woman embraced her fondly in welcome, that Beatrice Waverly had, either.

The parlor was pleasantly cool, although Philipa still felt very warm. Elliot commandeered the loveseat for their use, and Terence Gavilan selected, by design, she was certain, the brocaded wing chair directly opposite her position. Philipa seized a tall glass of lemonade offered by the serving girl and barely prevented herself from gulping the beverage down in her haste. Her mouth was as dry as sand, and the boulder in her throat had not diminished. The tiny sips which etiquette forced upon her did nothing to relieve either. She was glad the conversation centered on the doctor, his wife and Terence Gavilan. That kept Roger Waverly's watchful, analytical eye away from her.

After a time, Waverly asked Gavilan if he would like something stronger than lemonade, and the younger man wisely declined the invitation. It was almost as if Terence Gavilan had come courting, Philipa thought, except that the Waverlys had no daughter. In a moment of clarity, she realized that the charming and clever businessman had come courting, but it was not a person he courted—it was Roger and Beatrice Waverly's good opinions.

Terence Gavilan, Philipa decided, watching the performance before her, was not only a man who knew what he wanted, but how to acquire it, as well. It might be interesting, she thought, to watch events unfold during the course of the evening. Beatrice Waverly and her husband were no fools, and they would take some persuasion to admit a bold outsider like Terence Gavilan, along with his unconventional ideas, into their tight inner circle. But Gavilan was a man with a mission, she perceived. He would stop at nothing to ensure the approval of his plans to convert Braedon's Beach from a sleepy little seashore community of contented residents to a bustling seaside resort for tourists with money to spend. It remained to her, she realized, listening to the conversation before her, and to the inhabitants of the island, to see to it that this proposed metamorphosis did not get out of hand.

Dinner was served and consumed without incident, and Philipa relaxed her guard somewhat. Gavilan had made no allusion to their tryst of the previous evening. Oddly, Philipa actually began to feel slighted by his omission, annoyed at the notion that Terence Gavilan could so thoroughly ignore what had been, to her, a most disturbingly memorable event. Listening to the conversation over dessert and coffee, she began to notice a headache behind her eyes.

"I doubt you've said five words this entire evening, Philipa Braedon," Beatrice Waverly declared. "Not like you at all. Are you ill, child?"

Philipa felt all eyes, including Terence Gavilan's, upon her, and she pressed her white damask napkin to her lips before replying, staring at the half-eaten blueberry comfit in the dish before her.

"I—have a slight headache," she murmured in reply.

"A headache!" Mrs. Waverly exclaimed. "You are too young for headaches. Roger, why don't you give Philipa one of your powders?"

"No, please," Philipa declined, holding up her hands. "I think fresh air is all I need. Elliot, would you mind . . . ?"

Elliot and the other men were on their feet as she stood up. Excusing herself, she allowed the younger Waverly to escort her through the dining room to the parlor, where he unlatched the French doors leading to the side of the wraparound porch.

Night had come to the island. The moonlight reminded her of her late swim the night before. She wished Elliot would come up behind her and put his arms around her, perhaps to plant a loverlike kiss in the hollow of her shoulder. But not being one of Mrs. Emma Hunt's romantic heroes, he did not. Disappointed, she held her own arms, rubbing them with the flat of her hands. Goosebumps formed there as she did. Her rose-colored organza gown, with its off-shoulder capped sleeves, had been adequate in the warm evening, but she had left her shawl inside, and the air had turned cool, with a zesty breeze blowing in off of the ocean.

"Would you please get me my shawl, Elliot?" she asked without facing him. The pain in her head was already ebbing. "I am cold."

"Of course, Philly."

His footsteps faded and the door closed behind him as he entered the house again, and she sighed. The sigh came forth in broken little gasps, as though she could not take in quite enough air. Far too soon for Elliot to have returned, she felt the warmth of her shawl, then a pair of strong hands, light but firm, upon her shoulders.

"You sent him in for this, I believe."

Terence Gavilan was behind her. She started, pulling away from his gentle touch. He chuckled, a sound with which she was beginning to be all too familiar. She faced him with a vituperative remark that died upon her lips: He had done nothing to merit such treatment, except to provide her shawl.

"Mr. Gavilan," she managed, glad of the darkness, although she knew he could see her features, "you should not be out here."

"Neither should you," was his bold observation. He continued to monitor her steadily, a scrutiny she found most disconcerting. Under it, she felt, uncomfortably, like a hapless mouse whose tail was caught beneath the lazy paw of a big, hungry cat. Suddenly she was no longer cold, but unbearably warm. She rallied.

"Mr. Gavilan, why have you come here this evening?" She tried a challenging approach, hoping to place him on the defensive. He merely smiled at her, his generous mouth parted to demonstrate even, white teeth.

"Merely fate, Miss Braedon, I do assure you. Dr. Waverly was kind enough to extend the invitation when I chanced upon him this afternoon—"

"I think fate has played no part in this exercise, Mr. Gavilan," she interrupted him coldly. "I believe you forced this encounter for no better reason than to embarrass me!"

"Miss Braedon," he reproved lightly, after allowing a reflective moment. "Vanity does not become you."

She could not sustain his amused stare.

"Neither does embarrassment, I am sure," she muttered, half to herself, although she knew he would hear her.

"On the contrary," he contradicted her with exaggerated politeness. "I find your blush and your confusion most disarming. How very awkward for you to be confronted in the presence of your fiancé by the man who held you in his arms only the night before! And how very proper and dignified you have remained, in spite of it. My congratulations. But tell me. Does the Reverend Waverly know of his intended's—ah—breach of loyalty?"

She could not even pause to wonder how it was that Terence Gavilan already knew of Elliot's plans to enter the ministry.

"Shh!" she hissed at him, unwillingly meeting his gaze again. "Someone will hear you."

His dark eyes sparkled with devilment in the moonlight, like some leering satyr.

"So he does not," he mused. "Well, Miss Braedon, he shall not hear of it from me. I have merely come out here to assure you that my discretion may be relied upon. Does that satisfy you, or were you hoping for a reprise of last evening's events?"

Philipa was filled with an overwhelming rage. She raised her hand and swung it toward Gavilan's cheek, but he was too fast for her. He seized her wrist in a firm, lightning gesture and held it before her eyes as if to give her a moment to reflect upon her precipitous action.

"Why didn't you strike me last night, Miss Braedon?" he whispered, his serious gaze commanding hers in the darkness.

She had no answer for him. She could only watch, thoroughly mesmerized, as he pressed his lips to the palm of her hand without once taking his eyes from hers. They burned her, and she pulled her hand away quickly.

He was gone.

"Philipa! I looked everywhere for your shawl, but . . ." Elliot had returned, sounding like a schoolboy. She could barely see him.

"Why, Philly! You have it on!"

She looked about her shoulders. Why, so she did.

Chapter Five

Hazelnut brown. No, dark honey. Dark honey, with traces of spun gold . . . Gavilan wondered, playing with his fountain pen, if her hair lightened during the summer months of sunshine, or if Philipa Braedon, like most ladies, kept that profusion of soft, fragrant hair bundled beneath a straw hat. She had worn no hat at the Waverlys' the other night, and he'd sat across from her at dinner wondering if her hair felt as soft as it looked in the glow of Mrs. Waverly's crystal chandelier. Then later, on the porch, he had brushed against it with his cheek and had marveled at its warm, satiny texture, as well as its faint, wondrous aroma, like the first flowers of spring.

Dark honey, he imagined, closing his eyes. *Spilled carelessly upon the white mound of his pillow, warm and soft between his fingers . . .*

He opened his eyes to the papers on his desk, startled by his unanticipated reverie. Where was he? He realized, abashed, that Owen Parrish was staring at him from his own small table across the makeshift office on the second-floor walkup above the Promenade. His secretary's collar was loosened, his grayed cuffs pushed up to his elbows, and his narrow dark eyes sporting, with their thin, barely visible brows, their typically cynical expression.

"What's the matter, Brownie? Daydreaming, again?"

Gavilan tossed his pen onto the miasma of paperwork before him and raked his fingers through his own thick, unruly hair. He found Parrish's perceptions invaluable as a businessman, but nearly intolerable as an acquaintance. Besides, Owen knew he hated to be called "Brownie."

"We're nearly two months behind here," Owen went on to remind him. "The bathhouse alone was supposed to be finished by Decoration Day, and we won't even have the zoning we need by then. You still haven't gotten permission for the arcade and the casino, and we were supposed to have the extension of the Promenade in the works by now. You stand to lose a lot of money if that Braedon woman and her damned auxiliary get in the way of things."

That Braedon woman. Gavilan leaned back in his chair until the front legs reared up off of the floor, challenging his secretary with a direct gaze.

"I can handle Miss Braedon, Owen," he replied, arcing his fingers before his lips.

Owen Parrish smirked, a singularly unpleasant expression in an already unpleasant countenance.

"Yeah, sure," he retorted, his tone derisive. "Like you handled the Dean's niece at Princeton?"

Owen Parrish always knew just which buttons to push. Sometimes, Gavilan wondered why he'd kept him around for so long. He got up from his chair and strode to the window overlooking the Promenade, a journey that required but four steps. The niece to whom Owen referred had been well known in Princeton fraternity circles as a girl of astonishingly easy virtue. She was labeled the Junior Class Project that year, and had been more than willing to accommodate the class. It had merely been Gavilan's misfortune to get caught by the girl's uncle, the Associate Dean of Princeton's law school, who was widely rumored to prefer the young men with whom she romped. The girl, of course, had since married well, and her uncle had been named to the State Supreme Court. Such, Gavilan reflected bitterly, was justice.

"I could buy and sell that hypocritical bastard tomorrow, Parrish. And a dozen just like him," he reminded the other man tersely, jamming his hands into the pockets of his white duck trousers. "And don't you forget it."

Behind him, Owen chuckled. It was an intolerably patronizing sound.

"It still rankles, though, doesn't it, Brownie?" he drawled, his Brooklyn accent as thick as the hair on his round head was thin. "Probably the only time in your life when you didn't get exactly what you wanted. I'll bet you'd trade everything you own in a minute to have that Ivy League sheepskin he robbed you of."

Gavilan's hands in the pockets of his trousers were balled into tight fists. Below him, on the Promenade, women in spring pastels pushed enormous wicker perambulators in the bright May sunshine as the ocean breezes tugged like spoiled children at the hems of their draped skirts.

"History," Gavilan dismissed, forcing a light tone to his voice that he was far from feeling. "Ancient history, Owen. Although I must confess it was the most expensive piece of ass I've ever had. And certainly not worth the price. Of course, if my father had been richer, he might have purchased my way back into Princeton's good graces. How the hell did we lose so much time here already?"

He wanted to change the subject, his untimely dismissal from Princeton a decade before not being his favorite topic of discussion. Owen Parrish, annoyingly, laughed again, and Gavilan longed to bloody the man's already misshapen nose.

"You spent six weeks in Cape Cod following a red herring on Emma Hunt. Remember?"

Terence Gavilan faced his subordinate and former classmate, barely curbing his urge to seize him by the throat.

"A red herring *you* fished up," he flared, his anger surfacing like a leviathan on a stormy sea as he recalled yet another failure to ferret out the elusive author.

Owen Parrish, irritatingly, leaned back in his chair, folding his thick hands across his paunch.

"I only do what you pay me for, Brownie," he remarked,

his tone laced with sarcasm. "You're the one who's obsessed with the woman."

One of these days, you snide, self-satisfied bastard, Gavilan thought, considering the man who had gotten the diploma, when you are no longer of any use to me, I will take great pleasure in firing you, if not destroying you. He debated giving Parrish the afternoon off, just to be quit of his offensive company. Then he had a better idea.

"Grease some palms at the courthouse, Owen," he ordered the man, reaching for his own straw hat that hung on a peg by the door. "I want the permits for that casino by the end of the week. And I want a complete file on Philipa Braedon. The whole Braedon family, in fact. Back to the *Mayflower*, if necessary. I want to know about every skeleton in the Braedon wardrobe. And probe the Waverly armoire, as well, while you're about it."

"Anything else?" Parrish was laconic, having just been given several days' worth of additional work.

Gavilan smiled, his humor restored.

"Since you're so disdainful of my taste in literature, I expect you to return every volume of Mrs. Hunt's work you've borrowed from me recently. That would be four books, I believe. And send a messenger around with some flowers for Miss Braedon. White roses. And I guess a bunch to Jess Flaherty, too. With my name on the card, not yours."

One of the good things about having a bad reputation, Gavilan reflected as he bounded down the stairs for his afternoon off, was that no one ever expected any better of you.

The Promenade in Braedon's Beach was but four city blocks long and consisted of a fishing pier on the north end and a boat launch on the south. Sandwiched in between were the kind of quaint little shops that catered as much to permanent residents as to seasonal ones, including a restaurant, an ice cream parlor complete with wrought iron furnishings with umbrellas for dining al fresco, a milliner, a shop featuring all manner of attractive and utterly useless gift items, several clothiers, and a candy store whose sign proclaimed "Salt Water Taffy Available Here." Why anyone would consider that last to be an attraction was beyond Gavilan. He considered the uniquely New Jersey delicacy to be only slightly more appetizing than caulking cement, and often thought it would be better suited for that use than for consumption as a confection.

In addition to these establishments were two large storefronts which were boarded up. These were the buildings Gavilan hoped to use for his arcade and casino. Their locations were excellent, and he was relying upon their success to enable him to make additional land acquisitions along the Promenade in the near future, as well as to encourage expansion of the same for further enterprise. Surveying the scene from a bench near the fishing pier, he saw in his mind's eye the flurried activity of Coney Island and Atlantic City. He saw a wondrous confusion of wild amusements: roller coasters imported from Germany; roundabouts from Italy, and even a Ferris Wheel made by George Ferris, himself. He saw casinos and arcades, and paddleboat rides. He saw peanut vendors and lemonade stands and beaches full of bathers who sunned by day and spent by night.

He saw two women in white tennis dresses and hats pedaling shiny Columbia model safety bicycles energetically along the Promenade in his direction. He squinted, shielding his eyes against the glare of the midday sun, and perceived at once Miss Philipa Braedon in the lead, followed closely by an unknown companion. Recalling their encounter of several days before at the Waverlys', he wondered, as a grin meandered across his lips, if she would attempt to pretend that she did not see him.

Suddenly the woman in the rear stopped pedaling. They were still perhaps 50 yards away from him, and he heard her call "Philly!" in an excited soprano. He watched Miss Braedon adroitly maneuver her vehicle and return to her friend's position. He could not hear their words, but he could tell by their animated gestures that they were arguing about something, and he thought he saw the other woman nod in his direction. He watched with interest as Philipa shook her head vehemently, her hands planted firmly on her hips. A pleading whine could be heard above the sound of the wind and surf, and a plaintive gull high above responded to it with

a lonely cry. The other woman scrambled onto her bicycle
and Miss Braedon hurried to follow, calling "Essie! Wait!"
in frantic tones.

But Essie did not wait. She pedaled gaily in his direction,
staring straight ahead. Miss Braedon, with an unmistakable
expression of resignation on her attractive features, made to
follow, albeit slowly. The pretty, petite blonde in the lead
suddenly came to a halt about ten feet away, crying "Oh!"
with a look of not-quite-surprise on her face. She then dis-
mounted and began examining the rear wheel of her bicycle,
which had been operating perfectly. Gavilan smiled to himself, deciding to play along.

Rising from his indolent pose upon the bench, he strolled
up to the woman even as Philipa Braedon pedaled toward
them. He pretended to ignore her as he addressed her afflicted
companion.

"I beg your pardon, ma'am," he said politely to the woman
he'd heard called Essie. "May I be of some assistance here?"

"Oh," the little blonde fretted again, blushing becomingly.
"You are very kind, sir. My wheel—it seems stuck—this old
bicycle . . ." She allowed her helpless whine to trail off, batting her brown eyes at him.

Gavilan restrained himself from laughing. The woman,
whoever she was, was an outrageous flirt, but hardly an accomplished actress. Still, it might be interesting to humor her.

"Please, allow me." He bowed, and bent on one knee to
examine the offending object. There was, as he suspected,
nothing whatever wrong with it. He slipped a small piece of
gravel into his hand from the deck of the Promenade and
straightened even as Miss Braedon, her features a study of
chagrin, came to a halt beside her friend.

"This stone was your problem, I believe." He presented
the pebble to the woman, who looked completely abashed.

"Why, good afternoon, Miss Braedon!" He addressed Philipa next, touching the brim of his skimmer, trying to suppress
his smile. He affected wonder with, he was sure, far greater
thespian skill than Philipa Braedon's transparent little friend.

Philipa was, however, he sensed with no surprise, not in
the least deceived by his performance.

"Good afternoon, Mr. Gavilan," she responded in a grudging way that bordered on hostility. "May I present Mrs. Charles Tavistock. Esmaralda Tavistock, Mr. Terence Gavilan."

Immediately the pretty younger woman's eyes ignited with pleasure and undisguised triumph. This, thought Gavilan, was precisely what the two women had been arguing about. He took her gloved hand into his own and bent over it without kissing it, glancing once at Philipa as he did so. She was attempting to mask a scowl. The expression was surprisingly appealing, on her.

"Mr. Gavilan!" The artfully artless Mrs. Tavistock expressed astonishment and pleasure. "I have heard my husband talk about you in the most glowing of terms! You have come to our little island to make us all rich as kings, I hear."

Miss Braedon, Gavilan noticed, reddened profusely at her friend's rather bold remark. He wondered, watching her, how a man could look at Esmaralda Tavistock, pretty as she might be, while Philipa Braedon occupied the same room. He wondered further how he might respond to so bold and uncouth a statement so as to persuade Miss Braedon's unexpectedly attractive blush to remain.

"Not all," he replied with a measured amount of self-deprecation. "Only those with enough foresight to appreciate the opportunity. How refreshing," he went on, changing the subject, "to see women engaging in healthy exercise! You ladies are quite the Gibson Girls."

Miss Braedon's ensuing glower was elegant.

"We are hardly girls, Mr. Gavilan," she contradicted him in an unmistakably chilly tone. "And certainly not Gibson's."

Esmaralda Tavistock giggled, disproving the heart of her friend's preemptive comment.

"We ride every day in the fine weather, Mr. Gavilan," she assured him, tossing her head like a playful filly. "My husband tells me that you play tennis."

"Not as often as I'd like," he rejoined, still watching Miss Braedon blush.

"Philipa is a wonderful player," Mrs. Tavistock went on, cheerfully unaware of her friend's discomfort at their con-

versation. "Why, she has even beaten Charles, upon occasion.
And how he hates that! You must come and play sometime,
Mr. Gavilan. We have a brand-new clay court in our yard.
We tried grass last year, but it was impossible to make it
thrive in this horrid sand."

"I can imagine," Gavilan interpolated cordially.

Philipa Braedon tugged impatiently upon her friend's arm,
trying very hard, it seemed to him, to avoid his stare.

"We must be going, Essie," she said firmly.

Mrs. Tavistock shook her off, turning what she no doubt
believed to be a sweet smile to Gavilan.

"My husband and I are hosting a garden party on Decoration Day, Mr. Gavilan," she informed him, without even
glancing at Miss Braedon. "Please say you'll join us!"

Gavilan smiled, pleased at the thought of another social
engagement where he could campaign his ideas to the gentry
of Braedon's Beach at the same time as he could pursue the
granddaughter of its founder, with or without the presence of
her fiancé.

"I am honored by your invitation, Mrs. Tavistock, and I
will gladly join you. How kind of you to include a comparative stranger in your celebration."

Esmaralda Tavistock apparently enjoyed the role of society
grand dame.

"Not at all, Mr. Gavilan. It will be our pleasure to entertain
you, and I shall certainly introduce you to everyone who is
anyone in our little town. You may rely upon it. And—"

"Essie, we must go. *Now*," Miss Braedon interrupted her
friend, fairly tearing the younger woman's arm from its
socket. "Good day, Mr. Gavilan."

She did not even look at him as she uttered the words and
mounted her bicycle. Mrs. Tavistock, subdued, followed her
friend's example with a smile and a wave.

"Decoration Day, Mr. Gavilan!" she called over her shoulder to him. "Two o'clock!"

"I'll be there, Mrs. Tavistock," he assured her, curiously
invigorated by the afternoon's encounter. "Rely upon it!"

He added that last for Philipa Braedon's benefit. Interesting,
he thought. He had not exchanged more than a handful of

words directly with her, but he felt as though he had said far more to the delightfully proper Miss Braedon than he had to her considerably less rigid, and less interesting, companion. She found him attractive. Her steadfast avoidance of his eyes confirmed that. He wondered, watching the cyclists disappear down the Promenade, if she was aware of that attraction herself, or if she was too committed to the notion of marrying her brooding and dispassionate childhood sweetheart and would-be minister to allow herself to believe it. Ah, Miss Braedon, he thought, trembling with sudden anticipation. What a satisfying conquest you will be!

Chapter Six

"You are mine," the slave trader gloated, his words piercing her like sharp swords. "You will do my bidding now, and do it gladly, or you will see your lover die horribly before your eyes!"

Diana could not hide her terror any longer. This man was her captor, and her master. She bowed her head, unable to endure the undisguised lust in his sharp eyes. She would do anything for Adam. Even this...

Owen Parrish reread the passage, seeing before him the lovely, half-naked Diana, her white body glistening with exotic oils for the pleasure of her master. He could hear the distant music of heathen instruments, and smell the heavy, pungent aroma of incense in the trader's tent. Emma Hunt, whoever she was, had been a slave to such passions as this, he thought hungrily, ramming the book into its place on the shelf in Gavilan's library. *The Willing Slave*, this one was called, and ironically it had been the first Emma Hunt tome to which Gavilan had introduced him. It was not necessary, he had discovered, to read them in the order in which they had been published. It was best to read them as one's own erotic fantasies dictated.

How fortunate he was, he reflected, that Gavilan's obsession paralleled his own. With Gavilan's money and his own skill at ferreting things out, he knew it was only a matter of time before he could put the disturbing matter of Emma Hunt to rest. Why couldn't her life be an open book, like the Braedon woman's?

It hadn't taken much genius at all to uncover the fact that the town's founding daughter had graduated summa cum laude from Bryn Mawr College outside Philadelphia in 1898 with a degree in classical literature. It had, however, required a bit more persistence and a nose for scandal to find that her name had been remotely linked to a certain married professor who had been forced to resign because of allegations that he had compromised a student. Not Miss Braedon herself, unfortunately, but in interviewing certain willing subjects during the course of his investigation, he discovered that the said professor had made certain promises to her, including one of marriage, which was supposed to have been a secret. Apparently Miss Braedon had been unaware that the man was already married, and that he in fact had made similar offers to more than one of her classmates, including the one with whom he was eventually caught *in flagrante*, as the saying went. Philipa Braedon had escaped, at the time, with her sterling reputation intact.

So far, at least.

Of course, now that it was in Terence Gavilan's hands, thanks to him, there was no telling what might happen.

The Waverly investigation, sadly, had come up dry. But Gavilan had departed for the Decoration Day celebration appearing more than contented with the information at hand. Owen Parrish, satisfied with the results of his labors, sat awaiting Miss Jessamyn Flaherty, a social outcast like himself, in Terence Gavilan's favorite chair with a glass of his finest brandy in his hand. His Decoration Day celebration, like his master's, had only begun. He toasted his reflection in the globe of the snifter. Braedon's Beach was as good as theirs.

Now, he would be free once again to renew his efforts upon the elusive Mrs. Emma Hunt . . .

Charles Tavistock's friends were shallow and boring, just as he was. Philipa kept herself apart from the guests as much as she could, unable to endure their incessant jests ridiculing suffrage and women's rights, sure that her very presence inspired these men to new heights of bigotry. The women were no better, she reflected, watching as the wives of Charles's business associates huddled in cliques, gesturing and whispering behind fans. Elliot was off somewhere with his friends, involved in a serious game of croquet, a game she found only slightly less tedious than its cousin golf. And so she sat on a bench under a birch tree, like a wallflower at a debutante ball.

It was a thoroughly unpleasant sensation.

She found herself, by and by, mulling over her latest novel. Set against the backdrop of the Crimean War during the reign of Queen Victoria, it featured a fearless lieutenant and a young orphaned English girl who was to fall in love with him and follow him for years until she was old enough to marry him. The writing had gone smoothly for a time, until she suddenly realized that her hero, who had started his fictional life as a blond, blue-eyed Adonis, had become, somehow, a tall, chestnut-haired man with penetrating dark eyes and a wide, ever-smiling and sensuous mouth. This unexpected turn of events had alarmed her.

She couldn't be in love with Terence Gavilan. She barely knew the man. And she intended to keep it that way. Still, there was no denying that her heart had a way of reminding her just how attractive a man he was whenever he happened to be near, even if she could barely muster the will to look him in the face for fear he'd read her emotions as clearly as he read everything else about her.

The afternoon was warm and calm. It was breezy on the beach, but Essie's yard faced the bayside of the island. Bees buzzed in the honeysuckle that carpeted the latticework along the back fence. Philipa concentrated her attention on an army of large black ants at her feet foraging for crumbs of barbecue in the sand and yellowed pine needles. The activity of the ants was, in any case, of far more interest to her than the boorish conversation of the cultural Philistines around her. She wished, as was not uncommon for her, that she were home in her study with her typewriter and her characters, weaving their lives into the fabric of a romantic novel instead of here eavesdropping on half-heard conversations of ruined hopes and disappointments. It was rather more depressing a way than she cared to spend a holiday, but Essie had invited her, and she was obliged to attend.

Above her head a gray squirrel chattered. He scampered higher into the birch tree, knocking a twig onto the cream-colored cotton lawn of her favorite afternoon dress. She brushed it away with a mitted hand and looked up, as if on some silent signal, to witness the advent of Terence Gavilan on the arm of their hostess.

Essie was prattling away in her animated fashion, and Terence Gavilan, to his credit, appeared deeply interested in her chatter. Philipa was safe enough from embarrassment, she determined, staring at him from this distance. He looked more than usually handsome in his gray and white windowpane checked suit, white gloves and skimmer. The man's wardrobe of hats alone, she reflected, surely rivaled any woman's of her acquaintance. His sienna locks curled slightly about his collar, and Philipa was aware of a desire to smooth them with her fingers. The notion took her by surprise, and her face grew warm even as his eyes, from across the yard, met hers.

He held her gaze, persuading her blush to remain. Essie went on talking, apparently unaware of the visual exchange taking place before her very eyes. Terence Gavilan touched his hat, holding her gaze until Essie, completely oblivious, led him to a cluster of men who were drinking rum punch under the trees near the tennis court.

Philipa was gripped by a desire to get up from the bench and run from the yard, but she mastered herself. Philipa Braedon, you are twenty-five years old, engaged and a college graduate, she scolded herself. You are far too old and far too wise to behave like a foolish and flustered schoolgirl. Terence Gavilan is only a man, she went on, looking about for Elliot. And if he were going to make an issue of the episode on the carousel, he would have done so long before today.

Elliot was nowhere in evidence, the croquet game having been established some distance from the house. She had just decided to get up and go to find him when her path was suddenly blocked by the tall, broad-shouldered frame of the distressingly omnipresent Terence Gavilan.

"He's playing croquet, beyond the tennis court." Mr. Gavilan's light baritone sent an unwelcome ripple along her spine.

She could not help but stare at him. "Who?" she wondered, surprised that she had spoken.

"Elliot Waverly," he supplied helpfully, smiling. "That's who you were going to look for, isn't it?"

He was infuriatingly intuitive.

"No," she replied hostilely, staring at the group of women who sat near the house peering at her from behind paper fans.

"Surely, you weren't leaving on my account, then?" His astonishment was not quite genuine.

If only his voice were not so thrilling! She forced herself to meet his gaze again, and found him sporting an amused expression as he regarded her.

"Vanity does not become you, Mr. Gavilan," she remarked as sweetly as she could, even though it was a lie. Few things, she was discovering to her dismay, did not become the engaging Terence Gavilan.

He laughed out loud, causing several heads to turn in their direction.

"Touché," he declared, bowing to her. "Well, now that we've established that you are neither running away from me nor looking for your fiancé, shall we sit down awhile and chat?"

Not wanting him to believe he had scared her away, and unable to form a reasonable excuse for not joining him, she resumed her seat. He took the place beside her, sinking his tall frame onto the bench with a grace she could not help but admire.

"What have we two to talk about?" she murmured, all at once lightheaded.

Beside her, he shrugged. It was a careless, unstudied ges-

ture which she found very masculine, and more than a little
pleasing.

"The first thing that comes to mind," he replied easily,
stretching his long legs out before him, "is how you come to
be sitting here by yourself like the lone mourner at a wake
instead of participating in the festivities."

His question lacked the taunting quality of his earlier remarks, and she found herself wanting to respond to it in a
similarly straightforward fashion. She folded her hands into
her lap and tried to shrink away from him, for the bench was
small and his shoulders were broad. He, however, did not
seem to mind the proximity at all.

"At the risk of sounding snobbish," she answered in a
quiet voice, surveying the party, "I find that I prefer my own
company to that of most of the guests. Not being of a mind
to argue politics, I avoid the men. Uninterested in discussions
of dalliances and children's maladies, I find the conversation
of the women tiresome. There is no one here, except for Elliot, with whom I can converse intelligently on matters of
interest or concern to me, and I choose not to suffer anyone
else to bear my taciturn humor."

There, she thought, relieved to have expressed a forthright
observation to him. Let him draw whatever inference he cares
to from *that*.

To her surprise, he did not offer a disparaging comment to
her candid admission.

"How interesting that you should say that," he remarked,
his deep voice as soft as a gentle caress. "How often I have
found myself in that very same position. Tell me, Miss Braedon, do you suppose that may be because we don't allow
ourselves the luxury of behaving like mere mortals from time
to time?"

She stared at him, trying to determine the weight of his
question. He was regarding her with a steady and penetrating
gaze, his wide mouth relaxed and unsmiling. She perceived
in him, all at once, a kindred spirit which she had not marked
before. Had she created it, or was it authentic? There was no
way of telling. At least, not at the moment. She had, however,
the comforting sense that he knew, and understood, precisely

what she meant. And she, by turn, took his meaning, as well.

"Are we so hopelessly conceited, then, Mr. Gavilan?" she inquired lightly, unwilling to look away from his sober, magnetic dark eyes.

He flashed her a quick grin, as though hoping to conceal his deeper thoughts from her once again.

"I can't speak for you, of course," he responded with an unmistakable playfulness in his tone. "But I certainly am. And I think it only fair to warn you in addition that I have a nearly uncontrollable urge to flirt with beautiful women, a compulsion of which you are no doubt aware. And may I say, Miss Braedon, that I believe you to be the most beautiful woman here today?"

He had caught her off guard again!

"You may say it, Mr. Gavilan," she answered with what she hoped was an air of propriety, looking away from him again with warmth in her cheeks. "But you have little hope of being believed."

Beside her, he sighed, a bottomless sound which resonated in his expansive chest.

"More's the pity, Miss Braedon," he breathed at the end of it. "Many is the plain woman who has made herself beautiful merely by believing herself to be so. And you are by no means plain. I've no doubt that with your extraordinary wit, you could have been quite an accomplished coquette."

Philipa bridled. "How very interesting," she remarked icily. "And I was just thinking that, were you not quite so wearisome a flirt, you might actually have something of value to say."

"Philly!" Elliot trotted up unexpectedly, his thin face red from his run. "Essie and I have challenged all comers. What luck that you are here, Mr. Gavilan. Help me persuade Philly to play croquet. You can partner her. She's not half bad, really, when she applies herself."

Powerless against the combined persuasions of both Elliot and Mr. Gavilan, she accompanied the men around the side of the tennis court to a shaded yard set up with wickets. Already a cluster of spectators had gathered, and Essie, in her gay, cherry and white striped silk dress with matching bonnet, was trying out mallets.

"We mean to trounce you, Mr. Gavilan," the younger woman purred, her brown eyes bright as she tossed her head of blonde ringlets. "Elliot and I are the best players in all of Braedon's Beach. Perhaps in the entire state of New Jersey. I shall stake you out personally." She selected a red mallet and ball, more to complement her gown than for any other purpose, Philipa guessed.

"Now there's a woman who knows how to flirt," Gavilan remarked sotto voce, touching Philipa's elbow as he nodded and smiled at Mrs. Charles Tavistock. Philipa softened the glare she'd meant to bestow upon him. He was right. That Essie was her very best friend in all the world did not alter the fact that she was an outrageous flirt. Gavilan met her gaze with a frank, direct look. Philipa's mouth grew limp at the expression, as if in anticipation of a kiss. Gavilan's lightning-quick smile told her he was thinking the same thing.

"I think the green for you, Miss Braedon," he announced, taking hold of the green mallet and ball with authority. "For luck. It will complement your eyes. Your eyes are very green today, indeed. Don't you think so, Mr. Waverly?"

Elliot had been practicing his stroke, and he glanced up at the older man, his youthful face flushed and perspiring.

"What? Green? I—I hadn't noticed. Why, I suppose they are." He was nonplused for only a moment before returning his attention to his blue ball.

Philipa wanted to run from the yard and all the way home. She had, with that one intimate observation, been made all too aware of her treacherous feelings for Mr. Terence Gavilan at the same time as the older man had illustrated to her the comparative indifference of her own beau, the man whom she was supposed to marry. She was certain, glancing furtively at the comparatively polished Mr. Gavilan, that the wily man had intended to orchestrate just such a tumultuous state of affairs.

Interested spectators began putting up friendly wagers. Terence Gavilan confidently took up the yellow ball and mallet, ensuring for himself the second position. Essie stood beside him, sidling and smiling. With Gavilan's recent unvarnished observation ringing in her ears, Philipa was keenly embarrassed for her friend.

They each dropped their balls over their shoulders at the starting stake. Philipa's green one, sadly, rolled into a gopher hole. The other three players quickly threaded the wickets and were off. She surveyed her miserable lie, biting her lower lip, fighting a foolish urge to cry.

"Here, Miss Braedon." Terence Gavilan was at her side again, his tone harboring a note of intimacy despite the gathering crowd. "May I show you a clever trick?"

Philipa had the uneasy sense that he was not referring to a croquet stroke. As though it were the most natural thing in the world, he removed his jacket and his skimmer, tossing them carelessly onto the lawn at their feet. Before she could refuse, however, he positioned himself squarely behind her, pressing his body against hers. He made a show of seizing her mallet by placing his arms around her. She could scarcely breathe, imprisoned as she was by his instructive embrace. His bare, manicured hands closed upon her own gloved ones, and they were strong and hot. With a smooth, unbroken sway of his body, which she felt all the way into her toes, he guided the mallet to make contact. Their combined movement sent her green ball careening toward the stake. She did not move, and Gavilan made no effort to release her, seeming to be more interested in the progress of the ball than in relinquishing his custody.

"Your hair smells like honeysuckle," he whispered swiftly in her ear. He did not look at her again as he went off toward his own ball.

She nearly fell over when he let her go.

Philipa ordinarily was not a half bad croquet player, but her partner had completely shattered her concentration. She tailed during the entire match, and the final insult was Elliot croqueting her ball after he had completed the course. The winners graciously accepted congratulations from the losers, bets were paid, and new challengers came forward, relieving Philipa of the chore of providing further entertainment for Essie's guests. Utterly exhausted, she slipped away again, hoping to leave the party at last without attracting anyone's notice.

Her hopes were quickly dashed as she heard a voice at her ear.

"You play very well, Miss Braedon." Terence Gavilan was beside her, his baritone gently teasing. "I would be delighted to tutor you again sometime."

She swallowed hard and composed her features before facing him. He was still coatless and hatless, but he held a tall glass of lemonade in each hand, offering her one with a charming, boyish smile. His dark hair, overlong and impossibly unruly, begged her to tame it with her fingers. She resisted the urge by force of will alone, accepting the beverage instead.

"Thank you, Mr. Gavilan. For the lemonade, I mean," she said when she finally dared to speak, although her voice came out as no more than a whisper.

"But not for the lesson?" He appeared offended. "That was quite my favorite part of the game. Yours, too, I thought. Or hoped."

He was a tease and a flirt. She sighed. She was attracted to him, sadly. He intrigued her more than any other man she had ever met. Yet it was his very glibness, his perfect ease with a pleasing phrase, that convinced her of his capricious and fickle, not to say insincere, nature. Her heart had been trampled upon once, and that was enough for her. More than enough. She could not risk making a fool of herself again, especially not at this stage of her life. She was about to marry a man and settle down. She was no young college student, easy prey to a sophisticated older man who had professed his love for her while philandering with half a dozen other unsuspecting young women.

"I am sorry, Mr. Gavilan," she murmured, meeting his painfully tender gaze straight on. "I have wrongfully encouraged this kind of behavior from you from the very beginning. It is entirely my fault. I appeal to your sense of honor. Do not seek me out again. I cannot and will not be the kind of woman you apparently want, nor can I see any point in our continued contact. I—I am shortly to become engaged—"

"—to a man who doesn't even know what color your eyes are," he reminded her, not ungently, with a slight shake of his head. "Although perhaps you never allowed him to look. Prudery, you realize, is half a virtue and half a vice. There is nothing wrong in what we've done, Philipa. You find me attractive. God knows, I find you attractive. I kissed you once, because I wanted to. I want to kiss you again. Maybe more than kiss you. We're adults, and we're independent. There's no reason why we can't enjoy ourselves without feeling guilty about it, is there?"

His words made her all the more keenly aware of the vast chasm separating them in their perception of the world, and that he quoted Victor Hugo with ease impressed her not one whit. Men, after all, tended to seek the most outrageous excuses to defend their behavior. Every breath hurt her.

"Yes, there is," she said firmly, unable to use his first name as boldly as he had used hers. "There is a big difference between us, Mr. Gavilan. I would deny myself anything for the sake of my good name, and you, apparently, care nothing for yours, or for anyone else's. I could not possibly justify giving myself to a man who had so little regard for me, or for my values."

His dark eyes narrowed in an expression which seemed at first hurt, then disparaging.

"Spoken like the virtuous woman I know you to be," he offered, although his words sounded more like a taunt than a compliment. "You'll be the perfect wife for the Reverend Waverly. But ask yourself this, Philipa Braedon, if you dare: will he be the perfect husband—and lover—for you?"

Terence Gavilan walked away from her, not waiting for a reply. It was just as well, for she knew the answer to his question, and she did not like it.

Chapter Seven

1902, Gavilan thought as he netted Charles Tavistock's easy serve, was destined to be the summer of his discontent. His tennis game, among other aspects of his life at present, was abysmal. He restrained himself from slamming his racket to the clay. Tavistock was a marginal player at best, with the weakest backhand Gavilan had ever challenged. Yet the man was ahead, five-two, in the set. Cursing under his breath, he readied himself for another of Charles's deceptively slow serves.

And he netted it again.

"Game and set, Gavilan," Tavistock announced gleefully, mopping his brow with his handkerchief as he crossed the court to his opponent. "Pay up."

Gavilan could not even muster a word of congratulations for his host. He fished a ten-dollar bill out of his pocket and laid it carefully in the man's outstretched hand, hoping not to betray his annoyance by any excessive gesture.

"You are off your game," his host observed genially, pocketing the bill. "Does your work have you distracted?"

Gavilan considered him. Charles Tavistock was a business

associate, being a vice president of the bank with which he dealt. He was also a social acquaintance. It was obvious the man wished to cultivate a friendship with him, but Gavilan, who had few friends, was wary of taking Tavistock, or indeed any other resident of Braedon's Beach, into his confidence. It was too great a risk at this point. Perhaps at a later time, after he was sure there would be no obstacles to his plans, and when he had determined exactly what favors could be traded for his confidence. But not yet.

In any case, his business was proceeding nicely. The bathhouse was nearly completed and fully operational, and had already attracted a new tourist trade. Day trippers from Vineland, Millville and other inland towns had begun flocking to Braedon's Beach in record numbers, enjoying a convenience and economy not offered by Atlantic City or other resorts. The renovations to the building slated to house the arcade were progressing so that he could open the place as soon as the zoning was approved, possibly by the Fourth of July. His plans for a casino were as yet under wraps. He did not want to tip his hand. But other land acquisitions were quietly in the works. His timetable had been shifted by the unanticipated meddlings of Philipa Braedon and her Ladies' Auxiliary, but he was a patient man. He could afford to wait.

"No more than usual," he dismissed his host's question, bouncing the ball on the clay with his racket.

" 'Bluestocking' Braedon?"

"What?"

He must have registered surprise, for his host chuckled, to his chagrin.

"Philipa Braedon," prompted Tavistock, a knowing, if unpleasant, grin on his broad, smooth face. "Known in certain circles as 'the Bluestocking.' "

Gavilan affected disinterest with his next question, although he could not deny that his host had piqued his curiosity.

"How would a married gentleman be privy to the hue of another lady's undergarments?"

Charles did not respond to the vulgar inference.

"Bluestocking," he replied, removing his cap to scratch his balding head, "is what my mother used to call a bookish girl. A few of us have taken to referring to Miss Braedon as 'the Bluestocking.' Not to her face of course. Kind of a code.''

"A code?"

Tavistock shrugged, demonstrating rounded shoulders. "You've noticed that she pokes her nose into places where it doesn't belong—"

"—such as the welfare of her community?" Gavilan interjected politely.

"Exactly." Tavistock missed the point of Gavilan's shaded sarcasm. "So we devised this code to use when she pops up unexpectedly while we're discussing matters of importance. 'Let not thy right hand know what thy neighbor's left hand is doing,' so to speak."

How fatuously perfect, Gavilan mused, concealing his disgust. These men were behaving just like children trying to exclude an outsider from their play . . . the metaphor struck a little too close to home for comfort.

"Bluestocking," Gavilan echoed presently, wondering why the phrase, and its inferences, bothered him. He supposed, dismissing it, that it was because he, who had suffered from being labeled all his life, disliked labels of any kind, even when applied to someone else. Especially someone with honey-colored hair that smelled of fresh flowers . . .

He shook his head, hard.

"A bee?" Charles inquired, looking about.

"Yes," Gavilan replied firmly, scratching his chin. "A bothersome one."

"A few of us have been after Elliot Waverly to marry her once and for all, just to get her out of our hair." Apparently Tavistock was back on the subject of Philipa Braedon. "As it is, all the woman has to do is write her books and pester the Town Council with her petty concerns. It's become nearly impossible to get anything done."

"Write books?" Gavilan's ears pricked up. "She writes books? What kind of books?"

Charles Tavistock shrugged again, spinning his racket in his hands.

"I asked her once. 'Obscure writings on classical literature,' she told me, looking down her nose at me in that damnably superior way of hers. 'Only another academic would find them of any interest.' I swear, what that woman needs . . .'' He trailed off, shaking his head in disgust. Drops of perspiration fell from his cheek onto his white shirt.

Gavilan considered him thoughtfully.

''Why,'' he wondered aloud, ''hasn't anyone given it to her?''

Charles appeared startled by the bold question. Then he laughed.

''No one's wanted to, I guess. Except maybe Elliot, and I think he's afraid to. Why? Don't tell me that *you* . . .'' Charles allowed his voice to trail off, but his steady scrutiny betrayed his lewd curiosity.

The expression brought Gavilan back to himself sharply. ''I?'' He affected amusement.

''Well, you certainly demonstrated an interest in her on Decoration Day,'' Charles argued, and Gavilan did not like the sharp look in the man's gray eyes.

''She is an attractive woman.'' Gavilan found himself wondering why he was defending his actions to this man.

''I suppose so.'' Tavistock sounded as if he disagreed. ''But she's waiting for Elliot. Their families approved it long ago, and if that mama's boy ever does go through with it, he'll be going from one mama to another.''

''She has too much sense for him, if you ask me,'' Gavilan muttered, sliding his racket into its covering.

''That may be,'' Charles conceded, doing the same. ''But she'll marry him. He's safe, and she can manage him. So she thinks. That's what every woman likes to think. It makes them happy.''

Gavilan, however, was only half listening. Philipa Braedon writes books! What an interesting revelation. Some day, somehow, he would have to persuade her to show him her writings. But first, he would have to find a way back into her good graces.

He slapped his cheek with his hand. Why hadn't he thought of this before?

''Bee?'' Charles inquired.

"No, mosquito," he replied. "Where does Miss Braedon attend church?"

"Holy Innocents, same as us. Why?" Charles was mystified.

"I think perhaps it's time I found God," Gavilan declared in a soft voice, pressing a finger to his lips thoughtfully.

Charles Tavistock's laughter echoed in the birch trees.

"You are quite wrong, my friend. The way to that kind of woman is to sweep her entirely off her feet."

Gavilan was amused by this analysis from a man whose own wife would flirt with anything in pants.

"Really?" He expressed his disdain as wonder.

"She's my wife's best friend. Take my word for it." Tavistock nodded firmly.

Tavistock's conviction persuaded Gavilan that the man knew absolutely nothing about Philipa Braedon, and very little about women in general.

The Reverend Henry Michaels had become the second rector of Holy Innocents Episcopalian Church after the death of its first rector, Father Thomas Wharton, five years before. Father Wharton had founded the church nearly 25 years earlier, and Philipa's grandfather had been one of its first vestrymen. Parishioners hereabouts, having grown up, married, baptized and buried with Father Wharton for over a generation, still referred to Father Michaels as "the new rector," despite his half decade of tenure.

Philipa smiled to herself over that observation, watching as the refreshment committee argued, in Father Michaels's study, the advisability of whipping fresh cream for the upcoming Strawberry Festival. Father Michaels had suggested purchasing blocks of ice. Mrs. Waverly was adamant in her belief that the runoff therefrom would ruin the wicker hampers. Mrs. Moss argued strenuously that her hamper had been left in the rain numerous times with no ill effect, whereupon Mrs. Ames, a neighbor of the prolific Mrs. Moss, whispered to Philipa that the result of the occasions upon which this had occurred was probably each of the young Mrs. Moss's five children. Philipa, smiling at that, remained neutral, not caring whether cream was served, and not believing that the issue was worth alienating either camp. She was content to be the secretary, an observer rather than a participant, and to be well out of any debates which might, and often did, occur.

"Well, at least the problem of a location has been settled." Father Michaels silenced the argument with his booming, jovial voice. Father Michaels's resonant tones could bring a roomful of chattering parishioners to a dead calm merely by uttering the words, "Let us pray."

All eyes looked to the rector expectantly, even Philipa's. This was news, indeed. As of their last meeting, the Strawberry Festival committee had been unable to find a location offering both area and facilities, there being some necessity for access to fresh water and lavatories. For Father Michaels to have accomplished this was quite a coup.

"The Somers estate," he answered their unasked question, beaming his most benign smile. "Mr. Gavilan came round to see me yesterday. Seems he wants to join our parish. Which reminds me, Miss Braedon. I have a favor to ask of you."

Philipa froze in her seat, eyeing the rector with no scant trepidation. That Terence Gavilan's visit would remind Father Michaels of a favor he needed to request of her made her more than a little nervous. The handsome entrepreneur had not troubled her since their confrontation on Decoration Day the week before, and she had allowed herself to believe, with a combination of relief and regret, that he had abandoned his campaign for her attention. Suddenly, Father Michaels was announcing Mr. Gavilan's intention to register in the parish, and that he had a favor to ask.

"Philipa, are you unwell?" Beatrice Waverly's stern voice was shaded with agitation. "You look as though the devil himself were sitting upon your shoulder."

Mortified at having revealed herself, Philipa shook her head.

"I'm fine, Mrs. Waverly," she managed to murmur, concentrating on her notebook. "It must be the heat. Please, Father Michaels. Do go on."

Father Michaels did go on as if nothing were amiss.

"As you know, Miss Braedon, our ranks tend to swell in

the summer months, and I know that you never hesitate to share your family's pew under any circumstances. Would you be so generous as to allow Mr. Gavilan to sit with you on Sundays? He—''

''She most certainly will *not*, Father Michaels, and I am appalled that you would even think of asking!'' Beatrice Waverly huffed, her blue eyes wide and her wrinkled cheeks pale. ''The very idea that a decent unmarried woman and a—''

''Yes, Father Michaels, of course I will.''

Had that really been her voice? Philipa marveled at its clear, even sound. For a full minute the room was deathly still, and she became painfully aware of the unabashed and critical stares being sent her way. Beatrice Waverly wore an expression of such astonishment that Philipa thought she might be having an attack of apoplexy.

''Philipa Braedon!'' Mrs. Waverly's thin lips formed the first consonants several times before any sound actually emanated from them. ''What can you be thinking of? What will Elliot say?''

Philipa suddenly felt very lightheaded. Free. As if she were a bird which had just been released, quite by accident, from its lovely gilt cage into a clear azure sky. Drawing in a deep breath, she formed a polite but firm response for her future mother-in-law.

''Elliot,'' she began, not blinking as she met the woman's horrified stare, ''will be pleased to know that I am offering Christian courtesy to a fellow worshiper. Elliot, thank heaven, does not have quite so condemning an opinion of people whom he hardly knows.''

Beatrice Waverly was deathly silent, a hawk circling overhead. Philipa felt, oddly, more tranquil than she could ever recall in her adult life. Could it, she wondered, returning Mrs. Waverly's stare, have something to do with the fact that she had stood her ground against Elliot's mother, a formidable opponent? Or, as was more likely, was it because she so eagerly anticipated having Terence Gavilan beside her for an hour in church every Sunday, hearing his fine, rich baritone joining in the hymns, breathing air that harbored traces of his light but very masculine cologne?

She forced down her blush at those thoughts, successfully. Beatrice Waverly would have perceived, and condemned, such a crimson betrayal in an instant.

"Well, of all things, Philipa Braedon," Mrs. Waverly managed, although she sounded as though she were choking on a stale biscuit. "I never imagined—I'm quite glad that your poor mother, God rest her soul, is not alive to see this day. She would be appalled to think that her daughter—"

"I am hardly a child, Mrs. Waverly, and you have no right to treat me as such." Philipa, to her own amazement, felt stronger and more secure in her resolution. "I believe I am capable of making my own decisions in such matters as affect me, thanks largely to my mother, who did have the good sense to send her daughter to college. This discussion is now over. Will there be anything else, Father Michaels, or may we adjourn?"

She closed her notebook with a bang that made every other woman, including Beatrice Waverly, jump. Father Michaels, whose innocent inquiry had inspired the debacle, looked about as happy as a clam in a steam pot. And Philipa herself felt remarkably wonderful.

Chapter Eight

A letter arrived by special messenger later that afternoon. The young man had found it necessary to knock three times and call loudly before she responded. It was Arliss's afternoon off, and Philipa had sequestered herself in her study, having no inclination to recount the events of the afternoon or to suffer the advice, however well-meaning, of friends and neighbors pertaining to the issue. When she finally responded to the summons, she bade the man wait on her porch while she fumbled in her desk for a tip. After dismissing him, she fairly slammed the door in the face of a curious neighbor, whose distracted expression as she started up Philipa's walk convinced her that the woman already had an opinion on the proceedings which Philipa was in no mood to entertain. She had found that she was shaking with anger when she had returned home, and preferred to be alone.

She appreciated the cool breeze in the darkened hallway as she made her way back to the study, letter in hand. The study was a bit cooler as well, being in the rear of the house, away from the afternoon sun and facing the ocean. Shunning her typewriter, she sank into the wing chair which had been her father's favorite and caught several deep breaths before turning her attention to the letter in her hand.

The postmark was New York. Frowning, she tore open the envelope. The only people whom she knew in New York were her family's lawyers and her publishing agent. It was, as she had suspected, from the latter.

"My dear Miss Braedon," she read, then skipped impatiently over the obligatory salutations to the second paragraph.

> *It is with growing concern that I report to you a matter of some curiosity, an event which occurred some two weeks ago. At the time, I thought nothing of it, but have since been given cause to suspect that there might be due reason for worry. At that time, I was visited by a man who produced no credentials but introduced himself as a Mr. Thomas Goliard. He was of average height, slightly greater than average weight, and had no remarkable features of any kind. He claimed to be an attorney's representative with information on an inheritance for Mrs. Emma Hunt. He had somehow (he declined to say precisely how, upon gentle questioning) discovered, or guessed, at my capacity as her publishing agent.*
>
> *As I know that there is no possibility of such, I discouraged what I took to be an exceptionally ardent admirer of Mrs. Hunt's work and showed him the door.*
>
> *Since that time, however, I have marked the gentleman's name: Goliard.*
>
> *Does that not strike you as odd?*
>
> *Please extend my warmest regards to Mrs. Hunt, and remind her that we eagerly await "The Lady Lieutenant." Sincerely, etc.*
>
> *P.S.: "The Calumnious Count" was met with the usual enthusiasm.*

Philipa reread the letter several times, sinking further into her seat. *Mark the name*, her agent had said: *Thomas Goliard.* The name, she mused, fanning herself with the missive, strangely resembled Terence Gavilan, but her agent's descrip-

tion of the mysterious interrogator did not. In any case, her
agent would have no way of connecting the two: Gavilan.
Goliard. She was certain that her agent referred to *Goliards*,
which was the name given to certain Latin poetry written
between the tenth and thirteenth century. Poetry upon which
Philipa Braedon occasionally formulated learned, if esoteric,
academic treatises for scholarly use, and, not coincidentally,
poetry upon which Mrs. Emma Hunt also occasionally relied
for certain unspeakably erotic inspirations.

Goliard.

She held the letter to her lips, rapt in thought. Who might
be so conversant with both classical literature and the works
of Mrs. Emma Hunt to draw such an astonishingly ingenious
parallel between the two?

This was not good.

Fighting a knot in her stomach, she quickly went to her
desk and withdrew a sheet of vellum from the drawer to pen
a response. Then she stopped herself.

Thomas Goliard, whoever and whatever he really was,
would in all likelihood not have been put off by her agent's
polite rebuff. He might, in fact, be closely monitoring her
agent's movements and correspondence, even to bribing
postal officials . . .

Philipa got hold of herself. You are beginning to think like
Emma Hunt, she scolded herself, shivering as she placed the
letter in a locked drawer of her desk which contained other
correspondence from her publishing agent. There is nothing
to worry about, yet. Remain calm. This Thomas Goliard had
nothing, at this point, but suspicion, if he had even that. The
whole episode might be nothing more than an eerie coincidence.

Or it might not.

Perhaps, she reflected with an undeniable sense of foreboding, it was time for a trip to New York. The idea began to
appeal to her as she considered it. A few days away from
Braedon's Beach might allow the petty furor over her recent
confrontation with Elliot's mother to resolve itself. It would
also give her an opportunity to do some shopping, some tour-
ing of museums, and possibly of delivering her latest manu-

script, *The Lady Lieutenant,* to her agent in person, eliminating the necessity of relying upon the mails.

Her mood brightened. Charles Tavistock traveled regularly to New York on bank business, and Essie needed very little persuading to accompany him on these junkets. Philipa could simply invite herself along. Once they were there, Charles would proceed about his business, she would introduce her publishing agent to Essie as a dear family friend, and they would take tea with him. She could find an opportunity to slip him her manuscript, and they would be well away before her vivacious but lamentably unworldly friend could even question her motives.

Or so she hoped.

Elliot called upon her that evening, wearing a brand-new navy and white seersucker suit topped with his summer skimmer. Philipa invited him to join her on the back porch, overlooking the beach and the ocean. It was a cool and breezy evening, clear overhead but with a ribbon of low clouds spanning the horizon which obscured the rising moon. Philipa shunned the porch swing in favor of a whitewashed Adirondack chair, and Elliot selected the seat opposing. There was a small table between them, and Mrs. Grant, without waiting to be summoned, brought two glasses of fresh lemonade, each with a sprig of mint from her kitchen garden. Philipa felt curiously calm and relaxed in the presence of Beatrice Waverly's son, despite the tension which he seemed, uncharacteristically, to be radiating. In fact, she confessed to herself, only a little amused, she was rather enjoying the fact that her proclamation had caused such a stir.

There was no doubt of it, she reflected, hiding her smile from the agitated Elliot. Terence Gavilan was definitely a bad influence on her.

"My mother is furious, Philly," Elliot began in a quiet, almost awed tone. "I am most curious to hear your side of the story."

Elliot, Philipa knew, had always been a little intimidated by his admittedly formidable mother. She prevented herself from chuckling.

"I'm sure your mother reported events accurately, Elliot. I see no reason to offer further words which could only lead to conflict and contradiction, not to mention a compromise of your loyalties."

Elliot said nothing. For a full minute, the only sounds were the surf buffeting the beach and the raucous mockery of scavenging gulls as they glided lazily overhead. Philipa sipped her lemonade, thinking it quite the finest batch Mrs. Grant had ever concocted. She found herself wishing for one of the little chocolate cookies, called Toll House, of which she was so fond.

"Philly, it isn't like you to treat my mother's feelings in so cavalier a fashion. What has gotten into you lately?" Elliot's tone was reproving. Philipa bit back her irritation.

"Elliot, I consider the whole incident a tempest in a teapot," she replied, aware that it came out as a retort, but not caring. "You, and your mother, would do well to remember that I have feelings too, as well as a mind of my own, thank you very much!"

She must have been glaring at him, for he blanched visibly in the fading twilight.

"It's Terence Gavilan, isn't it?" Elliot said, his ordinarily soft voice hardening. The sound of it surprised her. She had never heard him speak thus to anyone. "What does he mean to you, Philly? As your fiancé, I think I am entitled to an answer."

Philipa's anger crested as abruptly and as inevitably as a storm swell. She was on her feet, facing him with her hands clenched in the folds of her ivory dress.

"My 'fiancé?' " Her voice rose in pitch, and she strove to control it. "My fiancé? I am humiliated beyond comprehension to be forced to remind you, Elliot Waverly, that you have never properly proposed to me! And as for your inference regarding Mr. Gavilan, in view of our undeclared status, I do believe I am well within my privileges as a lady to tell you that it isn't any of your business!"

The polite thing for her to do, she realized, panting with indignation, would have been to go into the house and leave him in solitude to ponder his response to her outburst. But

Philipa was in no mood to be polite. She stood her ground, her feet firmly planted on the painted planks of the porch, staring hard at Elliot Waverly, whose slack features betrayed his utter astonishment. Even in the fading light, she could see that his ordinarily pale cheeks were filling with crimson, and that his blue eyes were unblinking.

"I . . ." He paused and swallowed, for he sounded as though he might be having some difficulty breathing. "You are right, Philly. I'm sorry. I would—I would like to correct my unforgivable mistake right now, if I might."

That was the limit. The sole reason for his sudden action, Philipa deduced, was to enable him to question her further regarding Terence Gavilan, and subsequently to forbid her (as if he could!) from allowing the man to share her pew with her at Sunday services.

"Please leave now, Elliot." She maintained a low voice with what she viewed as admirable self-restraint, still staring at him.

He was on his feet, his hands at his sides clenching and unclenching.

"Philly, I—"

"Get off of this porch at once, Elliot Waverly!" she ordered again, louder than before. Her anger took precedence over her circumspection, and she could not entertain the slightest concern that her neighbors would overhear their discourse.

Elliot appeared to weigh her. He nodded in slow acquiescence, backing off.

"All right, Philipa. I will go. I—I am sorry to have upset you so. I will call upon you another time. I leave for St. Charles in two weeks—"

"Just go, for heaven's sake, Elliot!" she shrieked at him, her patience having found its limit.

The young man very nearly upset his chair in his haste to do her bidding, or to escape from her harridan's wrath, she could not be sure which. In any event, she didn't care. She was shaking, although she was not upset by her immediate actions so much as by the various ramifications thereof.

For one thing, Terence Gavilan was certain to hear, one

way or another, all about the events of the afternoon. And how, she wondered, suddenly filled with dread, would she explain her words and her actions to him?

Elliot felt like the emperor in the fairy tale "The Emperor's New Clothes." He strove mightily to maintain an even, erect carriage as he retreated from Philipa's house all along Ocean Avenue, but he felt the unseen eyes of the entire neighborhood upon his back like so many stones hurled by an angry mob. Confused, hurt and, yes, angry, he wandered the streets for a time, not wanting to go home to face his mother, nor wanting to return to Philipa to try to patch things up. He had blundered again somehow. Nothing he ever did turned out right in the eyes of his mother, or in the eyes of the vexatiously perfect Miss Philipa Braedon. Here he was, 23 years old, and between the two of them he constantly felt a boy of seven.

He walked, and he walked, shunning even prayer, which had often been his consolation in times of worry or strife. The act of walking helped to clear his brain, and to revitalize his will and energy to face the challenges of his life.

Walking also brought him, after a time, to the door of Miss Jessamyn Flaherty, who lived by herself in a walkup in the less savory part of town.

He knocked quietly, and she answered the door before his hand returned to his side. She was wearing a dressing gown of emerald green satin trimmed in ostrich feathers dyed the same outrageous hue. Her pert young face crinkled into a fond smile, the same smile he remembered from their childhood days. Jessamyn Flaherty, he thought, feeling the weight of his troubles dissipate in the face of that smile, always had a way of making him feel like a special person.

"Hullo, Elliot," she greeted him in her childlike soprano, sounding truly delighted to see him at her door. "Would you like to come up? I'm going out, but not until later. You could stay for a little while, if you like, and we can talk, and . . . whatever."

Elliot found himself smiling back at her. For what she was, she always appeared so innocent. So artless. So genuinely fond of him. He would never think of marrying her, of course. Not only because of her lack of social position and his family's rightful disapproval, but for the fact that she was not his intellectual equal, the way Philipa was. Nor could he envision her as the mother of his children, or, more to the point, of Beatrice Waverly's grandchildren.

Oh, but she was so good for him! He never felt so complete, so totally in command of himself as he felt when he left her door. He had begun wondering daily how he would manage, sequestered in the confines of St. Charles, without Jess to give him a boost every now and again. He followed her up the stairs and stayed with her longer than he should have. He always stayed longer than he should, but she never seemed to mind. She never asked him for money, either, but she never refused or returned the ten dollars he always left on the nightstand, whether they did anything or not. Usually they did.

The room was small and smelled like must disguised by an excess of some garish perfume. The bed took up nearly the whole of it, as though the bed might be the only thing in the world she needed. But no. Her small closet was crammed with clothing. Dresses and jackets and hats and various undergarments in brash and exotic colors, colors Philipa would no doubt have fainted to even think of wearing. But bold, free-spirited Jessamyn delighted in such colors, and he delighted with her. She dressed by the light of a tall floor lamp hung with rows of garnet colored beads all around the scalloped red velvet lampshade.

He liked watching her dress. Her heavy, rounded breasts seemed to have been poured into the firm cups of her corset like brimming champagne glasses. Her legs were plump and shapely, inviting his touch as she deftly pulled her cotton stockings up over her calves and thighs. She pulled a dress of pink satin, the deep, blushing pink of his mother's prized geraniums, over her petticoat and bustle, and he even helped her button the pretty thing up the back. She smiled at him, her sleepy, rosy grin with her blue eyes half closed making him want to pull her back on the bed with him.

''Time to go,'' she said, and he rose instead, collecting his things in an awkward and self-conscious manner.

He never regretted the leaving. Leaving, he knew, was as inevitable as his arriving had always been. Just as quiet a thing, like leaving one's shoes outside the hotel room and finding them freshly polished on the threshold in the morning. It always would be that way until Jessamyn drifted out of his life, away from Braedon's Beach. Or until she settled down with some likable fellow who cherished her, and didn't mind what she was or what she had been, a man who merely saw in her what she could be, just as Jessamyn saw in him.

He found his way out of her door as a noisy Hurricane rounded the corner.

Chapter Nine

Philipa was ill on Sunday morning. It had been warm during the night, and she had felt feverish and restive, fighting a queasiness in her stomach that would not relent, even to Mrs. Grant's tested home remedies. On any other Sunday she would gladly have remained at home in bed with a hot water bottle pressed gingerly to her abdomen, but that, she realized grimly, would be impossible today.

After all, having so boldly contradicted the righteous Mrs. Waverly in front of the woman's peers only a few days before, she had no choice but to appear at church and endure the icy stares which were certain to result from her brazen behavior.

She allowed herself extra time for dressing, bidding Arliss time and again to wait while she sat upon the bedspread striving mightily to curb her repeated urge to retch. This most unhappy and unanticipated state of affairs, she reflected morosely, was surely due either to the anger of the Almighty over her unforgivable pride, or to her mounting anxiety at the thought of facing Terence Gavilan, and indeed the rest of the congregation, after her presumptuous and, she had begun to believe, foolhardy performance at Father Michaels's. Why, she mourned in agonized silence, couldn't she have just done what had been expected of her and refused the priest's request?

At Mrs. Grant's urgent behest, she took a little tea and toast in the breakfast room after she had finished the arduous task of dressing. Happily, the small meal did make her feel a little better, although contemplation of the walk to church dimmed her brightening spirits somewhat. Mrs. Grant, more than twice Philipa's age, insisted that she take her arm, and indeed she did rely on the older woman's strength, and even bade her to slow down on more than one occasion. The price of this assistance, however, was to endure the remonstrance of her housekeeper for the entire journey for presuming to venture forth with so debilitating an illness. Philipa had not even the vigor to argue with her.

Holy Innocents was a welcome sight, even for all the stares which she received as they approached the doors. The white-washed frame building stood proudly on high ground and boasted the tallest bell tower on the island, taller even than the Town Hall's. Its windows glistened in the morning sun as it stood watch over a tiny churchyard speckled with dune grass and marble monuments. Philipa greeted her neighbors and fellow parishioners in her usual, if somewhat weakened, fashion, noticing immediately that the Waverlys were not present. They were, in fact, conspicuous by their absence. It was with great relief that she sat down in the Braedon family pew at last, near the window so she could enjoy any breath of air that might venture through one of Father Michaels's lengthy sermons. She closed her eyes, relishing the stillness of the place. Then the organ began to wheeze, robbing her of her peace. Distracted, she found her place in her prayer book, waiting for the arrival of Terence Gavilan, and for the next thing to happen.

The church bells rang their summons through the warm June morning. In moments, Father Michaels would call them to prayer. All of this she had suffered, and now Terence Gavilan was not even going to show up! She felt ill all over again. She might just as well have stayed at home in bed.

There was no procession, the choir having been dismissed for the summer, but the congregation stood for the opening hymn. Philipa read along but could not muster the energy to sing with the rest. He wasn't coming, after all. She didn't know which was greater: her disappointment or her illness.

"I think you should sit down, Miss Braedon." She recognized that strangely courteous baritone at her ear, and she was undeniably overjoyed at his arrival. "You don't look well."

She could not answer him. She swayed dizzily, then felt the warmth of his hand on her arm, gently guiding her to her seat. Philipa was aware of a sense of satisfaction. She had fulfilled her duty after all. Beyond that, she was aware of nothing else.

Terence Gavilan had arrived late on purpose, wanting to make Philipa Braedon believe he was not coming. But when he arrived, his careful planning was instantly set aside. She was not well. She looked as pale as wheat paste, and as fragile as an eggshell. Through the prayers and the readings, he kept a watchful but surreptitious eye upon her in her corner, debating the wisdom of carrying her out of the church before all of the congregation. He decided, during the reading of the Psalm, that she looked as though she had already fainted, and he took matters into his own hands.

Amid the stares of everyone in the church, including Father Michaels, who stopped reading to observe the spectacle, Gavilan lifted the limp form of Philipa Braedon easily into his arms and carried her to the rear of the small building. On his way down the lone aisle, he spotted Esmaralda Tavistock and Charles. Philipa's friend demonstrated true alarm and would, he was certain, have jumped up to assist him, had her husband not restrained her with a firm hand on her arm. An older woman who seemed to know Philipa sprang up from her seat in the back and opened the doors for him, just as Dr. and Mrs. Waverly, and their offspring Elliot, were about to enter the apse.

Gavilan did not wait for a greeting, nor did he waste one.

"She's ill, Dr. Waverly," he heard himself explain in a quiet voice. "She fainted."

"She was sick in the night," the woman behind him offered, her aged features stricken with worry. "I told her not
to come this morning, but . . ."

You know Philipa Braedon, Gavilan thought, supplying the
woman's unspoken codicil. Sweetly stubborn and quietly outspoken Miss Philipa Braedon, who cannot allow a trifling
thing like an illness stand in the way of honor.

Now, why in the world would he feel a twinge in his gut
at that thought?

"I'll take her to her home in the Hurricane." He was laconic and did not even look at Beatrice Waverly, whose opinions were already well known to him. "It's faster. But there's
only room for the two of us."

Dr. Waverly, unlike his judgmental wife, nodded his approval of this proposed course of action.

"Mrs. Grant and I will follow in the carriage. We will be
along directly. Elliot, would you see your mother inside,
please?"

Elliot Waverly, Gavilan noticed shrewdly, would not meet
his gaze.

"Of course, Father," the younger fellow mumbled, and
Gavilan was seized by an unreasoning desire to strangle the
lad, who resembled a weasel more than a human being.

How could Philipa's illness have upset him so? he wondered distractedly, proceeding to his vehicle with his armful.
It was probably nothing more than a female complaint, or a
grippe, or some such other temporary malady. Why, in a day
or two, he thought, trying to buoy himself, she would most
likely be up and about, in the thick of things once again as if
none of this had ever happened.

For now, however, she lay slumped against his arm as he
drove through the quiet Sunday morning. He liked the feel of
her head against him, and he could just catch a breath of the
scent of her hair from beneath her gay straw bonnet festooned
with tiny silk roses. Presently she was murmuring something
that he could not make out. The very sound of her voice, so
small and weak, made him want to put his arm around her
protectively. But he needed both hands upon the steering
wheel.

Dr. Waverly and Mrs. Grant arrived at the Braedon house minutes after he did, and Mrs. Grant admitted him as he carried Philipa into the house.

"Up the stairs," Mrs. Grant said tersely in a tone that told him she didn't trust him. "And straight back."

Gavilan was aware of an errant desire to look around the place. It was the first time he had seen her house, and he wanted, for some reason he could not fathom, to take in all that was Philipa Braedon. She was so light in his arms that he could almost have forgotten she was there as he gazed at the collection of stern portraits of her family that sentried the staircase. Behind him, the heavy, hurried tread of the doctor and Mrs. Grant, whom he now understood to be the housekeeper, reminded him that he had a mission to complete.

Entering Philipa's bedroom, he felt as though he were penetrating a forbidden realm. In stark contrast to the heavy, solidly Victorian fixtures in the lower regions of the house, her bedroom, he was flabbergasted to discover, was upholstered in a pink and cream floral print, from the voluminous skirts on the dresser and vanity to the dust ruffle on the cherrywood bed. A dried laurel wreath woven with a soft pink ribbon adorned the broken-arch pediment on the headboard like the captured crown of a wood nymph, and the whole light, airy room smelled of the ocean and of dried, aromatic flowers. Across the room, diaphanous curtains billowed in the gentle sea breeze like tender white arms reaching for a stolen embrace.

As he lay her upon the ecru coverlet, his gaze alighted upon her nightstand. There, beside a dainty crystal clock and atop a small white and gold Bible, was a single white rose, dried and tied with a white satin ribbon. White roses, he had said to Owen Parrish. He'd forgotten! The sight of it nearly caused him to drop her, but he mastered himself again and placed her carefully in the center of the bed.

She stirred as he withdrew his arms from their assignment, and her eyelids fluttered open, like some fairy-tale princess he'd read about as a child. He could not recall which one, and in fact, the simile amused him. All at once he was gazing into her eyes, which appeared almost gray this day. He felt, from a place he did not care to name, a lump form suddenly in the back of his throat. He was paralyzed by an alien emotion, and he could not look away from her.

"M—Mr. Gavilan," she murmured drowsily, sounding as weak as a child. "What—"

"The doctor is here," he assured her, barely above a whisper. "Rest now, honeysuckle. Rest."

Indeed, the doctor was there, behind him. As Gavilan turned to depart, suddenly wanting very much to flee the room, he nearly ran into the man, whom he found to be scrutinizing him in a most disconcerting manner.

"Thank you for your assistance, Mr. Gavilan." Roger Waverly offered his gratitude courteously, but Gavilan could sense the suspicion in the older man's sharp-eyed gaze. "I'm sure Miss Braedon will be fine. Mrs. Grant and I will handle things from here. Can you see yourself out?"

Gavilan stared at the doctor, who dismissed him as if he were a mere errand boy. If he himself had not been overcome by a bewildering and unexpected desire to flee the place, he realized, aware of a bitter taste in his mouth, the combined forces of heaven and hell could not have prevailed upon him to go. However, as it was, his wants overcame his pride, and he found himself merely nodding to the man in farewell before slipping from the room with a small sigh of relief, mingled with wonder. Had he actually called her "honeysuckle?"

As Gavilan reached the bottom of the steps, mired in contemplation, Elliot Waverly came bounding into the house, his hat gone, his fair hair disheveled and his collar loose. His face was beet red and perspiring. Gavilan guessed he'd run all the way from Holy Innocents church.

"Where is she?" he panted, pausing at the open door for a breath. "Is she all right?"

Gavilan surveyed the younger man with, he knew, a look of disparagement.

"Your father says she'll be fine," he replied curtly, not moving from the bottom step. "He's upstairs in her room with her now."

Elliot breathed a quick sigh and made a move to pass him

at the foot of the stairs. Gavilan put out his hand, arresting
the younger Waverly's progress. Elliot glared at him, his pale
blue eyes smoldering.

"Let me pass," he demanded in a cold but quiet tone. "She
is my fiancé!"

Gavilan, annoyed, did not need to be reminded of that fact.

"Just a moment, Mr. Waverly," he intoned, both intrigued
and bitterly amused by Elliot's fervent concern over Philipa's
condition.

Elliot looked positively furious, but said nothing. He
merely stared at Gavilan with a hostile and impatient expression on his smooth, young features.

"In the future," Gavilan began, keeping his tone soft but
with an edge of warning, "I expect you to stay away from
Miss Flaherty. Do I make myself clear?"

Elliot's jaw dropped. He quickly set it again.

"I guess Jess can make up her own mind about who she
sees," he retorted in a low voice, demonstrating rather more
spunk than Gavilan had thought him capable of, but still casting a worried glance upstairs, as though afraid someone might
have overheard them.

"It isn't Miss Flaherty who concerns me." Gavilan cor-
ralled his audience's attention once again, maintaining a civil
tone, although he realized, with some surprise, that he had
taken hold of Elliot's jacket lapel in a savage and uncompromising grip. "I was thinking of Miss Braedon's welfare."

Elliot stared from Gavilan's face to the hand crushing the
lapel of his seersucker suit.

"Release me, sir," Elliot demanded, his voice shaking with
anger. "I remind you that Miss Braedon's welfare is not your
concern."

Gavilan did release him, not because he wanted to but because he sensed that unless he did, he would be brawling on
the floor with the younger man. And as he had not forgotten
the boxing lessons so hard-learned in Princeton, he just might
kill young Waverly. The thought gave him pause.

"If you are as concerned about Miss Braedon's welfare as
you profess to be," Elliot went on, straightening his jacket
with a much-practiced look of righteous indignation, "you

would be well advised to stay away from *her*."

Gavilan flexed his hands to prevent himself from seizing the younger man's throat.

"Don't threaten me, boy," he warned, staring hard at him.

Elliot drew himself up. "Good day, Mr. Gavilan," he remarked in a tone of forced boredom, and he brushed insolently past him on his way up the stairs.

Gavilan closed his eyes as the younger man passed, wishing he were less of a gentleman than he was. Elliot was both a cad and a coward, but there was nothing more that he could do, he realized grimly, than to leave her house. For now. He took two pensive steps toward the door before the sound of Elliot's voice stopped him again.

"You are in love with her, aren't you, Gavilan?"

The observation rooted him to the spot. In love with her? Impossible! he thought. Wherever would Elliot have fished up an idea like that? Love! There had to be another more reasonable, rational and logical explanation for the chaotic feelings he'd experienced since leaving the church with Philipa in his arms. Love! Elliot Waverly was out of his mind. He had to be. And yet . . .

"Mr. Waverly," he began, still staring at the door through which it was his intention to pass, "I'd be a little more worried about that possibility, if I were you. Especially if, as I suspect, Miss Braedon shares that tender sentiment."

Behind him, Elliot sniffed loudly.

"You're mad if you think you could ever be anything to her," the younger man sneered.

Still staring at the door, Gavilan laughed.

"Why don't you ask her, when she recovers, about that white rose on her nightstand?" He almost regretted that revelation, but not quite.

"Oh, she may believe that she is attracted to you." Elliot was not phased by his challenge. "To your looks and your bold, devil-may-care mien. But make no mistake. She is an exceptionally intelligent woman. She sees you for exactly what you are, Mr. Gavilan. As do we all."

Remembering Philipa on the carousel and on the croquet

course, Gavilan smiled, and faced young Waverly at last.

"Miss Braedon is a woman of deep insight, indeed," he offered lightly, enjoying his audience's look of sudden suspicion. "All the more reason for you to mend your roving ways. As if your aspiration to the ministry wasn't enough of one. Good day, Mr. Waverly. My compliments to your mother."

In love with Philipa Braedon! he thought to himself again as he departed into the noonday sunshine. What a preposterous notion! Love played absolutely no part in his plans. Besides, how could he possibly be in love with Philipa Braedon while being so obsessed with Emma Hunt? It was almost as unlikely an event as Elliot Waverly being in love with Philipa while devoting his attentions to Jessamyn Flaherty.

Why did that notion disturb him so much?

Chapter Ten

Dr. Waverly pronounced her illness to be grippe, and Philipa
was much slower in recovering than she would have liked. It
was several days before she could get out of bed, and another
day more before she could tolerate the idea of solid food.
Mrs. Grant had turned aside all visitors, and Philipa had quite
a collection of calling cards to review when she finally felt
up to the task. They were spread all over her coverlet like
decorative tiles when Dr. Waverly called on Thursday afternoon, as he had every day since her illness began.

"Well, my dear, you are looking quite a bit better this
afternoon," he greeted her as he entered her room, his black
bag in hand. "Has that powder helped you at all?"

"I didn't take it," Philipa admitted, organizing her cards
so as to see how many times each visitor had called. "I was
feeling better, and that potion is so very noxious. Really, you
physicians should put your heads together and come up with
philters which don't taste quite so abhorrent."

"You are nearly yourself again, I see," Roger Waverly
quipped ruefully, withdrawing his stethoscope from his bag.
"Beatrice has asked about you. She feels badly that you two
quarreled."

Philipa's nose went up an inch.

"It was not my choice," she remarked in as offhand a tone as she could muster. She was still angry about the episode, she admitted to herself, feeling a little foolish. It was not like her, she knew, to harbor a grudge for so long. Especially against the woman who would some day be her mother-in-law. If she ever forgave Elliot, that is.

Roger was silent, listening to her heart with his instrument. His blue eyes regarded her presently with a somberness she had not marked before. Or had it just now appeared? It made her wonder if his medical instrument could detect things she was keeping to herself.

"You have argued with Elliot, too, haven't you?"

His voice was quiet. Philipa, startled, could see the pain this notion inspired in his face. Poor, dear Roger Waverly, she found herself thinking, wishing it would be appropriate for her to take his hand in hers. She could not bear the distress in his countenance, and so she looked away.

Her gaze happened to fall upon the bouquet of miniature pink carnations which had arrived that morning from Terence Gavilan. Their color was, remarkably, the exact shade of the floral print of her bedroom drapings, and she was sure it was not accidental. Her cheeks grew warm with the vague, pleasing memory of Terence Gavilan's handsome face above hers as she lay upon her bed, his spellbinding dark eyes reporting his concern for her . . .

"Philipa?"

She started, thoroughly embarrassed. Dr. Waverly was examining the card she had foolishly left on display with the flowers. By now, she knew its message by heart, having read it at least a dozen times: "Your room is very like you: an oasis of refreshing innocence amid the trappings of everyday life. Sweet dreams. T.G."

She watched, unable to speak as the doctor replaced the card among the fragrant blooms, slowly. His mouth turned down in a slight frown, and it was a moment before he looked at her again.

"This is serious, isn't it, Philipa?" he said in a whispered voice like a breeze across the salt marshes.

Philipa could not sustain his gaze. His quiet words had shamed her more than Beatrice's declamatory recriminations at Father Michaels's. She knew, on the face of it, that she owed no debt to Roger Waverly regarding her relationship with his son, in view of the state of that relationship, any more than she did to Elliot's mother. But she had always looked to Roger as a second father; indeed, a primary one, since the untimely death of her own father five years earlier. Even were she married to Elliot for fifty years, she was convinced that she could never think of Beatrice Waverly as anything but a mother-in-law. She could not form a response for Roger, except to nod.

Roger said nothing. Presently he sighed, and the sound caught in his throat.

"I have never told you about your mother and me, have I, Philipa?" he said at the end of it, and Philipa held her breath, sensing that she was about to learn the whole parable of Roger Waverly and Julia Wilson Braedon.

Roger settled back in his chair, removing his stethoscope from his ears and hanging it about his neck like a talisman. He stared at the cherrywood molding around the ceiling of her room, but she could tell he was actually gazing into the past, as if into a crystal ball.

"Julia Wilson was the most beautiful woman I had ever seen," he began in soft declaration, and Philipa could almost see her mother before her eyes. She suspected that she was going to be crying by the end of this tale, and tears, curiously, began to sting her eyes at the very thought of what was to come.

"She was seventeen, and I was twenty-five. I believe I loved her from the first moment I set eyes upon her. Her aunt had brought her to the seaside so that she might recover from the ague which had killed the rest of her family in Camden, and they were staying with the Hanfords for the summer. She was tall, like you, Philly, and she had the most glorious hair, the color of new honey . . . Well. You know what she looked like. It was my good fortune, as the only doctor on the island, just beginning my practice, mind you, to look after Miss Wilson."

Roger paused for a breath, and Philipa perceived that it was as though he were contemplating his happy assignment for the first time. Seventeen. The very age Philipa had been when her mother had died, and her mother had been but forty years old when she had succumbed to influenza. Roger was talking about an event which had happened thirty years earlier as though it might have been only yesterday.

"She was so bright, Philly. She was so unaffected by her own beauty, and really had no idea of how very beautiful she was. Again, like you. She used to tease me, but never in a flirting way, about how serious I was. But I could never find a way to tell her that I appeared to be so serious around her because being in her company robbed me of my ability to speak.

"I called upon Julia every evening, and we would sit together on the porch in front of the Hanfords'. Everyone knew, I think, that I was in love with her. Everyone spoke of us in ensemble, as though it was inevitable that we should one day marry when her aunt thought her old enough. I dreamed of the day when I would find the courage, and the wit, to reveal my heart to her; only dreamed of it. On that day, I thought she would understand why I behaved as I had, and she would be made to know how very much I—" He broke off, his swell of emotion having strangled him. She swallowed the lump in her own throat at the sound of it.

"Henry Braedon returned to the town on the Fourth of July. He had completed his education and his grand tour of Europe and was ready to take on the world. We had always been fast friends as children, although I was several years older than he. He was much more outgoing than I. Always the center of attention. Not that he was a showy man, mind you." Roger amended himself, she was sure, to highlight the differences between her father and Terence Gavilan, who at times seemed to crave the attention of others. "He was one of those personalities to whom people naturally gravitate, unlike myself, at that time. He was possessed of remarkable self-assurance, and weaker people like myself naturally find that irresistible in others.

"I suppose I was somewhat envious of Henry Braedon. Of

his stature, and his popularity. He was a brilliant civil engineer, as you know, as well as a keen reader of people. His plans for the Promenade, which at the time was but a strip of boards laid upon the sand, fired many imaginations. And he was extremely magnetic. I'll never forget the moment when he was introduced to Julia Wilson. It was at a social after the town meeting where Henry had put forth his plans for the Promenade. He took her hand so gallantly, and she demurred so charmingly . . . I think I knew from that time on that she was his. I began paying court to her in earnest as soon as I realized that I would lose her to Henry Braedon unless I acted quickly. But it was already too late. So you see, my dear," he wound up with a sigh, looking at her again with a sadness he did not even try to conceal from her, "it would break my heart to see Elliot repeat my mistake. For he does love you, Philly, I'm convinced of it. He just—he's just like his father, I suppose. We Waverlys have never been ones for putting ourselves forward."

There was a clumsy silence. Philipa could not help but feel pity for the man who had loved her mother so long ago, but had lacked the courage, perhaps even the depth of feeling, to declare himself. But her tears would not come. She could not help but wonder at the character of a man who would procrastinate on the single most important decision he might ever be called upon to make in his life. Nor could she help but admire her mother, who apparently had possessed the exceptional courage to do what was not expected of her. She thought, suddenly, of Terence Gavilan. There was a man, she knew. A ripple of excitement rose in her throat. Terence Gavilan was a man who possessed the courage of both his convictions and his emotions—even if these were occasionally misguided.

"I think these things are best discussed between Elliot and myself, Dr. Waverly," was what she said to him, glad, in a way, that he had told her the story, but sorry in another sense: she was convinced that there was still a great deal more to the tale he had decided not to impart, and his words, if he could but know it, had served only to remind her of her duty and her honor. Two words which, of late, had cost her rather more than they were worth. She found herself wishing for her mother's strength.

"May I," Roger Waverly ventured at length, "at least tell him that you will see him when he comes to call?"

Philipa stared. It was not like Roger Waverly to place her in such an awkward position, taking advantage of her fondness for him and her vulnerable emotional state to further the interests of his own brooding and somewhat secretive son. Why was he doing this to her? She collected her thoughts to form an answer for him. An answer which, she knew, would not mollify him in the least.

"I would be doing both myself and Elliot a disservice if I were to answer that question, Dr. Waverly," she murmured finally, looking down at all of the cards scattered upon the coverlet. "I think perhaps you had better go now."

Roger Waverly realized that he had overstepped his bounds as physician, friend and father figure. He nodded quickly, rising as he removed his stethoscope from around his neck.

"You are quite right, child. I am sorry. I am getting as bad as my—" He stopped himself, she realized with some amusement, before he committed an act of disloyalty to his wife, however deserved. "I am taking liberties which not even my age should permit me. I promise I will not speak of the matter again, Philipa, unless you bring it up. Only I do hope," he added his postscript, as Philipa had half-known he would, "that before you act precipitously, you will think carefully on Mr. Gavilan's character and intentions. For my sake, and for the sake of your family's good name, if not your own."

Mr. Gavilan's intentions. Philipa, filled with renewed confusion, blushed. Terence Gavilan had never expressed any intention to her other than the fact that he wanted to kiss her. More than kiss her, she recalled him saying at Essie's Decoration Day party. She grew warmer by the minute. Lying there upon her bed, staring at the enchanting bouquet he had sent, along with its captivating sentiment, she found herself thinking, not of Elliot and her duty, but of what it might be like to have Terence Gavilan "more than kissing" her.

"Oh," she murmured, lost in the fiery and unexpected stirrings surging through her at the thought like the flood of a storm tide. She had not experienced these feelings in a very, very long time, and she'd thought she had forgotten them. And it had taken Terence Gavilan to remind her of them, for better or for worse.

Blessedly, Roger Waverly completely misread her reaction.

"I have tired you," he remarked by way of apology. "Get some rest. I will look in on you again tomorrow."

"That won't be necessary," she told him, focusing her attention on his face, forcing her shameful thoughts to one side. "The Strawberry Festival is tomorrow afternoon, and I must attend. You see, I promised Mrs. Ames that I would help with the hulling and with the strawberry shortcakes. So look in on me at the Somers Estate, if you are so inclined."

Dr. Waverly examined her, his gaze critical. All at once he softened, like ice cream melting in the warm sunshine.

"I know better than to caution you not to tire yourself with so much work, Miss Braedon." He wagged his finger at her fondly, his humor apparently restored. "I will look in on you, if only to be sure that you do not."

He took his leave of her, and she was left alone with an accumulation of calling cards in her lap, Roger's gentle warnings in her ears, and bold impressions of the roguishly handsome Terence Gavilan "more than kissing" her in her heart. And other places.

Chapter Eleven

Philipa was able to sit at the large oak table in Terence Gavilan's kitchen as she hulled and sliced strawberries, and that was a good thing, because she was still weak from her illness and she very soon discovered that she tired easily. Her hands were quickly reddened and swollen by the juicy, aromatic fruit, but the work was nevertheless a balm for her. It was both a mindless task and a solitary one which enabled her to plan the middle chapters of Mrs. Hunt's upcoming work, *The Lady Lieutenant*, without interruption, except for the workers who brought colanders full of freshly washed berries for her attention, and others who came to whisk away full bowls of hulled and sliced fruit and replace them with empty bowls for her to fill. The entire scenario reminded her of the Greek fable of a king, Sisyphus by name, who had been doomed in the afterlife, for some offense or other, to roll a huge boulder to the top of a hill, only to have it slip from his fingers just before reaching his goal and having to start all over again at the bottom.

In another part of the kitchen, women in starched white aprons were whipping cream in big copper bowls with wire whisks. Thank goodness it was not too hot, she reflected, watching their brisk, efficient motions as they turned the liquid into mounds of white heaven, or they might just as well have been churning butter. Other workers were slicing sponge cake as it cooled from the ovens. Still others ladled the nearly liquified berries onto the mountains of cream and cake and carried trays full of the dessert out into the immense yard behind the house, where tents and chairs had been set up. A floor had even been laid down for dancing, as soon as Tom Hanford and his brothers arrived with their banjo, accordion and clarinet. The affair, as far as she could tell from her little corner in the kitchen, was a rousing success.

All the moreso, in her opinion, for she had not encountered Terence Gavilan, Elliot Waverly, or indeed any other Waverly all afternoon.

At that moment, however, Beatrice Waverly entered the spacious kitchen like a general overseeing troops preparing for a battle. She was using her cane. Apparently her lumbago was troubling her again. Philipa, glancing at her, had an amusing image of the woman some twenty years hence, when Mrs. Waverly would, indeed, be every inch the curmudgeonly dowager after which she so diligently styled herself even now.

"We are running out of lemonade," she announced crisply, her very tone accusing the refreshment committee of gross negligence. "And the cream is beginning to run."

That last was added with an unmistakable note of triumph. Mrs. Waverly had disapproved of the use of whipped cream. Philipa, in spite of a twinge of annoyance, could not help smiling to herself as she remained in her corner hulling and slicing strawberries, happy to have no part in the dialogue.

A brief argument ensued, as stiffly formal as cardboard and overly polite, which was interrupted by the clamorous advent of Terence Gavilan's secretary, Owen Parrish. He was perspiring in his clover green jacket and necktie under the weight of a flat of strawberries upon his broad but rounded shoulder. She noticed a distinct red stain against the green linen, and wondered if the man was aware of the ruin of his garments by the overripe fruit. In any event he looked, Philipa thought, like a man who wished himself anywhere but a church Strawberry Festival amid the bickerings of its volunteer distaff management.

"This is the last one," he announced curtly, not looking at any of the women. He did, however, glance once at Philipa, and she returned his stare only long enough to see a glint of recognition in his small, narrowing eyes. She looked away quickly. She did not like him. She could not fathom why.

"And where is Mr. Gavilan?" Beatrice Waverly, without missing a beat in her tirade, turned to Parrish with a critical glare. "There are one or two matters regarding the placement of the pavilion which I would like to take up with him—"

"He's just had sod laid down by the garden," Parrish cut her off with a terse explanation. "He told the men to set it up nearer to the house."

His tone was tolerant, nothing more, and he did not address Mrs. Waverly by name, although Philipa was certain the woman was known to him. That slight was not lost on Philipa. He was panting like an old dog from his labors, and he mopped his dark brow with a well-used handkerchief. The squarish man, who, with his average build and dull, dark looks appeared more suited to physical labor than to the work of a secretary, tried to escape the room after dropping his burden onto the dry sink, but was halted by the imperious tones of the event's chairperson once again.

"You are his secretary, are you not?" Beatrice inquired, or perhaps more accurately, accused. "Please fetch him at once. It is of gravest importance that I speak with him."

Owen Parrish's ensuing stare of amazement was almost comical.

"I am under orders not to disturb him," he said firmly, his Brooklyn accent emphasizing his resolve. "He received a shipment of new books this morning, and whenever he gets his books, everything else grinds to a standstill. He'll be down when he's finished. But don't worry. It shouldn't be long. He chews those things up like an orphan with a bag of penny candy."

So Terence Gavilan was a weekend scholar! Philipa was discovering more and more pleasant things about him every

day. Like the way he had remembered the exact color of her
bedroom . . .

"You've gotten that strawberry juice all over your face,
Miss Braedon." Owen Parrish, to her alarm, was addressing
her, in a cordial tone laced with derision. "Don't get it on
your clothes. I'm told it stains. Oh, damn . . ." His attention
was happily diverted by the vast stain on his own jacket, and
he addressed no further comments, kind or otherwise, in her
direction. She knew in what regard Owen Parrish held her
and the Auxiliary. The Auxiliary, to a woman, held an equally
low opinion of him. How typical of men of his ilk, she reflected contemptuously, not to guard their tongues in the presence of ladies. It was with no small relief that she watched
him leave the room without offering either greeting or farewell.

"Your cheeks are rather red, my dear." Beatrice Waverly
addressed her, her manner markedly softer than that which
she had earlier used upon the other workers in the kitchen.
"Are you ill again?"

These were the first words Elliot's mother had spoken to
her since their public disagreement more than a week earlier.
Mrs. Waverly, in her Ashes of Roses afternoon dress with its
complementing millinery and gloves, leaned heavily on her
cane as she walked slowly toward Philipa in the corner of the
kitchen. The woman's step was a little heavier and her limp
slightly more pronounced as she approached, possibly to garner sympathy for herself as she sat to partake of crow with
her daughter-in-law to be. In the face of the impending dialogue, Philipa's blush receded, and she strove to wipe all emotion from her features as she met Mrs. Waverly's frankly
conciliatory gaze.

"Thank you, Mrs. Waverly. I am quite well," she replied,
aware of the sudden silence in the room as all other parties
ceased their chatter to better eavesdrop upon the two women.
"And thank you for calling upon me on Monday. I am sorry
I was too indisposed to receive visitors."

Outside the kitchen door, Owen Parrish grinned to himself.
These people were as stiff as painted plywood cutouts, like
the kind that people in Coney Island and Atlantic City often

had their pictures taken behind: strong men, fat ladies, circus clowns. He was amazed, listening to the Braedon woman and that pompous, overbearing Waverly hag converse, at how they fell all over themselves in strained politeness. He remained on the other side of the door, wondering if either of them might let fall something which could be of use to him, or of interest to Gavilan. It became apparent, however, after a minute, that the two women had nothing of any significance to say to one another, much less anything that might be of value to him or his boss. He slipped away up the back staircase to Gavilan's second-floor study, where he entered without knocking.

Gavilan was still where he had left him over an hour before. Coatless, his tie loose about his open collar like a fawning blue snake, the brilliant entrepreneur, the Wunderkind of resort developers, was lounging on the divan, his dove gray shoes planted on a silk brocade pillow, his stare intent on the page of a book. Mrs. Emma Hunt's newest tome, to be precise. This one was entitled *Destiny's Darling*. Parrish had brought him the book as soon as it had arrived, wrapped, that very morning. Gavilan was a fast reader, and even now looked to be almost finished with it. Mrs. Hunt's books tended to be short, often no longer than 250 pages, and as quick and satisfying as an afternoon romp with a skilled and willing courtesan. Parrish ached to get his hands on this one, and he could tell, monitoring his boss, that he would not have long to wait. Gavilan would be eager to get to the social event taking place in his own backyard as soon as he finished his book, so Parrish would have it and a few hours all to himself in a very short time. He did not speak. He merely waited for Gavilan to notice his presence, not wanting to disturb the man from his reading any longer than was necessary.

"What?" Gavilan's tone was abrupt. He did not look at Parrish.

"The Braedon woman is in the kitchen with Mrs. Waverly. The others are about finished, until cleanup time. You going down?"

"In a minute."

Parrish shifted his weight to his other foot. He felt as if he were standing in line at a urinal in a public washroom. Presently, Gavilan snapped the book shut and held it to his breast, closing his eyes tightly. He sat up abruptly, his chestnut hair falling into his face, which was a study of determination.

"This woman," he said in a low, deliberate tone, shaking the book at Parrish, "is the very devil herself. You are going to New York again next week, Owen. And you are not coming back until you squeeze the truth out of that prissy little agent of hers."

Parrish could barely contain his anticipation of the event, but he mastered himself. It would not do to allow Gavilan to guess that their obsessions paralleled one another. He contrived, in fact, to appear resigned at the assignment. But his efforts were wasted. Gavilan was not even looking at him. The younger man slowly got to his feet, shaking his head.

"I thought this time I might be free of her," he was muttering, half to himself. "But each time she returns, she imbues me with new resolve. By God, I will find her, Parrish! I will!"

His determination scared Parrish for a fleeting instant. The secretary had never before seen his boss in such a wild and unguarded state. But Gavilan mastered himself again, the flush over this new novel having apparently abated somewhat. Parrish hid his sigh of relief. After all, Gavilan was not crazy. Merely obsessed by the woman who had written it, like himself.

"Write a good one this time, did she?" he ventured to opine, even offering a conspiratorial grin.

To his surprise, Gavilan glared at him. Almost jealously, Parrish thought. As if he knew his secretary intended to read it next, and as if he resented that Parrish still had the whole of it to look forward to. Instinctively the secretary feigned contempt, a defense he found infallible against Gavilan's angrier moods. He shook his head slowly, deliberately broadening his smile.

"My mother always used to say it's bad to want a thing too much, Brownie," he dared to taunt the younger man, folding his arms across his chest. In satisfaction, or for protection? He did not know which. Gavilan regarded him with a dark look, an easy thing for Gavilan to do. His brown eyes were nearly the color of charred mahogany, and his dark eye-brows were veritable crossbeams of the same substance against the white skin of his forehead. His puckish nose flared once, and his wide mouth turned down at the corners.

"It was Oscar Wilde," Gavilan corrected him disparagingly, tying his necktie. "The two great tragedies in life, remember? One, not to get your heart's desire, the other, to get it."

Gavilan's humor, and his composure, had apparently been restored. Saying nothing further to his waiting secretary, he donned his powder blue pinstriped seersucker jacket and pushed a comb through his unmanageable sable hair without benefit of a mirror. He then obscured those rebellious locks with a white skimmer and fished his white gloves from the pocket of his coat.

"What's on the docket for Miss Braedon this afternoon?" Parrish wanted to change the subject. He could not risk angering Gavilan so much that the younger man would send him on another quest. Who knew how long it might be until he got his hands on the new book if that unhappy event occurred?

Gavilan, however, was smiling, as though he was looking forward to deviling Philipa Braedon again. Parrish was aware, presently, of a not unfamiliar twinge of enviousness of his boss, whose way with women was epic, and even a mote of pity for the innocent and unsuspecting Miss Braedon, troublesome as she was. From outside, the sounds of musical instruments, slightly out of tune and handled by amateurs, could be heard.

"A dancing lesson, I think," the tall, well-heeled entrepreneur remarked deliberately, straightening his tie. "And send a note around to Jess, Owen. After all of this piety on my own grounds today, I feel like a trip to Long Branch this evening."

Owen Parrish recalled, watching his boss stride from the study in his trademark arrogant gait, having taunted the man recently with his lack of a university degree. He realized, with a spasm of jealousy too great to ignore, that he himself would trade his own Princeton sheepskin willingly for Gavilan's looks, money and position.

Gavilan waited patiently, silently, beside the kitchen door until he heard the indomitable Beatrice Waverly take her leave of Philipa Braedon. Judging by the quiet, melodious tones of their parting discourse, the two women had amicably reconciled their differences regarding him, although he could not make out their words. He wanted to allow enough time to pass after Mrs. Waverly's exit to make his own entrance seem entirely unplanned, but not enough time for Miss Braedon to have left the kitchen as well. He counted to twenty, took a deep breath and breezed through the swinging door as though he intended to continue into the backyard.

Miss Braedon looked up at him, wearing the expression of a startled doe. Over her simple blue shirtwaist she wore a white bib apron, stained with the red, almost sickeningly sweet-smelling juice of the strawberries she had been slicing all afternoon. In her hands was a tea towel she was wringing to dry her fingers. He stopped short, as if he were as surprised to see her as she him.

"Why, Miss Braedon!" he exclaimed as a smile widened his mouth. "Had I known you were in here all by yourself, I would have come down much sooner to keep you company. I am glad to see you have recovered from your recent illness."

"I—" She was delightfully flustered, and obviously could not sustain his gaze. "Yes, I have. Thank you for the lovely flowers. And thank you for your—your intervention last Sunday."

"Miss Braedon." He took a step closer to her, and she edged back until she bumped into the sink. "I do assure you, it was my great pleasure to be of assistance. However, it is I who am indebted to you for allowing me to share your place in church. I understand there were some . . . complications?"

She was blushing, and had no place left to run. God, but she was an unexpectedly fetching spectacle, if she only knew it!

"That is . . . that has all been resolved, Mr. Gavilan," she stammered, gazing fixedly at his lapel, as if something were wrong with the garment.

He was seized by a sudden, compelling desire to rescue her from her awkward circumstance, even though it had been he who had knowingly thrust it upon her.

"I am glad of it," he remarked, even more quietly than he had planned. "I would not like to believe I had caused you any distress."

An awkward silence ensued—awkward, at least, for him. The conversation had hit a sandbar, and not even his glib tongue could break them free of it. It was an unnerving situation. Thankfully, Philipa Braedon found a redirective comment.

"It was kind of you to offer your home for this event, Mr. Gavilan," she murmured, daring to glance at him. "You have gone a long way in these last weeks toward convincing people that your intentions to settle are genuine. That will count heavily in your favor, I imagine, when the council meets to approve your plans."

Approve his plans! Gavilan the businessman pushed aside Gavilan the romancer. *When*, she had said. *When!* Her words were a welcome sign. In them, he sensed sanction for his further development. A little goodwill, he was discovering, went a long way in these sleepy little gold-mine towns. Who among them would guess that his master plan for the Somers estate was to convert it, eventually, into a grand and elegant gaming house which would rival anything in Long Branch, complete with lavish and discreet upstairs rooms?

"Is that music I hear?" Gavilan, the romancer, cocked an ear.

Philipa Braedon's smile was wry.

"If you can call it that," she replied, glancing out the window.

Gavilan sighed, affecting an expression of regret.

"Then I may as well go back up to my study." He shook his head sadly.

"Why?"

Her question was ingenuous. This was going to be too deliciously easy.

"Because," he lamented, turning away. "I am almost embarrassed to say this—"

"What?"

The woman was putty in his hands! He could barely contain his delight.

"I never learned to dance," he admitted in a whisper, even managing to blush a little.

She laughed with delight, enabling him to redden further.

"Really, Mr. Gavilan. Do you honestly expect me to believe that a man of your experience—"

"But it's true!" he lied earnestly, facing her again. He fixed a stricken look on his face, and her softening expression told him she was relenting in her disbelief. Not wanting to wait until they were interrupted, as they surely would be, he decided to take the initiative. After all, everything had been going better than he could have hoped, so far.

"Say!" He brightened, removing his skimmer and tossing it to the clean table, where it skidded to an unceremonious stop. "Perhaps you, Miss Braedon, could succeed where others have failed!"

Her lovely features clouded with appealing confusion.

"What do you mean?" She sounded skeptical.

He maintained his hopeful gaze.

"Do you think you might teach me the steps?"

God bless his unruly hair! A lock of it fell obligingly onto his forehead at that precise moment as if on a signal, underscoring the sincerity of his request. Nevertheless, Miss Braedon shrank from the suggestion, physically as well as mentally.

"I . . . suppose," she conceded doubtfully. "The dance floor does not appear too crowded—"

"Oh, no!" He contrived to look horrified. "I could never let these people know that so simple a thing as a polka has confounded the infamous Terence Gavilan for all these years! I do have my pride, Miss Braedon! But how difficult can it be? Surely you could show me the steps . . . right here?"

He had her. She could not refuse him without making herself look foolish or timid, and he knew that, along with dishonor, Miss Braedon would prefer a slow death to either option. She regarded him with a penetrating look which made him feel, for an uncomfortable moment, that she had divined his intent precisely.

"Very well, Mr. Gavilan," she said presently, an unmistakable note of cool distrust in her normally sunny alto. "It continues to astonish me, however, this predilection of yours for tutorial situations."

"You are by nature a suspicious woman, Miss Braedon," he told her, unable to repress a smile. "But you will discover me a most willing pupil."

"I have no doubt," she averred ruefully, narrowing the space between them. "It's ridiculously simple, really. It's all in the timing. The polka is just one-two-three-and. Four beats to the bar. You step on three of them and hop on the last one. Like this. Watch."

With that concise synopsis, she lifted the hem of her skirt to reveal her feet, to the tops of her pale blue kid shoes with matching covered buttons, and proceeded to demonstrate. Gavilan knew the steps, but he watched her, feigning complete bafflement.

"I don't know," he protested doubtfully. "I think I'm hopelessly clumsy."

As he had anticipated, retreat was, for Philipa Braedon, unthinkable.

"Oh, really, Mr. Gavilan! I would have thought you'd have more backbone than that! Here."

She took hold of his hands in hers. Neither of them was wearing gloves. Her hands were warm and soft, in spite of the wet work they had been doing all afternoon. He felt them tremble in his own, betraying her. He tightened his hold upon them as though completely unaware of her timorous reaction.

He took a few fumbling steps at her behest, then pressed his lips together ruefully.

"This just isn't working," he declared, shaking his head. "I'm sorry, Miss Braedon. This isn't your fault. Many have tried before you—"

"Don't be absurd." Her voice was barely a whisper, escaping past his ear like a gentle breeze. "Try again. I never took you for a quitter, Mr. Gavilan."

Without hesitation, Gavilan released her left hand and pulled her close, securing his own left arm about her waist firmly. She gasped at his sudden motion, but did not, to his triumph, attempt to pull away from his embrace.

"Nor I you, Miss Braedon," he replied, his own voice equally breathless as he gazed down into her wide, startled eyes, inches from his own. They were green today, as they had been on Decoration Day, like deep, refreshing pools into which he wished, fancifully, that he could plunge . . .

In moments he was whirling her around the deserted kitchen in perfect time to the lively, if off-key, melody, holding her closer than he ever had before, even on the night when he had kissed her. Her slender body was surprisingly pliant and willing, and he found that willingness, to his amazement, to be even more tantalizing than her previous reticence. Philipa Braedon, he realized, her bosom pressed gently against his own, had certainly taught him something this day. Although not, perhaps, what she had intended. Or himself, either, he realized, only a little alarmed by this unexpected turn of events.

"Oh! My! Excuse me! I thought . . . that is . . ."

Gavilan had anticipated being interrupted, but he had rather hoped that Elliot Waverly would have been the one to come looking for her, or, failing that, one of the other Waverlys. But it was only Father Michaels, his round face blanched. In his arms, Philipa tensed and tried to tear herself away. He held her fast. What she was intending to do, he knew, would only serve to confirm whatever wild opinion Father Michaels had formed upon entering the room. And Gavilan had no wish to compromise the estimable Miss Braedon's reputation. Yet.

"Do come in, Father Michaels." He greeted the priest in a cordial, if not jovial manner. "Miss Braedon is educating me in the mysteries of the polka, at my request. Perhaps you could counsel me on the sin of pride, as well, since I refused to demonstrate my ignorance of the step in public."

Father Michaels endeavored, with some success, to smile.

"Oh. Oh, yes. Oh yes, of course," he laughed, a tad nervously. "I would be most happy to. Well, it appears that in any case the polka lesson was a success. Let us hope my counseling will satisfy, as well.''

Gavilan relaxed his hold, and Philipa, perceiving his intent, eased away from him. By God, she was a bright woman. Naive, in some ways. But undeniably bright.

Philipa did not know whether she was furious with Gavilan or tremendously amused by him. She had not been deceived by his little ruse, although she had gone along with it, wondering where it might lead, half knowing it would only lead to trouble. But the thought of being in his arms had been too enticing to resist, and he had willingly provided her with the perfect rationalization for the activity. What she had not anticipated was the bolt of raw desire his presumptuous embrace had engendered within her, and she could tell by the expression in his wide, dusky eyes as he had held her close that he had been unprepared for it, as well. So much the better, she thought, stealing a glance at the wily entrepreneur again, only to find him looking at her even as Father Michaels babbled on in a painfully self-conscious manner about the nature of the sin of pride. Perhaps Mr. Gavilan, that brazen scoundrel, would be more cautious about trifling with her in the future.

Although a part of her, she realized, quivering, certainly hoped not.

Chapter Twelve

When Elliot sought Philipa out later that afternoon, she thought for certain he had heard about her and Terence Gavilan and the impromptu dance lesson in the kitchen. Father Michaels had a reputation for discretion, but even clerical prudence, she realized pragmatically, had its limits. But Elliot, to her surprise, not only did not mention the incident, but merely expressed a desire to walk her home. The refreshment committee had returned to the kitchen to begin the task of cleaning up, but Philipa begged her leave of the women, discovering that she was worn to the bone between her labors and the episode with Mr. Gavilan.

It was a fine afternoon, warm and sunny, but not in the least humid. Philipa, though tired, looked forward to the half-hour walk home. Walking always invigorated her, and helped her to clear her thoughts. And her thoughts, could Elliot have but known it, were in dire need of clearing. Elliot, however, his pleasant features thoughtful under the brim of his cream-colored skimmer, had other matters on his mind. He had not, after all, spoken with her since their argument on her porch before her illness, when she had ordered him away. Perhaps,

Philipa thought with a twinge of annoyance, his mother had
reported her own happy conclusion to her son, and Elliot pre-
sumed it might be prudent, or at least safe, to approach her
again.

Elliot gathered her hand into his as they walked. Her surprise at his bold and relatively intimate gesture displaced her
annoyance. It was several minutes more, however, before he
risked speaking to her.

"I'm glad you're feeling better, Philly," he remarked dif-
fidently, not looking at her. "I was worried about you. I was
afraid that, perhaps, our recent quarrel had brought on your
illness."

What an astonishingly arrogant thing for him to presume,
she thought, her annoyance renewing itself. Glancing at his
youthful yet solemn profile, she realized it was exactly what
he had wanted to think. A rude response sprang to her lips,
but she closed them tightly to prevent its untimely escape.

"Your father said it was grippe," was what she eventually
said, hoping she sounded clinical and aloof.

"Yes, I know."

What else, Philipa wondered suspiciously, recalling Roger's reaction to Terence Gavilan's flowers and note, had Elliot's father told him?

Elliot interlaced his fingers with hers. It was not an unpleasant sensation, but something told her that if it were Mr.
Gavilan's hand that held hers thus, her heart would be thump-
ing to a loud and lively beat similar to the polka they had
danced together a scant two hours earlier. The notion made
her face feel hot, and caused her to wonder why she was even
allowing Elliot Waverly the liberty of such an intimate gesture
at this time. After all, she was supposed to be angry with him.

Upon closer examination of her feelings, though, she realized she was not. In fact, she was experiencing no emotion
whatever, except for the weariness which accompanied a long
day's work after an illness. The thought occurred to her: here
she was, walking hand in hand with the man whom she was
allegedly going to marry, and she was able to conjure no
emotion whatever save exhaustion. What in the world was
wrong with her?

"It was a lovely day for the festival," Elliot observed presently, looking up at the cloudless blue sky.

A pair of gulls hovered, motionless, overhead.

"Elliot, in view of the fact that you are leaving for St. Charles on Monday, I would hope you have more to say to me than to make superfluous remarks about the weather!" she snapped irritably, no longer able to restrain herself.

He laughed, a merrier sound than she'd heard from Elliot Waverly in a long while. The sound both startled and annoyed her.

"Whatever do you find so amusing?" she demanded, pulling her hand away from his, hard.

He was undaunted by her humor. In fact, he continued to chuckle, and took her hand once again, more firmly in his own.

"You," he replied easily, bestowing a fond glance upon her as they walked. "You are the absolute antithesis of a flirt, my darling Philipa. Did you know that? One wonders how you manage that, being so intimate with Essie Tavistock!"

Elliot took one or two more steps, but Philipa's own feet had stopped as though sealed to the bricks beneath her shoes. Elliot's words were reminiscent of words she had heard before. Not very long ago, either. But whose? She could not recall, but she was sure it would come to her. She remembered to walk again, and she quickly caught up with Elliot, who had waited for her to recover. Unperturbed, he took her hand for a third time. Philipa found the gesture very possessive. Not an entirely unwelcome sensation, she realized, to her surprise.

They walked on, saying nothing for a time. They passed clusters of bathers returning from the beach bearing buckets and shovels, and small children who were so completely covered with sand as to appear to be made of the stuff. They waved to Mr. O'Reilly in the mail cart, and to Mrs. Freemont, whose husband kept the lighthouse in Ballard's Inlet. They reached the intersection of Fourth Street and Ocean Avenue and Elliot tugged on her hand, pulling her toward the beach rather than her house. She went along without protest. The afternoon was fading into evening. The bathers had mostly gone, and all but a few surf fishermen and beachcombers. There was a stiff breeze blowing in off the ocean.

"I think it will rain tomorrow," Elliot remarked casually, helping her over a dune. "Orsy said it was showering in Baltimore."

Daniel Orsy, another of their mutual childhood friends, managed the telegraph office at the train station. He had a practice of wiring brief weather reports along the line to whatever location he might be asked to send a wire. His fellow operators enjoyed returning the favor. The telephone had not yet made it to Braedon's Beach, and until it did, Orsy was their most reliable link to the mainland, and to information, since the only newspaper was local, except for the Atlantic City paper which came out four times a week and always arrived in town a day late.

That would change, Philipa reflected, negotiating the sand skillfully despite the tiny stack heels on her boots. The advent of Terence Gavilan to the island was a guarantee that progress was not far behind. Soon there would be an arcade on the Promenade, a place her father had envisioned as a stately and provincial walkway, a thoroughfare for social intercourse. And there would be a carousel, and other amusements to attract locals and out-of-town tourists. And a nickelodeon. And who knew?—possibly even a vaudeville theater. With people and progress, she knew as she and Elliot watched the hungry gulls scavenging a supper from the leavings of low tide, came all of the trappings thereof: Telephones. Increased train service. More automobiles, like Mr. Gavilan's Hurricane. Land agents and policemen and schools and poor unemployed people who would look for jobs and find what was once a pleasant little noplace on a map to be a bustling commercial enterprise where employment, except to the most enterprising, was limited to low-paying service jobs, and was not quite all they'd hoped it would be . . .

She shuddered at the image she had conjured, supposing it to be inevitable. She felt Elliot's hand squeeze her own. She had forgotten he was with her. She must have appeared startled when she looked up at him, for he smiled at her affectionately.

"Are you cold?" he asked, making a motion as if to remove his periwinkle blue jacket for her.

"N-no," she managed after a small sigh. "I was just thinking. Things have remained as they have been in our town for so very long. Since before we were born, in fact. And now it appears that, in a very short time, everything is going to change rather rapidly." She sighed involuntarily, watching a third gull snatch a stranded crab out from under two others who were busy quarreling over the morsel.

"Oh, I don't know." She could hear a smile in his voice, but did not look at him. "From what my folks tell me, your own father shook things up here thirty years ago. It's progress, Philly. Change. It's like the tide. We can watch it, I guess, but we can't do much about it. And I'm not sure we should, even if we could."

"I suppose you're right," Philipa conceded, troubled. "But I can't help wondering: what do you suppose our town will be like in another thirty years, Elliot?"

Elliot did not answer her immediately. He turned his gaze outward to the horizon, where a small party fishing boat steamed north toward Brigantine.

"I can't imagine, Philipa," he said, his voice as quiet as the rustling of the dune grass. "But I do know that it is unlikely that we will be here to see it."

She stared at him. His expression was contemplative, and not at all unpleasant or morose, as she had seen it so often in the past. He looked, she thought, fascinated, more mature than he ever had before.

"What do you mean?" she wanted to know.

He drew in a long breath, and let it all out at once.

"After I am ordained, I must go where I am called," he reminded her, massaging her hand with his thumb in a most distracting, almost arousing manner. "And after that, I will be looking for a congregation of my own, if it is God's will. I must go where my vocation takes me, Philly." He breathed, his blue eyes regarding her steadily. "And I hope you will go with me. Philipa, my darling, will you marry me?"

Philipa's breath caught in her throat. Indeed, she felt as if the air had suddenly been taken away from her, and as if the solid ground beneath her feet had fallen away to reveal a black and bottomless chasm. Elliot's features remained constant and unbearably hopeful, and she could not begin to imagine what message her features might be imparting to him.

He was asking her to become his wife. He was finally willing to make formal the commitment they had so earnestly discussed and worked toward throughout their adolescence and young adulthood.

And now, remarkably, she was not at all sure it was what she wanted.

She found herself looking at the sea, watching the gray waves of the receding tide scrape away at the beach, as if clawing in desperation for a foothold in the smooth, wet sand. Beside her, Elliot Waverly made no sound. He was still holding her hand, rather more tightly than before. Her palm in his felt damp. She thought, for an eerie moment, that she heard the hauntingly off-key music of the Hanford brothers again, but she realized it was only the steady, if irregular, cacophony of the gulls combined with the sound of the surf in her ears. And of her heart racing in her breast. With confusion, not excitement.

"Philly?" Elliot's quiet, respectful voice prompted her gently.

Will he be the perfect husband—and lover—for you? Terence Gavilan's mocking question, his sensuous baritone acutely recalled, taunted her, and it was as though the tall, magnetic Gavilan were there himself, watching their tableau with that familiar rakish, derisive grin on his darkly handsome face. No, she confessed to herself, permitting herself a private disloyalty as she eased her moist hand out of Elliot's grip. Elliot, she knew, would not be perfect. But he would be constant, and appreciative. He would be a good father to their children, and a warm, affectionate companion for her. She was 25 years old, she realized with neither regret nor enthusiasm. If she refused Elliot Waverly now, after all these years of waiting, she knew it was unlikely that she would receive another offer of marriage, especially if she remained here in the tiny community of Braedon's Beach. Oh, possibly when she was older, much too old to consider children of her own, some widower might make her an offer of convenience, enabling her to raise another woman's children. But she wanted children of her own. Desperately. Bright children, handsome and full of the devil, with dancing brown eyes and wide, reckless grins, like their father . . .

She gulped. The father whom she had conjured in her brief reverie was definitely not Elliot Waverly.

But Terence Gavilan had not asked her to marry him. *We are adults, and independent,* he had said to her on Decoration Day. These were not the words of a man with an eye toward home and hearth, and a family, and children, she knew. These were the words of a man accustomed to having his own way. Of a man accustomed to selecting only what he wanted from life, and from women—and for men like Terence Gavilan, only the very best would do—and then discarding the dross without a care. And part of that dross, she knew instinctively, was the commitment of marriage and family.

She thought, whimsically, of Roger Waverly and Henry Braedon, each vying for the affection of the beautiful young Julia Wilson. They had both been gentlemen with the most honorable of intentions. She, Philipa, was neither young nor, she felt, exceptionally beautiful. And Terence Gavilan was not Henry Braedon. There were some similarities, she admitted. But the important ones certainly appeared to be lacking, at least from everything he had thus far demonstrated. Could she afford, after the crushing and nearly devastating error of judgment she had committed in college, to trade a lifetime of contentment for a few moments of rapture?

She opened her mouth, intending to say, "Yes, Elliot, I will marry you." But instead, to her own wonder, she heard a voice that sounded remarkably like her own saying:

"I must ask you to allow me some time before answering you, Elliot. I don't mean to be coy, but certain recent events have made it impossible for me to accept your offer with my whole heart, and in fairness to us both, I—"

"It's Gavilan, isn't it?"

Elliot's interruption was quiet, but there was an edge to it like a newly honed blade.

Philipa lowered her head. She could neither lie nor force

herself to utter the truth to him. Beside her, Elliot sighed.

"I'd hoped you would not have been taken in by him," Elliot began, but Philipa placed her hand on his again in restraint. She could not bear to hear him malign the entrepreneur, nor to cheapen himself by so doing.

"Don't, Elliot," she begged him softly, searching his darkened features. "You are too noble for such meanness. And I am not saying no. I am merely asking you to wait for a time. A few days at most. You would not want me to enter into such a contract with any burden upon my conscience, or an entailment upon my affection. Nor do I wish to. When I become your wife, I want to do so willingly, with a full heart and with no encumbrances. Can you understand that?"

She was standing inches away from him and had, without realizing it, taken hold of his lapel. His blue eyes were stormy, like the sea reflected therein, and his small mouth was drawn into a thin, tight line. Presently his features softened again and his mouth grew slack.

"I'll take you home now," he said, and she was deeply moved by his unexpected understanding.

She patted his cheek and even managed a smile.

"No, Elliot. I think it best if I walk alone. I'll walk on the beach. I need to think. Perhaps it will clear my head."

He covered her caressing hand with his own and kissed it tenderly.

"Do what you think best, my darling," he told her, trying hard to smile in return. His effort fell just short. "May I call upon you this evening?"

She felt obliged by her own inconstancy to make the concession.

"Of course." She nodded, withdrawing her hand again from his.

He walked away from her and she watched him go. I will marry him, she thought with a small, broken sigh, slipping her hand idly into the pocket of her skirt. She was surprised to discover that there was something small and hard inside it. Fingering it, she realized that it was a ring. Curious, she withdrew it and examined it in the fading afternoon light.

It was the brass ring from her ride on Terence Gavilan's carousel.

Elliot arrived just before dusk, driving the piano box buggy he normally used only for longer trips to the far end of the island, or to cross the causeway to the point. Philipa came out front to greet him, having been alerted all the way out back in her study, where she had been working on a new book, by the clatter of hooves and creaking wheels on the otherwise quiet street.

"Elliot!" she exclaimed, gazing with some confusion upon the dapple gray gelding and the shiny black vehicle to which it was harnessed. "What—"

"I thought we'd take a drive," Elliot interrupted her by way of greeting, an engaging grin enhancing his youthful looks. "Get your hat."

Philipa was bewildered, but pleased, by this side of Elliot Waverly she was seeing for the first time. Normally acceding to her wishes, he was usually slow to assert a desire of his own, much less to invite her, in so raffish a manner, to go along with him. Without another word, she went back inside, retrieved her gloves from the hall etagere and fetched her straw hat from the hatrack, securing it to her head by way of a broad blue ribbon under her chin as she hurried out the front door.

Elliot was waiting for her at the curb, feeding the placid gelding half of a green apple. He helped her in with one hand lightly upon her waist and then climbed in himself. He released the brake and set off with a flick of the reins.

"Where are we going?" she wondered aloud, waving to Mrs. Grant, who had come out to the porch to see her off.

"I thought we might take a ride to Ballard's Inlet," Elliot ventured, guiding the vehicle along quiet Ocean Avenue. "It's going to be a fine, clear night. I thought we could view some stars."

Ballard's Inlet! Philipa's stomach knotted nervously.

"We can see all the stars we want from my back porch, Elliot," she murmured with, she knew, not quite the degree of protest a lady should express.

Ballard's Inlet, Philipa was all too aware, was a popular place for young couples to frequent on fine summer evenings such as this one. She herself had been there upon occasion, but never at night, and never with a beau. The place was widely rumored to be a haven where young lovers could communicate their deeper sentiments to one another with a privacy not offered by their own front porches. Ballard's Inlet had, so far, been untouched by scandal, but Philipa nevertheless felt a brief flush of trepidation at the seemingly innocent suggestion, which she quickly denied. Perhaps it was about time that she discovered the secrets of Ballard's Inlet for herself, she thought with no small apprehension.

Elliot placed an arm about her shoulder, tentatively at first, then with greater authority when she did not immediately protest.

"Not the way we can at Ballard's Inlet," he answered with a rich undercurrent of unmistakable sensuality in his light tenor. "But first, I have a favor to perform for Orsy. A quick errand. You don't mind, do you?"

"Not at all," she conceded, folding her hands tightly in her lap to prevent them from trembling visibly.

Elliot's "errand" took them, to Philipa's alarm, to an unsavory part of town along the bay near the causeway. He pulled to a halt at a curb before several boardinghouses in obvious need of a coat of paint. It required no education to know that these were not respectable establishments, and she was stunned that Elliot would subject her to the neighborhood under any circumstances. She was about to voice this sentiment when he turned to her with an apologetic grin on his attractive, if narrow, features.

"This won't take but a minute, Philly. Stay in the buggy and keep out of sight. I promise I'll be back in a moment."

He did not even give her an instant to protest his departure. She was alone in the buggy, parked in a bad neighborhood. Stay in the buggy, Elliot had cautioned her. Indeed, she had no inclination to get out of it. What business could Orsy possibly have here for which he might enlist Elliot's aid? Shrinking as close as she could to the rear of the buggy, she waited.

And waited.

And grew annoyed. What was Elliot doing? Where had he gone? And how could he even think of allowing her to wait alone in a buggy on the street, especially in this district? In the distance, she heard a noise that sounded like the racket of an automobile. She listened as the sound grew closer, approaching from behind her. She recognized it presently as Terence Gavilan's Hurricane. Indeed, who else on the entire island drove such a vehicle?

She listened with growing wonder as the conveyance drew near, whirring like an overgrown cicada. She was horrified at the thought that Gavilan might find her thus, huddled in a buggy like a pile of discarded laundry in such seedy surroundings. But as she listened, her worry was displaced by wonder: what, after all, was Terence Gavilan doing there, anyway?

The Hurricane pulled to a halt directly behind the buggy. Philipa scarcely dared breathe. The horn sounded, a startling and atrocious noise that made her jump.

"Come on, Jess! We're going to be late!"

She froze. Terence Gavilan's lusty baritone was unmistakable, even over the din of the idling engine. Jess. Jess Flaherty. Jess Flaherty, of the stunning, if scandalous, red dress and equally scandalous reputation. Philipa had known, of course, that Gavilan and Jessamyn had been companions when he had first arrived in town. Their first meeting at the town hall had told her that much. But she had allowed herself to forget that spectacle. She had wanted to forget it, she admitted miserably. And she had wanted to pretend that he had ceased paying calls to that woman, or indeed to any other woman, when he began to pay so much attention to her. But this evening, the blinders were stripped mercilessly from her sight.

She could not pretend any longer.

Philipa choked on the import of what she was hearing behind her. Terence Gavilan spent his days tempting her, and his nights in the arms of the lovely, and obviously willing, Jessamyn Flaherty. The realization was as crippling, and as painful, as if she'd been struck by a speeding train.

She could not prevent herself from stealing a glance out of the side panel, careful to keep out of sight. She need not have worried about that possibility, she discovered at once, to her devastation: she had looked in time to see the radiantly lovely Miss Flaherty emerge from her door in a sapphire blue gown from which her ample, snow-white bosom swelled forth like snow-capped mountains, and in time to see Terence Gavilan take the woman masterfully into his strong arms and buss her full on the mouth most indecently. Philipa's own breast tightened as if she were strangling.

"You look good enough to eat, sweetheart," she heard him say in his familiar velvet baritone, and his words penetrated her heart like barbed gaffing hooks.

Your hair smells like honeysuckle, he had whispered into her ear only a few short weeks ago in that very same warm and promising tone, sending her into a flustered tizzy. She had been making a fool of herself over him all the while he had been brazenly romancing this bit of fluff, and apparently making no secret of the fact! She shuddered. How could she have allowed herself to believe that his intentions might have been serious, not to say honorable? How many people had known of his entanglement with the shameless and wanton Miss Flaherty? How many of her own friends and acquaintances, who had said nothing but had shaken their heads in private and among themselves. *Philipa Braedon is making a fool of herself over that man*, they had probably been saying. *And she is old enough to know better!*

She shrank back against the rear of the buggy again, feeling faint, aware of an intense desire to be dead. Minutes later, without further public demonstrations, the Hurricane drove off, past the buggy and down the street. Quiet settled on the avenue like a heavy, tangled fisherman's net thick with noxious seaweed. Many emotions fought for precedence in her, prominent among them anger, humiliation, bitter disappointment and, yes, a measure of relief. Her decision to accept Elliot Waverly's proposal had just been validated, and she had not yet, she convinced herself, made so much a fool of herself as she might have, had she not been reminded of Terence Gavilan's true nature in time.

"I am truly sorry it took so long, my darling." Elliot returned suddenly, having materialized from nowhere. He climbed into the buggy beside her again, and the vehicle listed curbside with his weight.

She tried desperately to compose herself, but she could not bring herself to speak. She was too full of the burdensome weight of her discovery, and of the magnitude of her folly. She felt Elliot's gaze upon her, and she was not able to meet it for the tears that pricked her eyes.

"Philly, are you all right?" His voice was quiet and urgent, although not quite surprised at her state.

She did stare at him then, repressing the tears that glistened on the threshold of her lashes by widening her eyes. Elliot's youthful, narrow features demonstrated concern, and no hint of deceit, yet she perceived at once that this dreadful scenario had somehow been orchestrated for her, if not by Elliot, then by someone else who had wanted to make her aware of Terence Gavilan's fickle nature. She could not challenge Elliot with her suspicion, either, she realized bitterly, without betraying her own injured feelings in the matter. Indeed, on the surface of it, Elliot had no idea of what had just occurred. But for Philipa, all of her interest in Ballard's Inlet had completely vanished in light of what she had recently witnessed. She could not even think of spooning with Elliot on a dark and secluded inlet while her heart was in tatters. She desired nothing more from the evening than to lock herself in her room, or better yet her study, and to have a thorough, purging cry.

"Take me home, please, Elliot." She tried for a cool and indifferent tone, but in her devastation could manage only a broken whisper.

"Whatever you say, Philly." Elliot Waverly, to her vague curiosity, did not even challenge her wish.

It was but a ten-minute ride in the darkness, and she addressed no remark to him, having no faith in her ability to sound calm and untroubled. She was, she knew, not that good an actress. She was glad of the darkness, too, for she knew that her dejection must be plainly etched upon her features.

Far too soon for her to regain her composure completely, Elliot reined the buggy to a halt before her house and got out to help her down. She heard his heels click on the cobblestones as he went around the back of the buggy to her side. She extended her hand as she alighted, and he took it gently but firmly to help her out. She compelled herself to look up into his serious, searching features, as profoundly sad as she had ever felt in her life.

"I have decided that I will marry you, Elliot," she said quietly, at the end of a painful, broken sigh.

Chapter Thirteen

The day following the strawberry festival was overcast with an intermittent drizzle, but not wet enough to force Terence Gavilan to leave his uncovered Hurricane in the shed behind Somers House. The Town Council was to meet in a rare Saturday session to accommodate the peculiar and demanding schedule of Braedon's Beach's newest and most prominent citizen, there being some important news to impart regarding his zoning petitions.

Rumor hinted that all of his primary requests had been approved, with certain restrictions which would cause delays in construction. Having great faith in that rumor, Terence Gavilan had brought along with him to this small meeting a magnum of fine imported champagne in an iced silver bucket, as well as half a dozen crystal goblets, packed decorously behind the facade of a wicker picnic hamper. Good champagne, in his experience, went much farther than goodwill alone, particularly among small-town politicians with unwarranted self-importance.

Owen Parrish muttered a quiet oath, grabbing the enormous hamper containing the bounty as Gavilan jerked the Hurricane to a halt on the curb before the Town Hall.

"Christ, Brownie," Parrish swore under his breath. "You nearly lost the wine. One of these days you'll kill one or both of us."

Gavilan ignored him. Neither the variable weather, his own hangover nor Owen Parrish's perpetually taciturn humor could dim his jubilation. From this day on, he knew, Braedon's Beach was his. And how much longer could Braedon herself—Philipa, that is—hold out against his tender siege?

"Don't drop it, Owe," he cautioned his secretary as the latter labored up the steps of the building even as he himself bounded like an athletic youth. He felt, he realized blithely, like a joyous young schoolboy with the world at his feet. Like he had as a sophomore at Princeton, pledging for his place in the fraternity.

He had expected half a dozen men to be present to impart the good news to, and was surprised to find more than twice that number in the small room with a large walnut conference table. Among those present were Charles Tavistock and several of his friends and associates, as well as Dr. Waverly and his hypocritically pious son. The elder Waverly Gavilan held in no particular malice, except that he was the sire of the younger, but the younger one he had found intolerable ever since Jessamyn Flaherty had confided to him that Elliot was one of her regular visitors. Gavilan paused in the doorway, wondering at the crowd, and aware that he was now short several glasses for his celebration. Charles was the first to notice him standing there.

"Gavilan!" he greeted in his usual overly cordial fashion. "About time you got here. You'll be late to your own funeral, I swear!"

"Don't swear here, Tavistock," Mayor John Brewster admonished him cheerfully. "We have a man of the cloth present, remember? Come in, Mr. Gavilan! You are just in time to offer congratulations to this lucky young man. He has finally popped the question, and—"

"—and Miss Braedon," Elliot interrupted with a note of triumph aimed, Gavilan suspected, only at him, "has made me the happiest of men."

Philipa Braedon to marry—actually marry!—Elliot Waverly! When had this calamity occurred, and how?

Gavilan realized, discomfited, that the room had gone silent. Every man was staring at him expectantly. And Elliot Waverly, the worm, had his hand outstretched toward him confidently, a smug, detestable grin on his clean-cut and perennially youthful face. Elliot Waverly, who less than a week ago had accused him of being in love with Philipa Braedon— most improbable of events—had proposed marriage to the same woman at some time during the last two days, either before or since his polka lesson. And she had accepted him! It must have happened afterward, Gavilan mused somberly. Philipa Braedon, honorable as she was, would have been forced to reveal such an occurrence to him on the spot.

Behind him, Owen Parrish cleared his throat as a loud reminder. Gavilan remembered to extend his hand, but he discovered, to his further dismay, that his fist was balled. Tightly.

He relaxed it with conscious effort and finally took the younger man's hand, aware of a desire to twist it behind the insufferably sanctimonious fellow's back. Possibly to break his arm . . .

By God, what was the matter with him? Why should he care that Philipa Braedon, who had only yesterday allowed him to hold her in his arms, was going to marry this duplicitous fool of a boy?

"Congratulations, Mr. Waverly." That was Owen Parrish somewhere behind him, and there was a maddeningly instructive note in his secretary's amused voice.

"Yes, yes," Gavilan stammered, to his exasperation. "Of course. Congratulations, Mr. Waverly. I am sure you'll both be very happy. One hopes, of course, that you're not breaking any hearts by your decision to wed the fortunate Miss Braedon?"

The others laughed, as he had intended, at what they perceived as a jest. Only Elliot, he knew as the younger man's triumph changed fleetingly to apprehension, was aware of the true ramifications of his offhand remark.

"Quite the opposite, Mr. Gavilan," Roger Waverly declared, moving to his son's side proudly. "At least, as far as his mother and I are concerned. We have considered Philly to be a part of our family for years. This will only serve to make it official.''

"Well, I must be going," Elliot said hastily. Rather too hastily, Gavilan thought, mastering an instinctive scowl. "Philly and I must have a talk with Father Michaels—"

"The wedding will be soon, then?"

Gavilan could have bitten his tongue off for that unguarded outburst. Indeed, Charles Tavistock and the others were regarding him in a probing manner he found intolerable. To make matters worse, his face grew warm under their frank scrutiny.

"We haven't set the date yet, Mr. Gavilan." Even Elliot's raw tenor had gone soft with surprise. "But it will be as soon as we can manage. You may rely upon it. And we'll be delighted to have you dance at our wedding."

Gavilan could not prevent himself from staring hard. Had Elliot somehow learned of the episode in his kitchen? The younger man's face, smooth and bland, yielded no clue.

"I look forward to it," he said lamely, because he knew he had to say something. He would sooner burn in perdition.

It had suddenly become stiflingly hot in the small room, and he ached to loosen his collar, which seemed to be strangling him. His hands, however, remained obediently at his sides. He watched in silence as the other men congratulated the young Waverly again and escorted him and his blatantly pleased father out of the room. Charles Tavistock lingered behind, sporting a broad, almost leering, grin which Gavilan found grossly offensive.

"He'll be taking Bluestocking out of our way at last." The man's remark was childishly gleeful. "The way has been cleared, Gavilan. I only hope this wedding will be soon!"

Charles joined the others in bidding the newly engaged Elliot Waverly a hearty farewell.

"You'd better watch yourself, Brownie." Owen's thin, reedy voice at his ear was taunting in its obvious enjoyment of his boss's predicament. "You look like somebody just hit you in the gut with a sixteen-pound sledge at a full swing."

Gavilan did not look at his secretary, but he did finally give in to his urge to scowl.

"Shut up, Parrish," he growled under his breath, realizing, to his chagrin, that he felt exactly as Owen had described him. "Take the champagne back down to the Hurricane. I've changed my mind."

"Sometimes, boss"—Parrish chuckled—"you are so predictable."

Parrish was gone before Gavilan could form a retort.

Philipa Braedon to marry Elliot Waverly. And soon. Gavilan almost did not hear the rest of the proceedings, his official sanction to take Braedon's Beach and run like a thief in the night. He could not get his mind off of this unexpected catastrophe, nor could he shake the disturbing image of the distressingly bright and enigmatic woman with keen and variable eyes and soft, fragrant hair the color of apple-blossom honey actually married to that dolt, who hadn't even the sense to realize his good fortune. Why, a man could spend an entire lifetime discovering all of that woman's tender secrets, and still find it to be not enough time. And Elliot, he knew instinctively, believed, fool that he was, that he knew everything there was to know about her . . .

He could not allow this disaster to take place. It wasn't that he himself was in love with her, he told himself. It was just that he could not endure to see Philipa Braedon shackled for life to a man as thoroughly undeserving of her as Elliot Waverly.

He did not even care that the council and the mayor stared at him throughout the proceedings as though he might have contracted the bubonic plague. He was able to go through the motions, for his part, and escape the meeting quickly with his zoning rights in hand. Elliot Waverly would press for an early wedding, he was certain, just to spite him. He needed to work fast.

Carefully. But fast.

The Tender Trap, which Philipa had begun only the night before, was going to be Emma Hunt's final book. She could complete it, she was certain, well before she and Elliot actually wed, and forever after put the scandalously erotic Mrs. Hunt to rest and retirement. Philipa sighed, rereading the last few paragraphs she had typed.

She had not anticipated the furor her engagement caused among her friends and other interested spectators in the town. Why, only that morning, no fewer than half a dozen women had come calling, separately and in pairs, to offer their congratulations and advice, and to try to glean more details of the engagement itself. Philipa, surprised at her own reluctance to discuss the matter, was evasive, even to Essie, who had stamped her foot and pouted at her friend's reticence. Essie had left in a huff, certain, Philipa was sure, that everyone in town knew more about Philipa's and Elliot's plans than she. Philipa, however, was equally certain that Essie in fact knew more about the whole matter than did she and Elliot themselves. Such was the grapevine in Braedon's Beach.

The most tiring visit was from Beatrice Waverly. Having had no daughters of her own, Beatrice chafed at the bit, as the saying went, to secure Philipa's permission to handle the wedding arrangements, since Philipa herself had no surviving relatives to whom the chore (or honor, depending upon one's point of view) could be assigned. The older woman seemed surprised at the willingness with which Philipa granted this boon. Could she have but known that the reason was Philipa's utter indifference to the task, Philipa realized wearily, seeing her out, Beatrice might have been more concerned.

Philipa, unable to sleep during the night, had indulged in one of her usually soul-cleansing moonlight swims again. But the previous night's ablution, rather than liberating her spirit, had served only to remind her, dismally, of the unalterable fact that the nights of her moonlit adventures were numbered. Still restive, she had repaired to her study, her refuge, to write, and was reminded, to her further discontent, that Emma Hunt was another issue with which she would have to come to terms, as the wife of a minister. Scandals had a way of finding ministers and their wives, she knew. She could never forgive herself for ruining Elliot's dreams of the ministry by continuing to compose the romantic and frankly erotic tomes for which Emma Hunt had become notorious, thereby risking exposure.

Another catharsis which would be denied her.

She questioned, through the night as she hammered away at her typewriter, whether it might be God's intention to punish her for these sins by taking them away from her and then denying her the children, which she so desperately wanted, in trade, anyway. She was, after all, 25 years old. Most married women of her age had several children already, and continued having them well into their thirties. But perhaps there was some medical reason why a woman of 25 who had no children might actually be unable to conceive.

She wished there was someone with whom she could discuss these things. Essie was a dear, but she was a featherheaded gossip, and Philipa would never dream of baring her soul in that manner, unless she also then wanted unsolicited advice from every matron on the island. She could ask Roger Waverly, but the very idea chilled her: could she ask the man to tell her whether he thought she might be capable of giving him the grandchildren which he, no doubt, earnestly desired? The most desirable option, of course, would have been to consult her own mother. But Julia Braedon had abandoned her for death long before such a question would even have occurred to Philipa.

Philipa often, of late, had found herself wishing she could confer with her mother on matters involving her heart. What, for example, would Henry Braedon's wife have advised her to do in the matter of Elliot Waverly's lukewarm proposal, as compared with Terence Gavilan's fiendishly tempting embraces? She could not even begin to conjecture.

By the time Elliot arrived at noon to take her to Father Michaels, she was completely played out, from visits, from lack of sleep and from melancholy contemplation. She begged off from the visit that day, pleading fatigue. The following morning, after church, would be soon enough, she persuaded him. Elliot, obviously concerned, exhorted her to rest and did not leave her before extracting a promise that she would dine with him and his family that evening.

He was sweet, she reflected, feeding another page into the

roll. He would, she was painfully aware, never inspire in her
the tumultuous passions which Terence Gavilan, during their
brief acquaintance, had been able to arouse with seemingly
little effort. But Elliot was sweet. And she would rest, she
promised herself. Just as soon as she had completed this next
chapter.

"Miss Braedon, you have another caller."

Arliss Flaherty's timid, wavering soprano, obviously reluctant to disturb her, called her away from her brooding, and
from the wilds of the Canadian Rockies, the improbable backdrop against which her latest epic was set.

Philipa swiveled her chair to face the young girl, feeling a
frown come upon her features like a shadow. It was Arliss's
sister who had unknowingly broken Philipa's heart the night
before, with the help of the perfidious Terence Gavilan. Of
course, it was not Arliss's fault that her sister was what she
was. Still, Philipa could not prevent herself from addressing
the simple girl more sternly than usual.

"Arliss, I specifically told you that I was not to be disturbed
again this afternoon!" she said briskly, narrowing her eyes at
the girl, even taking some perverse pleasure from the fact that
Arliss shrank from her wrath. "I don't care who it is, and I
don't care what you tell them. But turn them awa—"

"If you imagine that I can be 'turned away' by a scrap of
a serving girl, you are sadly mistaken, Miss Braedon."

Philipa's breath stopped. It was Terence Gavilan's undeniably thrilling voice, and Terence Gavilan's tall, broad-
shouldered form, in an immaculate silver gray suit,
completely obstructing the doorway to her study. Her heart
swelled into her throat. Arliss shrugged in her helpless and
unfailingly annoying fashion, standing stupidly between the
two of them like some awkward young bird which had not
yet solved the mystery of flight.

Philipa forced herself to think, staring at the comely man.
His sable eyes burned into her even from across the room,
and his stark, angular jaw was working furiously. She realized
at once, to her amazement, that he was angry, although she
could not comprehend why, nor what his anger could possibly
have to do with her. All too aware of her treacherous feelings

for the bold entrepreneur, and of the page in her typewriter and the partial manuscript exposed upon her desk, she stood up on remarkably steady feet and moved toward the door, toward both Arliss and her unexpected visitor.

He has made a fool of you, she told herself grimly. *But there is no reason to give him the opportunity to make you more of one, or to give him the satisfaction of knowing that he has succeeded in his mission. Get him out of the study, quickly!* an inner voice urged her. *He has already shattered your heart. Imagine the havoc he could wreak with Emma Hunt!*

"Mr. Gavilan." She managed, to her relief, a cool and even tone. "Please allow Arliss to show you into the parlor. I will join you momentarily."

He took in a quick breath and looked as though he were going to protest. His dark eyes were bold and penetrating, and reminded her fleetingly of the terrible storm clouds of a northeaster. Whatever could he want from her?

He nodded curtly, then followed the hapless younger Miss Flaherty out of the study. Philipa, aware that her heart was racing, tried to command her breathing. His appearance here had caught her completely by surprise, and had made her painfully aware that, no matter what had transpired on the previous evening, she was still hopelessly, desperately infatuated by him.

Now she rallied, taking a deep breath, to try and persuade Terence Gavilan, who seemed to know her so very well, otherwise.

He was standing in the middle of the parlor when she entered, looking about the place as a ruthless tax assessor might. He did not look at her, but he did address her in a faintly mocking tone.

"How can someone with such romantic and exquisite taste in boudoir furnishings abide the dreary and cumbersome effects of this room?" he wondered aloud, shaking his head.

"If you have only come here to insult my home, you may leave it at once, Mr. Gavilan," she responded in a stiff and formal manner. She clenched her hands within the folds of her navy blue poplin skirt and stared at him with forced indifference.

He faced her like a thunderous wind, the power of his bewildering anger nearly bowling her over.

"You know damn well why I'm here!" he snapped, taking three steps toward her.

His humor frightened her, but she took only one step backward before she mastered herself again.

"I'm sure I have no idea," she replied coldly, her chin going up as she forced herself to meet his uncompromising scrutiny. "And I won't have swearing in my home. Now please state your business, and leave. I have work to do."

Her chilly, imperious demeanor tempered his rage somewhat, and his dark brow unfurrowed itself. She watched as he opened his mouth and breathed as hard as a winded athlete. He moistened his lips with the tip of his tongue. His gaze, serious and piercing, pinned her like a pitiless warlord's.

"Why are you going to marry Elliot Waverly?"

His outrageous question was like the hiss of hot air escaping from a lanced balloon. Philipa drew herself up, feeling a tremor of heat through her breast.

"I don't believe my reasons are any of your business, Mr. Gavilan," she retorted, folding her arms before her chest. "You, of all people, must be aware of *that*."

She checked herself. She had no intention of discussing the distressing events of the previous evening with him, then or ever. She flexed her hands in a steady rhythm, thus mastering her impulse to strike him with both fists.

He was obviously not intimidated by her cold words or her haughty, determined posture.

"Why are you doing this, Philipa?" he asked her again in a much softer tone, coming very close to her. His nearness was undeniably exhilarating. He took hold of the yielding flesh of her upper arms with a firm, almost desperate, grip. His touch was an inferno. "You can't love him," he continued, barely above a whisper. "What other purpose would prompt a beautiful, intelligent and sensitive woman to engage herself to a selfish, conceited fool like Elliot Waverly?"

In his grip, Philipa swallowed hard. His hot breath rushed

past her ear, and his commanding scrutiny bored into her. She was incapable, returning that gaze, of lying to him, or to herself. In any case, she knew full well that he could read her discomfiture, and that she was powerless to conceal it from him.

"Honor, Mr. Gavilan," she breathed, returning his steely gaze across the inches separating them. "A discipline about which you apparently know very little. Not that my plans are or ever have been any of your business. Now please leave, or—"

"I'll leave when I'm satisfied, Miss Braedon!" he said roughly, shaking her once, although not hard enough to hurt her. He had already done that the night before with Jessamyn Flaherty, without uttering a word or laying a hand upon her.

"And what will satisfy you, Mr. Gavilan?" she challenged him, angered by his presumption. "What reason can you give me not to marry Elliot Waverly?"

Gavilan stared into her infuriatingly cool hazel eyes, tinted with a misty green that matched her disdain.

"Because," he heard himself begin to reply, not really knowing what words were going to escape his lips next, "you should marry me instead."

Had he actually said that? he wondered in astonishment, releasing her arms abruptly. He must have, he decided, for Philipa Braedon's enchanting eyes widened in amazement and disbelief.

But he had no wish, he realized, further dumbfounded, to retract them.

She issued a brief, contemptuous laugh that sounded like a choked sob.

"Mr. Gavilan," she said slowly and deliberately, as if to try to prevent her voice from shaking. "At this moment, you are the very last person on earth with whom I could be prevailed upon to marry!"

He felt, at her words, a cutting pain press into his chest like a rusty scalpel. That he had proposed marriage to a woman—he, Terence Gavilan!—and she had refused! Actually refused! Two situations to which he had never in his life given a second thought . . . He straightened. His pride simply could not endure this scornful treatment.

"Uttered like a true Jane Austin heroine, Miss Braedon."
He mocked her, trying desperately for a tone of urbane indifference so as to deny her the satisfaction of knowing she
had lanced him.

Her immobile expression gave him no hint as to the success
of his effort.

"You must think me quite the little fool, Mr. Gavilan,"
she said. Her stare was bold and constant, but her quiet voice
trembled. "But this absurd exercise has gone far enough.
Leave my house at once, before I call Mrs. Grant to summon
the police."

What, he wondered, his frustration mounting, had gotten
into her?

"That won't be necessary, Miss Braedon," he replied flip-
pantly, issuing a small bow to mask his bitterness. "I won't
be darkening your doorstep any longer, except to wish you
the happiness of your foolish decision. Good day."

He turned away from her, shaking with unbridled anger and
injured pride. He was aware of an almost instinctive desire to
hurt her somehow, as deeply and as carelessly as she had hurt
him. Elliot and Jessamyn? he contemplated, feeling her stare
upon his back as he stood planted in her drawing room for a
minute, not moving. No. She would never believe it. The Bryn
Mawr scandal! Perfect! He faced her again with the cruel
revelation on the tip of his tongue, but caught in her stare an
expression of such forlorn vulnerability that the words refused
to come forth.

"What has happened, Philipa?" was what came out instead, to his own surprise, in a whisper that was more thought
than sound.

Her pale, smooth cheeks glistened with escaped tears that
he longed to brush away, but would not allow himself. She
did not retreat from him, or from his question.

"I suggest," she replied in a small, suffocating voice, "that
you ask Miss Jessamyn Flaherty. Now get out! Just get out!"

A hard lump gathered in his throat. Jessamyn Flaherty!
How had she learned . . . of course, he realized at once,
stunned. Elliot Waverly apparently was not as stupid as he

had believed him to be. Oh, the self-righteous pup wouldn't have told her straight out. He wasn't man enough for that. But he had certainly been instrumental in demonstrating the relationship. Gavilan was suddenly overwhelmed with a peculiar desire to do himself some bodily harm. Never again, he vowed in silence, watching the brave and perennially noble Miss Braedon equal his gaze, would he make the mistake of underestimating Elliot Waverly. Or any other opponent.

He did leave her house then, without another word. There was, he knew with a sickening certainty, nothing he could tell her which could ever redeem himself in her eyes. And he remained exasperatingly bewildered as to why her opinions had begun to matter so much to him in the first place.

Chapter Fourteen

Philipa sat with the Waverlys at Sunday service, and the congregation was too full of the news of her engagement to Elliot to remark upon, or even to notice, the flagrant absence of Mr. Gavilan from the Braedon pew. Flagrant at least to Philipa, who, with Elliot, suffered the effusive congratulations of the entire congregation, including all of those who had extended their good wishes previously. Even Essie appeared, miraculously, to have gotten over her snit, although Philipa suspected that the younger woman's magnanimous behavior was partly due to her own fervent desire to be designated Philipa's matron of honor.

The detente, however, presented Philipa with the ideal opportunity to inquire as to Charles's next planned excursion to New York City. The ultimate disappearance, if not the demise, of Emma Hunt was still uppermost in Philipa's mind, and her engagement had not altered her resolve to visit her agent. Indeed, it had reinforced the idea. Blessedly, Charles was going to New York that very week, Essie informed her blithely. That coming Tuesday, in fact.

Other than expressing mild surprise at Philipa's unusual

interest in visiting the metropolis, Essie displayed no unto-
ward curiosity regarding Philipa's motives, as Philipa had anticipated. Essie was singularly unconcerned by the
motivations of others, unless she suspected a grain of interesting gossip. To Essie, Philipa was, she suspected, a predictably boring topic. Just as well, of course.

Mrs. Tavistock seemed delighted at the prospect of visiting
New York again and acting as chaperone to the as-yet unmarried Miss Braedon, several years her senior, especially
since Philipa had never been there, and had hinted at a desire
to shop for a trousseau. She felt only a twinge of regret at
her deliberately misleading remarks and made a mental note
of keeping to the spirit of her promise, if not to the letter.

The timing of the trip could not have been more perfect.
Elliot, Philipa knew, was leaving for his first term at St.
Charles on Monday, and their plan, made only the evening
before, was to wed just before Christmas, at the end of that
term. That left her fewer than six months to conclude her
business with Emma Hunt and to prepare, with Beatrice Waverly's enthusiastic guidance, for her nuptials. With Elliot
safely out of the way for the duration, she could leave the
details of where they would live in Philadelphia to him and
manage her own affairs at home without having to contend
with a rush of engagement parties in their honor, and without
the usual restrictions that society placed on the behavior of
betrothed couples.

Unless, of course, Beatrice Waverly undertook to play duenna to her until December. But that was a possibility about
which Philipa preferred not to think. Anyway, she could make
the trip without even mentioning it to Beatrice Waverly, and
would gladly suffer any reprisals after the fact as long as her
mission was completed.

She bade a serious and reserved Elliot a fond but tearless
farewell on Monday and spent the remainder of the afternoon
in preparation for the following day's journey to New York.
On Tuesday morning a cab already containing Charles and
Essie Tavistock arrived for her at seven sharp and whisked
her and a small valise packed with necessaries and the completed *The Lady Lieutenant* to Atlantic City, where they

caught the 8:15 express train to New York.

Philipa adored train rides, and she could never take one without wondering why she did not travel more often. As a writer who spun tales of locations both exotic and domestic, she knew she really ought to have traveled more. She probably would have, too, she realized with no remorse, had her parents lived longer. They had always talked of taking her to Europe to view the centers of art and culture and antiquities when she had completed her schooling, to give her the opportunity of seeing the originals of timeless Latin and Greek documents about which she had only read. But alas, neither of them had lived to see that wish come true. Perhaps, she mused, looking out the window of their first-class compartment at the sentinels of pine trees, Elliot would be the one to share that glorious experience with her.

The notion made her smile ruefully. Elliot had struggled with Latin and Greek. Indeed, with every language. His forte, if one could call it that, had been forensics. As a debater, he had few peers during their schooling, leading everyone to believe that he was going to dedicate himself to a life of public service as a congressman or senator. However, along with this gift of dissembling came the curse of being able to sympathize with both, if not all, sides of a given issue, a trait not considered compatible with contemporary political thought. Forsaking politics, the next logical step, Philipa thought with the benefit of hindsight, would have been the clergy.

But it had taken Elliot a few additional years of searching to arrive at the same conclusion. She smiled, and caught the reflection of her expression in the train window beside her. Dear Elliot. Poor, dear, confused Elliot. *And look*, a naughty voice inside of her taunted, *at who's marrying poor, dear, confused Elliot.* The smile in the window vanished.

She closed her eyes against the glare of the glass and allowed her head to rest against the back of the seat. She drew in a deep, shuddering sigh. She had not slept well again the night before. Indeed, it had been many nights since she had slept through. The gentle, rocking motion of the train soothed her into a pleasant reverie. She remembered, feeling the firm but yielding seat behind her, the curious and wonderful sensation of Terence Gavilan instructing her in the art of croquet.

She found herself daydreaming about Terence Gavilan in Europe, squiring her to the most awe-inspiring sites of antiquity and romance. What a perfect guide he would be, she mused longingly, certain, for no particular reason, that his facility with languages equaled his skill in flirtation. She found herself sitting in a swaying gondola with him in a Venetian canal, and felt his warm, strong lips steal a kiss from hers beneath the celebrated Bridge of Sighs . . .

''Coffee, Philly?''

Philipa sat bolt upright, disappointment paralyzing her. It had been a dream, after all. She shifted in her seat, forcing a hot blush from her cheeks even as Essie allowed the porter to wheel in a small, narrow cart. The table was laden with china, a silver coffee urn and a small tray of cakes. Philipa was about to decline the invitation when she spotted among the offerings a chocolate croissant, always a favorite of hers. Chocolate, she reflected, contemplating her treat even as she pushed aside her treacherous fantasy, had a way of assuaging even the most troubling of circumstances.

And, as she recalled from her college days, chocolate from Hershey was available in Philadelphia like a bountiful year-round crop. Oh, happy prospect! If she could not have Terence Gavilan, and passion, and romance, that naughty voice intruded once again, at least she could have chocolate.

New York City was hot, and smelled at Grand Central Station of creosote and the exhaust of a veritable parade of horseless carriages. These noisy conveyances, to Philipa's surprise, had made huge inroads into replacing the elegant hansom cabs as a preferred mode of transportation in the city. There even appeared to be more streetcars than horse-drawn vehicles. She was reminded unpleasantly, as Charles led the way to an attendant vehicle, of Terence Gavilan and his Hurricane, and of waiting for Elliot outside of that horrible place on the bay. Many things, she observed sourly, were reminding her of Terence Gavilan this day. But mostly her still-aching heart.

''I expect you both back here at six o'clock sharp.'' Charles, to Philipa's annoyance, was speaking to both her and his wife as though they were truant and irresponsible children, liable to stray. "The train to Atlantic City leaves at six fifteen, and I intend to be on it, with you or without you. Have I made myself clear?"

"Abundantly, Charles, as usual." Philipa could barely prevent her response from sounding like the retort it was. "For heaven's sake, go attend to your business so we can be about ours."

"Go, Charles," Essie exhorted him sweetly, presenting her cheek for him to kiss. "We shall be prompt. Have no fear. Philipa is with me this time, and you know how punctual she is."

Charles merely scowled at both women, drawing his skimmer down on his heat-wrinkled forehead.

"Humph," he replied, glaring at them in turns before administering the awaited kiss to his wife's cheek.

"Have a good day, dear," Essie bade him gaily, waving her handkerchief at him as the cab pulled away from the curb. When she returned her attention to Philipa, her pert features were thoughtful.

"He worries so," she fretted with a small sigh. "He's such a dear. And I'm so glad he's gone!"

Philipa could not express her astonishment at her friend's disloyal remark except to stare with mouth agape. Essie laughed with childlike glee at the expression.

"You'll discover," she began in a matronly, almost condescending tone which Philipa recognized as instructive, taking the older woman's arm in a comradely way, "that you are much happier, as husband and wife, when you see as little of each other as possible. Now, where shall we go first? Fifth Avenue?"

They strolled along the sidewalk in a leisurely fashion toward the next waiting cab, Essie prattling on about their impending shopping adventure. Philipa was not listening, for the most part. She was ruminating on her friend's casual dismissal of the marital relationship.

Essie's declaration would certainly be true, Philipa reflected grimly, staring at her friend, if she were married to Charles Tavistock. But what about Elliot? Or Terence Gavilan? Surely marriage could not automatically turn someone from being compellingly fascinating, as she found the magnetic Mr. Gavilan, into something so incredibly ordinary as Charles Tavistock.

She had not forgotten that Gavilan had rather abruptly proposed marriage to her the other day, nor had she mentioned the bizarre incident to anyone. She considered confiding it to Essie, but thought the better of it at once: she had no wish, as she was certain that Mr. Gavilan did not, either, to have reports of the event circulating the entire eastern seaboard. What could he have been thinking of, to offer marriage to her? An answer occurred to her which both frightened and intrigued her.

Could the distressingly sensual and unpredictable Terence Gavilan actually be in love with her? And what if he were? she wondered further, feeling a heavy mass in the pit of her stomach, as if the croissant therein might be engaged in mortal combat with the coffee she had consumed. That did not alter the fact that the man's morals were little better than a tomcat's. In fact, to her mind, it only made matters worse.

Gavilan again! She could not keep her mind off him!

"Good morning, Miss Braedon. Mrs. Tavistock. I thought I saw you boarding the train in Atlantic City. A bit far from home, aren't you?"

Philipa stiffened, jolted from her meditation most unpleasantly by a familiar and unwelcome voice. Before them on the sidewalk, like some evil troll from a children's fairy tale, stood the presumptuous and contemptuous Owen Parrish, secretary to Mr. Gavilan. Essie, Philipa noticed, gave him a look which approximated that of a dowager peering through her lorgnette. As infatuated as Essie was with her own perceived position in a decidedly gentrified society, Philipa knew that her friend abhorred being treated in a familiar manner by those she did not acknowledge as her social equals.

"Mr.—Parrish, isn't it?" Essie's non-answer was chilly, and admirably regal. "Our compliments to Mr. Gavilan. Is he with you this morning?"

Essie craned her neck slightly to look around as if knowing the answer would be no but hoping the man would take the hint, bid them good morning, and allow them to go on their way without attempting to engage them in conversation.

"No." Parrish deliberately ignored Essie's valiant effort. "He stayed behind. He always sends me on these missions, unless he has personal business in the city as well. What brings you ladies to New York on such a scorcher as this?"

Parrish's gaze strayed to Philipa, and her cheeks grew warm. It was as if the man knew the extent of her knowledge of Gavilan's "personal business," and further, as though hers and Essie's dealings in New York might actually be of concern to him. She held herself tightly to avoid shuddering visibly. She did not like this sardonic, probing, rude little man. He was altogether too familiar in some odd way she could not define. He made her feel as though she wanted a bath.

"We must be off," she said in a light but firm voice, with no hint of rancor. "Good day, Mr. Parrish."

She did not wait for Owen Parrish's valediction before tugging Essie, who was most willing to go, away from him toward the next waiting cab.

Owen Parrish simply could not comprehend what Gavilan saw in that Braedon woman. Unless it was merely the challenge. If that was it, he mused, monitoring the haughty gait of the tall, slender woman as she walked away with her companion, then Gavilan had obviously lost. A true rarity. Philipa Braedon was without a doubt the stuffiest bitch he had ever laid eyes on, arrogant and not even all that pretty, as far as he was concerned. Too thin. He preferred busty women, like that Tavistock tart, and Jess Flaherty.

Besides, he had never met a college-educated woman he had liked. Maybe it was just him. Maybe he just liked his women to be simple. College-educated women, in his experience, always acted as if they had something to prove, or as if they were better than men. Often they made him want to prove to them just how good a man could be, but not in the Braedon woman's case. It had surprised him to discover that his and Gavilan's tastes were so very different in this respect.

He had wondered, these last weeks, about his boss's involvement with the Braedon woman. Their ensuing relationship had not unfolded the way he had envisioned it, nor, he was certain, in the way Gavilan had originally intended. Terence Gavilan was either losing his touch, losing his edge, or was actually in love with the woman. Parrish had not yet figured out which.

Parrish found her appearance in New York, along with her winsome tease of a friend, to be a rather interesting event. And he had some time to kill. Why not, he thought as he watched them climb into a cab, ride around for a while and find out what they might be up to? It was only time and money—and Terence Gavilan's, at that. And where Philipa Braedon was involved, Parrish had a sneaking suspicion Gavilan would not begrudge either.

Philipa was agitated. She had not anticipated feeling so anxious about her upcoming rendezvous with her agent in the presence of Essie. The manuscript in her small valise, which had seemed so inconsequential in bulk this morning at home, suddenly, after their disturbing brush with Owen Parrish, began to feel like a millstone around her neck. And she'd had to concede several shopping stops along the tour in order to persuade the younger woman to pay what she, Philipa, had characterized as a polite social call upon a long-time family friend.

To complete the dismal picture, New York was every bit as hot and inhospitable as she had dreaded it would be. She found herself wishing she had stayed home in Braedon's Beach and risked a letter and a parcel to the man, instead. She could not help feeling, as she sat very still in the noisy, rattling automobile and surveyed the grim, set features on every man, woman and child in the streets through which they rode, that she did not belong in this alien place. Casting a glance at her younger friend beside her, she knew, with no small sense of irritation, that Essie did.

Essie had apparently forgotten all about Owen Parrish, and Charles Tavistock, and was totally engrossed in absorbing the sights of the throbbing metropolis, with its confusion of automobiles cramming the streets like huge humming insects on a castoff sweet. There was an undeniable expression of pleasure, bordering on rapture, on the woman's face, as well as a hint of satisfaction. *Finally*, the look conveyed. *A place big enough and brassy enough for me to find, and to express, who and what I am.* Philipa experienced a feeling she had never had before about Essie: envy. Essie, secure in her marriage to the respectable, not to say dull, Charles Tavistock, obviously enjoyed a freedom greater than any which Philipa herself, bound like a helpless slave to her reputation and to her family's good name, did not. She behaved like an actress might, or some bold, brazen adventuress. Why, Philipa thought, amazed, Essie made a far more convincing Emma Hunt than she did herself!

Like a skilled and enthusiastic guide, Essie gaily led her on a whirlwind tour of her favorite clothiers, milliners, hosiers and a host of other establishments along Fifth Avenue, featuring fashions from the very latest to the most baroque, especially in lingerie. She would not rest until Philipa had indulged, nay, gorged herself, in the various emporiums, which appeared to be patronized by, if not the cream, certainly the rich milk of society.

Philipa allowed Essie to talk her into several fine dresses of watered silk and velvet in the most wondrous shades— colors she had heretofore never considered but which, she had to confess upon examination, suited her fair coloring and light brown hair, with its faint coppery highlights, perfectly. Peach and royal blue, and even a daring fuchsia boasting an illusion neckline sure to tantalize even the timid and pious Elliot Waverly, as Essie put it. Perfect for the picnic on the beach on Independence Day, Essie had pronounced, ordering the clerk to wrap it up for Philipa.

"But Elliot will be at St. Charles on Independence Day," Philipa reminded Essie, admiring in the mirror, to her own embarrassment, her profile in the form-fitting garment with the merest of bustles.

"How sad for him," Essie dismissed quickly, even though her very argument for purchasing the exquisite and provocative (for daytime) garment had just been stripped away. "As if you need an excuse to treat yourself to something so wonderful as this gown! Really, Philly, you are no better than a spinster. I should have brought you here years ago. Perhaps it would not have taken Elliot quite so long to make up his mind about you. Perhaps Terence Gavilan would have offered more of a challenge to him! Now take it off, dear, so the girl can wrap it.''

Dear, thoughtfully thoughtless Essie.

Package after package at shop upon shop was wrapped and forwarded to the train station, to be held until their departure later. It was Essie's own hunger, eventually, which led her to yield to Philipa's wishes. Relief, commingled with apprehension, flooded Philipa at the prospect of the impending meeting with Royal Godfrey.

Philipa had never met Mr. Godfrey face to face. She had never desired to, and he had never insisted upon it. She would not have been meeting him now were it not for the alarming letter he had sent to her two weeks earlier. He was, thanks largely to Emma Hunt, one of the most successful author representatives in the business, she knew; an occupation of solitude and comparative obscurity to which, in her opinion, only a confirmed hermit must aspire. Much like writing.

He was not expecting her. That would create an awkward situation, although Philipa had begun to hope that he would not be in. That way, she could simply leave the unidentified parcel with the doorman, express a degree of feigned regret to Essie, and the two of them could go on about their business for the remainder of the day, unfettered by the burdensome manuscript.

Mr. Godfrey was in, however. The doorman rang up his apartment while Philipa nervously readied her monologue for the man and Essie folded her arms across her breast, shifting her weight from one foot to another. Essie, it appeared, would have preferred that Mr. Godfrey not be in, either. The younger woman was no doubt eager to get out and spend as much more of Charles's money as she could, Philipa mused wryly.

Minutes later, through the glass doors of the foyer, Philipa perceived the approach of a short man with an abundance of gray whiskers about his jaws and under his comical, bulbous nose. His small dark eyes peered at her through gold-rimmed spectacles, and his surprisingly unwrinkled face erupted into a warm, grandfatherly smile. He was wearing a black vest over his rumpled white shirt and cravat, but no jacket, as though he had been abruptly disturbed from his work. Philipa endeavored to return his smile, swallowing several times as she waited for him to open the doors. She would need to identify herself quickly so that an awkward confusion could be avoided. Her stomach knotted as the doorman performed his task for the man.

"My dear Miss Braedon!" he greeted, his voice as warm and deep as a tidal pool in August.

"Please, call me Philipa. I feel as though I know you so well, Mr. Godfrey. Good afternoon. My friend Mrs. Tavistock and I were in town for a little shopping, and I felt I must pay you a call. My parents both spoke so highly of you."

She tried to convey, in her desperate smile, the awkward-ness of the situation. Mr. Godfrey's gray brow furrowed in misunderstanding for an instant; then it was as though a bolt of sunshine had emerged from a bank of dark clouds.

"Of course, of course!" He grasped her hand warmly and sent a brief glance in Essie's direction. "Do come inside, ladies. It is so nice of you to visit me. I get so little company. You must take luncheon, or at the very least tea, with me."

Mr. Godfrey then led them, in a surprisingly vigorous, al-most athletic pace for a man of his years, past the lift to a narrow staircase just beyond it. He lived, mercifully, only on the second floor, and Philipa managed to produce enough small talk to eliminate the necessity of Mr. Godfrey's speak-ing, thus preventing any slipups which might have otherwise occurred. Once safely inside his apartment, Philipa allowed herself the fleeting luxury of an examination of Royal God-frey's charming, if eclectic, furnishings.

The drawing room featured a pair of glistening windows rising twenty feet from floor to ceiling on the east. They were framed by exotically brocaded crimson portieres, held aside by heavy gold braids. The wallpaper was black silk spattered with bold red roses the size of melons. The room was crammed with furniture, including a Gramophone and a carved rosewood music chest, a secretary desk literally stuffed with papers, a pair of mismatched loveseats, one Chippendale, the other Queen Anne. A sumptuous Persian rug the color of blood and veined with blue and gold covered the floor, and a variety of odd wing chairs and wicker rockers were strewn about with the carelessness of blown autumn leaves. There was not a single flat surface in the large, cluttered room that did not support some curio which looked to be both exotic and antique. Mr. Godfrey, she deduced, was a collector. A veritable pack rat. The showpiece of the collection was an elaborate wooden cage near one window, where a large green macaw preened its emerald plumage.

Philipa recalled her mind from its distractions and issued proper introductions. Mr. Godfrey then solicitously, and sagaciously, invited Essie to freshen up in his lavatory down the hall. As soon as she was gone, Philipa gave way to the panic she had successfully held at bay up until that moment. A stream of perspiration trickled down the small of her back, just beneath her stays, and she shook with apprehension.

"I'm terribly sorry about this, Mr. Godfrey," she began swiftly, but he silenced her with an upheld finger as he glanced down the hallway through which Essie had passed.

"Nonsense, Miss Braedon." He spoke in a low tone. "I have always enjoyed a little chicanery now and again, and I am glad to meet you at last. We will not speak of your parents, since I know nothing about them. You will simply tell me about yourself, and give me some sort of sign when you are ready to leave. I believe I am perspicacious enough to take the hint. Now—"

"Nonsense, Miss Braedon," cackled the bird in interruption, in an astonishing imitation of Godfrey's own gravelly voice.

Philipa started at the sound, and Royal Godfrey chuckled.

"Don't mind Willy," he assured her. "He's a rude creature. You were saying?"

"I've brought along *The Lady Lieutenant,*" she ventured, casting a wary eye at the creature before fumbling in her valise with trembling fingers. "After your letter, I didn't want to risk mailing it. Have you had any other—visits?"

Mr. Godfrey shook his head thoughtfully.

"No," he admitted. "And I'm beginning to believe that I

may have alarmed you over nothing.''

"Nonsense, Miss Braedon,'' the bird chirped again. ''Don't mind Willy.''

Philipa ignored the bird this time and allowed herself a small sigh of relief.

"That isn't the only reason why I needed to see you,'' she went on quickly. ''Mrs. Hunt must stop writing these books, Mr. Godfrey. You see, I am going to be married, to a minister, and I can't allow—''

"Good heavens!''

Royal Godfrey's features clouded over at that. It was only natural that he would not be pleased by this turn of events, she thought grimly. After all, it was his living, as well.

"I've analyzed this thoroughly, Mr. Godfrey, and there will be no discussion about it. I am quite resolute,'' she declared, hoping to derail his protest. *The Tender Trap* is to be Emma Hunt's last work, and will be published posthumously. I expect to finish it by September, so we can proceed to eliminate her at any time. The sooner, the better. She is to have perished on safari in Africa while researching a book. I've sketched out the entire scenario, including a bogus obituary. It's all in here with the manuscript. I hope I may rely upon you to handle the particulars?''

"Of course,'' he replied, looking troubled as he scrutinized her with sage, charcoal eyes. ''But what will you do, Miss Braedon? For your creative outlet, I mean?''

Philipa managed to smile. Royal Godfrey, like the grand-fatherly figure he resembled, was, in spite of his own impending loss, still thinking of her well-being. She could not help but be pleased that she had chosen her representative well, if not her future mate.

"I'm sure that, being the wife of a minister, I shall be kept quite busy,'' she predicted, trying to sound enthusiastic about the prospect. ''Perhaps I shall take up the needlepoint in which my mother so judiciously schooled me many years ago. I may even pursue my academic research once again. I am never bored, Mr. Godfrey. I see to that.''

"Nonsense, Miss Braedon,'' the bird screamed again. ''Good heavens!''

Philipa was seized by an urge to throttle the annoying thing.

"Still," the man interjected reflectively, disregarding his obnoxious pet, "one can't help but wonder at so disproportionate a sacrifice. You have been so very prolific, and so consistently innovative, that I cannot believe you to have run out of tales to spin for us. What kind of compromise is your future husband prepared to make for you?"

Philipa drew herself in. This was precisely the kind of provoking conversation into which she had not wanted to enter.

"As I have said, I am quite resolute on this matter, Mr. Godfrey," she repeated in as cool a tone as she could without being rude. "It will serve no purpose to discuss it further. Here is the material."

She handed him a stationery box, carefully wrapped in plain brown paper and marked with his name. He accepted it with both hands, looking solemn.

"It will be as you wish, Miss Braedon," he intoned, gazing sadly at the box as though it contained the remains of a departed companion.

"As you wish, Miss Braedon." Willy continued his mindless monologue. "What a silly bird!"

"Philly!" Essie had returned, and Philipa started in dismay. "Is that what you have been lugging about with you all morning? And I thought it was a change of—oh, my!"

Essie gravitated toward the bird as a child might have. She chattered and prompted the creature, who then, perversely, was as silent as a statue.

"Just some old letters Miss Braedon has graciously given me," Mr. Godfrey said smoothly, even though Essie's attention was already diverted. "Thank you, my dear. Let me put these away, and ring for our luncheon."

As the man padded off, Philipa could not help but admire the fluency with which he had thought of a lie for Essie. She stifled a sigh of relief, curiously mingled with remorse, as she listened to Essie's coaxing of the exasperating macaw, and watched Emma Hunt's penultimate opus leave her own hands.

It was over an hour before Philipa Braedon and Mrs. Tavistock emerged from the building where Royal Godfrey resided and maintained his business, but Owen Parrish waited patiently at the window of the cafe across the street. This most interesting turn of events might be, he knew, the greatest discovery in his four-year search. Or it might be mere coincidence. After all, the building no doubt housed nearly a hundred residents. But it sure looked like Royal Godfrey who had met them just inside the door. And his gut told him, as he watched the two women clamber into the cab the doorman had summoned, that there was definitely a story behind this seemingly innocent little rendezvous.

He roused himself from his half-consumed coffee. It was time, he judged, straightening his wilting collar, for Thomas Goliard to pay another call upon Emma Hunt's representative, Mr. Royal Godfrey.

Chapter Fifteen

Gavilan spent the days following his scene at Philipa Braedon's home fiercely mired in work. He left Somers House early in the morning, before his cook had even started the stove, and did not return until near midnight. He spent the long hours in between at his office above the Promenade and on site at his multifarious construction and rehabilitation projects, arguing with contractors and suppliers and generally being unpleasant. He had packed Owen Parrish off to New York almost at once, knowing he would have been unable to endure his subordinate's incessant ridicule and insufferably snide innuendo so close on the heels of his own ignominious defeat. Braedon's Beach, which had once been a juicy plum ripe for the plucking, had been transformed overnight into merely another old prune to be stewed. Not even the rapid metamorphosis of the hamlet from a small, quiet provincial town to a bright, lucrative tourist haven could inspire Gavilan to his former enthusiasm for civic rapine.

Nothing was worth the effort.

He stared out his window to the Promenade below. The Promenade which, if reports were true, had been engineered and executed by Miss Philipa Braedon's father, Henry Braedon himself.

Gavilan's hands were tightly clasped behind his back. It was as hot as a blast furnace in the dreary little room, and outside barely a breath of air was being granted by the exceptionally penurious Atlantic Ocean to ease the blistering heat. He tore at his collar savagely with one impatient finger. Its tiny bar clasp popped, flying across the room and landing somewhere on the uncarpeted floor with a faint tinkle, like the drop of a penny. Grimacing, he yanked the remaining accessory from his sweating neck, along with the hopelessly limp tie, and flung both to the cluttered surface of his desk.

If Philipa Braedon was fool enough to marry Elliot Waverly, he reasoned, his jaw stiffly clenched, well, what concern was it of his? He didn't care. It was nothing to him.

Three times since Saturday he had roused himself to go and seek out Jess, just to prove that very thing to himself. Three times he hadn't even gotten as far as the Hurricane before deciding he had better things to do than to prove things to himself, or anyone else in this miserable excuse for a town.

You should marry me, instead, he had said to her. What a fool he had been! He should have known Philipa would have rejected him out of hand. She was too scared of what people might think. And he had been out of his mind, anyway, even for asking. Marriage! My God, next he would be thinking about a permanent home, and children!

Perhaps a daughter: a pretty, quiet, serious little girl, smarter than she should be. Maybe a little taller than other children, in a white pinafore with a blue sash, her tea-colored hair done up in ringlets that bounced behind her as she skipped down the walk to greet him in the evenings. An adoring daughter, whom he would swing easily up into his arms and carry home to her mother, who would be waiting at the door wearing a fond, enigmatic smile for them both. A mother with keen, changeable eyes and soft, honey-hued hair done up in a simple, alluring chignon that he would relish taking down, and an ordinary shirtwaist which her tall, regal figure would render exceptional, and which he would willingly help her out of before they retired . . .

He spun away from his window, seized the empty inkwell from his desk and hurled it as hard as he could. It ricocheted off the wall behind Parrish's empty place with a loud crack. The sound shattered his preposterous reverie, and the bottle landed on the wood floor in front of his own desk. He listened to it roll before it finally came to rest somewhere.

"What the hell's going on in there, Brownie?" From outside came the sound of Owen Parrish's scornful voice as the older man's footsteps approached the door. "Target practice?"

Christ, he was back. Gavilan smoothed his thick hair with the splayed fingers of one hand while trying to arrange his features into a detached expression before his secretary invaded the sweltering gloom with his all-too-knowing stares. He turned to the window again just as Parrish tipped the lever.

"I hope to hell you have something for me," Gavilan greeted him hostilely, without granting him the courtesy of a look. "What have you been doing in New York for these past three days, besides spending my money on whores and absinthe?"

Parrish did not reply, but Gavilan could hear him stride into the room and stop before his desk.

"Have you seen the paper?" The question was abrupt, the voice parched gravel.

"What paper?" Gavilan was impatient.

"The *Times*." Parrish was laconic.

Gavilan frowned, turning to him, his hands upon his waist. "No. Why?"

"Have a look." Parrish, staring grimly, tossed a folded newspaper onto the mound on Gavilan's desk.

Scowling, suspicious, Gavilan picked it up, noticing immediately that it was the *New York Times*, and that it was opened and folded to the obituary section. There was a sixth-of-a-page article staring back at him, headlined "Novelist Emma Hunt Perishes on Safari in Congo."

What!

He gripped the paper mercilessly, scanning it. It was dated that day, July 2. "Emma Hunt, author . . ." and a story that read strangely like one of Mrs. Hunt's own novels, about how she had traveled to the Congo to research a book and had been gored by a rhino on safari. "Tragic," it said. "A freak accident," it went on.

But nothing whatever about her age, her place of residence, surviving relatives . . . no personal information at all. Nothing.

Gavilan's face filled up with heat, then flushed with cold. A shudder went through him like an icy knife, followed closely by a swell of utter disbelief. Emma Hunt—dead?

"This can't be," he muttered, dropping the paper as if it had some deadly, communicable disease. Then he quickly picked it up again. "This can't be, Owe. It's not right. It's a mistake. It has to be."

Before him, Parrish sucked in a deep breath.

"That's what I thought, Brownie," his secretary replied on the expelled air. "But Godfrey was wearing a black armband when I paid him a call yesterday. You can bet your backside he's in mourning. The man just lost a gold mine."

"Christ, look at it, Owe!" Gavilan argued, slapping the page with the back of his hand. "It doesn't say anything! According to this obit, she was a woman without a life. Without a past. How in hell can that be? I understand that 'Emma Hunt' was in all likelihood a pseudonym, but that's usually mentioned in these things."

Parrish shrugged, shaking his head.

" 'Emma Hunt' probably didn't want anyone ever to know who she really was, Brownie," he offered. "She made damned sure her tracks were covered, I'd say."

But Gavilan scarcely heard him. Emma Hunt. Gone. Gavilan sank into his high-backed chair and dropped the paper down before him. He was recalling a passage from her most recent book, *Destiny's Darling*, the one he'd read only Friday. Only Friday, the day of the Strawberry Festival. The day he had danced the polka with Philipa Braedon in his kitchen. The day before he had learned of her intractable intention to marry Elliot Waverly. Mrs. Hunt's heroine, Crystal, had been tending to her lover's aching back, which he had injured by saving her from a fall. In the scene, she was massaging him with a fragrant lotion and a tender touch. The descriptions of her activity, and of her hero's response thereto, had completely unmanned him when he'd read them the first time.

And now the creator of those haunting, titillating words; the unashamed pagan priestess of those vibrant, erotic images, was dead.

He breathed deeply. Emma Hunt was dead.

Why, he wondered clinically, could he not dredge up any sense of loss, or despair, over the fact? Why would such an event, which only a short time ago would have caused him untold distress, now inspire merely a sense of fleeting regret?

Gavilan sighed again, trying to focus his sorrow. To harrow his grief. But all he could think of was the image he himself had conjured immediately prior to Parrish's untimely invasion of his office: the image of a child and her mother, and the bitter recollection of a nameless yearning deep in his gut as he thought of these things.

He cupped his hands behind his head, closing his eyes as he leaned his back against the chair.

"Oh, well, Owe," he dismissed, remarkably, a four-year fantasy obsession with seven little words. "That's that, I guess."

Owen Parrish, before him, said nothing for a full minute. Gavilan did not look at him.

"I guess so," the man replied, sounding more subdued than Gavilan had ever heard him before.

Parrish took his place behind his own desk, hardly able to credit his good fortune. He had spent an entire extra day in New York, wondering how he was going to placate Gavilan without telling him what he had discovered, and the solution, by grace of Providence, or Satan, or whatever, had dropped into his lap in the form of the obituary only that morning as he had headed out on the train.

Royal Godfrey hadn't had to say a word to him. Indeed, Thomas Goliard had not even had to pay the man a formal call. Parrish had merely stood outside the man's door and listened for several minutes at the cackling sound of a bird inside the apartment, screaming, "Nonsense, Miss Braedon!" over and over, like some kind of a certified lunatic. He'd hung about as long as he dared, hoping the loquacious animal might say something else, but it never did. It didn't matter, though.

It hadn't taken long for Parrish to convince himself, with the evidence he had already garnered.

The sultry, eloquent Mrs. Emma Hunt was, in fact, none other than the frosty, and highly literate, Miss Philipa Braedon.

Given that, Terence Gavilan was the very last person with whom he wanted to share this startling discovery. After all, it was obvious to him that Brownie already had the woman eating out of the palm of his hand, even for all of her protests that she was set to marry Waverly. He, Parrish, wouldn't stand a prayer of getting close to her if Gavilan knew, or even suspected, the truth.

He risked a look at his boss. Gavilan, sans jacket, vest and collar, sat with his elbows upon the cluttered surface of his huge desk, his hands arched together before his face. The newspaper sat atop the mess, ignored. Gavilan was not looking at him. He appeared to be rapt in contemplation of some event to which Parrish was not privy. The expression both disturbed and relieved Parrish, who allowed himself a small sigh.

He realized all at once that he was sweating like a mule skinner, and mopped his brow with his limp handkerchief. It felt as if it were a million degrees in the room, although Gavilan hardly seemed to notice the fact. Quietly, Parrish removed his jacket and spread it carefully upon the back of his own chair. He loosened his collar and removed the marcasite cufflinks at his dark, hairy wrists. He pushed up his damp, wilted cuffs as he slipped into his place. Goddamn it, say something, Brownie! he thought, sweltering with the heat of the room and the heat of his deception. Prove to me that you believe this bullshit story!

But Gavilan said nothing.

Parrish began sifting aimlessly through the paperwork upon his desk, work Gavilan had apparently thought could wait for his return. He was unable to focus upon it. He eyed his boss again surreptitiously, eager for Gavilan to speak next so that he could gauge the younger man's reaction to the news of Emma Hunt. Gavilan, however, had already pushed the newspaper aside and was poring over a blueprint. Damn Gavilan!

He was like a crack poker player. His expression seldom revealed anything about the deliberations behind it. Finally Parrish could no longer endure the silent suspense.

"You look like hell, Brownie," he remarked, although it was a lie. Gavilan, damn him, always looked good. In fact, the man's appearance had changed very little from their Princeton days a decade before, except that Gavilan's had matured favorably whereas his own had merely aged. He, Parrish, had grown heavier. Balder. There were, he knew, sacks beneath his own eyes. True, he had earned them with his dissolute behavior. But Gavilan, he noticed, had not one dram of excess flesh under his eyes, or anywhere else on his body, for that matter. And the man, only two years his junior, had certainly led as wanton a life-style as he had. Where, he asked himself, grinding his teeth as he monitored his boss steadily, was the fairness in that?

Gavilan took his time looking up.

"I haven't been sleeping too well," he muttered, his obsidian eyes staring at the wall behind Parrish's head as if they might drill a hole therein. "Too damned hot, even at night."

The question seemed to nudge Gavilan back to his work, which was not exactly the response Parrish had hoped for. But he was not surprised: Gavilan had never been the sort of man who volunteered a lot of information about himself. Parrish realized that he would have to draw him out—carefully, like an apothecary measuring morphine, so as not to appear clumsy or overly curious. For his next question, he mustered a sardonic tone.

"Let me guess." He attempted a snicker. "Philipa Braedon."

Gavilan's gaze riveted suddenly to his own, and it was a chilling one. The snicker had succeeded.

"*Oh.*" Parrish chuckled, relieved to have found Gavilan's new weakness, but alarmed at the same time. They would now become rivals: he knowingly, and Gavilan unknowing. Parrish considered him, not moving. He was, he knew, no competition for Gavilan in the arena of amour. He would have to shift the odds in his favor somehow. The most logical medium, he quickly deduced, would be to play upon Gavilan's unprecedented sense of pride. "So she has got you on a string after all, huh, Brownie?"

Gavilan's scowl predictably darkened.

"How is it you purport to know so much about women, but you can never get one of your own without waiting around for my hand-me-downs?" Gavilan was disparaging.

That remark would ordinarily have incensed Parrish, but he steeled his mind toward his goal. He laughed instead.

"My guess is, everyone from Cape May to Atlantic City knows it by now, boss." He pumped as much disdain into his tone as he dared. "It would have taken an idiot not to see that something was wrong with you on Saturday at that meeting. A dozen men saw you stand there like a steer at a slaughterhouse when Elliot told you he was going to marry her. Then you didn't show up at church the next day, and I bet the rest of the town buzzed. But I give you credit. You're no hypocrite. You claim you've never cared about what people thought, and I guess you've gone ahead and proven it. I guess you really don't care who knows that you're thoroughly deranged over that hard-assed Braedon woman."

Gavilan stared blankly at his subordinate for nearly a minute. Then, to Parrish's dismay, he smiled. Slowly. That wide-mouthed, hungry crocodile grin Parrish knew all too well. Whenever it appeared, it meant Gavilan had gotten an idea. The ideas it presaged were, more often then not, radiantly clever. The kind of an idea that made one slap one's head with one's hand and wonder why they had not thought of it themselves. These notions were always entirely unforeseeable. Like quicksand. Parrish could only sit back and hope that this one, whatever it might prove to be, would not irreparably alter his own plans.

"Every time you push me to the brink of firing you, Owe, you say something or do something which reminds me of why I've kept you around for so long," Gavilan declared in a far more jovial tone than any he had used earlier.

Chapter Sixteen

Prior to his discourse with his secretary, Gavilan had utterly dismissed the idea of attending the Fourth of July picnic and fireworks display on the beach, the idea of encountering Philipa Braedon in public so soon after her recent rebuff being somewhat more than his pride could tolerate. Fortunately, however, Owen Parrish's return to town the day before had granted him an entirely new perspective. Careening along the cobblestone streets in the Hurricane with the hot July wind whipping his face, he envisioned her discomfiture as she watched him approach, and her hurt and confusion as he completely ignored her presence. Perhaps he would even select some other attractive, eligible young woman upon whom he could lavish his attention, just to demonstrate publicly his supreme indifference to Philipa Braedon and her asinine engagement.

Perhaps, he thought, feeling deliciously reckless, he would even flirt with Charles Tavistock's charming, if brainless, young wife. He doubted Charles would even take note of the fact, and he was certain that Esmaralda, Essie, would respond most favorably.

The picnic, set up just above the Promenade at Seventh Street, was already in full vigor. It was four o'clock. The sun was westering over the bay, and the gentle, late day breeze had begun to drift in over low tide. The heat of the previous four days had abated somewhat, and with the clement salt zephyr, it was positively refreshing on the beach. The constant rumble of the surf was a soothing backdrop to the festivities. Bright quilts dotted the sand where families had set up picnic blankets and staked out their parameters. Kegs of root beer nested in iced troughs, and busy yellow jackets hummed about the taps. A short way away, the clang of quoits and the hollow clatter of bocce balls added to the clamor of laughing men and children and scolding mothers. Barbecue smoke rose from deep pits in the sand and from long metal stoves set up like tables just under the Promenade, away from any threat of rain.

But the afternoon was as fine as anyone could have wished, and spirits were high, even his own. Gavilan's buff kid shoes sank to his ankles in the hot gray sand and he fixed a jaunty smile on his face as he approached a group of acquaintances including Tavistock and Mayor Brewster. He risked a glance about him to try to determine Miss Braedon's whereabouts in the mob, but was unsuccessful. Disappointment stung him like a greenhead fly. In order to achieve the full benefit of ignoring her in public, he thought, he must first know that she was present to notice him performing the exercise.

"Gavilan!" Charles greeted him with an outstretched hand and a red-faced smile. "Where have you been keeping yourself these last few days?"

Gavilan accepted his hand, aware of a measure of relief: Charles Tavistock obviously had not learned of his errant proposal of marriage to the prudent Miss Braedon. She, then, had not even mentioned the occurrence to her good friend Essie, or the garrulous Essie would surely have told Charles, who would have been unable to prevent himself from gloating over Gavilan's unhappy predicament. *Thank you for that, at least, Philipa*, he thought.

"Working, Charles," he answered the man in good-natured reproof. Charles's hand, he noticed, was sticky with root beer.

"Unlike you, I haven't the time for excessive jaunts to New York."

Suddenly from under the Promenade came the irregular c-c-crack of loud firecrackers. Charles started at the sound, and several nearby women cried out in surprise. Gavilan grinned, recalling an occasion from his own youth when he and several co-conspirators had literally scared the pants off a schoolmaster in a privy with a few well-placed small explosives. The punishment, which he could not now recall, had definitely been worth the commission of the offense. Sure enough, four youths, who looked to be about fifteen, ran out from under the Promenade wearing suspicious expressions of triumph. Gavilan reached out and collared the last of these, pulling the lad to an abrupt halt between himself and Tavistock.

The boy knew when he had been bested. He stared at his toes, his flat cap hiding his eyes. His stained gray knickers were buttoned below the knee, and his chambray shirt was unbuttoned at the throat. He held his hands behind his back in the manner of a prisoner awaiting sentence. Gavilan felt his mouth curl down at the corners as he tried to suppress his grin.

"What's your name, mister?" He affected a stern tone.

The boy did not reply.

"Mr. Gavilan asked you a question, boy!" Charles Tavistock barked at him, but Gavilan held up his hand for patience.

The boy did not move. "Freddy Hanover, sir," he mumbled.

"Freddy is a child's name, son," Gavilan chided him roundly. "You're a young man. Did your mother raise you to be a gentleman, or a hoodlum?"

There was a moment of repentant silence.

"A gentleman, sir. Mr. Gavilan," he corrected himself. His cap brim went up slightly, and he stole a furtive glance at his captor.

"Good," replied Gavilan, releasing his collar and extending his hand to the lad. The boy accepted it shyly. "You have too much time on your hands, Mr. Frederick Hanover. What you need is a job. For the summer, of course, until you go back to school. You do go to school, don't you?''

The boy was now staring openly, his mortification at having been caught apparently overwhelmed by his amazement.

"Yes, sir. Else my ma'd take a switch to me, sir."

Gavilan decided he liked the lad.

"There's a good man, Hanover. Now." He fished in his pocket for several tokens, and held them out to Frederick Hanover. "Take these on up to the arcade. Play yourself some skeeball. Take a look at a nickelodeon. Then find Mr. Jarrett and tell him I sent you. You'll be sweeping floors to start, but unless I miss my guess, you'll be fixing machines and making change by August. Pay is twenty-five cents a day. And Mr. Hanover," he added, fixing a stern look upon him even as the boy grinned at him from ear to ear, "there'll be no more terrorizing the population with those pyrotechnics, y'hear?''

"Yes, sir." The boy straightened his heretofore rounded shoulders. "I mean, no, sir. I mean—heck, thanks, Mr. Gavilan!"

Jingling the tokens in his hand, Frederick Hanover swaggered off down the beach like the lone bantam cock in a crowded chicken coop. Charles Tavistock looked on in amazement.

"Since when are you running a charity, Gavilan?" Tavistock's tone reflected his disbelief. "Twenty-five cents a day! To a—to a—"

"To a promising young man with a lot of energy and not much to put it into except mischief," Gavilan interrupted him calmly. "You heard him, Charles. He's respectful and fairly well-spoken. Goes to school. So he raises a little hell. At fifteen, I guess he's entitled to some wild oats."

"Wild oats!" Charles huffed disparagingly. "You'll find out he's stealing from you within the week, I'd wager."

"That's a wager I'll take, Tavistock." Gavilan felt the hackles rise on the back of his neck. He considered himself a pretty shrewd judge of character, and Charles not at all. He was willing to take the risk.

Charles raised his round chin smugly.

"Name the stakes."

"If I win, you have to hire one of Hanover's friends to work in your office for the rest of the summer, at twenty-five cents a day."

Charles smirked, as though he thought that an unlikely result.

"And if you lose?" he prompted skeptically.

Gavilan shrugged and grinned at him.

"I'll give you the Hurricane."

Charles's blue eyes widened, then narrowed again.

"It's a bet," he agreed, extending his hand as though the Hurricane were as good as his. "You're a fool, Gavilan!"

"I've been told that before, Tavistock, by—"

Out of the corner of his eye, Gavilan saw a blaze of deep rose amid the pastels of ladies' dresses. He looked away from Charles in mid-sentence in time to see Philipa Braedon make her way to the sweet table a short distance away, bearing a basket covered with a red and white checkered napkin. She had not noticed him, so he allowed himself to watch her as she handed her contribution to an older woman behind the table. She wore an eye-catching dress of deep rose, draped and bustled, with puffed sleeves and a fetching neckline that made her appear positively gay and girlish, but for her regal deportment. She held a matching parasol with one hand, and her attractive straw bonnet was trimmed in complementing colors, framing her face most becomingly.

The woman behind the table, whom Gavilan did not know, smiled at her and offered some remark that Gavilan could not hear. Philipa's rose-petal lips moved in brief reply and she returned the woman's smile, but Gavilan detected a hint of sadness in the expression which might, he realized, have been his own invention.

"If I didn't know better, I'd swear you were in love with Bluestocking, Gavilan!"

Gavilan heard the comment and was about to retort when Philipa Braedon turned suddenly in his direction and actually took two steps toward him before looking up. When her gaze met his, he felt his face heat suddenly, as though he faced an open flame. Her exquisite mouth opened slightly, and her clear, bright eyes widened becomingly. Then she turned away

quickly and hurried off in the other direction in a flurry of
pink. He felt his face grow warm. He'd meant to ignore her,
and had not gotten off to a very good start. He remembered,
too, that he had wanted to answer Charles sharply, but—damnation! He had forgotten what Charles had said to him! He
steeled himself for Charles's mocking laughter, but when
none was forthcoming, he looked at the other man expectantly.

Charles, however, to his dismay, was returning his stare
with one of sober, unconcealed incredulity.

Philipa walked quickly through the crowd of picnickers,
upbraiding herself even as she felt herself flush with shame.
She'd hoped she had sufficiently prepared herself to encounter
Terence Gavilan once again after their disturbing confrontation in her parlor. She had devoted a great deal of time during
the last two days reconciling herself to the fact that she would
run into him now and again. In a town as intimate as Braedon's Beach, one had to expect it. Thus she had schooled
herself carefully, fantasizing a variety of situations in which
their paths might cross: at church, on the Promenade, or even
at a social gathering of a mutual friend or acquaintance. She
had conducted elaborate silent dialogues, practiced gestures
and facial expressions. She was confident, in the end, that she
had mastered every foreseeable variable, and that she would
be able to face him with equanimity and great presence of
mind when next they met.

Why, then, had her composure completely forsaken her
when she looked up and saw him staring at her, not twenty
feet away on a crowded beach?

She made a conscious effort to slow her walk, and discovered, blushing again, that in her haste she had made a wrong
turn. She was to have met Essie and other mutual friends in
the vicinity of the makeshift baseball diamond, set up as usual
behind the sweet tables where she had seen Terence Gavilan
conversing with Essie's husband. Annoyed, she felt herself
glow to the very roots of her hair. She managed a clumsy and
self-conscious greeting to Father Michaels, whom she nearly
ran into in her distracted state, and turned around to head,

once again, in the opposite direction.

On her way, she spotted Beatrice Waverly from afar, holding court among a gaggle of frowning matrons. The women were deeply engrossed in conversation, no doubt decimating someone's character for some lapse in morality, real or imagined. None of them appeared to have noticed her. She cut her future mother-in-law a wide berth, having no desire to endure the woman's probing inquisition regarding her scarlet complexion, and hastened to join Essie and her own contemporaries.

Resplendent in crisp navy blue bathing bloomers which, she knew, Essie entertained no thoughts of testing, her friend reclined idyllicly in a green canvas deck chair from Abercrombie and Fitch. She displayed matching stockings and shoes, her blond curls subdued by a red-trimmed blue bathing bonnet. She waved gaily to Philipa from her rustic throne. Around her, seated on an enormous patchwork picnic blanket like devoted ladies in waiting, were several of their friends: Emily Moss, whose children were off digging for clams in the low tide; Sally Brewster, who had married the mayor's cousin only the previous year; Alice Beecham, who was a cousin of Beatrice Waverly's, and several other young matrons with whom Essie and Philipa had grown up. Philipa greeted them all warmly and realized, sinking into Charles's unoccupied chair, that, aside from the schoolteacher Wilhelmina Stoner, who was several years her senior, she was the only unmarried female in the group.

"I was just telling them all about our little trip to New York, Philly." Essie obviously adored being the center of attention. "Everyone was admiring your gown, and I was about to tell them about Gaultiere's. Would you like to tell them, or shall I?"

"You tell, please," Philipa begged off with a sigh, greatly relieved to be among a fortress of friendly faces who would surely buffer her from Terence Gavilan if the need arose. She had begun to feel exceedingly warm in spite of the pleasant sea breeze, and she wished that she had worn her bathing costume so she could go in for a cooling dip. No, she thought suddenly. She would certainly have died of mortification had she met Terence Gavilan in such garb. She detested the things anyway. Later, she promised herself. When the beach was deserted and touched by moonlight. Then she would indulge in her aquatic endeavors to her heart's content.

She leaned back in the chair and found it deceptively uncomfortable. It forced her back, accustomed to a rigid uprightness, into a deep, curved slouch that made her feel as awkward as an overturned horseshoe crab. When she tried to get out of it, the chair held her back like a great unbalanced weight, so she decided to remain where she was. Essie was prattling on about the shopping highlights of their adventure, and Philipa's restive mind began to wander.

What had Mr. Gavilan thought when he'd seen her take off like a frightened deer minutes ago? she wondered grimly, feeling a slight warmth encroach upon her neck again. Certainly he must have noticed her foolish reaction—he'd been looking right at her at the time. She successfully held her blush at bay and glanced about. She had no desire to encounter Terence Gavilan again this day without being forewarned of his presence. The effect upon her had been too unsettling, not to say devastating. She felt a little like an unsuspecting swimmer in shark-infested waters, constantly looking over her shoulder for that telltale fin slicing through the waves. Not that Gavilan was in any way menacing, she realized, feeling a little silly about the simile. But there was a certain undeniable similarity in their predatory temperaments.

"... did you, Philipa?" Essie wound up her recitation, unfortunately, with a query directed at Philipa.

"Elliot isn't here, Philly," Emily Moss teased her in a knowing whine.

"I think she's watching for Beatrice," Sally volunteered. "She must be careful to look as though she isn't having any fun."

"You're both quite wrong," Essie sniffed with a distinct air of condescending superiority. "*I* believe she is looking for Terence Gavilan."

Philipa started. Essie wore an insufferably knowing grin on her annoyingly pretty face. Philipa was seized by a nearly uncontrollable urge to slap her. She did manage to curb her corporal instinct, but was unable to stay herself from glaring at her best friend.

"I think your bathing cap must be too snug, Essie!" she snapped, rather more loudly than she had wished, causing the other women to stare at her in wordless wonder.

Philipa, looking from one astonished face to the next, realized too late the forcefulness of her words.

"Come, ladies." Charles Tavistock's patronizing words split the tension abruptly, rescuing Philipa from her mortification without being aware of it. "It's time for our annual exercise in absurdity. Not you, Essie," Charles restrained his wife, who had already begun to rise. "It wouldn't do. Not— not in that getup. I won't have you displaying yourself. Besides . . ." Charles allowed his voice to trail off, and he held his wife's gaze for a moment longer than was usual for him.

Essie, to Philipa's surprise, returned his gaze with a demure smile and a fond blush.

"Of course, Charles," she murmured in an uncharacteristic display of wifely acquiescence.

Charles, seeming anxious to escape, withdrew. The attention of the ladies was immediately drawn from Philipa, mercifully, to Essie Tavistock, who looked like the cat who had eaten the canary.

"Something is in the wind, Essie," Alice Beecham scolded her playfully, wagging a finger at her.

Essie blushed harder.

"More like something's in the womb, I'll wager," Emily Moss, who knew of such things all too well, declared baldly.

Sally Brewster gaped at those words.

"Emily!" she exclaimed, her gloved hands upon her cheeks.

"It's true," Essie purred, Philipa's outburst apparently forgotten. "Dr. Waverly confirmed it yesterday. I had wanted to tell you, first Philly,"—she sent an apologetic glance her way—"but . . ." Her voice trailed off, and she shrugged with a coy little smile.

Essie was expecting a child. Essie, a mother. Philipa's throat swelled unexpectedly with some strange emotion that

was part joy, part envy. Amid the laughter and the congratulations of the other women, Philipa managed to get up out
of her chair and go to her friend, bending over to give her a
warm hug.

"I'm so happy for you, Es," she whispered, choking on
the emotion that caught her unawares, overjoyed for her
friend. "You will be a wonderful mother. I'm certain of it."

"Thank you, Philly," Essie whispered in return. "I hope
that may be true."

The crowd upon the beach began shifting, like a school of
mackerel, toward the baseball diamond for the exercise of
which Charles had spoken. It had become a tradition at the
Independence Day festivities for the men to engage in a game
of baseball. Somehow it had also become a tradition to allow
the women to compete against them in the first inning. Philipa, being somewhat athletic, had come to look forward to
this tradition, even though it was intended by the men as
indulgence, if not jest. The blot on this year's demonstration,
for Philipa, was the presence of Terence Gavilan. Her enthusiasm for the game being well known, she could not beg off
without inviting a lot of questions. But perhaps, she thought
doubtfully, Terence Gavilan would not play.

Besides, she rallied herself, there would be eight other men
upon the field besides him. Even assuming that she hit the
ball, chances remained excellent that she would not even cross
his path. Buoyed by this prospect, she joined the other women
who queued up at home plate.

It was not the dare of the men which drew these women,
she knew. It was the more appealing challenge of whacking
a small sphere with a long wooden stick and sending it sailing
through the summer air. It was, she sensed as she watched
their faces light up with anticipation, as close to Camelot as
many of these women would ever come.

Thirteen women, ranging in age from 19 to 33, drew lots
to see who would hit first. Traditionally, all of the women
batted in the first inning, regardless of the outs, and then
played the other half of the inning in the field before yielding
to the men for the more serious game. Philipa drew last place,
a position that pleased her. She conversed with the other play-

ers, watching with one cautious eye as the men took their
positions in the field. Terence Gavilan, she noted with some
dismay, had removed his impeccable pale blue jacket and
white skimmer and had taken up his position at first base. Her
participation in the chatter ceased and she watched with fascination as he assumed the pose of a vigilant fielder: legs
apart, back bent forward, the long fingers of his ungloved
hands splayed upon his knees. He had the lean, competitive
look of a true athlete. The sea breeze teased his sable locks,
and she realized, all at once, that he was staring at her again,
unabashedly, unapologetically. She quickly looked away as
her face grew warm.

George Moss was pitching. He threw the ball in a generously slow manner to the women, even though Philipa knew
him to possess a fastball that many a professional ballplayer
would have envied. Even so, the first seven batters struck out
on five pitches apiece, amid cheers and good-natured teasing.
John Brewster, who stood behind home plate calling balls and
strikes, proceeded to allow his cousin by marriage to walk to
first base, as she had not seen fit to swing at any of the pitches
offered. Wilhelmina Stoner then sent a fly ball sailing over
the infield, only to have it bagged by the short fielder. She
retired amid respectful applause.

Philipa longed to hit the ball in that manner. She had only
ever managed ground balls, and even though she had gotten
on base with these once or twice, she thought it must be a
glorious feeling to watch a ball take to the air once it left her
bat. And anyway, a fly ball would eliminate the necessity of
her running all the way to first base, where Gavilan stood,
looking like a serious player.

While the next batter stepped to the plate, she stole another
look at him. He was bantering with George Moss in an easy
manner, as though he had known George all of his life, even
though they had only met at Essie's on Decoration Day. She
envied him his ease with people, his natural self-assurance.
And she could not help but admire the way in which he had
in so short a time become a lively part of their usually aloof
little community.

And suddenly he was looking directly at her again, as

though her gaze had attracted his attention like a beacon from a lighthouse. His mahogany eyes seemed to perceive her very soul from across the distance that separated them. She was unable to look away from him, although she desperately wanted to. She felt her throat constrict, as though a child's balloon had gotten caught there and was slowly inflating.

"Batter up!" John Brewster declared, and Gavilan, to her relief, released her from his gaze.

The women had not scored, although Sally Brewster had advanced to third base and Emily Moss had made it to first on a ground ball to her husband. It was finally Philipa's turn, and she removed her gloves to take hold of the Louisville Slugger Emily had dropped at the plate. The bat felt good in her hands, warmed from the heat of the sun, and from the hands of her teammates who had come before her. She took a few swipes at the air. It was a heavy bat, but she could get it around quickly, feeling her shoulders and back stretch against the unaccustomed movement. George Moss eyeballed her, and she felt the way she was sure a professional ball-player would feel facing his adversary. It was thrilling. Now, if she could only send the ball into the air . . .

Hanford threw the ball. She swung, hard.

And missed.

She tried to ignore the encouragement of her teammates and steeled her concentration once again. Again she missed. And again. Anxiety crept in. *Please, don't let me strike out*, she prayed, watching George Hanford wind up.

She hit the fourth pitch solidly. She stood watching as the ball went up, up, over the head of the third baseman and just beyond him into shallow left field.

"Run, Philly! Run!" Essie's high-pitched squeal reached her ears.

Philipa, overjoyed at her success, began to trot toward first base in her cumbersome skirts. She glanced back, certain that the outfielder would catch it. Remembering what awaited her at first base, she suddenly prayed that he would. Blessedly, he did.

But Charles Tavistock dropped it.

The spectators made much noise over this, both cheering

and whistling, but Philipa scarcely heard them. She was now, thanks to Charles's clumsiness, required to continue running toward Terence Gavilan.

Gavilan stood just at the corner of the base, watching for the ball. Philipa could not look at the play any longer, lest she run into him as she reached the base. She was but three steps away when she saw Gavilan stretch out his long, lean body while his toe remained upon the base, and she heard the sound of the ball smack into his palm just before she ran into his shoulder, hard.

She was out.

Instantly she felt his strong hand close on her arm to steady her.

He could not know, surely, that the effect upon her was anything but steadying. While the spectators cheered the play, he continued to hold her for what seemed a lifetime.

"Are you all right?"

Those were the first words he had spoken to her all afternoon. She could barely bring herself to respond to them, she was trembling so badly.

"Yes," she nodded hesitantly, staring at his collar. "Th-thank you."

She looked up at him, against her will. He was not smiling in a teasing way, as she had expected. He was monitoring her steadily, and even reached up with a tentative hand to pluck a strand of dune grass from her hair.

"Nice hit," he offered with a brief smile, releasing her.

She flushed.

"Nice catch," she managed to return the compliment breathlessly.

"Sides!" John Brewster bellowed, and the gossamer spell was broken. Gavilan placed the ball in her hands, and the tips of his fingers touched hers, where he allowed them to remain for an instant. Then he was gone, with no further remark to her.

The men were to be allowed two outs; barring that, eight hitters. Women with husbands or beaus participating pitched to them, and any unmated players remaining took pot luck. Emily Moss pitched a creampuff to George, which he grounded to third, where Wilhelmina handled it nicely and threw it to Philipa at first. But George was fast. In fact, one spectator offered a not too obscure analogy to Moss's prodigious feat of five children in six years. Charles Tavistock was next, and Wilhelmina Stoner did the honors, as Essie was indisposed. In no time, there were three runners on base, nobody out, and the fourth man stepped to the plate. It was Terence Gavilan, and the women in the field looked as one to Philipa. In spite of the late afternoon heat, her feet felt as though she were standing ankle-deep in a lake which had frozen all around her.

There was nothing to do, short of a scene, but to pitch to him.

Tentatively, she approached the mound, although in the sand it was more of a depression. Marshaling her wits, she faced the batter. He stared back at her, poised to swing, his dark eyes yielding no emotion whatever. Thank God, she thought, winding up.

To her astonishment, Gavilan struck out swinging on three pitches. And judging by the look of disgust on his features, she suspected that he had not done so on purpose.

Philipa was so unutterably relieved when the little exhibition was over and the men's game began in earnest that she slipped away completely, seeking a few moments of solitude on the cold sand under the Promenade. The sand under the boards, unlike the warm beach, was cool and damp, but from her secluded vantage point, she was able to survey the crowd unnoticed, and try to garner her composure again.

The simple fact, she realized bleakly, was that she was thoroughly smitten by Gavilan. Nothing had altered that. Not her own engagement, nor her discovery that he was calling upon Jessamyn Flaherty, who was conspicuously absent from this gathering of respectable company. Philipa had hoped to cure herself of this terrible, wonderful affliction, but her efforts, admittedly half-hearted, she finally confessed to herself, had been to no avail. It had required but one touch of his hand; one innocently tender gesture on a ball field to remind her most acutely of that attraction. She remembered, all at once, his abrupt and unexpected proposal, and she wished she could have that moment back so she could answer him differently. The truth of the matter was that she did not care about anything anymore except the fact that she loved him, and that she would accept him no matter what his shortcomings, or her own. Had she not been such a prude, such a coward . . .

No. She would not weep. She had the remainder of the afternoon to get through, as well as the rest of her life. And anyway, regret, she was certain, would make for poor company in a marriage bed.

Chapter Seventeen

Philipa had disappeared immediately after the exhibition inning, and Gavilan could not look for her. He had endured much good-natured ribbing regarding his performance at the plate. *Can't connect with Bluestocking?* Charles had teased. *He's much more skilled with the mallet,* George Moss had allowed broadly, referring, Gavilan was sure, to the croquet game at the Tavistocks' on Decoration Day. He'd had to smile at these and many more vulgar, if veiled, jibes, all the while simmering inside. To compound difficulties, he was then more or less obliged to play in the baseball game that followed instead of being free to seek out Miss Braedon. The only consolation to this occurrence was that his hitting improved considerably, since he no longer had to look into Philipa Braedon's lovely and changeable eyes as he chased a pitch.

Her mysterious disappearance, however, gave him cause for concern, and rendered him a surly companion on the playing field. The more churlish he became, the more his teammates, and opponents, harassed him about his behavior. He was glad, therefore, when the cooks clanged the dinner bell terminating the game, for he had reached the end of his patience and was certain that he would have flattened someone, most likely Charles Tavistock, had the game, hence the ribbing, gone on any longer.

There was one bright spot, however, if one could view it as such, he thought, tacitly amused by the irony. The events of the afternoon had finally forced him to acknowledge what several independent sources, among them Charles, Owen Parrish, and even Elliot Waverly himself, had already suggested: Philipa Braedon did indeed, as Parrish had so eloquently put it, have him thoroughly deranged. He had been made aware, as he had placed the ball into her hands at first base, that he had fallen madly, hopelessly in love with the woman.

The feeling had been quite remarkable. It was as if some huge, unseen hand had seized him, shaken him to attention, and then pointed a finger at her. *She is the one*, a thunderously silent voice had told him. The breakthrough, which was in reality only a little disturbing, had left him with but one pressing question.

What to do about it?

Find her, was the first answer that occurred to him, although pride quickly prevailed over that option. The barbecue was ready, he reasoned, looking about for her as he stood a little apart from the gathering with his own uneaten plate of food in his hand. Surely she would surface for supper.

Tell her, was the second idea; impossible to execute, he realized, unless the first was accomplished. Nor was he altogether certain that it was the prudent course of action at this time. She had, after all, less than a week before rejected his proposal of marriage, and in a vehement and debasing manner. He tried to recall her exact words: he was, if memory served him, "the very last man" with whom she could be prevailed upon to marry. How did one set about wooing one's fair lady when said fair lady entertained such an unfortunate opinion of one?

He set his plate down on a weathered pylon and folded his arms across his chest, biting his lower lip as he surveyed the picnickers. Her words rankled, that was certain. But he could not help but wonder, recalling her charming, blushing confusion at first base, whether they had been inspired by true feeling, or by the jealousy and hurt of a woman who had discovered that the object of her affection was carrying on with another woman, in this case, Jess. If the latter were true, he mused, with a new surge of hope, it might require nothing more than an earnest conversation with her to set straight the record, determine her true feelings and clear the way for him to declare himself to her.

But what of her engagement to Elliot?

He dismissed it at once. Philipa did not truly love the younger Waverly. Of that, he had no doubt. And if Elliot's behavior was any indication, and he was certain it was, then Elliot did not truly love her, either, although the man might believe that he did. But in any case, Elliot's feelings were not his concern. Elliot was 75 miles away in a seminary outside Philadelphia. He, Gavilan, was here. As was Philipa. Any man, he rationalized with no small sense of self-righteousness, who would go off and leave his affiancéd alone during the period of their betrothal deserved to have her stolen away from him.

Damn it, where was she? He rubbed his jaw, considering the possibility that she might have gone home. Piqued by the notion, he abandoned his dinner to the noisy gulls which had been circling like hungry vultures and walked up the beach, away from the picnic, in the direction of her house some three or four blocks away. If he found her at home, he would know she had left the gathering to avoid him, and that she was a coward, after all.

But no. The house was deserted. He peeked boldly in every visible window, knocked, and even called to her eventually. All to no avail. Not even the housekeeper was there. Feeling his discouragement keenly in his gut along with his hunger, he made his way slowly back south along the beach again to the picnic area, where he discovered with no surprise that the plate he had left on the pylon had been ravaged by the gulls.

Twilight began as a deep blue line along the horizon of the Atlantic Ocean and crept slowly across the sky as the sun retreated past the bay on the other side of the island. It was but half an hour until sunset, he judged, and therefore perhaps another thirty minutes beyond that until the much-touted fireworks display on the beach would begin. Philipa Braedon, he thought, growing annoyed, where have you gone?

The popping of small firecrackers could be heard below the deck of the Promenade again, some distance away. Gavilan experienced a shudder, thinking fleetingly of Frederick Hanover and his three friends, hoping he had not been wrong about the lad after all. He would hate to see Charles Tavistock tooling along the avenue in his Hurricane, gloating over him at every opportunity. And besides, the automobile would be expensive to replace. He forced thoughts of Philipa Braedon aside and ducked under the joists of the Promenade to try to determine the source of this new disturbance.

It was dark and cavelike under the Promenade, but he could see, a block away, three tall, lanky silhouettes, obviously three young men, dancing around two taller, rounder figures in long skirts. One of these, he realized at once, was Philipa Braedon. The other, by her square and solid aspect, might have been Wilhelmina Stoner, the schoolteacher. Bright flashes of golden white light sparkled around the two women, followed almost instantaneously by the sharp crackling noise of small explosions. This racket was met with high-pitched shrieks, more of annoyance than of fear. Gavilan broke into a run, cursing under his breath. If you are among them, Freddy Hanover, he thought grimly, I will have your hide!

Before he had even made it halfway there, he saw another silhouette interrupt the scene, that of a tall, gangly youth he recognized as Fred Hanover. Relief challenged his alarm for the women. The fireworks abruptly ceased, replaced by the din of a heated exchange in which everyone shouted at once.

"—to torment defenseless women—"

"—ought to be ashamed—"

"—Freddy's sweet on—"

"Take them Black Cats on down the beach a ways, Tommy!" He was finally able to distinguish Freddy's voice, hard and sure, and a good octave lower than where it had started earlier in the day. "I wouldn't want to be in your boots if Mr. Gavilan finds that you been botherin' his lady!"

Gavilan pulled up to a halt behind them, suddenly glad of the darkness under the Promenade. *His* lady? Whatever had given Freddy the idea . . . He collected himself and caught his breath.

"You'd best do as he says, boys," he said, his voice resonating under the deck as if in a cathedral. "Be on your way. And don't let me—or Mr. Hanover—find you bothering ladies that way again, or we'll forget we are gentlemen. Have I made myself clear?"

Freddy, and the two women he had so gallantly defended, had turned to him as one when he had started to speak. He, however, did not look at them. He had fixed his stare upon the three perpetrators of this fortuitous confrontation with Miss Braedon. Could they but know it, they would have been amazed to discover that he felt like tipping them all handsomely for their mischief, including Hanover.

Gavilan did not look at Philipa as he came around to join Fred Hanover's barrier between the ladies and their attackers, but he could feel her stare upon him, almost as if she were touching him with her fine, graceful hands. The young men, whose shadowed features he could not make out, once again hastily retreated in the face of challenge. Gavilan, suddenly angry without fully understanding why, directed his attention next to Fred, whose large, flat hands were shaking.

"Your friends' manners leave a little to be desired, wouldn't you say, Mr. Hanover?" he remarked, striving mightily to keep his ire in check.

He saw the youth suck in a hard breath. Relief was evident on the earnest young face.

"Yes, sir," he panted, and Gavilan could see a rivulet of perspiration make its way down the youth's smooth and hairless cheek. The sight melted Gavilan a little: Fred had been afraid, but he had stood his ground defending the ladies, and had not betrayed his trepidation to his adversaries. Gavilan stuck his hand out with the full force of his arm. Fred accepted it wordlessly, even shaking it bashfully twice.

"I knew you were a good man, Hanover. Have you spoken to Mr. Jarrett?"

"Yes, sir, I have."

"And you'll start Monday."

"Yes, sir." Hanover was starting to relax a little.

Gavilan released the young man's hand and clapped him on the shoulder.

"Fine. And, ah—Mr. Hanover."

"Sir?" Fred looked at him expectantly.

"I have not the pleasure of calling either of these ladies my own."

Yet, he thought, controlling a wayward blush.

"Oh. Sorry, Mr. Gavilan. Miss Braedon." There was a pregnant pause. "Miss Stoner."

Miss Stoner spoke next, relieving some of the tension. For Gavilan, at least.

"I had not imagined you to possess such noble qualities, Frederick." Miss Stoner's tone was all business, with a faint tint of admiration skillfully infused. "I am most pleasantly surprised. Thank you for taking our part. And thank you too, Mr. Gavilan." She nodded at him with a gracious, proper smile.

Gavilan nodded his acknowledgment in return. In her way, he perceived with some irritation, Miss Stoner was as short-sighted as Charles Tavistock.

"I find that most people tend to live up, or down, to the expectations we have of them, Miss Stoner," he remarked dryly. "Perhaps you might wish to employ that theorem in your classroom."

He tipped his hat to soften the harshness of his words, but not the sentiment behind them. Miss Stoner's mouth popped open; then she closed it again. And he could not tell for certain, but he suspected she was blushing, as well.

"Why, yes. Yes. Thank you. I just might do so. Good evening, Mr. Gavilan. Miss Braedon, I'll wait for you with Mrs. Tavistock."

No! Wait! Philipa wanted to call out to her, terrified at the prospect of being left alone with Terence Gavilan. The words, however, stuck in her throat like the overcooked steak she had nibbled upon earlier. She was still trembling from fear and rage in connection with the earlier incident, and she had not the presence of mind to compose herself as she would have liked. But Wilhelmina had hastened away without a backward glance and left her to the lion. Beside her, she heard him breathing in the deep, regular, untroubled respiration of a disconcertingly healthy male animal. There was a long moment of silence.

"They didn't hurt you, did they?" His tone was respectful. Almost reverent.

She swallowed hard before attempting to reply.

"No," was all she could manage in an exasperatingly weak tone.

The wash of the surf and the restful blanket of chatter from the picnickers echoed under the Promenade like a whispered taunt. Beside her, Terence Gavilan cleared his throat and shifted his weight on his heels.

"Where did you go after the baseball game?" he inquired lightly, although she would have sworn she detected a note of injury in his quiet, deep voice that rent her heart.

"For a walk," she answered, oddly touched by his curiosity.

"Oh," he said, and from the corner of her eye she saw him nod quickly.

She rifled her conversational repertoire for something else to say, but this proved difficult as she did not know whether she wanted him to go away or to stay. She suspected the latter. She wished fervently that she could quiet her heart and command her shallow, erratic breaths, but she felt as though she had no mastery over her own body. It was both a terrible and an extraordinary sensation.

"The fireworks will likely begin soon," Gavilan observed, his baritone suddenly brisk and neutral.

Philipa thought he might say more after that. She prayed that he would. But he did not. Disappointment lanced her breast.

"I believe I'll just go home now," she sighed finally. "I have had enough of fireworks for one Fourth of July."

She bitterly enjoyed the deeper meaning behind her sentiment. Beside her Terence Gavilan chuckled softly, as if he thoroughly understood both interpretations. She felt his hand, firm but gentle, on her elbow. The sensation paralyzed her, and she perceived his intention at once.

"Really, Mr. Gavilan, it isn't necessary for you to walk me

home," she said, a trifle too quickly, she realized. "I'm just up the beach."

But he began to walk with her anyway, north under the Promenade and away from the watchful eyes of the population of Braedon's Beach.

"I am well aware of your address, Miss Braedon, having found your home on at least one other occasion. Don't try to order me around the way you boss your fiancé," was his abrupt response.

She bridled, blushing at his thinly veiled rebuke.

"I don't know why you are angry with me," she retorted in what she hoped was a bold voice. "I didn't invite that attack."

"No, you didn't," he agreed, in a tone that suggested otherwise. "But neither did you handle it in the proper fashion. Honestly, Miss Braedon, did you learn nothing at Bryn Mawr about dealing with people? Or was it your aim merely to attract my attention?"

Her cheeks burned. She had, on the face of it, wanted to avoid him completely at all costs throughout the day. But she had realized very quickly that she was powerless to prevent her gaze from seeking him out, from perpetually straying to his tall, lean, splendidly attired figure. And every time she had found him, she had discovered, to her embarrassment and wonder, that he had been looking at her with a searching expression on his handsome, animated features.

He did not alter his pace, but her own step faltered.

"I..."

She stopped, unable to go on. Her sense of honor would not permit her to lie, nor her sense of pride to confess the truth. He waited for a long time before making a remark.

"You need not reply to that, Miss Braedon," he allowed, apparently pleased to bestow the favor. "I have my answer, after all."

He did not speak for a time. His hold on her elbow neither tightened nor relaxed as they continued in a leisurely pace up along the Promenade, finally emerging from under its shelter after having left the picnic far behind.

The beach there was quiet, except for the ceaseless rush of

the surf and the lonely cawing of the gulls. Philipa might almost have enjoyed the walk, with her elbow secure in Terence Gavilan's grip, were it not for the palpable tension between them. Her step wavered in the shifting sand, and he tucked her arm into his, covering her trembling hand with his own in an authoritative manner which would brook no protest. His protective gesture sent a burning weight into the pit of her stomach, like a load of brimstone: she had seen him escort Jessamyn Flaherty in precisely the same manner only the week before. The memory, to her surprise, triggered not so much anger as pain.

"Was your trip to New York a success?" he broke the silence by inquiring.

Unwillingly, Philipa looked up at him for the first time since he had joined them under the Promenade. That he had learned of her junket to the city did not startle her so much as the way in which he had elected to frame his question. She quickly mastered her suspicion to reply in as oblique a fashion as she could.

"Yes," she said shortly. Then, deciding that her response had come out as rather abrupt, she sought to embellish it. "Yes, it was."

Looking away again, she felt like a fool. What was it, she wondered miserably, about Terence Gavilan that robbed her so often of her usual articulation?

"If this new gown of yours is a product of the excursion, I would have to agree with you." He, fortunately, supplied the flourish. "It is quite the most flattering frock I've ever seen you wear. Gaultiere's, on Fifth Avenue?"

His question intensified the confusion which his compliment had incited.

"Yes," she replied a trifle breathlessly, sounding, she knew, amazed. How was it that he knew so much about the fashionable seamstresses? Then she had a dreadful thought: was it possible that Gavilan had visited the place himself, with Jess Flaherty on his arm, for the purpose of purchasing that outrageous blue creation the younger woman had been wearing on that awful night?

"Really, Miss Braedon, you should not talk so much," he

was saying with exaggerated politeness. "I can hardly get a
word in."

He was teasing her again. Flirting, as he used to just after
they'd met. Only they had not just met. Something had passed
between them. Something so powerful that it had induced him
to propose marriage to her, and something so disturbing that
it had forced her to reject that proposal, even though she now
bitterly regretted it. He, as far as she could tell, had already
forgotten. But she would remember for as long as she lived.
She sighed brokenly, incapable, she knew, of responding to
him in the same light manner of address he had used.
Therefore she elected not to respond at all.

They were still half a block from her home, and she could
see that the lights within were not lit. Mrs. Grant, she thought,
must still be at the picnic. But of course: why would she have
left? The fireworks display was yet to come.

"I wish," Gavilan was going on in a soft, almost wistful
voice, "that we might converse again. I wish we could forget
our recent—unpleasantness, and go back to where we were
on Decoration Day. I had begun to think of you as a friend
in this strangely formal and remote hamlet. I miss that friendship. More than you can know."

His words pierced her heart, like the careless claws of a
playful cat. Part of her yearned for that same friendship he
had described, almost a kinship of the spirit, unlike any she
had ever felt for another human being. But part of her, the
greater part, yearned for something much more. But Jessamyn
stood between them now like a winsome, dark specter, and
Elliot like a blinding flash of pure, cold, white light.

They had reached the porch, and it was dark already. The
darkness had descended upon them quickly, like a heavy purple drapery drawn across the evening sky. It would be a good
night for fireworks, Philipa observed with some distant portion of her mind that was still concerned about such things.
Clear. The breeze had died, but the salt air was still comfort-
ably cool. The sound of their combined footfalls upon the
wooden porch steps kindled, for a fleeting, painful instant, a
vivid childhood memory of her own parents mounting those
same steps together from the beach upon many a Fourth of

July evening while she, awake in her bed in the room above, had listened to the comforting sound of their voices:

"The fireworks were inspiring this year, don't you think, Julia?" her father would declare in his clear, robust baritone.

"They inspire you every year, dearest," her mother always replied fondly in her soft and melodious alto. And she, the child Philipa, would drift off to sleep after hearing that familiar, loving exchange between her parents, secure in their love, and in her perception of the world.

"You'll miss the fireworks if you don't get back," she cautioned him. Her voice, to her dismay, was but a whisper.

She felt his eyes upon her in the darkness, and she could imagine the tenderness in his gaze. She did not want to look at him. She was afraid the tenderness might have been of her own invention, but more afraid that it was genuine, as real as the gentle touch of his hand upon hers in the crook of his arm.

"I thought we might watch them together from your porch," he replied quietly, and his flagrant omission of her name was as intimate as if he had called her "darling."

"Very well," she murmured, although she had meant to say no, should have said no.

She chose to sit on the porch swing, a wooden affair painted forest green like the shutters, eaves, gables and fretwork about the outside of the house, suspended from the porch roof by sturdy chains. He sat down beside her, his very proximity reminding her of why she should have refused him. She felt as though she had long since lost control of the situation—that Terence Gavilan was, in fact, commanding her every move with cool assurance. His thigh brushed hers. His broad, solid shoulder pressed against hers. His ungloved hands, with their long, strong fingers, were folded in his lap in a loose and relaxed manner.

Her own hands were tightly clenched at her stomach. She felt like a ball of twine too tightly wound. So tightly, in fact, that the explosion from the very first spray of red sparks which appeared in the sky a quarter of a mile down the darkened beach made her jump.

"Why, Miss Braedon! You're as nervous as a cat!" Beside

her, Terence Gavilan sounded surprised and amused. "Here. Perhaps I should . . ." he paused, and she felt, to her alarm, his hand alight upon her own.

She was so astonished at this bold gesture that she did not even resist as he wove his fingers possessively around hers. She was fascinated by the wave of heat his gesture generated within her, spreading quickly from the very center of her breast throughout her extremities, even into her face and her loins, like sweet, hot cider being poured into a bowl. She feared for her composure. She wanted to protest his intimate demonstration, but her tongue was paralyzed by the heat he had incited, a heat that did not diminish. On the contrary, it renewed itself, layer upon layer, with each passing moment.

She stole a glance at his profile: did he feel it, too? He appeared to be concentrating on the display down the beach, and she could gain no clue from his rapt, sensuous features. But how could he not feel it? Her own hand felt as hot as an iron. She was glad of the darkness, for she knew that in it he could not possibly note her fevered blush. Several more fireworks erupted screaming into the dark night. Still he maintained his firm but gentle grip upon her hand and said nothing.

She was beginning to feel slightly faint, and she knew it was because of the imprisonment of her hand. She should pull it away, she realized, or, that being improbable due to the strength of his grip, she should ask him to release it. But he had been holding on to it with no protest from her for several minutes, at least. It would be decidedly odd for her to make such a belated request.

"Well, I must say, I'm a little disappointed." Gavilan spoke up presently in his familiar urbane way. "I expected something more, based upon reports. Who sponsors these festivities?"

She was made aware, all at once, that the fireworks display had concluded. She had been so rapt in her contemplation of him, his possession of her hand, and of her own chaotic emotions, that she had completely missed the program. She swallowed hard at the realization.

"The merchants on the Promenade," she replied faintly.

"Then," he remarked in a quiet but resolute tone, "I shall

have to join them. I intend for Braedon's Beach to become the showplace of the New Jersey shore, and memorable Fourth of July fireworks, complete with a ground display with pinwheels and sparklers, is both an economical and effective means to that end. Don't you agree?''

Philipa could not help but stare at him. The fireworks must have been lackluster, she reasoned, if she could have completely missed them for thinking about the hand that still held her own so possessively. Suddenly he was looking at her, his dark eyes demonstrating their familiar intensity and intimacy that never failed to make her quiver like aspic.

"My father was fond of fireworks," she said quietly in reply to his question. "I believe he would have approved of your ideas."

In the darkness, she saw him smile, a smile that touched her heart perilously. The smile, however, faded quickly at his next question.

"Would your father," he queried softly, his fingers tightening upon her own, "have approved of Elliot Waverly?"

Chapter Eighteen

His unexpected question rendered her speechless even as his tender gaze imprisoned her. *No*, she realized in a startling moment of clarity. As a matter of fact, Henry Braedon probably would not have approved of the Elliot Waverly who had proposed marriage to her. As she recalled, her father had never expressed any opinions at all regarding Elliot and his suitability as a husband for her. On the other hand, Philipa had the idea that, with the exception of his moral character, Terence Gavilan would have been much more to her father's liking. Henry Braedon, like Gavilan, had been a man of action. A born persuader, he was thoughtful and concise, but deliberate and decisive in his business and personal relationships.

Her mother's opinion, of course, would have been an entirely different matter. Terence Gavilan, after all, was a proven libertine who consorted with the kind of woman her mother would have crossed the street to avoid, and he did not even take the trouble to conceal the fact.

The engaging libertine's unswerving gaze compelled a response from her, but she resisted, turning her face aside.

"I think it best that you leave now, Mr. Gavilan." She hoped to sound chilly and imperious, and was dismayed by the weak and breathless quality of her voice.

She felt, to her shock, the fingers of his left hand trace a soft, lacy pattern on the back of hers, still firmly clasped in his right. She could feel the tingling of his caress reverberate to the very base of her spine.

"And why," he inquired in a tone similar to the one she had used, "is that?"

He was seducing her. The notion shocked her. If she allowed it to continue, he had every chance of succeeding. She wrenched her hand away and got up from the swing, escaping to the back door of the house. But she did not go inside.

"Because, Mr. Gavilan," she replied, when she trusted herself to speak again, "you must return to the picnic before you are missed. It would not do to allow people to think that . . . that . . ." she hesitated.

"That what?" He filled the void, his deep, contemplative voice at her ear. She felt the heat of his lean and muscular frame directly behind her like a veritable wall of flame. How had he moved so swiftly, and so silently?

"That I am pursuing you?" he went on in an urgent and unbearably sensuous whisper. "That I am in love with you? That you are attracted to me, in spite of your professed feelings for your fiancé?"

She was dreaming, or hallucinating. She had to be. This wasn't happening . . .

"No, I—"

All at once she felt his strong hands upon her arms like a gentle but irresistible vise. She could not go on, nor could she fight him as he turned her, inevitably, toward him.

"Miss Braedon," he began, maintaining that rich, promising whisper as he commanded her gaze. "Surely you, of all people, must realize by now that the petty conjecture of other people factors not at all into my conduct. Let them think what they will," he continued, his warm hands cradling her face like a treasured prize as his thumbs caressed her cheeks. "I, for one, have no fear of their mean speculations."

Philipa's throat constricted, and every muscle in her body

went soft as chocolate left too long in a summer sun.

"Please," she whimpered. "Let me go."

There was no trace of amusement or compromise in his probing dark eyes, eyes which made her feel dangerously vulnerable to their bewitching and forbidden enticements. He did not back off, and so she was obliged to do so, until she felt the hard wood and the windowpane of the door at her back.

There was no place left to run.

"I have always respected and admired your honesty. And if I thought for one moment that you really wanted me to leave, I would go," he told her, leaning his left hand upon the door just above her shoulder. "But I don't believe you want me to. Tell me," he urged, barely above a whisper, his right hand still caressing her cheek with a faint, delicious touch. "What do you really want, Philipa? What? Tell me, and I promise I'll do it."

Her feet had dissolved beneath her, and her legs were quickly following the lead. She floated above the ground. Above reality. Above the cold, level-headed common sense for which she was so celebrated. Terence Gavilan had become her reality, standing inches away from her. The only part of her he was touching was her face, and that but lightly, yet she had never felt closer to him than she did in that sweet, tortuous moment. His command became her dearest wish.

"Kiss me," she pleaded in a weak voice, powerless in the face of his unyielding dark eyes. "Please kiss me . . . Terence . . ."

He smiled with no trace of mockery.

"With greatest pleasure," he breathed, drawing her chin upward with his fingers.

Her chin remained poised, and his hand moved to the nape of her neck, where he gently massaged the sensitive hollow just below her hairline. His motion inspired a fluttering need within her, and of its own accord her body arched away from the door frame and pressed itself against his. He welcomed her, and she thrilled at the nearness of his strength supporting her. He paused, his face within a breath of her own, his lips parted with anticipation. He wanted her to make the next move.

She did. With a sureness that left her gasping for breath, she glided her hands up along the crisp lapels of his jacket and around his neck to the back of his head, where they lost themselves in his pleasingly soft chestnut locks sifting through her fingers like spun silk. The slightest pressure of her hand justified his spanning of the small breach between them until their lips touched softly. And again.

Philipa felt herself falling through time and space, and yet, as he held her back for an instant, she knew she was still on solid ground. She opened her eyes, and all she could see was his handsome, angular face, serious in contemplation of her own. His mouth came down upon hers like a torrent, flooding away any belated protest she might have offered.

But she was not inclined to protest. Indeed, she held him to his design, abandoning propriety and decorum as she allowed him to take her mouth. He tasted her, nipping her gently with his lips, seeking her with his tongue. His kiss was demonstrative of his reckless, adventurous nature. She had never been kissed in such a way before, and she knew, by his deliberate exploration, that he knew it, too. He delighted in her tremulous responses, cradling her jaw, teasing her earlobe with a bold finger as his kiss retreated again.

No! her mouth protested. She wanted more of him. So much more! She grew aware of why he had backed off: he had been tantalizing her into wanting him, into making her seek him out. And indeed she was, even before she herself had been aware of it. Small sobs issued from her as though she had no control over them, for she did not. He had taken her over. He had completely usurped her will, and she knew, with a bolt of terror coupled with unreasoning desire, that she would grant him anything, anything at all . . .

His hands glided slowly along her arms, and hers along his, until their hands met at their sides and their fingers entwined tightly. His mouth withdrew. She could not look at him. She heard him take in a hard, shuddering breath.

"I must go," he whispered hoarsely.

"Why?" she purred in protest, rubbing her cheek against his shoulder, loving the feel, the aroma of him, all around her.

"Because, dear lady," he said after a hard swallow, slipping his hands from hers and grasping her arms again, more firmly than before. "I fear you have made a gentleman of me."

His words, spoken in his warm and sensuous baritone, sent a new ripple of shivers all along her spine. He slipped his arms about her again, his hands finding a fit upon her shoulder blades. She wanted to feel those fine, strong hands on her skin, and for a long moment in his arms that yearning was more than she could bear.

"Why must you be a gentleman tonight?" she murmured in weak protest that sounded like a groan to her.

"Because, my love," he said, his voice husky with bridled desire. "I—" he paused, kissing her temple and her eyes and her earlobes—"I don't remember why."

He gave up finally, finding her lips again, to her delight. His mouth was a wellspring of new and fanciful pleasures, and the small sound that issued from his throat played upon the strings of her heart, which he had so finely tuned.

Her hands found his hips, and she wanted to reach around to his buttocks to pull him closer again, but she dared not. It was too bold, too deliciously forbidden. . . .

"God, if you touch me there again, Philly, I'll—no, don't" he pleaded, taking her hands quickly, purposefully, into his own. She was at once disappointed and wickedly titillated: she had never suspected that she might possess such power over a man. Over this man, in particular. It was an exhilarating, almost a frightening, sensation. But he was gazing down at her again, his dark eyes serious and adoring.

"This is"—he paused, kissing the backs of each of her hands. "This is the most wondrous thing that has ever happened to me, my sweet Philipa. And I want to—I want everything to be as it should be. I want to court you. To woo you, like a proper suitor. I feel as if, with this love, I've been granted a great and precious gift which I must treat with utmost care. Does that make any sense to you at all?"

He was all around her like a soft, protective blanket as she lay her head once again upon his lapel.

"It does," she sighed, feeling both cherished and frustrated. "You are a very wise man, Mr. Gavilan. A wise and wonderful man. Funny," she mused. "I have always been considered so wise, and so prudent. And yet here I stand, ready to abandon every tenet I have held so dear just to be with you for one night."

"It will be many more nights than that, Philly, my darling, my sweet," he promised her with a kiss on her upturned nose. "And you will be glad in the morning for this exercise of prudence tonight."

She sighed again, for it seemed to be the only way she could breathe.

"I know that you are right, Terry, my darling," she admitted to his cravat. "But I—"

"Say that again," he urged in a whisper, releasing her hands to hold her close again.

"What?" She pressed her palms softly against his chest.

"My name," he invited, raising his chin, closing his eyes. "It started a ringing down deep inside of me, like a—well, never mind like what. Just say it, Philly. Please."

"Terry," she ventured, reveling in the surges of desire that coursed through her as his name liberated her. "Terry, Terry my love, my darling . . ."

He gripped her arms again, hard this time. Almost painfully hard.

"I must go. Now," he said firmly, and his voice was like a warning. "Because you are altogether too tempting, and my imagination is altogether too active."

"Will I see you tomorrow?" She caressed his cheek with the back of her fingers, gazing at him, trying to memorize every detail of his face as it looked in this moment of unfulfilled passion.

"And tomorrow." He took hold of her hand and pressed a kiss into its palm. "And tomorrow, and tomorrow. All of our tomorrows for the rest of our lives, I hope, Philipa. Philly. My sweet, sweet, Philly, how I do love you!"

Across the street, in the shadow of a street lamp, Owen Parrish observed all with alarm. He fully expected, holding his trembling rage in check, to see Gavilan and Philipa Braedon—Emma Hunt—disappear into the dark house together.

If that happened, he contemplated bitterly, it would all be over. In fact, it might all be over already, if she had confessed her secret to him.

He rallied. Why would she have done that? Surely she had no foreknowledge of Gavilan's fixation with Emma Hunt. Still, a woman, he suspected, could do strange and unpredictable things under the influence of passion. And Philipa Braedon was very obviously under the influence of passion. All he could do was wait, he realized, flexing the hands with which he longed to throttle Gavilan, the devil. Gavilan, the fool. Gavilan, who stood there on the dark porch defiling Emma Hunt's own mouth, while in all likelihood not even aware of the fact . . .

Parrish was compelled by the tender scene, and repulsed by it. He watched as Gavilan and Philipa/Emma exchanged another fond, lingering kiss. Then Gavilan spoke again, saying something his ears could not detect. He watched Philipa/Emma nod in return, her eyes plainly adoring the man before her. Parrish choked back his emotion. It was not jealousy he felt, exactly. He had never experienced the remotest attraction to Philipa Braedon, nor could he ever discern what Gavilan apparently saw in her. It was Emma Hunt who intrigued him. Emma Hunt whom he must possess, if not materially, then in some other less obvious, more insidious way. After all, he was no competition for Terence Gavilan in this arena. That much was apparent. For Gavilan had, in his usual overpowering fashion, already won the tournament.

Gavilan's tall, lean form bent over her hand once again. Parrish watched Philipa/Emma's small shoulders shiver slightly, and damned his own shortness, as well as his shortcomings in the domain of romance. He had never once, to his knowledge, made a woman quiver at his touch. Even Jess Flaherty, the cheeky tart, seemed bored by him more often than not. What kind of a man it must take, he marveled with a fleeting sense of detachment, to cause Emma Hunt—Emma Hunt!—to tremble.

Suddenly, to Parrish's utter astonishment, it was all over. Philipa/Emma was clinging to the porch post, wearing a sleepy and sensuous smile as she watched Gavilan bound down her front steps in a buoyant, almost giddy, gait. If her expression was seraphic, his was positively enraptured. The sight disgusted him. But it was odd, he mused. It looked as if Philipa Braedon had been the one who had wanted Gavilan to remain, but that Gavilan, for once in his depraved life, had been a gentleman.

Could Brownie, he wondered, as he had jokingly intimated to his boss in the recent past, actually be in love with the woman?

Parrish instinctively shrank back against the lamp post as Gavilan passed by across the street, but he knew he needn't have worried. By the look of both participants in the recent tryst, neither of them would be thinking too clearly for some time to come. He continued to watch, though, not moving. Gavilan proceeded up the street toward Somers House, turning once to wave foolishly to Miss Braedon, whose eyes followed him as if he were the Second Coming. She even withdrew her handkerchief from her sleeve, waving it at him like a tiny white banner of surrender. The fool!

Surrender . . . surrender to me, Emma Hunt, he thought, hungrily recalling Diana and her pitiless captor. He mastered himself, straightening. How uncharacteristically obliging of Gavilan to yield the amphitheater to him, even if only for a brief time. If he tread carefully, he mused, watching Philipa Braedon/Emma Hunt enter her as yet unviolated fortress, the day—or at least a part of it—might yet be his.

Chapter Nineteen

Philipa, charged with new emotions, was utterly unable to lure sleep. She forsook all attempts in favor of a retreat to her study after midnight, where she lit all the lamps and filled the typewriter with a fresh sheet of paper. Arliss and Mrs. Grant slept on the third floor, and she knew there was little chance of the noise of her typewriter awakening them. She sat for a time at her desk, staring at the virgin bond poised upon the platen, her mind racing with the wondrous images of Terence Gavilan—*Terry*, she thought, smiling to herself, and feeling a bit sheepish for it—and the events of the evening. *I want to woo you*, he had said, his luscious baritone a thick, sensuous whisper. Like a proper suitor.

She closed her eyes, trying to envision what it would be like to be wooed by him. She remembered the gentle touch of his hand upon the back of her neck and the radiant heat his intimate, but not bold, gesture had induced. Her face grew warm all over again just thinking about it. She thought of his mouth over hers, warm and soft, and yet strong . . . She opened her eyes quickly, her hands on her burning cheeks. She wondered, trying to calm her rapid breathing, if she was capable of waiting for all of this wooing. She giggled at the notion, and the sound of it in the still room startled her. Mrs. Grant, if she happened into the room, would think she had lost her mind. Well, perhaps she had, she thought, touching the typewriter keys lightly. And if that were indeed the case, perhaps she should have lost it a long time ago . . .

Elliot.

She sighed, lifting her fingers from the keyboard again. No matter how she rationalized her behavior, it was cruel. Elliot was going to be hurt. And Roger. Dear Roger. And Beatrice. Beatrice would probably never speak to her again, and half of the Ladies' Auxiliary with her. Braedon's Beach was a small, tightly knit community with explicit standards of conduct. Her jilting of Elliot Waverly would, she realized grimly, likely cause social repercussions which could very well span generations.

Assuming, of course, that she and Terry would continue to make their residence in Braedon's Beach.

Terry. Mrs. Terence Gavilan. She felt a sudden rush of energy that seemed to expand her entire body until the room was simply not large enough to contain it. She pushed away from her desk and ran toward the large windows facing the ocean. She pushed the drapes aside and worked the latch until it gave way, swinging the window wide to admit the night breeze into the stuffy room. *Mrs. Terence Gavilan.*

She sighed, shivering with the breeze and with the anticipation her reverie had invoked. For better or for worse, she decided, hugging her arms to her chest as she looked out beyond the porch to the dark beach, her life would henceforth never be the same. But as long as Terence Gavilan was to be a part of the better, surely she could tolerate the worst.

The sound of the waves on the incoming tide was inviting. It was a perfect night for a swim. But she felt oddly weak— weakened by desire, and by the bedeviling images of Terence Gavilan that she could not prevent herself from conjuring. She could not trust her body to the caprice of an undertow in such a state. Instead, she would write.

She returned to her typewriter resolutely, placing her fingers once again atop the keys, intending to resume work on

Mrs. Hunt's finale, *The Tender Trap*. It had been a week since she had written anything, and so much had happened! Emma Hunt had died—and Philipa Braedon had been reborn. She giggled again at the comparison, but her giggle was cut short by a strange sound out back, as though something had bumped into one of the wicker chairs and had pushed it some distance across the porch. She wanted to get up and investigate, but was somehow frozen to her chair. Instead, she gripped the sides of her typewriter.

"Is someone there?" she forced herself to call out in an overly loud way which, she was sure, telegraphed her alarm to the intruder.

She immediately felt foolish for doing so. If there were, indeed, someone out there, they did not belong there, hence would not admit to being there. Especially if it were someone who had come with the intention of entering a dark house quietly to commit burglary, but had been stymied by her midnight wakefulness. She waited, listening for another sound. The porch remained quiet.

Almost too quiet.

She sat perfectly still for a minute, trying to decide on her next course of action. She was reminded of blind man's bluff, a game she had played as a child, and had always hated. Finally she resolved to close and lock the window again, which she did, without hearing any further sound from outside. She felt safer, but unsettled. She would never know whether in fact someone had been hiding on her porch. Moreover, if someone had been hiding, they would know she had suspected their presence. She had never believed in ghosts, nor did she have any inclination to credit this phenomenon to the supernatural. She tried to put the event out of her mind and concentrate on her work.

Sarah, the heroine, was confined in a log cabin by a blizzard, and Jack, her hero, was fighting his way through to rescue her. Philipa bit her lower lip. It was no use. The words would not come tonight. Her mind was too full of her own adventures to concentrate on the fantastic and lunatic escapades of her fictional characters. There was too much to be done . . .

A letter to Elliot. A very constructive enterprise, she congratulated herself. She would have to deliver it herself, of course, as it would be unconscionable to break their engagement by mail. But a letter was the very thing to help her organize her thoughts, and to buffer the truth for him. She began to type.

She typed for some time, filling three pages until the words began to blur before her eyes. She lay her head down upon the desk to rest, then resumed her composition. It was going so well . . .

Suddenly from outside there came another noise, a louder one. Philipa frowned. She marveled at her boldness as she got up from her chair and strode to the window which, she was surprised to discover, was open. Hadn't she closed it before? Alarm caused a tightening in her breast, and all at once she felt very heavy.

"Who is out there?" she demanded smartly, peering into the darkness, although she really did not want to know. What she wanted to do was bolt the window and run to hide in her bed. But her body, sluggish and contrary, would not yield to her wishes.

"It's me, Philly."

Elliot stood before her, wearing the same gray suit he'd been wearing when she bade him goodbye at the train. Her shock at seeing him now was tempered by suspicion: it was not Elliot's voice she heard, but a low, oddly familiar and unpleasant one. She tried desperately, but unsuccessfully, to place it.

"Elliot," she heard herself murmur strangely. "What are you doing here?"

She extended her hand to him and realized, with a shock of terror, that her hand passed through him.

Her eyes popped open with a start, and she found herself staring at the top of her desk. She shook herself and looked at the window. It was closed fast.

It had been a dream, and a strangely disturbing one. Of course she would have dreamed about Elliot, she scolded herself, briskly removing the last page of her letter from the platen. Hadn't she been writing to him just before she dozed off? But why had the dream disturbed her so much? And the noise. What about the noise on the porch? Had it been real, or just another part of the dream?

She could not answer any of those puzzles. The only thing she knew for certain was that she was profoundly weary. Tired enough to try to sleep, and to leave the mystery of the noise on the porch for another time.

"Miss Braedon!" Mrs. Grant's urgent, grandmotherly voice prompted her to consciousness. "Miss Braedon! Wake up!"

The bright light hurt Philipa's eyes even though they were closed. She could tell without opening them that it was daylight, and probably quite late. Her eyes refused to open at first, and it was a few moments before her sluggish tongue would move to speak.

"What is the matter, Mrs. Grant?" She wrested her eyelids apart and focused her gaze upon the anxious face of her housekeeper, slowly raising herself to a sitting position in her bed.

Mrs. Grant's serious expression did not change.

"I think you'd better see for yourself."

Philipa was jolted instantly to a sickening awareness, and she hastily followed Mrs. Grant's short, solid figure through the hall and down the stairs, tying her robe about her as she went. They had gained the first-floor landing when she saw it.

There, hanging on the outside of the open front door, was an enormous black crepe wreath, like the kind displayed upon a house of mourning. The very sight of it both bewildered and chilled Philipa, and momentarily rooted her to the stair.

"I'd gone out to fetch the milk," Mrs. Grant explained in an admirably even tone. "Mr. Isley leaves it around front in the warm weather, in the shade, so it won't turn by the time we bring it in. You can well imagine my shock to find it hanging there. And by now, Mr. Isley's asking all around, wondering who died in the Braedon family. I call it a wicked prank, if you ask me."

Philipa was only half listening. She was compelled by the

sight of the death wreath, filled with a sense of foreboding. But perhaps it was a mistake. She dismissed that idea at once. There was but one florist, and one undertaker, on the entire island, and she doubted, considering the tiny population, that such an error was possible. There was a small envelope nestled in the eucalyptus, and she plucked at it with trembling hands, not wanting to touch the wreath itself. Aware of Mrs. Grant's expectant gaze, she opened it and read:

"R.I.P. Emma Hunt—An Admirer."

She gasped, and very nearly dropped the note.

"What is it, miss?" Mrs. Grant's question seemed prying and mean.

Philipa mastered herself, swallowing hard several times before answering.

"It's—it's a joke," she managed, crushing the note in her hand. "A ghastly, horrendous joke. And if I discover who is responsible . . ."

What? What would she do? What could she do? she wondered bleakly. To make a public issue out of it would be to admit that she was, indeed, Emma Hunt, whereas to ignore it would render her helpless against further such assaults. What could she do?

She could confide in Terry, she thought. He was well schooled in handling mean, dark threats, she was certain. A man in his position would have to be. But—what would he think of her if she revealed her secret to him? He knew her, and loved her, as the very proper and comparatively innocent Philipa Braedon. How might his opinion of her change with this revelation?

"Miss Braedon?" Mrs. Grant prompted her again, sounding very far away.

Philipa resolutely lifted the large and surprisingly heavy wreath from the door and handed it unceremoniously to her housekeeper.

"Destroy it," she ordered the woman briskly. "Get it out of my sight."

"But what did the—"

"Remove it at once, Mrs. Grant!" she shrieked, although she was immediately sorry for her outburst, for the woman looked as stunned as if Philipa had struck her. Silently the housekeeper took the wreath and left the room without a backward glance.

Philipa wrung her hands, trying to think. Someone knew, or suspected, her secret. Someone fairly close to her, and possessing a macabre sense of humor. She might check with the florist, but that might yield no result. It was likely that the perpetrator of this horrific jest had taken great care to cover his tracks, and all that her investigation would do would be to confirm his suspicions, as well as draw unwanted attention to herself. She struggled to still her body's trembling. *Remain calm*, she told herself. After all, what is the worst that could come of this? She had the uneasy feeling as she slowly mounted the stairs that she could not even begin to plumb the depths of that question.

It was mid-morning and she was at work in her study when Mrs. Grant interrupted her again to announce a caller, her address betraying no hurt at Philipa's earlier harsh treatment.

"Where is Arliss, Mrs. Grant?" Philipa inquired, wondering at the girl's absence. Normally it would have been the younger woman who reported such events to the mistress of the house.

Mrs. Grant's aged features revealed no emotion.

"A messenger came round this morning. Her mother was taken ill again."

Philipa sighed. Mrs. Flaherty's decline in health during the past few years was widely known to be agonizingly slow, with especially serious setbacks every so often. Dr. Waverly, ever the circumspect physician, would say only that the woman suffered from a variety of ailments, none of them life-threatening in and of themselves, but debilitating in combination. There were a catty few who suspected that the greatest of these ailments were a wayward daughter, a jailbird son, a late husband who had been inordinately fond of spirits, and the fact that she had borne a dozen children, only five of whom, Arliss among them, had survived past infancy. In light of all of this, Philipa acknowledged that her own problems were trivial indeed.

"Who is the caller?" Philipa pressed the housekeeper, not wanting to dwell upon the decline of Mrs. Flaherty.

Mrs. Grant's glower of disapproval was unmistakable.

"In the parlor. Mr. Gavilan," she answered in a bold huff, making a quick exit, Philipa supposed, to avoid another rebuke. But Philipa hadn't the time or the inclination to chide her.

Terry was here!

Philipa restrained herself from breaking into a run at the news, instead managing a serene gait down the hall and into the parlor.

Terence Gavilan stood in the center of the room, his arms laden with what seemed to be dozens of red roses. In an instant the blooms fell to the floor, replaced by her own body as his mouth commanded hers with a deliciously improper kiss. She felt herself become fluid in his embrace as her mouth responded urgently to his.

"I've needed to do that since we parted last night," he murmured by way of greeting, his dark eyes caressing her. "I worried as soon as I left. I was afraid that perhaps I'd dreamed every event of last evening. I couldn't sleep for wanting to hear your sweet voice again, telling me that you love me . . ."

He found her mouth again with his own, and she settled her arms about his neck like a wreath. She did love him, she knew. More than reason should allow. She permitted herself to respond to his kiss, even though his words kindled the memory of her unsettling experiences of the previous night: the bizarre and strangely frightening dream, the unexplained noises on the porch, and the grotesque decoration which had mysteriously appeared upon her front door.

Terry pushed her back a little, but still held her close. She felt his dusky eyes now searching her. Afraid that her face would reveal her worrisome thoughts, she looked away from him.

"Something's troubling you," he asserted, raising her chin with his fingers so she could not look away from him. "What is it, Philly? Please, tell me."

Unwillingly, she met his gaze, and found in his eyes a

warm shelter in which she could take refuge from all of her woes, if she would only allow herself the luxury. She drew herself in. *Not yet*, she told herself. She felt a wan smile tease her lips, and she placed her hand on his.

"I had some difficulty sleeping, myself," she declared softly, loving the intense, adoring scrutiny of his sable eyes. "Perhaps, Mr. Gavilan, we ought to reevaluate this courtship of which you spoke."

Terry grinned at her, his wide, sensuous mouth parted to reveal his even, white teeth.

"Perhaps, Miss Braedon," he said on a shallow breath, "we ought to pick up these flowers before someone happens in here and decides that we have both lost our minds."

He released her and stooped his tall, lean form to begin recovering the mistreated roses.

"Who would come in?" she wondered aloud, bending to assist him. "Only Mrs. Grant, or—"

Arliss, she thought, but could not bring herself to mention Jessamyn Flaherty's sister to him. Terry did not seem to notice her hesitation.

"Mrs. Grant," he declared, continuing about his project, "doesn't like me."

"Mrs. Grant," amended Philipa, finishing the job, "doesn't trust you. I doubt she trusts anyone who wasn't born and reared within a five-mile radius of Braedon's Beach. There. That appears to be all of them. Whatever were you thinking of, to purchase every rose on the island?" She laughed at the notion as he handed her his bundle.

He did not reply immediately. She watched him touch one of the blooms with a remarkably gentle finger, tracing its soft, delicate red curves. She was fleetingly aware of an odd pang of jealousy of the flower.

"I suppose," he said in a deliberate, tantalizing tone, still studying the blossom, "I was thinking of your lips."

He raised his eyes to her, observing her mouth intently.

Philipa's breath caught in her throat. He had woven his sweet spell about her again, like the most skilled of magicians. She marveled at his ability to beguile with a word, a small, tender gesture. She longed to respond to him, but realized that her arms were full of roses. She managed a smile.

"I must get a vase for these," she murmured, feeling her spine lose its starch. "I'll be right back."

She found Mrs. Grant in the kitchen snapping beans for supper. She deposited the flowers on the sideboard, charging her housekeeper to trim them and find a suitable vessel for them. Mrs. Grant merely nodded in reply, and Philipa slipped out again, eager to get back to Terry, trying his sweet words out in her own mouth . . .

She stopped suddenly in the hallway.

She had heard those words, or words very like them, before, or seen them, she could not recall which. But where? And when? Certainly no one had ever before spoken them to her. Then where . . . ?

". . . they are very like your lips, my darling," someone had said.

In one of her own books!

She shook herself mentally. How could she be so conceited as to believe that no one had ever thought of that romantic simile on their own, before or since? She was still smiling at her foolishness as she returned to the parlor, where Terry was waiting for her with his graceful, long-fingered hands resting at his waist.

"Let me take you to dinner this evening," he said, coming forward to take her hands into his own. "I want to have you entirely to myself. I want to talk with you. To learn all about Philipa Braedon from you, and to tell you all about Terry Gavilan. Please say yes, Philly. I promise to return you at a respectable hour that not even Mrs. Grant would frown at."

Philipa closed her eyes to allow herself the most thorough pleasure of the feel of his warm hands holding hers so securely. Slowly, reluctantly, she shook her head.

"Not yet, Terry," she whispered, although she was loath to decline such an enticing offer. "I must break my engagement with Elliot first, before—"

"I'll drive you to Philadelphia myself today!" he declared savagely, his eyes ablaze with a passion which, for lack of a better word, she had to label as jealousy. "If you could only know how it galls me to think that—"

"Shh!" She placed a finger upon his lips. His ferocity frightened her, but her playful gesture seemed to temper his humor.

"I've written him a letter," she told him, taking hold of his lapels as he enfolded her possessively in his magnificent arms. "It needs a few refinements, but in it I request that he make a trip home, and tell him that I need to speak with him urgently. I wish it could be over, too. More than you know," she told him, smoothing his furrowed, dark brow with a crooked finger. "For until it is, we are caught in limbo, as it were. I—"

Suddenly she perceived that he was looking directly into her eyes, that his arms had tightened about her, and that his mouth was tempting her. She felt as utterly helpless, as vanquished by an overpowering need, as she had the night before on her porch, and the sensation rendered her limp as jelly. She could not go on. She could only summon the strength to form his name with her lips before his mouth was upon hers again.

This time he teased her with it, alternately tasting and devouring her in unceasing surges which threatened to rob her of her very sensibility. He seemed to know exactly what he was doing to her, and the notion excited her unbearably even as it frightened her a little. How could he know her so very, very well? She felt her body press against his, and she felt his body welcome hers, almost tormenting her with the promise of what awaited her, and what awaited them both, once the specter of Elliot Waverly no longer stood between them.

"Your flowers, Miss Braedon."

Philipa gasped, tearing herself away from Terry, who was himself obviously too startled to do anything but stare. Mrs. Grant glanced once at them, placed the overburdened vase upon the mantelpiece, and said nothing more. When she left the room, Philipa began to breathe again, but the breathing was difficult.

"This is already becoming complicated, isn't it?"

Terry's voice was quiet. Light. Philipa turned her stare upon him and discovered that he had blanched. Mrs. Grant's unceremonious entrance had taken him by surprise, as well.

Well, it was her own fault, Philipa reflected glumly. She should have thought to close the parlor doors. But then that would have given rise to all manner of wild speculation . . . Oh, why couldn't it all be over? she worried with a small sigh, seeking once again the comfort of Terry's steadfast embrace.

Chapter Twenty

Philipa completed her letter to Elliot as soon as Terry left. Satisfied that the wording would cause him no undue alarm, she decided to post it that very afternoon. It was best to make the break as quickly and as cleanly as possible.

She was on her way out the door when a breathless young man bounded up her porch steps, red-faced and perspiring. He very nearly ran into her, and would have, had she not stepped aside just in time.

"Miss Braedon," the boy panted. "Doc asked me to come quick. Mrs. Waverly—she had a spell of some sort—apop—apolex—"

"Apoplexy!" Philipa was instantly flooded with dread. "Oh, no! How bad is she? Is she at home? When did this happen?"

She seized the boy's heaving shoulders, impatient with his breathlessness, although she realized he must have run the entire way.

"She's at home." The boy's breathing was quieting somewhat. "He wants you to come."

Of course Roger would want her to come. She was shortly

215

to be a daughter-in-law. Who more natural to have in attendance? She fumbled in her purse with shaking hands and withdrew a nickel.

"Go inside," she instructed the lad, handing him the coin. "Tell Mrs. Grant where I have gone. And tell her what has happened. Ask her for something to drink. Then go round to Mr. Gavilan's office on the Promenade—do you know where that is?"

The boy gulped and nodded, a lock of brown hair falling into his eyes.

"Tell him . . ." She stopped. Tell him what? That Roger Waverly had summoned her, and that she had dutifully obeyed? That she was attending Elliot's mother, as would be expected of Elliot's future wife? *Please understand, Terry*, she prayed silently.

"Tell him exactly what you have told me," she said finally. "And that I will see him when I can. Have you got all that?"

The lad nodded again, licking his lips, Philipa supposed, at the thought of the "something to drink" she had mentioned. It was a hot day and he had run a distance, after all.

Philipa did not wait to watch the boy slip into her house. She folded her letter to Elliot into her purse. She suspected she would not need to post it. A shiver of dread crossed her shoulders. His mother's dire illness would be all Elliot required, she was certain, to bring him home on the very next train.

And then what?

Damn that sneaky, underhanded Charles Tavistock!

Gavilan fumed inwardly, striding so hard upon the deck of the Promenade that the boards rattled with each step. Behind him, Fred Hanover was running to catch up. Gavilan heard his quick trotting steps following his own.

"He said he would meet you here? At the arcade?" Gavilan paused before the swinging doors of the place, doors which, the contractor had assured him, were exact imitations of those on casinos and saloons in the formerly Wild, now tamed, West. He considered young Hanover with, he knew, a severe and measuring look.

Fred Hanover nodded vigorously, not avoiding Gavilan's eyes. That alone, thought Gavilan, was a good sign. The boy was not trying to deceive him.

"He said he'd make it worth my while if I could just bring him some of those picture postcards outside—you know the ones I mean?" Fred Hanover blushed profusely, demonstrating his sexual innocence. Gavilan watched as the lad swallowed and plunged bravely on.

"He said he couldn't just go in and buy them. That he had a reputation to consider, and that a man of my experience would surely understand that. He said don't mention it to Jarrett, or to you. If 'e was anybody else, Mr. Gavilan, I'd a just told him to take a hike. But Mr. Tavistock could make trouble for me. And my family. His bank holds our mortgage. That's what my ma says."

Gavilan trusted Hanover completely. He was not sure why, except that it might have something to do with the fact that Hanover reminded him so much of himself at the same age.

"Did Mr. Tavistock mention anything about a wager?" he challenged the young man.

Hanover shook his head, his gaze steady.

"No, sir. What wager?"

Gavilan grimaced. He had never liked Charles, but this clinched it. The man was a liar and a cheat as well as a thief. His hands itched to take him down.

"Do just what he says, Mr. Hanover," Gavilan said, scanning the Promenade quickly in both directions to be certain that Charles was nowhere in sight, yet. "And don't worry about a thing. Play along with him. You can do that, can't you?"

Fred nodded again, this time hesitantly.

"But what are you going to do, Mr. Gavilan?" he wanted to know, looking afraid for the first time since he had appeared in Gavilan's office with this tale of deception over half an hour before.

Gavilan forced a grin, hoping to relax this unwilling participant in his little sting. He needed to catch Charles at the most precise, most incriminating and most embarrassing moment in order to appreciate the fullest revenge.

"Don't worry," he replied, slipping through the swinging doors. "Just disappear immediately after I come out. Go back inside the arcade and don't come out again. Understand? And for God's sake, try to look nervous!"

Fred laughed, just as Gavilan had intended. The lad needed to be loose, but it was crucial that he behave as though he himself were involved in the criminal mischief. Gavilan was confident, glancing at Fred's large, trembling, callused hands, that the lad would have no difficulty with that.

When Charles Tavistock came strolling down the Promenade with his cane and skimmer and immaculate white gloves, even Gavilan, observing him from seclusion by a window, marveled at the man's composure. No doubt, he mused with disgust, Charles Tavistock was a practiced con artist. Gavilan, watching him, realized he did not mind so much even that Charles was trying to cheat him out of his Hurricane. It was more the manner in which the man was going about it: to use an innocent boy to gain his own ends. To potentially ruin a young life over so petty an issue. The very notion sickened him. Well, he thought with a distinct burn of anticipation, Charles Tavistock was about to obtain his comeuppance. In spades.

Charles idled by the arcade doors, not standing too close. He withdrew a tortoiseshell cigar case from his inside breast pocket and, in a very casual, almost arrogant manner, proceeded to select a cheroot from within. His supercilious ritual of nosing the thing, then snipping off the end with a tiny pair of scissors made for the purpose was quite comical, and Gavilan had to prevent himself from laughing outright as he beheld it.

"That's the signal," Fred, beside him, whispered.

Wordlessly, Gavilan nodded once. Fred then proceeded through the doors.

"Light, Mr. Tavistock?"

Gavilan heard Fred's words as clearly as if he were still beside him. He remained perfectly still, although a slight cramp was beginning in his left leg. He willed it away.

"Thank you, Freddy." Charles was overly cordial, and he bowed slightly over the flaming match Fred had struck.

"Have you brought what we discussed?"

Gavilan tensed. He watched as Fred glanced over his shoulder, in the direction of the doors, not the window from which Gavilan watched the comedy unfold.

"Right here in my pocket, sir."

Fred patted his shirt front. Good lad, thought Gavilan, waiting.

"Well?" Tavistock, his cigar clenched in his teeth, was suddenly impatient. Almost, Gavilan thought, as though he were picturing himself driving off in the Hurricane already.

"You, uh, mentioned that it'd be worth my while, sir."

Gavilan could not see Charles's face from where he stood, but he could picture its porcine features narrowing with avarice.

"I don't buy merchandise I haven't seen, Hanover!" he snapped. "Where are they?"

After another glance around himself, Fred slipped his hand into his shirt pocket and withdrew a small stack of the glossy, racy postcards to which Charles had referred. Art postcards, they were called among gentlemen. Pictures of scantily clad young women with fetching smiles and a not-so-innocent allure. They were quite a scandal, hence very popular as arcade prizes, although Gavilan had a strict rule about not dispensing them to minors. For Fred to even have his hands on them was forbidden. Gavilan waited, watching as Fred slowly extended them to the nauseatingly eager Tavistock. Not yet, he thought. Not quite yet . . .

Now.

"I never took you for an art lover, Charles." Gavilan strolled through the doors smiling, enjoying Charles's expression of utter shock. "And I don't believe they have been paid for. Would you care to explain this situation to me? Or shall I summon a constable?"

Fred, as planned, disappeared. Charles Tavistock's ordinarily parchment-like face flushed a deep scarlet. His mouth hung open and the cigar fell to the Promenade. The cards in his hands were spread like a fan of guilt.

"Gavilan!" he got out after a false start. "It was your boy.

He—he came out here a moment ago and solicited me for these. He—''

''Don't lie, Charles. You're no good at it,'' Gavilan interrupted him tersely. ''I watched the whole thing. If there's one thing I manage to command from my employees, it's trustworthiness. Hanover came to my office this afternoon and told me the whole story. Aren't you even a little ashamed of yourself, using an innocent young man as a pawn in this despicable attempt to con me out of my Hurricane?''

Charles, still holding the cards, seemed to search desperately for something to say.

''I—I was just trying to prove to you that he couldn't be trusted.'' He choked on the words. ''Really, Gavilan, it was for your own good that I—''

''My own good.'' Gavilan managed a snicker, because he could not punch the man as he wanted to. ''Really, that is too considerate of you. But I believe I've just proven the boy's sincerity, have I not?''

Charles scowled, still blushing to the edge of his receding hairline.

''The week's not over yet, Gavilan!'' he cried, waving the postcards at him as though they might be a dangerous weapon.

Gavilan folded his arms across his chest, staring hard.

''It is for you, Tavistock,'' he said in a low voice. ''You're the one standing here with art postcards which you haven't paid for. Ask yourself this: can you more afford two bits a day to hire a young man for your office for a few weeks, or to disgrace your family by forcing me to press charges for petty larceny? And of such merchandise?''

Charles's hand shook, and his eyes widened like those of a great fish.

''You wouldn't!''

Gavilan felt a faint smile of triumph flicker across his mouth.

''My, you are a gambling man, aren't you?'' he declared softly. ''I'd think very carefully on it, Charles. After all, see how your last wager turned out.''

Charles closed his mouth tightly, shaking his fists like a

small, helpless infant batting at the air.

"You haven't heard the last of this, Gavilan!" he sputtered, backing off.

"I certainly hope not," Gavilan rejoined casually. "I'll expect proof within the week that you've kept your end of the wager, since it's obvious I can't take you at your word. Oh, and keep the postcards. A gesture of good will."

Charles stared from Gavilan to the postcards he was still clutching, then back to Gavilan's face. Uttering a wordless cry of disgust, he hurled the incriminating objects to the deck of the Promenade and stormed off. The excessive gesture reminded Gavilan of a cheap vaudeville theatrical device. As he stooped to retrieve the cards, he was joined by his erstwhile partner, Fred Hanover.

"Good work, Hanover," Gavilan offered, handing the lad the rest of the cards as he straightened. "I am in your debt. Now put these things away, safely."

As Gavilan fished in his pocket for a monetary token of his appreciation, Fred Hanover cleared his throat.

"Uh, Mr. Gavilan . . ." he began, sounding uncertain.

"Yes?"

"If you don't mind, sir, I'd like to talk with you right now about that debt."

The boy was bold; Gavilan gave him that.

"What is it?"

Fred straightened his sloping shoulders, making himself an inch or two taller.

"I'll be sixteen next month, sir," he began, his voice a shade deeper than it had been. "And I've heard you're planning to open a casino here in Braedon's Beach. I'd just like to have the guarantee of a job there, sir. If it—if it isn't asking too much."

Fred was not looking at him by the end of that brazen little speech. Gavilan would have been amused by his temerity except that he was pulled up short by the import of the lad's words.

A casino in Braedon's Beach. So word had leaked out. A week ago that would not have bothered him very much, he realized, staring mutely at the top of Fred Hanover's head.

But something had happened to him in that week. A profound change of heart, and priorities. He had not thought about it before, but he suddenly realized that he had no desire whatever to effect so fundamental a change in the charming milieu of Braedon's Beach. And he had no desire to condemn a bright young man to the unhappy bondage of a life in a casino, whether that young man desired it or not.

He smiled as he realized further the reason for this reversal of opinion, wishing quite suddenly that he could take her into his arms again and kiss her sweet, compliant mouth.

"No, I am not building a casino in Braedon's Beach, Mr. Hanover, now or ever," he said firmly. "And even if I were, I'd be doing you a greater favor by turning down your request. That's no life for anyone. Education is what you need, whether you believe it or not, and I'll make a pact with you right now: you remain in school, get good grades, and I'll continue to pay you at your current salary throughout the year. You'll work for me when you can, when it doesn't interfere with your schooling. And by the time you're ready for a university, you'll have a good leg up on the tuition. Does that sound fair enough?"

Fred Hanover looked up at him again, his face alight with a grin.

"It'll sure make my ma happy, sir," he declared, rocking back on the heels of his hobnailed boots as he crossed his long, lanky arms across his hollow, youthful chest.

Gavilan nodded, unexpectedly overcome by embarrassment at Fred's unabashed appreciation of the gesture. It seemed so small a thing. It was barely the cost of a fresh flower in his lapel every day. But it reminded him of something else.

"One more thing, Hanover."

"Yes, sir?" Fred seemed to wait upon his word.

Gavilan drew his eyebrows together in an effort to look threatening.

"Not a word of this, any of it, to anyone but your family," he said in a low tone, not smiling. "Agreed?"

Fred's grin had faded to a wide-eyed stare, disclosing the success of Gavilan's expression. The boy nodded, looking as though the devil himself might have been standing behind him.

"Agreed."

"Your word as a gentleman?" Gavilan extended his hand to the boy.

Fred stared at it uncertainly. Then he accepted it with a surprisingly strong grip and a single, hard shake.

"My word," he intoned in a practiced deep, unbroken voice, "as a gentleman. Thank you, Mr. Gavilan."

It was, Gavilan reflected, swallowing a lump in his throat, probably the single most responsible thing he had ever done. Philipa Braedon had obviously influenced him even more than he had suspected. And how he loved her for it!

"You'll earn it, my young friend. Make no mistake about it!" Gavilan tried to sound gruff, but he could not restrain a smile as he thought of Philipa again. "Now, back to work."

Fred Hanover disappeared into the arcade again and in no time was plying his mop with unmistakable vigor. The sound of it quickly faded into the wash of the surf as Gavilan headed back to his office, still smiling to himself.

Dr. Waverly was a staunch advocate of the restorative properties of sunlight, therefore unlike other sickrooms in Philipa's admittedly limited experience, Beatrice's convalescent chamber was pleasantly bright and airy. Upon entering the bedroom, she found Beatrice Waverly on the bed in a great, rigid mass, like some effigy of an ancient king. Her gray hair was amassed on her pillow in wild confusion, in spite of the ministrations of her personal maid. Her pale blue eyes stared vacantly at the canopy overhead, and had Philipa not heard the faint wisps of air which were her breathing, she would have believed the woman to be already dead.

"She has been like this since last night," Roger, ashen, greeted her. He sat by his wife on the edge of the bed. His coat was off. His sleeves were rolled up. His stethoscope hung about his neck like the yoke of a poor beast of burden. He looked careworn and exhausted, and Philipa knew from the moment she laid eyes on him that he had not slept since his wife's seizure. She was aware of a deeper sympathy for him than for Beatrice, who appeared to be beyond such meager affection.

"Why didn't you send for me immediately, Roger?" she inquired softly, and she realized that she had never before addressed him by his first name. The thought embarrassed her, but Roger did not seem to notice. He shook his head slowly, staring at Philipa without seeming to see her.

"She was overcome almost instantly," he began in a quiet voice, as if he had not heard her question at all. "We had just returned from the fireworks, and were getting ready to retire. One moment she was speaking to me about the most recent gathering of the Ladies' Advisory Committee, and the next moment she was staring at me from her vanity bench, her eyes as vacant as you see them now."

Roger sighed, casting another long, sorrowful look at his wife.

"Have you notified Elliot?" Philipa went on, unable to look for long upon Beatrice's paralyzed form.

Roger nodded.

"I telegraphed him straightaway. He should arrive late this evening, or on the morning train." Roger sighed brokenly. "I hope she holds out until he comes."

Roger's quiet words chilled Philipa.

"You don't mean that she—oh, Dr. Waverly, surely she will—"

"Each minute that passes with her in this state makes it less likely that she will survive, Philipa," he interrupted her, sounding painfully clinical. "I have seen numerous patients in this condition. The first twenty-four hours are critical. If there is no radical improvement within that time, the patient succumbs. Sometimes immediately. Sometimes the victim lingers for a few days, perhaps a week. But never longer than that. In many ways it's a blessing, I suppose. Survivors of apoplexy are almost always paralyzed, partially or completely. Often they cannot speak, and cannot perform certain basic tasks by themselves. It is not an existence I would wish on Beatrice. You know how vital she is . . . was."

Philipa moved beside Roger and placed her hand tentatively on his shoulder.

"What can I do, Roger?" she managed, dreading his answer.

Roger turned to her, his hands clinging desperately to her skirt, his gray head pressed to her abdomen. His lean, almost fleshless shoulders shook with sobs.

"God help me, Philly, I did everything I could. Everything I could, except love her enough . . ."

Philipa's throat constricted. Her limbs shuddered. *No, Roger*, she wanted to tell him. *Please don't tell me these things. Please don't. I can't bear them. Not now. Not considering what I am about to tell your son.* She tried to touch him, to stroke his dear head. But his remorse so numbed her that she could not will her hand to move.

"I tried to be a good husband to her. I so wanted to be, for her sake, and for Elliot's. But I believe I failed her, Philly, in so many ways, so many ways . . ."

He was sobbing again in wordless sounds. Philipa wanted to stop her ears. A great weight pressed her from all sides, and her stomach knotted. *Please, no more, Roger*, she wanted to cry out, feeling as helpless and as paralyzed as poor Beatrice there on the bed. *You will hate me for hearing these things, after what I must do to Elliot, and to you.*

"No, Roger," she said in a small, strangling voice. *No, don't tell me any more.* "No, you mustn't allow yourself to say that, or to believe it. She found no fault with you. You—and Elliot—have been her whole world. Please don't do this to yourself."

Or to me, she thought, utterly miserable. She glanced at Beatrice, who remained as impassive as stone. Beatrice, who had always represented duty and propriety, and responsibility. Beatrice, who had tried to dictate Philipa's moral conduct, as if Philipa's own parents had neglected to educate her. Beatrice, who would not have hesitated to grind someone under her heel for any perceived mistreatment of her family. It seemed to Philipa that this was Beatrice's revenge upon her, as if the woman had somehow known that she was about to break her son's heart, and that she had done the most drastic, the most terrible thing she could conceive of just to prevent that from happening.

Staring at the virtually lifeless form, still cradling Roger's shoulders, Philipa realized that she hated Beatrice, and that she always had. She gasped, pressing her hand to her mouth. How could she think of such an awful thing at a time like this? But it was true, Philipa realized, a growing rage inside her. Beatrice Waverly had proven to be a nagging thorn in her side on many occasions, but never more so than right now, when she was about to break her engagement to Elliot.

Dear God, forgive me, she thought, closing her eyes tightly. *Forgive me for hating Beatrice Waverly. Forgive me for thinking only of myself in this terrible, terrible hour. Forgive me for being so angry that I just want to scream . . .*

"Did you fix Tavistock's wagon?" Owen Parrish greeted Gavilan as the latter returned to the office. It was an unnecessary question, really. Judging by the satisfied grin on Gavilan's face, Owen guessed he had.

"Naturally." Gavilan's response was condescending.

Parrish waited for him to say more, but Gavilan did not. The secretary watched him remove his jacket and skimmer and hang them upon the coat tree by the door before taking his place at his own desk. Parrish stared at him. It was not like Gavilan to miss a chance to gloat over a vanquished foe. Something had gotten into him. Parrish suspected that he knew what—or, more accurately, who—that something was.

"You missed the fireworks last night, Brownie," he offered, hoping to draw his boss out.

Gavilan did not look up from his paperwork.

"No, I didn't," the younger man replied obliquely.

Goddamn it, he is in love with her! thought Parrish, feeling a scowl distort his features even as he balled his fists. There was no other explanation for this uncommon prudence. Ordinarily, Parrish knew, Gavilan would for certain have been regaling him with tales of the tender conquest Parrish had witnessed the night before with his own eyes.

Okay, Brownie, Parrish deliberated, massaging his jaw. *We'll play it your way. For now.*

"Oh, by the way." He watched Gavilan carefully while pretending to examine a lease document. "I nearly forgot. A messenger came while you were gone. It seems Miss Braedon wants to see you. I told the kid, if she wants to see him so badly, she knows where his office is.''

"Goddamn it, Owen, you didn't!" Gavilan was on his feet in an instant, the familiar storm clouds of anger having gathered over his accusing dark eyes.

Parrish, grinning inwardly, affected surprise.

"Well she does, doesn't she?" he countered righteously. "I mean, is her time any more valuable than yours?"

Gavilan seized his jacket and hat from the peg with two quick jerks.

"If you've made any trouble for me with this, I'll have your hide on a fence, Parrish!" was his dark threat, which did not faze Parrish in the least. "From now on, I'll take my own messages, no matter who they're from. Jesus, Owen!"

Owen smiled to himself as Gavilan stormed out, slamming the door behind him. Even if Gavilan did discover that the message had been inaccurate, and in all likelihood he would not, Owen could easily blame it on the messenger who delivered it. The only certainty about it was that Gavilan would not be pleased to have gone on a wild goose chase at the caprice of a woman. Nor would he, Parrish suspected, be particularly happy to learn of his lady-love's whereabouts, no matter what her motivation.

Chapter Twenty-one

It was near midnight by the time Philipa finally took her leave of Dr. Waverly. Elliot had not yet arrived, but she could not wait any longer. She ached with the fatigue of one who could only sit by helplessly and watch another suffer. The "other," of course, was Roger. She doubted that Beatrice was suffering. Beatrice seemed to be beyond all pain. She had, as far as Philipa could tell, not even blinked in all the while Philipa had been there.

Philipa had done virtually nothing during the last ten hours, she reflected wearily during her brief walk home, except to sit and hold Roger's hand and listen to his bitter self-recriminations regarding his life with Beatrice. And yet, she realized, trudging along the darkened street, she was exhausted. Drained. Stiff and aching, as if she had overexerted herself physically. She recalled, from some unknown source, an old expression: the burden of those who console. She had never truly understood its meaning until this day.

Mounting the steps to her porch seemed as difficult as scaling sheer rock. Gaining the top, she straightened with a sigh, closing her eyes.

"You look exhausted."

She could not immediately identify the voice, and recalled at once the strange noises from the porch the night before, and the macabre wreath on her door that very morning. She would have screamed, but had not enough breath to accomplish it. All she could do was utter a weak cry and pull her arms close about herself as if to defend against an attack.

"I'm sorry," the voice went on gently, sounding surprised. "I thought you saw me sitting here."

She recognized it as Terry's, but could not will herself to relax, or to respond to it right away. Indeed, she could summon no emotion at all to replace the terror that had flashed through her, not even relief. She took in another deep breath by degrees, and he was standing before her. She felt his hands on her arms, and she allowed him to guide her to one of the wicker chairs. Still unable to speak, she watched as he sat down on it. Then she willingly sat upon his lap, laying her head gratefully against his broad, firm shoulder. He smelled, wonderfully, of cedar and mint.

"I think Mrs. Grant has gone to bed," he said, his brown velvet baritone like a gentle caress to her ears. "And I'm sure the neighbors, if they are awake, can't see through your rhododendrons in the dark. I understand Mrs. Waverly is ill?"

Philipa nodded, rubbing her cheek against the crisp linen of his jacket.

"Yes." She tried her voice, and was not at all surprised by its tenuous quality. "Apoplexy. Roger believes that—that she will die."

Terry made no remark for a time, and Philipa knew he was reflecting upon the import of this situation. The thought made her feel very heavy again inside.

"I came here earlier, after I got your message," he said, his voice as quiet and soothing as the chorus of crickets under the porch and the distant sound of the waves in the darkness. "Mrs. Grant said you'd gone right over to the Waverlys'. Has Elliot come home?"

Philipa knew he did not intend his question to sound mean, impatient or demanding. But it seemed to her that Elliot's very name became something hard and menacing in Terry's voice.

She wished he had not mentioned Elliot at all.

"Not yet," she replied reluctantly. "Roger thought he might be in late this evening, but I couldn't wait any longer. In any case, he may not arrive until the morning, and I couldn't bear to stay in that place for the night, although Roger offered me a room. I just couldn't."

His arms were around her like a warm and comforting cloak, and his cheek pressed against her forehead. For a heavenly instant, all her cares were set aside.

"Of course you said nothing to Roger," Terry commented, his tone bland.

Philipa sat up, staring at him, trying to apprehend his expression in the darkness. How could he even think she might mention it to Roger? The notion appalled her, and she suddenly no longer wanted to be near him. Tell Roger! Under the circumstances! And before she even spoke to Elliot? In a quick motion, she got up from his lap.

"Of course I didn't!" she snapped, unable, even unwilling, to curb her irritation. "How could you even suggest—"

"Keep your voice down!" he interrupted her in a stern whisper, a stark contrast to her own rising dynamic. "I only meant that—"

"Beatrice Waverly is dying, Terry! Dying!" She spoke over him, her anger boiling over. "How could you be so crass, so insensitive as to suggest that—"

"You're tired," Terry interrupted her in a tight voice, standing up. "I know, because I'm tired too, from waiting here for you half the night. And if I stay here and listen to much more of your scolding, I'll start saying things I don't mean. Get some rest, Philipa," he wound up, brushing past her to the porch steps. "I'll talk with you tomorrow, when you're thinking more clearly about what you're saying. Good night."

She watched him start down the steps, and a feeling of helplessness overwhelmed her. She was angry, and hurt, and tired, and suddenly she realized that *he* was all of those things, as well. She wanted to call him back. To apologize to him. To scold him further. To cry, and to beat her fists upon his chest. To sit upon his lap again, and to feel him stroking her hair . . .

Something prevented her from speaking, though. She suspected that it was her pride, although in her exhausted state she could not be sure. She watched him leave her, her own hurt overruling her empathy. She bit her lip to keep from speaking, for she did not know what would come out if she did. She saw him pause at the bottom of the steps and turn to her again. She saw his handsome features, more angular than ever in the pale light of the street lamp, and they were sober and unflinching.

"I love you, Philipa," he said simply, and turned away without waiting for a reply.

Gavilan did not want to go home. Not just yet. He needed to walk, and walk hard. His heart was too full of the anger and frustration of his first argument with Philipa, and he suspected that a walk, the salty night air, and the sound of the surf would all help to assuage his turbulent emotions. At the corner of Fourth Street and Ocean Avenue, he turned not toward the bay and Somers House, but toward the dark beach and the ocean.

There was but a half moon, and that obscured by occasional clouds. Far to the north, Gavilan made out the pale golden lights of Atlantic City across the expanse of water which separated the islands. He walked in that direction first, on the harder, packed sand left by the receding ocean in the low tide. His pace was brisk, and he scarcely heeded his surroundings for ruminating on the unpleasantness with Philipa.

He'd been angry when he discovered that she had gone to the Waverlys'. He admitted that to himself at last, although he had tried valiantly to deny it earlier. But of course, being Philipa, she had gone. She would have gone even if she and Elliot had not still been officially engaged. And had they not been engaged, had Elliot not even existed, he realized with some chagrin, he, Gavilan, would not have been angry at all. He would not even have questioned her act of compassion. After all, wasn't that one of the things he so loved about her?

He sighed, and the sound startled him for its insignificance amid the ceaseless rush of the sea. The contrast reminded him of his own pettiness, and his arrogant magnification of his own feelings and concerns. A smile skittered across his mouth, like the rill of a small wave on the sand. He was, he knew, monumentally selfish. He had always supposed that to be a natural result of being an only child. That is, until he'd met Philipa Braedon. She was an only child as well, and he had never met a more selfless individual in his life. Perhaps too selfless, he thought, pausing in his stride. Perhaps he would do well to yield some of his selfishness to her, and to take some of the opposite trait in compensation . . .

He stooped and found a broken clam shell half buried in the damp sand. It was smooth, worn down by sea abrasion. He straightened and hurled it far out into the water, so far that he could not even hear it splash. The strain of the exercise felt good in his arm and shoulder muscles. The moon emerged from its seductive veil of clouds, and Gavilan looked out over the dimly lit waters. He recalled the words of Emma Hunt, and the fanciful moonlight ablution of her Arianna. He closed his eyes, and a warm shiver rippled through his core.

He shook himself. He had renounced Emma Hunt, even as a drunk might renounce Demon Rum. Still, he could not deny a twinge of regret, gazing out over the dark waters. No Venus would emerge from the sea for him. And if she did, he was unable to prevent himself from wondering, whose face would she have?

Only the noise of the crickets and cicadas met Elliot Waverly as he got off the train at midnight, but then he had not expected a reception of any kind. It was only a half-hour walk to his home from the station, and he required no help with his one small valise. He had only been gone from Braedon's Beach for a week, but it seemed to him, returning so unexpectedly, as if he had been away much longer. His father's telegram had, of course, alarmed him: his mother had never, to his recollection, been sick a day in her life; at least, not that she had allowed him to see. He had secured the priorate's permission to leave and had caught the first available train. Even so, more than 24 hours had passed since he had received his father's terse message. The urgency he'd felt at first had diminished somewhat. And now, he was all but home. Everything would be fine. How could it not be?

His walk took him along Bayside Avenue, right past Jess's door. Looking up, he noticed with some surprise that her light was still on. Wondering why she was not out with Terence Gavilan, he decided to pay her a quick call. Perhaps she was alone. Perhaps she had heard of his mother's illness and could provide him with some additional news before he showed up at home. And anyway, he felt remarkably free. He was not expected until the following morning. No one even knew yet that he was back in town. For the next few hours, at least, he was completely his own man.

The very notion made him dizzy with anticipation.

He shifted his small burden to his left hand so he could knock with his right. In moments, Jess appeared in a peacock blue dressing gown, her pretty face puffed with drowsiness. She grinned at him in unabashed delight.

"Elliot!" she whispered, leaning her lush form against the doorjamb negligently. "I didn't expect to see you here."

Elliot's mouth fell into a smile at her words.

"Same here, Jess," he replied, keeping his voice low. "I thought you might be out somewhere with Gavilan."

Jess shrugged. Her whole lush form became involved in the gesture.

"I haven't seen him much lately," she dismissed, as though it really didn't bother her. "What about you? I thought you were in Philadelphia, although I hear your mother's sick. How is she?"

Elliot loved the soft, sensuous sound of Jess's voice. It was so soothing and so musical. So completely untouched by trouble or care. He looked beyond her, but could perceive, on the staircase, nothing but the pale pink light and shadows from her floor lamp upstairs.

"Can I come in, Jess?" he asked, aware that he wanted to very much.

She made a face.

"I'm sorry, El. I have company right now. I expect I won't be available until later. I don't know when."

A heavy curtain of cigar smoke billowed down the stairs, and from above came a single word in a petulant voice.

"Jess!"

It was a command, and Elliot couldn't swear to it, but it sounded like Charles Tavistock's voice. He sighed heavily, looking down at the marabou-trimmed mules on her feet. His disappointment rendered him speechless for a moment.

"Maybe I'll come around later," he mumbled, still not looking at her face. "Just to talk. If you're still up, that is."

He did look at her then, and he was glad, for her face wore a fond smile.

"Any time, Elliot. You know that."

She blew him a kiss, then closed the door quietly. Elliot stood outside for another minute, listening, but he heard nothing. He wasn't even sure why he wanted to listen, or what he had expected to hear. He suspected that he had merely wanted to hear her footsteps on the stairs inside, to console himself that he was not really alone in this dark, empty place.

Philipa Braedon, for a well-mannered, spinsterish woman, kept very peculiar hours. Owen Parrish, watching her house from the alleyway across the street, wondered if Gavilan was aware of that fact. It was long after midnight, in fact long after Gavilan had left her porch, that the light in her study had gone out. Then, soon after, the upstairs lights. Parrish had noted, with no small satisfaction, that Gavilan had not stayed long on the porch after Miss Braedon had returned from the Waverlys', and that when he had left, his back had been ramrod straight and he had not so much as glanced over his shoulder. Proof, Parrish was certain, that the lovers had quarreled.

So far, things were going even better than planned. He was vastly amused by the fact that the Waverly biddy had even been so obliging as to experience a life-threatening condition at this most opportune time. No doubt, Parrish considered, Gavilan's own timetable had undergone a radical revision because of it.

So much the better.

Glancing once each way on the deserted avenue, Parrish emerged from the alley. He moved quickly along the street, careful to stay out of the dim light offered by the street lamps. He slipped through the rhododendrons and onto the porch of the Braedon house, wondering if Philipa had remembered, after the previous evening, to lock her first-floor windows. He tested one, and smiled to himself.

She had.

Locks will not keep me out, my dear Mrs. Hunt, he thought, trying to envision her alarm in the morning when she made that discovery for herself. The funeral wreath had been a lark. Thomas Goliard was not about to stop at so mild a torment.

It required but a few well-placed jabs with his pen knife to violate the lock on the window, and the hinge gave way soundlessly. Naturally, he reflected with some amusement, slipping quietly into the darkened study. Unoiled hinges were the sign of a slovenly household, and Miss Braedon was obviously careful to retain the most conscientious domestic help.

Parrish stood facing the room, allowing his eyes to adjust to the darkness. Then he closed the window and surveyed the private domain of Emma Hunt.

The air inside was alive with the aroma of rosewood and mahogany, finely polished with lemon oil. He inhaled deeply, even detecting the scent of fresh paper and ink, mingled with a trace of some womanly scent. The birthing place of the passions of Emma Hunt. Parrish thrilled to the feel of his own blood surging in his veins, and he surveyed the dark room as though it were a woman whom he was about to have for the first time. It was, he realized, panting, a rape.

Within moments, the outlines of objects in the room became clear to him, and he abandoned his fancy for the business at hand. He made his way to the desk in small steps, striving to be as silent as a thief. For thief he was.

The surface of the desk was clear save for the typewriter, covered, like an unfinished sculpture, with a bit of flannel. Parrish lifted the skirt, then tore it away, casting it to the floor. The typewriter seemed to stare back at him in the darkness. *I have known her fingers,* it seemed to say. *Touch me.*

He did. It was surprisingly warm, as though it might be alive, although he knew it was merely the heat of the day retained by the object.

The creak of a beam above his head reminded him that he had a task to complete. Quickly reaching into his breast pocket, he withdrew a rolled document. Deftly he unsealed it and inserted it into the platen. The white paper was like a banner she would not fail to notice when she entered the room.

Parrish sighed, shaking his head. How he wished he could be present when she learned that her caller had entered her home and violated this very room! He could almost feel her shudder to discover that she was so very, very vulnerable . . .

He straightened, looking about the darkened room again. How he would love to take something of hers. Something small, but personal. Something he could keep in his pocket, like a talisman. Something she would know was missing. Something that could give him some power over her that not even she could guess at. That, he decided resolutely, must be for another time. It was obvious she kept nothing so personal in this room. It was almost as though Emma Hunt and Philipa Braedon were two entirely separate and distinct individuals, who shared nothing other than a body.

Parrish retreated the same way he had advanced, even managing to lock the window, after a fashion. *Good night, Mrs. Emma Hunt*, he thought, satisfied with his night's work. He glanced once more through the window at the quiet chamber before slipping away in the night.

Chapter Twenty-two

Philipa passed a miserable night in her bed and arose early the following morning feeling as though she had not slept for a week. Her fitful rest had been marred by the recollection of Beatrice Waverly's deathlike visage, by Roger's horrifying self-recriminations, and by the disturbing argument she had had with Terry immediately before retiring. She felt, rolling over in her bed to face the cloudy dawn, like the princess from the old legend of the Princess and the Pea. But the pea was represented by her own collection of distressing thoughts.

And Elliot, she remembered, was coming home today.

The aroma of freshly brewed coffee met her in the stair-well. She tied her dressing gown as she descended slowly, rolling her shoulders and nodding her head from side to side to relieve the stiffness. Mrs. Grant, she knew, would not be expecting her down quite so early and would probably still be at her own breakfast.

To her surprise, Philipa found Arliss alone in the kitchen, pressing out fresh dough for blueberry scones on a flat baking sheet.

"Good morning, Arliss," she greeted the girl, stifling a

yawn. "I'm surprised to find you back. I hope your mother is better?"

Arliss always seemed diffident around her, if not downright frightened. This morning was no exception.

"Oh—ah—good morning, Miss Braedon." She fumbled with the breakfast dough, where before she had seemed quite adept. "Yes, thank you. Much better. I'm sorry about yesterday . . ."

Her timid, girlish soprano trailed off. Philipa, pretending to ignore Arliss's sudden clumsiness, took a cup from the china closet and poured herself coffee from the steaming pot.

"Nonsense, Arliss," she said, placing the heavy pot back on the stove. "Mrs. Grant and I managed quite well, I assure you. I have no objection to you taking care of your mother. In fact, I respect you for it. My, those scones look good! Your own recipe?"

Arliss, Philipa was pleased to note, smiled shyly and flushed with pleasure at the simple compliment.

"My mother's," the girl admitted, deftly scoring the square of dough with a large floured knife. "Mrs. Grant seemed to want to sleep a bit this morning, so I thought I'd—that is, if you don't mind . . . ?"

Once again, mercurially, Arliss looked fearful and tentative.

"Not if those scones taste as good as they look," Philipa declared, peering once more over Arliss's shoulder as the girl worked. "Really, Arliss, you ought to have more confidence in yourself. You have so many fine qualities, after all."

Arliss gawked. Philipa nearly laughed at the comical expression on her maid's charming young face.

"It's true," she went on, settling into one of the ladderback kitchen chairs which faced the girl. "You are a devoted daughter, a conscientious worker, and you seem willing to learn. Those are very valuable assets that will serve you well in whatever you do in this life. Hasn't anyone ever pointed that out to you before?"

Arliss abandoned the scones and stared out as if trying to recall.

"Dr. Waverly, once," she replied, her tone serious. "And my mother appreciates whatever I do for her. But"—the girl cast her gaze downward—"Jess just thinks I'm a fool."

Jess. Jessamyn. The very name made the coffee turn bitter in Philipa's mouth, although it was apparent that Arliss put a lot of stock in her older sister's opinions. She considered her next words very carefully.

"And has Jess made such a success of her life that her opinion is preemptive?"

Arliss's confusion was evident in her blue-gray eyes as she looked up at Philipa.

"'Scuse me?"

Philipa smiled, resisting an urge to shake the girl in a sisterly fashion.

"Surely, Jess is your sister, and you love her. And I'm sure she loves you, as well. But does her opinion count for so much that you can only see yourself reflected through her eyes?" Philipa enjoyed the rare chance to speak so frankly with the girl. "Don't you realize that many people, even sisters, use ridicule and insult merely to cloak their own jealousy?"

Arliss laughed, a trifle nervously.

"Jess? Jealous? Of *me*?" She sounded doubtful.

"Why not?" Philipa retorted, warming to her topic. "Jess may seem to you to lead a glamorous life, with her beautiful clothes and her admirers, but I can't believe she is truly happy in it. She has cut herself off from friends and from family. It seems to me there is one thing, above all else, which you possess that your sister may never aspire to. And that's—" Philipa stopped herself just before she said "respectability." Surely Arliss was aware of her sister's tainted reputation in Braedon's Beach, and there was no need for her, Philipa, to highlight it again. "That is the good opinion of one's friends and neighbors, and the knowledge that one is behaving in a manner in which one's family can take pride."

There. She hoped she had delivered that properly. She had no wish to hurt or offend the girl, or to make her defensive about her sister. Looking at her, Philipa thought it would be nice to have a sister, and to be a sister. She wondered if Jessamyn appreciated the fact that she had a sister. Arliss stared at her scones in a thoughtful manner, her thin lips pursed.

"I love my sister, Miss Braedon," the younger woman said, sounding to Philipa rather unhappy. She turned away and opened the oven door.

"Of course you do, Arliss," Philipa said softly, resisting a powerful urge to go to Arliss and embrace her. "As well you should. There can be no more powerful bond than that of sisterhood, unless it is that of mother to child."

Philipa wondered at her sudden wish to coddle the girl. Arliss, it seemed to her, was one of those people who seemed to invite protective behavior from everyone around her.

"Do you ever wish," Arliss ventured in her timid but engaging way, "for a sister?"

Philipa started. Arliss, while sweet, had never before seemed quite so perceptive to her.

"I confess to having enjoyed being the center of attention as I grew up," Philipa admitted, unable to keep from smiling at the thought. "But I have found myself wishing, lately, for such a confidante, and supporter. Are you and your sister very close?"

Arliss lifted the tray of dough from the sideboard, shrugging.

"We were, once," she remarked in a bland voice.

There was something sad about her. Perhaps it was her astonishingly large blue eyes, set in her thin, pale little face like beacons of pain. Arliss, Philipa was sure, did not lead a very happy existence. Her mother was all but invalid, and her sister a source of family shame. Philipa wondered, watching Arliss slide the tray of dough into the hot oven, whether Arliss's sister Jessamyn appreciated her good fortune in having a sibling. She wondered further, sipping her coffee, whether in fact Jessamyn ever confided in Arliss at all, about anything, and what Arliss might know of her sister's relationship with Terence Gavilan.

She set her coffee cup down quickly and pressed her hands to her cheeks, which suddenly felt excessively warm. How could she even think such wicked things? How could she even dream of spying on Terry in so mean a fashion? Of using

Arliss, innocent, guileless Arliss, to gain information on matters in which she should trust in Terry completely? Separately, the ideas were reprehensible. In concert, they were appalling, and unworthy of any well-bred lady, not to mention one in love.

Instantly, she was both deeply ashamed and profoundly confused. She did trust Terry, didn't she? Her stomach knotted painfully and she held her hand over her eyes, reluctant to allow Arliss the opportunity to guess her misgivings. Surely, Terry loved her. Surely he had terminated his relationship with Jessamyn, whatever it might have been, after he had confessed that love to her, if not before. Even to ask him about it would be unthinkable. To even entertain the idea of questioning Arliss . . . She sighed, wishing, fleetingly, that she were a Catholic. Then she could go to anonymous confession to Father Pierce, where she could beg forgiveness for her disgraceful thoughts, and be assessed a penance for her lapse of faith and morality.

But no. Perhaps it would be enough to attend morning prayer service at Holy Innocents instead, to make her peace with God and with herself. Perhaps the exercise would renew her strength before she returned to the Waverlys' again to stand vigil with Roger. And Father Michaels might, by some quirk of fate or breach of grapevine, still be unaware of Beatrice's dire condition. Certainly, the priest would want to know about it. It would be a perfect opportunity to tell him.

Or perhaps she was merely using the church as a rather lame but admittedly innovative excuse to avoid seeing Elliot this morning.

She sighed, suddenly uncomfortable in the comparatively small kitchen with Arliss, who was taking oranges from the icebox to squeeze them for juice. She had to leave the room, to escape, so the younger woman could not read her dark thoughts. In any case, she could not resume her pleasant, if intimate, discourse with the girl. She rose, coffee in hand.

"I'll be in my study, Arliss," she said with a small, shuddering sigh. "Please bring breakfast in whenever it's ready."

"Yes, Miss Braedon."

Their moment of frankness had gone. They were once

again a lady and her serving girl. Philipa, though she did not look back at Arliss as she left the kitchen, was certain that the young Miss Flaherty executed a brief curtsey.

The curtains were drawn in the study. It being an overcast day, the room was quite dark when Philipa entered it, which suited her. She was full of remorse over her shameful thoughts, and the darkness seemed appropriate. She sat in her favorite wing chair near the window and closed her eyes, thinking of Terry. His face formed in her mind: his wide, sensuous mouth smiling, his dark eyes adoring. She loved him. Of that she had no doubt. He loved her, as well. She was equally certain of that. But would the fact of that mutual love be enough to overcome whatever flotsam might emerge from either of their pasts to challenge it?

Her own past, she knew all too well, was not without taints. The near scandal at Bryn Mawr. Emma Hunt. And, most recently, her doomed engagement to Elliot. The follies of her youth could, if she allowed them, destroy the chance for happiness she so desperately wanted with Terry.

And what of his past? He was, after all, older than she, by at least five years. He had, she knew, lost his place in his class at Princeton for one scandalous episode of which she did not know the details. Jessamyn Flaherty, she was certain, must be but a small part of his past excesses; a life-style at which she could, unfortunately, with Emma Hunt's help, guess rather shrewdly. Living in Braedon's Beach as his wife, as Mrs. Terence Gavilan, she would have to look upon Jess Flaherty and know that she had not been the first. Even Arliss, Philipa suspected grimly, would be a reminder of the relationship. She closed her eyes and choked down a hard swallow. Did she possess the strength of character necessary to rise above such knowledge? Or was she, in fact, plummeting headlong into a monumental error which, through no fault of her own, or Terry's, would result in a lifetime of bitter regret for both of them?

She got up from the chair slowly, feeling far older than her 25 years. She would look to morning prayers for answers to these troubling questions, she decided, feeling a little better for the thought. But there was plenty of time to get ready for that. It was still quite early. Perhaps a turn at the typewriter would do her good. She had but a few dozen more pages to go to complete Emma Hunt's final work, to close that chapter of her life.

Philipa opened the doors from the hallway, wanting to admit as much light as possible without having to resort to the artificial illumination of a lamp. She took a deep breath of the tantalizing aroma of Arliss's scones coming from the kitchen, then moved toward the windows. She went from casement to casement, drawing back draperies and unlatching the windows to admit the morning sea breezes. The last casement gave with far greater ease than she had anticipated, but she attributed that boon to a recent oiling by Mrs. Grant. She stood before the last opened window and filled her lungs several times, hoping the fresh sea breeze would do for her what her restless night had not. It was not raining, and the damp, salty breeze made her shiver in her dressing gown. Somewhat refreshed and relieved of her earlier troubling thoughts, she turned from the window and headed purposely for her desk.

She frowned at the sight of a sheet of paper set in the carriage of her typewriter, its white tail waving in the light breeze. She was not in the habit of leaving papers in the platen when she retired, and the thought that she might have done so both annoyed and alarmed her. Suppose Mrs. Grant, or Arliss, had come in and found it there? She pulled the page from the typewriter with a quick jerk, and the machine rattled in protest.

Staring at the page, she froze to the pine floor.

On the otherwise pristine bond were the neatly typed words:

"You are mine Emma Hunt"

The import of its message struck her like the shock of an icy bucket of water in the face. Someone, probably the same person who had been responsible for the funeral wreath on her door the day before, had stolen into this very room during the night, and had even violated her typewriter. She felt, suddenly, as if she had been personally assaulted. The paper fell from her shaking hands, and she knew that the piercing sound which shattered the peace of the room was her own scream.

She backed slowly, clumsily, away from the desk like a wounded, hunted animal caught in the deadly sights of a ruthless, methodical, invisible stalker. She could no more prevent her screams than she could still the violent trembling that shook her entire body. Through her gathering terror she heard the sounds of running footsteps in the hall and on the stair. Arliss burst into the room, followed closely by Mrs. Grant.

Both women spoke at once, shouting, it seemed, to be heard over Philipa's own unceasing din. Philipa could neither hear nor understand them, but she suspected they were asking her what was wrong. Oh, God, some sane part of her being thought. What will I tell them? How can I tell them the truth? How can I keep this to myself? It was partly self-mastery which had by then reduced her screams to gasping sobs, but the transition was mostly due, she realized, to the fact that she was out of breath. She remained paralyzed by fear, unable to move her feet except to retreat, and powerless to retrieve the damning document on the floor where it had fallen.

"What is it, Miss Braedon?" She made out Mrs. Grant's anxious question. "A mouse? A rat?"

Silently Philipa blessed her housekeeper for providing her with a plausible excuse for her excessive reaction.

"A m—a mouse," she managed to get out, still unable to control the asthmatic pant of her breathing. "It startled me. I f—feel so foolish," she gasped, trying desperately to stop trembling.

With a great show of authority, Mrs. Grant quickly took her elbow.

"Come," the older woman said firmly. "Out with you. If the thing has upset you this much, we must get you out of here at once. Arliss, run across the street and ask Mrs. Dawson if we can borrow that cat of hers for a day or two. And run 'round to Peabody's and buy some traps. Here, Miss Braedon. We'll take care of everything. Perhaps you'd best go on back upstairs and lie down. I'll bring up your breakfast . . ."

Philipa did not hear the rest of her statement. Staring at the innocent-looking paper still on the floor, she resisted her housekeeper's earnest efforts to evacuate her. Her mobility returned. Hoping to retrieve the note before Mrs. Grant or

Arliss noticed it there, she quickly stooped and snatched it up, crumpling it in her hands. She pressed the paper to her breast as she allowed Mrs. Grant, finally, to lead her from the contaminated study. Her movements were as wobbly and uncertain as a new filly's.

A mouse. If only that were all, she thought, still gasping for breath. Dear God, if only that were all!

Chapter Twenty-three

Philipa could not even make herself comfortable in her own room, after the disturbing discovery in her study. If the burglar was able to infiltrate her study without detection, she thought, still trembling, could he not also violate her bedroom, as well? Mrs. Grant had left her alone to rest, but she could no more rest than she could fly. Rest! With her secret, if not her very life, in such imminent danger?

She dressed hurriedly behind a screen, feeling only a little foolish for the precaution. The burglar was long gone, she told herself. The burglar, in all probability, desired to maintain his anonymity as earnestly as she desired to uncover it. Her reasoning persuaded her mind, but not her emotions. Her home had been violated. She had to get out.

Mrs. Grant seemed surprised when, within the half hour, Philipa reappeared downstairs, dressed in a modest Wedgwood blue shirtwaist with a snow-white blouse and matching peplum jacket. Philipa congratulated herself that she moved with steady grace as she applied her straw hat to her neatly coiffed hair, and she stared at her reflection in the mirrored etagere while she addressed her housekeeper.

"I must apologize for my outrageous demonstration, Mrs. Grant," she began, pleased that her voice remained low and steady despite her racing heart. "I can think of no better excuse than that I was completely taken by surprise by the—the event. I am on my way to morning prayer service, and I shall go directly to the Waverlys' thereafter. If—if anyone should call, please tell them I will be home for dinner, and that they may call then. And please tell Arliss"—Philipa faced Mrs. Grant, whose gently wrinkled features, thankfully, betrayed no emotion whatever—"that I am sorry I missed her scones. I have no appetite this morning. I could not possibly even think of eating."

Mrs. Grant drew in a deep breath, and her short, stocky frame expanded with it.

"Suppose Mr. Gavilan should call?"

Philipa could only stare at her, a rush of warmth invading her neck. Mrs. Grant, she realized, remembering the scene in her drawing room the day before, knew there was something between her and Terry. She was neither blind nor stupid. Philipa found herself concentrating on the bib of Mrs. Grant's crisply starched apron.

"I—" She hesitated, remembering Elliot, and what she had not yet told him. "Things are very complicated just now, Mrs. Grant," she said softly, straining her hands into her gloves. "I hope I may resolve matters shortly, but there are certain elements that are out of my control. Please tell Mr. Gavilan, if he calls, where I have gone."

Mrs. Grant's gray eyes narrowed shrewdly, and she folded her arms across her bosom.

"You think very highly of him, don't you, miss?"

Philipa started. It was not like Mrs. Grant to make such a personal inquiry, although she had known the woman for years. Perhaps it was because of that very longevity that Philipa could not bring herself to chide the woman for voicing her observation. Her blush came to fullness, and she was powerless to prevent it.

"I do," she admitted, looking away.

Behind her, Mrs. Grant issued a noise that sounded something like a sniff.

"I hope he may be worthy of it," was all she said.

Philipa could only mumble a "good day," and leave the house quickly.

Father Michaels's morning prayer services were usually as brief and satisfying as a light spiritual breakfast. The theme of his short sermon that morning was that one had to have the courage to abandon the way things were in one's life in order to change them to the way one wanted them to be. Philipa knew, after listening to him and praying for guidance, that she must break her engagement with Elliot even if she did change her mind about making a life with Terence Gavilan. But as the service ended, she realized that she was no closer to a solution to her latest and most gripping dilemma.

Father Michaels met with each of his parishioners outside the church after services, usually exchanging cordial greetings and light pleasantries, sometimes arranging for formal or informal meetings regarding church business. Philipa delayed her departure so she could be the last person out of the church, and she hoped Father Michaels would not have pressing business elsewhere.

She needed to talk with him. Desperately.

"Good morning, Miss Braedon!" Father Michaels grasped her hand, his smile becoming a look of concern. "I hear that Mrs. Waverly is failing. In fact, I am just on my way over there now. May I offer you a ride?"

He moved as if to withdraw his hand from hers, but she held onto it. She needed to speak before she lost her nerve.

"Please, Father Michaels, I must speak with you, first. I— it's quite urgent."

A light rain had begun to fall. Father Michaels's normally tranquil brown eyes clouded with concern.

"Of course, Miss Braedon," he murmured, beckoning her into the sanctuary of the church. "Wait here. I won't be a minute."

Philipa sat in the last pew, grateful for the few moments to try and organize her speech. When Father Michaels returned, striding down the aisle in a brisk, businesslike pace, he had shed his vestment and was shrugging his shoulders into his black topcoat.

"Now then, Miss Braedon." He sat in the pew beside her, leaving several feet between them. "I am at your service. What is troubling you, aside from Beatrice's illness?"

Philipa was glad for his cool, clinical address. She stared at her hands, folded in her lap, and took a deep breath.

"I hardly know where to begin," she said softly, shaking her head. "Two months ago, my life was so simple, and now it has become so complicated that—that I am quite overwhelmed. Father Michaels, I cannot marry Elliot Waverly. No, please let me go on." She raised her right hand to abbreviate the beginnings of his protest. "If I pause, I don't think I'll be able to finish. You see, I am—I have fallen in love with another man, and I don't know if I will marry him or not, but I can't marry Elliot, feeling as I do about—the other. And the reason I don't know whether or not I will marry—this other man is that there are things in his past, and in my own, that I may not be able to reconcile. To overcome. And one thing is—Father, have you ever heard of Emma Hunt?"

Father Michaels frowned.

"She is—a writer, I believe. A novelist. Why?"

Philipa swallowed a lump in her throat. "Do you know what *kind* of novelist?"

Father Michaels shifted in his seat.

"She writes romances, I believe. Rather—descriptive ones, as I understand it. Father Pierce has told me, without naming names, that several of his parishioners regularly confess to reading her works."

Philipa could not help but smile, even as her face heated.

"Father Michaels," she said, ruing her pride, "Would it shock you very much to learn that—that *I* am Emma Hunt?"

There was a moment of silence.

"I beg your pardon?" His whispered question convinced her of his astonishment.

"It's true." She clasped her hands tightly in her lap. She could not look at him. "I can furnish you with proof, if you don't believe me."

"No, no," Father Michaels said quickly. "That will not be necessary. I—of course I believe you, Miss Braedon. Why would I not? But I don't understand—what has this to do with—your other problem?"

A sigh caught Philipa unawares, shuddering through her body like a cold wave.

"Someone has discovered my secret." She tried to keep her voice calm, but it came out as a trembling whisper. "And is tormenting me with the discovery in very sinister ways. Last night, this person even broke into my house. I am afraid. I planned to retire Mrs. Hunt—in fact, I have already done so—but I am afraid that this person, whoever he or she is, will continue to plague me, and may even threaten my relationship with—with this other man."

Father Michaels leaned back in the pew, and the wood creaked under him. He rubbed his hands together and entwined his fingers, pressing them to his lips. He sighed.

"Elliot knows nothing of this?"

She shook her head.

"And what about Terence Gavilan?"

She could only stare at the priest in open-mouthed astonishment. Father Michaels, in turn, smiled in a benign way, apparently pleased that he had surprised her.

"Who else could it have been?" he remarked gently, chuckling. "I recall very vividly the polka lesson I interrupted at Somers House. I think Mr. Gavilan is a fine man, Philipa. Not perfect, mind you, but a fine one, nonetheless. And after all, if we were perfect, there would be no need for men of my vocation, would there? But this other problem of yours . . ." He paused, shaking his head. "This sounds very serious, Philipa. You may be in danger. This person must be found out, and stopped."

"But how?" she countered, looking away from him again. "It would mean bringing Emma Hunt out in the open, and—think of the scandal, Father Michaels! I don't think I could bear it."

"Yes, you can, Philipa." Father Michaels's voice was strong and convincing.

She stared at him in surprise. He was looking at her with a stern expression.

"You are a strong woman. Perhaps stronger than you know. You knew there was a possibility of this kind of thing happening from the moment you undertook to write as Emma Hunt," he told her firmly. "You simply have to trust in your strength to weather this. You have to trust in your friends to accept you, and you must trust that your love for Terence Gavilan, and his for you, if love it is, can endure it. And above all"—he placed a firm, bracing hand upon her shoulder— "you must believe in God's higher purpose for this. It may not be for us to understand right now, or tomorrow, or ever, why He has given you this burden, but you must accept that God grants certain gifts in measure. The only way we can come to grief is by denying our gifts, or by fighting God's purpose for us, and trying to bend things to our own will. Remember the Lord's Prayer? Not '*my* will,' but '*Thy* will be done.' This is quite a can of worms you have here, Miss Braedon, I have to agree. But the best thing for one to do when one has a can of worms is to go fishing."

Philipa could not speak. She had her answer, but she did not like it. She was not disappointed, however, because she had not really expected to like it.

"You must tell Elliot about your change of heart as soon as possible," Father Michaels went on as if he did not notice her introspection. "Would you like me to be with you when you do?"

She shook her head, staring at her hands again.

"No, Father, thank you," she said. "I have gotten into this mess by myself. I will get out of it by myself."

"Well, not entirely by yourself," he corrected her, rising. "Thank you for confiding in me, Miss Braedon. You have a very interesting journey ahead of you, and I will be happy to help you in any way I can."

Philipa, too, rose.

"You won't—say anything to anyone?" she felt obliged to ask him, and felt ashamed for having done so.

"Of course not," he reproved, tucking her arm into his.

"Come, now. Dr. Waverly is expecting me, and you too, I believe. Shall we?"

It was Elliot who greeted Philipa and Father Michaels at the door, looking, Philipa thought, surprisingly calm and un-worried, although a bit pale. In his black frock coat he looked like a minister already, or at least like a child playing at one. She was more than a little self-conscious in his company, having disclosed her feelings to Father Michaels, and was glad that he merely took her hands and kissed her lightly on the forehead in a brotherly fashion in lieu of a more overt demonstration of affection. Father Michaels, Philipa was pleased to note, did not betray her confidence by so much as staring at her for an extra moment. He merely followed El-liot's brief direction and started up the stairs to Beatrice's room. Philipa placed a foot on the stair but felt, to her dismay, Elliot's hand on her arm, restraining her progress.

"Let's leave them alone for a few minutes, Philly." He spoke in a whisper, pulling her toward the parlor. "We can talk. In here."

Philipa was powerless to refuse. Elliot closed the doors behind him and came to her, taking hold of her arms. Elliot, Philipa realized for the first time, looked very much like his mother. She wanted to pull away from him, but could not muster the courage.

"She is dying, Philly," he said in a low, sorrowful voice. "Father says she has not improved. It's only a matter of time, now."

He sounded desolate, and she wondered why that should surprise her. Probably, she thought, detached, because he so seldom exhibited any extreme of emotion.

"He told me that yesterday," she heard herself say as if by rote. "He's very distraught, Elliot. I'm glad you've come, for him."

Elliot waved his hand, dismissing her remark.

"I am no comfort to him," he said with an edge of bitter-ness. "I have always been my mother's son. And you have been his daughter. Didn't you realize that? We will need to make the arrangements, Philly, you and I. He is—he is . . ."

Elliot did not seem able to go on.

Dear God, thought Philipa. Did he mean to say that Roger had lost his reason? She seized Elliot by the shoulders, shaking him once.

"What, Elliot?" she demanded, gripped by fear. "What is wrong with Roger?"

But Elliot only looked at her with his sad eyes, Beatrice's eyes, shaking his head. She uttered a small cry of disgust and ran from the room to find out for herself.

Father Michaels was on his way down the stairs even as she started up. His grim countenance filled her with dread.

"We must get a doctor from the mainland," he said quickly, answering her unasked question. "I have done all I can for Beatrice. But Roger needs us now, desperately. Elliot!"

Elliot, looking forlorn and hopelessly young, appeared in the foyer.

"Take my rig and get over to the Point. Fetch Dr. Kraus as quickly as you can. I'm going to get Mrs. Ames and one or two of Beatrice's other friends. Philipa, Roger is asking for you. He's exhausted, but I think he'll be all right. Just stay with him. Do whatever you can."

Father Michaels paused to grasp her hand as he passed her on the stair, and he held her gaze.

"For some things, there is no 'right time,'" he said to her in a quiet voice.

Then he was gone.

Roger was, indeed, exhausted. He looked old. Older, Philipa realized, stunned, than she had imagined him to be, although she knew he must be sixty years old, at least. But he had never seemed old before. Now, sleepless, unkempt, haggard, he might have been eighty. He barely moved from his vigilant pose in the chair by Beatrice's bed when she entered the room, except to raise his head slightly.

"Good morning, Philipa," he croaked in a weak voice.

Beatrice, Philipa noticed, had not moved from the position in which she had seen her the previous evening. The tableau struck something deep within Philipa; something that made her at once angry and unutterably sad.

"Roger, this will not do." She spoke lightly at first, but her resolve grew within her as she went on. "You must get some rest. You have done all you can. It's time to start thinking of yourself."

She approached him with a firm and deliberate step, noticing an untouched tray of breakfast on Beatrice's nightstand.

"And you haven't eaten, either," she went on, realizing that she sounded like a scolding mother, but unable to stop herself. "Come, Roger . . ."

Somehow she was able to persuade him to eat some of the oatmeal and toast, which were both, by then, probably as cold and unappealing as wallpaper paste. He appeared to be exhausted, and dangerously weak from lack of food and water. He was, she thought, remembering his bitter remorse, deliberately killing himself. Not if she could help it, she vowed, helping him to his own bed.

Mrs. Ames and other of Beatrice's friends came to the house straightaway and took over her care until the doctor from the Point could get there. Philipa placed herself in charge of Roger's well-being, supervising his food and drink, helping him to bed and sitting by him to ensure that he would remain there. It was not until late that afternoon that Dr. Kraus finally arrived. He saw Roger first, gave him a sedative and complimented Philipa on her care. When Roger fell into a sound sleep, Philipa escaped the room and went downstairs, hoping to slip away before anyone could detain her.

She got as far as the front door when she heard Elliot's voice behind her from the foot of the stair.

"Philly!" he exclaimed in a loud, reproachful way. "I've been calling you all the way down the stairs! Didn't you hear me?"

She released the lever of the door. So near and yet so far, she thought, turning to face him.

"I'm sorry. No, I didn't, Elliot," she replied with a sigh. "What has Dr. Kraus said?"

Elliot wore a troubled expression. She was amazed again at how much like his mother he looked. It seemed to her as if Beatrice's ebbing life were somehow entering her son.

"He is examining Mother now," he said, setting his shoulders back as he jammed his hands into his pants pockets. It was a childlike gesture that she found annoying. "Where are you going?" he went on, his expression accusing.

She squared her shoulders and leveled a frank stare at him. *No right time*, she told herself.

"I am going home." She pronounced each word deliberately. "I have done all I can do here, for now."

He stood before her, his expression hopeful and piteous.

"For my father, perhaps. But please, stay and dine with me," he pleaded in a soft voice that was almost a whine. "I don't want to be alone in this, Philly. I couldn't bear it."

Philipa stared, remembering what she herself had borne only the day before. How typical of Elliot, she reflected bitterly, to think only of himself under these circumstances! She was about to say so when she remembered, to her shame, that it was Elliot's mother who was dying, and Elliot's father who lay ill with grief. Her own parents had not died so long ago that she could forget the unremitting emptiness and incalculable anguish. She bowed her head and sighed.

"Very well, Elliot," she replied. *Although you may not like what results from it*, she thought, shaking inside.

Dinner was a thick, rich soup and freshly baked bread which the Waverlys' cook had prepared especially for Roger's failing constitution. It was served in the dining room despite Philipa's protests. It seemed a frivolous exercise of energies, under the circumstances. But Elliot insisted, taking his father's place at the head of the long, polished table which was set only at one corner. Philipa sat beside him in the place normally reserved for Beatrice.

She was cold, sitting in that chair. She was reminded of the tales of the Knights of the Round Table. The Siege Perilous, the chair reserved for the best knight in all the world. It was a silly reverie, she knew, but she could not help but think: what a perfect milieu for Mrs. Hunt's next novel! Then she remembered.

Emma Hunt was dead.

And the late Emma Hunt had a persistent, and perhaps dangerous, admirer.

The soup was fine, but she was surprised to discover that she had little appetite for it. Elliot, conversely, ate with a gusto unlike any she had ever seen him exhibit. She stared from him to her own barely touched bowl and realized that the time, right or wrong, had come. She drew in a deep breath.

"I can't marry you, Elliot," she said woodenly.

Elliot's spoon halted in midair.

"What?"

She forced herself to look up at him, knowing that she owed him at least the courtesy of looking at his eyes when she repeated it.

"I said, I can't marry you, Elliot," she said again, surprised that her voice seemed stronger the second time.

Elliot, never florid, paled nonetheless. "Philipa, what are you saying?"

She clenched her fists in her lap in concert with the tightening in her stomach.

"I believe you heard me that time," she replied, still maintaining his gaze.

He lay his spoon down and put his napkin to his lips briefly. "It's Gavilan, isn't it?"

Dear Lord, it seemed everyone knew it, even Elliot. How obvious she must have been! She compelled herself to return his stare, which had become quite unnervingly piercing.

"Partly, yes," she admitted. "But it was mostly us, Elliot. I have been made to realize that I am not in love with you. We both deserve more from a marriage than what we would have."

"Do you mean to say that you deserve no better than a womanizing libertine whose business is to ravage small, unsuspecting communities?"

"Elliot, this is not worthy of you." She curbed her anger at his brutal and unfair assessment of Terry's character. "Don't you realize what I'm saying? How could I become your wife, after admitting that I don't love you in that way? How could you even want to enter into a marriage with so reluctant a partner? You deserve more than that, Elliot. We both do."

"How kindly you express your concern for my feelings."

Philipa heard the seething rage simmering just below the surface of his calm. "And how inexcusably insensitive of you to begin this with me now, when my mother is dying, and my father too ill to care for her! Imagine how he will feel, Philipa, when he recovers to learn of the viper which we have nursed to our bosoms! You, whom he treated as a daughter! Imagine his hurt, and his shock when he learns of this betrayal. I knew that you and Mother never quite saw eye to eye, but I never dreamed you could be so cold, so selfish, so unfeeling—"

"I am leaving now, Elliot." Philipa rose. It required every ounce of her strength and her dignity to do it, but she was resolute. Having made the break, she had no option but to move forward or, like the shark, die. The analogy did not please her.

"I am sorry—sorrier than you will ever know, for the pain I have caused." She met his cold, angry stare with more confidence than she would have dreamed she possessed. "But I firmly believe that because of it, the greater pain has been spared, for both of us. I had intended to send you a letter requesting that we meet and talk. Your mother's illness intervened. But it would have been unfair of me to delay informing you of my decision because of it—"

"How glibly you talk of fairness," he mocked her in a hissing voice. "You, who tried for years in every way you knew to force a proposal of marriage out of me! You, who threw me off your porch the very first time I even uttered the words! You, who—"

"Good evening, Elliot," she said as calmly as she could, drawing herself up.

"How dare you, Philipa?" he was shouting behind her.

Philipa, aware of the many ears in the house, became hot with shame. She had arrived at the dining-room doors, although she had no recollection of having walked the distance from the table. She was filled with hurt, and with rage, and with an odd sense of relief: it was over. She had done it.

But what, exactly, had she done?

She felt like a small boat whose moorings had been torn off in a violent storm.

"I am sorry, Elliot," she whispered, unable to look at him, or to bear the expression of hatred in his voice. "I'm sorry it had to happen like this. I—"

"Get out," he said coldly, abbreviating her apology. "Just get out!"

She was in the hallway, moving toward the door. Behind her, she heard the sound of the maid scurrying like a frantic mouse. Upstairs, she was sure, Mrs. Ames and her compatriots huddled their gray heads over the commotion below. She could not escape quickly enough.

"A moment, Miss Braedon." Dr. Kraus's thin, very correct German accent halted her progress at the door. "You may want to know that Mrs. Waverly has died."

Philipa, feeling one weight leave and another press upon her, could not even look at the messenger of death.

"Her son is in the dining room, Doctor," she told the man, amazed at the serenity in her address. "Please tell him yourself."

Outside, a heavy mist hung in the evening air like a shroud.

Chapter Twenty-four

It was a miserable evening for a walk, and therefore a perfect reason for Philipa to take one. She had never felt so utterly alone and desolate. Having cast off Elliot and her cumbersome vow of betrothal, she had also forsaken the connection to Roger that she had valued so highly, and quite probably other of her friendships, as well.

She thought of paying a call upon Essie, whom she had always been able to count on for affirmation of her decisions, and of her very being. But she rejected the idea at once. She hated calling upon people uninvited at the dinner hour, even as good a friend as Essie. And besides, Essie was expecting a child. Her head would be full of her own thoughts and plans, as well it should be. It was not a time, Philipa reflected gloomily, climbing the steps to the Promenade, to be burdening Essie with problems which she, Philipa, had brought upon herself.

The Promenade was wet and deserted. The sky was a single shade of gray, and the sea beyond the beach a darker shade. The mist was heavier than it had been inland, and it rolled in off the waves like billows of steam. The air was cool and wet, and thick with the aroma of brine.

Philipa carried neither parasol nor umbrella, and soon she could see, from the corner of her eye, tiny beads of moisture clinging to the strands of hair that had escaped the confines of her straw hat. Her heels made little noise on the wet boards as she slowly made her way past the brightly lit arcade and the deserted, half-finished amusement area. The carousel was covered with a tarp, and the uncompleted Ferris Wheel stood like a random assemblage of bones of some prehistoric behemoth against the gray sky. She walked the length of the Promenade without encountering another soul and turned around to walk back again.

It was growing darker, making the white figure some distance up the Promenade much easier to see. She knew at once that it was Terry walking toward her. He did not seem to be hurrying, but his long legs and efficient stride carried him quickly nonetheless. She paused, watching him, remembering their argument the night before, and all of the things that had happened since then. She moved toward him, wanting very much to hear him speak her name and to feel his arms around her.

She saw, as he grew closer, that he was wearing pale blue, not white, and that his handsome features were searching and unsmiling.

"What are you doing out here in the rain?" he asked her in an incredulous whisper, stopping three feet in front of her.

She looked at him. His hands were clenching and unclenching at his sides, as though he wanted to take her in his arms but dared not. His lips were parted in panting anticipation, seeming to await some signal from her. His eyes were probing and intense, as though merely by looking at her he hoped to divine her inner thoughts. Her heart was so full that she could not answer him at once. She was free, she realized, considering him steadily. She was free of Elliot, and of Beatrice, and of every obstacle to his affection.

But at how great a price? she wondered bleakly. And had she merely traded the bondage of duty and obligation for that of a heartbreaking, and possibly dangerous, love?

She closed her eyes, closing the door on that frightening notion.

"It's done," she sighed as a sob threatened the back of her throat. "I am no longer engaged, Terry. And Beatrice Waverly—has died."

She did not open her eyes. She could not. Terry's hands were on her arms, gently pulling her toward him as if he wanted to warm her with his own nurturing heat. She allowed his tender gesture, welcoming the feel of someone else's strength. Her own had just about reached the limit of its endurance. Her head rested against his shoulder, and he tugged her hat down the back of her neck. In a moment she knew the warmth of his hand against her head.

"Let me take you inside," he whispered, pressing a light kiss upon her temple. "You're wet, and shivering."

She had not even realized she was shivering until he said so. She allowed him to guide her the short distance along the Promenade to his office, and she managed the outside stairs slowly, like an invalid old woman.

Terry's office was illuminated by lamps, and the yellow glow was warming. His secretary looked up from his work like a guilty thief caught in some illicit act. Owen Parrish, Philipa remembered, staring even as he stared at her. She further remembered, taking a step back against Terry, that she did not like the man.

"Good afternoon, Miss Braedon." He greeted her respectfully enough, although she perceived a note of mockery in his address.

Behind her, Terry gently nudged her inside.

"Go on in," he invited her softly. "Owen won't bite."

Monitoring the man's steady, unsettling scrutiny, Philipa was not so sure. She did take two or three uncertain steps into the room, waiting for Terry's next command, her own will having deserted her. Parrish made no pretense of returning to his work, and Philipa could not continue to look at him. His small, narrow eyes were upon her like a case of poison ivy as she allowed Terry to guide her elbow to a chair behind a large, cluttered desk.

"Drop in at Fantucci's and ask him to send some coffee

up here on your way out, will you, Owen?'' Terry remarked to his secretary, who had not seemed, to her, as if he had any intention of going anywhere.

"I was going to finish comparing these bids,'' Parrish replied, sounding as though he thought it a most important project.

"It's after six,'' Terry prompted him, and Philipa could hear the impatience in his forcibly calm baritone. "There's no hurry for those. You can finish tomorrow. Miss Braedon and I have some business to discuss right now. I'll see you in the morning.''

Please leave, Philipa thought, closing her eyes but not daring to lean her head back against the seat. *Please leave or I will scream* . . .

Parrish did so, at an iced crab's pace. It was not until Philipa heard the door close and the footsteps fade down the stairs that she allowed herself the luxury of resting her head. Terry's strong hands gently massaged her shoulders.

"Was it awful?'' he asked in a warm, gentle tone that made her feel like crying.

"Very,'' she admitted, almost willing to confess that the activity of his hands made it worth the anguish. "He accused me of terrible things, Terry. I could almost hate him for it, except—'' She broke off, unable to go on for the sudden lump in her throat.

"Except what, Philly?'' Terry continued to knead the aching muscles of her neck and shoulders.

"Except,'' she choked in a whisper, "I feel as though I deserve every horrid thing he said to me. Terry, I knew this wouldn't be pleasant, but I had no idea it would be quite so painful, either!''

His arm was about her neck, and his face in her hair.

"I'm sorry, my love,'' he said his voice low. "I should have been there with you. I should have—''

"No,'' she told him tiredly, reaching for his hand. "You really had no place there, Terry. I should never have agreed to marry Elliot from the beginning. I think I've always known that I didn't love him. I'm not certain why I even agreed to marry him at all, except that I knew that I wanted to marry and have a family, and he was the only option I could foresee, once I discovered that you and Jessam—''

She stopped herself, aghast. She'd had no intention of mentioning Jessamyn Flaherty to Terry, ever. She closed her eyes, her mortification complete.

''Jessamyn,'' he finished for her in a quiet, serious voice, squeezing her hand tightly. ''I offer no excuse for that, Philipa. All I can say is that it all happened before I knew you, before I realized I was in love with you. And I know you would never ask, but I'll tell you anyway: I haven't seen her since the night before I came into your house like a raving madman and asked you to marry me.''

Through her pain and confusion, Philipa had to smile. She remembered the events of that afternoon, and the whole episode seemed so ridiculous to her. And yet it reminded her once again of how uncanny was Terry's knowledge of her, that he should have realized, even when she herself had not, that she had no business marrying Elliot Waverly, even then . . .

A polite knock on the door interrupted their earnest discourse. It was Fantucci's son with a huge pot of steaming coffee and two mugs on a sturdy wooden tray. Terry handed the boy a coin at the door.

''Did you hear that Mrs. Waverly passed on?'' the boy, probably no more than fourteen, offered conversationally.

''Yes, I did, John,'' Terry answered politely. ''My compliments to your father. Please thank him and have him put it on my bill. Good evening.''

The young Fantucci disappeared. Demonstrating a magnificent disregard for his things, Terry put the tray on top of the papers on his desk and poured coffee into the two mugs. His movements were graceful and efficient. Philipa felt as though she could watch him all evening, even if he did nothing more than serve coffee. She settled back into his big, cozy chair, reveling in the knowledge that he sat there, in that very place, so often. The chair, and the notion, were both so comforting that she was able to begin to set aside her dark, troubling memories of her day at the Waverlys'. He held the mug out to her, and there was a suggestion of one of those endearing, raffish grins on his handsome face.

"Feeling better?" His intimate tone reminded her that they were completely alone.

She nodded, accepting the mug he offered, allowing her fingers to linger on his.

"For some reason, I always feel better when I'm with you," she confessed, unable to sustain his gaze as she said it. "It seems as though the whole world could go to perdition, but somehow, in your company, I find it all tolerable. Why is that, Mr. Gavilan?"

"Could it be, Miss Braedon," he inquired in a teasing tone, coming around to sit on the edge of the desk before her, "that you are in love?"

His voice was like rich, brandied cream, and it brought a swell to her breast. She was compelled to look at him again and found him studying her with no trace of mockery, however gentle.

"I believe, Mr. Gavilan," she replied, her alto hoarse and breathless, "it is altogether likely."

He was smiling again, that quicksilver grin that stopped her heart. He leaned toward her, and she was drawn to him, as well. They could do nothing more than kiss, lightly, in their circumstance, but it was all she needed to reaffirm the wisdom of her decision to abandon her engagement to Elliot Waverly. Her most passionate exercise with Elliot could not begin to compare with even this simple demonstration of tenderness with Terry for the way in which it transformed her into a quivering mass. His touch so charged her that she remained perfectly still after his kiss had been withdrawn, savoring the smallest ripples of sensation until they diminished like receding waves. When she opened her eyes, she saw him smiling at her, with a suggestion of longing in his eyes that he tried to mask with amusement.

"Shall I walk you home now?"

His baritone was so lush, so warm, and so soft that for a dizzy moment she fancied he had asked her to make love to him. She drew in a deep breath and shook her head, hard.

"This coffee is so warm, and so good," she murmured,

staring into its dark depths. "Let me finish it first. It will warm me."

But not as you could, she added a codicil to herself, stealing a glance at him again as she sipped the hot brew.

Dusk had completely masked the dull sky with a slate gray, and the dampness had not abated when they left his office. Terry took her hand in his, and she realized that the worst was past, and that no amount of whispered rumor on the island could mar the feelings she had for him. She was glad he did not speak, and she offered no remark until they mounted her front steps to the porch, where Mrs. Grant had left a light for her.

"Terry, will you do something for me?" she asked when they stood before her door.

He lifted her hand to his lips and touched it lightly, his eyes searching hers.

"What?"

She moistened her lips with her tongue and took a deep breath. Gavilan, looking at her, knew he would have done anything for her.

"Will you accompany me to Beatrice's funeral?"

Her whispered plea tore at his heart. It was among the very last things he would have chosen to do, but he forced himself to nod. After all, she had already performed the most difficult task, alone. The least he could do would be to support her at that most trying of public events, especially when word got around, as it inevitably would, of the broken engagement.

"Of course," he managed to reply, even finding her a smile. "I won't leave your side. It will be a good thing, in any case, to get people used to the idea of seeing us together, won't it?"

She did not smile. In fact, she appeared troubled.

"It will be very awkward, you know," she said quietly, staring at his shirt collar. "And I'm not at all certain that it will be in the best of taste for me to appear on your arm so soon after jilting Elliot, at his own mother's funeral . . . No. Perhaps it would be best if I went alone, after all. And Roger—"

"Philipa." Gavilan dammed her stream of logic firmly, taking hold of her arms as he trained her gaze to his. "Elliot's delicate sensibilities don't matter to me. You are my concern, and I won't have you on display for public censure for having the courage to speak your mind. Roger is a gentleman. He cares for you. He'll understand. If Elliot isn't man enough to accept what's happened, then that's his problem, isn't it?"

She did not reply right away, and he thought she might protest his argument. Then, to his mild surprise, she nodded, issuing a small sigh. A smile widened his mouth, and he was pleased at his victory over her excessive selflessness.

"I promise I'll behave myself," he teased, enjoying the rueful expression that crossed her features. "Of course, if Elliot calls me out, I won't promise I'll allow him to kill me—"

"Oh, Terry, stop." She abbreviated his tirade with a weak, resigned laugh, covering his mouth with her hand. Her touch was gentle, and her fingers soft and fragrant. He held her hand in place with his own and kissed the tips of her fingers lightly. A delicious burn ignited deep within him.

"I want," he began, examining her hand, "to give you something. A token of my intentions. What would you like? A ring?"

She pulled her hand away, smiling in an engaging, impish way as she slipped her fingers into the slim pocket in her jacket.

"You have already done so," she told him, withdrawing a small object. "Remember?"

She opened her hand and displayed a plain, brownish ring which he did not recognize. His mouth turn down at the corners, beholding such a base ornament.

"The carousel ride," she reminded him, her smile widening. "The brass ring?"

He closed his hand around hers, deeply touched.

"A mean token," he grumbled, unable to keep from smiling. "An embarrassment. A diamond, I think. Or perhaps an emerald?"

She shook her head gently. Her smile made his legs weak.

"There's nothing you could give me that could mean more than this, for now," she told him. A thrill rippled along his spine at the sureness in her voice, and the softness in her gray-green eyes.

"Philipa." He murmured her name like a charm, his arms finding their way around her. "My love . . ."

Her lips expressed themselves to him in a far different, although no less comprehensible, manner.

Chapter Twenty-five

Beatrice Waverly had been, if not popular, then certainly well known in Braedon's Beach, and on the entire island. Attendance at her funeral attested to that fact, filling Holy Innocents to the very seams. Philipa sat in her family pew with Terry for several minutes after the church had cleared for the burial, her gloved hands folded tightly in her lap. She was warm in her black taffeta gown, even though it was not an especially hot day. Terry, beside her, looked splendid and not at all crow-like in his black suit. He had worn a black derby with his ensemble, a skimmer being inappropriate for a funeral, even in summer. The derby rested in his lap, as did his hands. He wore gloves, which was also unusual for him. She suspected that he had made an extra effort to meet Braedon's Beach's exacting standards of decorum, just for her benefit. The thought, if she could only get beyond the covert stares of her neighbors and whispers behind fans of her friends and acquaintances, was a comforting one.

She had not seen either Roger or Elliot during the service. The Waverly pew was several rows behind her own, and she and Terry had arrived early, before the bereaved father and son. Philipa fancied that she could feel their stares upon her back throughout the service, and she had not dared to turn around.

Roger, she had learned to her relief, had recovered from his weakened state. She had expected a summons from him during the two days that had elapsed since her passionate scene with Elliot, but all had remained quiet from the Waverly camp. Almost unnervingly so. In fact, had the perennially curious Esmaralda Tavistock not visited her the day before, she would not even have known of Roger's improvement.

Essie herself, Philipa was pleased to note, appeared healthy and glowing and all the other positive adjectives which one could hope to apply to a woman with child. She had expressed, for Essie, an inordinate level of sensitivity regarding Philipa's broken engagement, as well as a high degree of aplomb regarding the reasons therefor. Charles, she confided to Philipa, had lately had some sort of "falling out" with Gavilan. Her husband had not divulged the reason for this occurrence, but Essie, in her typically singleminded manner, expressed her firm belief that they would have it all sorted out "in time for the wedding," as she put it.

"After all," she had said, her eyes as bright and lively as if it were she herself who were looking forward to the eventuality, "if I am still to be your matron of honor, it won't do to have the groom and my husband glowering at one another throughout the celebration!"

When Philipa had reminded her that she and Terry were not yet even engaged, Essie had waved her hand in an elegant gesture of dismissal.

"Terence Gavilan," Essie had asserted with a knowing nod, "is not a man who pursues lightly, either in business, or in love. You will be safely married to him before the year is out, or I'm not Esmaralda Wambush Tavistock!"

"We should go outside," Terry prompted her when all other sounds had faded from the sanctuary. "It's time."

As the images of Essie's declaration faded into the recesses of her memory, she could only nod to him in reply.

Father Michaels had already begun his eulogy when Philipa and Terry took their places on the fringes of the assemblage.

The white sand churchyard had been converted to a veritable sea of black crepe as the mourners stood about the gravesite in silent homage to the deceased. The rector's remarks were somber and brief, touching on Beatrice's prominence in the community, her steadfast support of the church, her fierce devotion as a wife and a mother (of which Philipa was all too aware), and what a great sorrow to have so fine an example to the women, young and old, of Braedon's Beach torn so abruptly from their midst. However, he exorted them to remember, such was the will of the Almighty. As the priest went on about the happiness Beatrice would no doubt enjoy in the company of the saints, Philipa found herself conjuring vivid images of Beatrice Waverly in heaven, diligently schooling those same saints in her view of proper deportment.

The "Mighty Fortress" borrowed from Bach's Lutheran tradition seemed an appropriate farewell hymn for Beatrice, and as she was laid to rest, Philipa silently asked her forgiveness for hating her, and for hurting her son and husband. From the grave came only the sound of earth on wood as ashes returned to ashes, and dust to dust.

The churchyard began to clear of mourners. Elliot and Roger stood like two lone sentries in black, accepting the brief, somber condolences and farewells of friends and neighbors. Philipa would have liked nothing more than to slip away, unnoticed by either of them. But she knew she would have to face them both sometime. Better sooner than later. Reluctantly, she removed her hand from inside the crook of Terry's elbow.

"I'll speak with them alone," she whispered to him, aware that Father Michaels was coming their way.

"I'll wait for a better time to offer Roger my condolences," Terry agreed with her, and she approached the elder and the younger Waverly alone.

Elliot, as she had half expected, saw her and abruptly turned and walked away, wearing a scowl. Roger, however— dear, frail-looking Dr. Waverly—did not take his sad eyes from hers as he opened his arms to welcome her embrace. Philipa felt his hands press against her back, and she was crying for the first time.

"Philly," he barely whispered, holding her desperately, as if he feared she might run from him. "My dear, dear girl, I don't know what to say to you."

"Roger, I'm so sorry." She breathed, embracing him tightly in return. There was a small, tight pain in her throat. "I'm so sorry for everything. For Beatrice, and for—for—" She could not go on. The pain, quite suddenly, overwhelmed her.

"I am sorry, too," he said in his hoarse, sorrowful voice. "I am sorry for burdening you with my grief. But most of all, I am sorry you will not be my daughter, after all."

Gavilan watched the tableau unfold from a discreet distance, aware of a surprisingly strong pang of empathy for the older man that caused him to press his fingers to his eyes and utter an involuntary sigh.

"Roger, I think, will feel the loss more keenly than Elliot."

He recognized the voice as that of Father Michaels beside him. Gavilan faced the priest, surprised that he had not heard the man approach. Father Michaels, who did not appear to be much older than himself, smiled in an open and congenial manner. Gavilan found himself wondering whether the remark had reflected Beatrice's death or Philipa's by-now epic jilting of the woman's son.

"It was good of you to come, Mr. Gavilan," he went on, smiling. "Very appropriate. And courageous. I am sure Philipa appreciates your—support."

"Good afternoon, Father Michaels," he said cordially, thinking that the priest merely intended to be polite. "I didn't know Mrs. Waverly well, but from what I did know, it seems to me that your eulogy captured her essence."

Father Michaels's smile widened slightly, then receded to a more pastoral beatitude.

"It was too long," he observed, glancing again at Philipa and Roger, who seemed still to be engaged in earnest conversation in spite of Elliot's unceremonious withdrawal. "I have a tendency to get too caught up in my love of the language. I do so enjoy creating my sermons, almost more than delivering them. Do you write, Mr. Gavilan?"

Gavilan stared at the man, hoping to gain some clue as to

the priest's deeper meaning. It seemed to him that there was a specific purpose behind the clergyman's presumably off-hand inquiry, but he could not divine what it might be.

"No," he answered, squinting his eyes against the glare of the sun before applying his hat. "But I do read. Reading happens to be one of my favorite pastimes."

"Ah," Father Michaels responded, nodding in a very clerical and somewhat annoyingly knowing manner. "And what sort of literature do you prefer?"

Gavilan glanced again at Philipa, who was still deeply engrossed in her dialogue with Roger Waverly. Then he frowned and looked down at his shoes.

"I'm fond of poetry," he allowed, neither wishing to lie nor to be completely truthful. "Byron. Keats. The sonnets of Shakespeare."

"Ah," Father Michaels said again. "A romantic. How nice. Miss Braedon is, I think, a romantic, as well. Although she might deny it. Tell me, Mr. Gavilan, do you read many novels?"

Gavilan could not prevent a fleeting grin as he glanced at the man, thinking of Emma Hunt.

"Now and again," he replied. "I do enjoy the classics, and perhaps one or two more contemporary novelists. Why do you ask?"

Father Michaels shrugged his bearlike shoulders under his cassock.

"I should think it would be a most rewarding vocation, to write," he replied, not quite, Gavilan noticed, answering his question. "Miss Braedon has, I believe, published some scholarly works. Did you know that?"

"So I've been told," Gavilan rejoined, wondering where this rather odd conversation was headed. "I must remember to ask her to show them to me."

"Yes, you must," Father Michaels agreed, somewhat more emphatically than Gavilan considered usual, or polite. "Quite an extraordinary woman, our Miss Braedon. Don't you agree?"

Gavilan stared at the man again, remembering suddenly that Father Michaels had stumbled upon the impromptu polka instruction in his kitchen, what seemed a lifetime ago. Did the priest know about Philipa's reasons for breaking her engagement with Elliot? He was burning to know, but could not, out of respect for Philipa, ask him. He was beginning to feel more than a little uncomfortable under the priest's disconcerting scrutiny.

"Yes," he replied, because he thought it to be the truth and, moreover, what the man had wanted to hear. He found himself wondering why he, who had always been able to find the perfect words for every occasion, should suddenly discover his own glibness stymied by this gentle, careful dissection by a parish priest.

"Yes, she is," he repeated lamely. He wished Philipa would have done with her conversation with Roger, so that he might escape further velvet inquisition.

"In fact, I shouldn't wonder," Father Michaels went on, blithely unaware, it seemed, of Gavilan's discomfort, "that there are many, many as yet undiscovered facets to her personality. What a joy to learn that a person whom you think you know so well should in fact continually surprise you, in so many pleasant ways. I believe the element of surprise in love, as in warfare, is truly an asset. Don't you think so, Mr. Gavilan?"

Gavilan, while somewhat nonplused by Father Michaels's pointed and unabashed observations, could not prevent himself from staring openly at him. What the hell was the man trying to say? The priest's pleasant features, still smiling, yielded no clue to his deeper meaning, if there was one. But there had to be one. If there was not, the rector had just babbled on stupidly to pass time. And Father Michaels, he knew, was not stupid, even if he did enjoy babbling now and again.

"Still, I would hope not to confuse the two," Gavilan made shift to reply. "It seems to me that unpleasant surprises can turn love into warfare."

Father Michaels chuckled, seeming to think it a clever response to his exasperatingly obscure remarks.

"I find it difficult to imagine that Miss Braedon could conceive of an unpleasant surprise. Don't you?"

Gavilan did find it so, although, remembering Elliot's re-action to her approach, he rethought his answer. For a chilling instant, he pictured himself in Elliot's position. *I can't marry you after all*, he could almost hear Philipa say in that low, melodious voice of hers. He shook his head and blew off a hard breath. He fancied he could see, quite clearly and with great disquiet, how Philipa Braedon might blindside one with an unpleasant surprise.

Philipa took her leave of Roger fondly, having pulled her-self together with great effort. The worst part of the whole affair, as she saw it, was that Roger had been hurt. Doubly. Triply. The loss of his wife, his personal remorse, and finally, Philipa's own betrayal. He had said that he understood her reasons, of course, but Philipa, returning to the place where Terry and Father Michaels stood waiting for her, knew she would remember the sorrow and the veiled reproach in his eyes as long as she lived.

Father Michaels took his leave of them at once and walked with Roger to his carriage. Philipa wondered at Terry's thoughtful expression as he monitored the rector's retreat.

"A penny for your thoughts," she volunteered, shaking off her own somber ruminations.

Terry quickly turned his head toward her, for an instant still wearing an intensely probing expression which frightened her. His handsome features relaxed to a brief, fond grin. Her fear vanished.

"I can't decide," Terry said, glancing once more at the rector's back, "whether Father Michaels is completely insane or merely the most brilliant man I've ever met."

She frowned.

"I doubt he is either," she remarked, puzzled, and anxious, although she could not tell why. "Whatever were you two talking about?"

Terry, to her surprise, stared after the departing priest again, his wide mouth pursed to a small, tight line.

"Love and warfare," he answered her finally, taking hold of her arm. "And literature."

By that time the churchyard was deserted but for the laborer who was finishing the task of laying Beatrice to rest. Philipa allowed Terry to lead her away to the waiting Hurricane and help her in. In moments they were off, the warm summer wind whipping about their faces. But Terry, to her alarm, did not aim the vehicle in the direction of the Waverlys'.

"You're going the wrong way!" she shouted at him, hoping to be heard over the grating din of the engine.

"No, I'm not," he called back, his smile creating a deep cleft in his cheek.

"But the Waverlys' is—"

"We aren't going to the Waverlys'," he said firmly and loudly.

Philipa, tired of shouting, decided not to debate the issue with him until he stopped, which he did not do until they had crossed the causeway to the mainland and driven some distance along the western shore of the bay. Terry finally braked to a halt before a tidy bungalow smartly painted in tones of brown and cream with long boxes of gay red and white impatiens decorating the railing of the wrap-around porch. The roar of the engine died, and the only sounds to be heard were the cackle of the riotous gulls and the gentle chirping of sparrows in the towering pines around them. The place seemed, to Philipa, to be a blessed oasis of calm and anonymity.

"Like it?"

She started, turning to Terry. His grin was mischievous.

"I discovered it some time ago." He did not wait for her to answer. "Quite by accident. I got lost on the way to the island when I first came to town, and I stopped here for directions. It's an inn, Philly. It's run by a Mr. and Mrs. Minnick, and they serve just about the best food money can buy. And not being much of a cook, I've eaten in one or two places in my life, so I know."

Philipa could not speak. She felt like a character from one of her novels. A heroine who had been spirited away from the watchful eye of her guardian, or her duenna, or—as in her case—a diligent, if not meddling, community to a verdant, secluded haven from all common cares. She felt at once unutterably safe, and paradoxically vulnerable.

But she could not deny that she adored being there with

him, alone, miles from the rigid constraints of Braedon's Beach.

Terry had climbed down from his side of the Hurricane and was coming around to help her down when a stocky woman of an indeterminable age appeared on the porch, wringing her hands on the skirt of her bib apron. Her hair was pulled back in a soft bun and netted in the manner of Eastern European immigrants, and she wore a pair of wire-rimmed spectacles on her broad, pleasant Slavic face.

"Ho, Mr. Gavilan!" the woman called out in a loud, deep, almost masculine voice. Her accent was apparent in those few words, as she said Terry's name with a slight over-exaggeration of each syllable so that no part of his name enjoyed more prominence than any other.

"You come here in your noisy machine and scare away the squirrels. Good! And you bringet your wife, too."

She pronounced "wife" as though it began with a V. Philipa smiled and accepted Terry's help down, noticing that he had not contradicted her.

"Good afternoon, Mrs. Minnick," Terry greeted her, escorting Philipa by the elbow up the neat gravel walk to the porch steps. "It's good to see you again. How is Mr. Minnick?"

"Fine, fine," the woman replied, ushering them to the porch with several waves of her large, work-worn hand. "He taket children swimming. He teachet them to swim. You livet near water, you teachet children to swim, yah?"

Climbing the steps, Philipa had the odd sense that she was visiting someone's mother. The woman grasped her hand as she approached, and her grip was warm and surprisingly strong. She smelled of yeast and kitchen spices and of things freshly baked, and her smile was genuine.

"You sit," she invited them, showing them a pair of newly caned rockers on the cool, shady porch. "I bringet you something to drink. Coffee? Tea? Lemonade? You come for dinner? Stayet for night?"

Philipa trembled, suddenly chilled. She did not dare to look at either Terry or the unknowing Mrs. Minnick. Was *that* why Terry had brought her to this place?

Chapter Twenty-six

"Lemonade," Terry, beside her, replied casually. "I'm parched. All right, Philipa?"

His omission was, to her, glaring. Philipa swallowed a hard, sandy bubble in her throat. She tightened her grip on Terry's elbow and sensed his stare upon her.

"Terry," she ventured, striving valiantly for a calm, normal tone but managing only a strangled whimper. "I don't—"

She stopped, confused and utterly disgusted with herself. Less than a week ago, while still engaged to Elliot, she had abandoned all propriety and had practically invited Terence Gavilan to seduce her, right on her own back porch. Here, today, in a secluded little hostelry where she had willingly come with him, and where there was little if any chance that an indiscretion between consenting adults might be uncovered by residents of Braedon's Beach, she was behaving like a foolish virgin who had forgotten to put oil in her lamp. Her face was hot, and she knew, even in the shade of the eaves, that her cheeks must be blazing red.

"It's all right, Philly," his soft baritone reassured her. "Sit down out here. I'll take care of everything. I promise."

It was not his words so much as his warm, gentle tone that made her feel better. She did sit down in one of the cane rockers as Terry entered through the screened storm door of the bungalow with Mrs. Minnick. The chair was comfortable, and she began to relax in spite of herself. Minutes later she heard the door close again with a slight, hollow bang. Terry had returned, alone.

"I know what this looks like," he said, settling his long, lean frame into the chair beside her own. "But allow me to explain. I thought some time away from Braedon's Beach would be good for both of us. You're worn out with everything that's happened in the last few days, and it's no wonder. You've put yourself through so much. And I've wanted to have you all to myself for few hours. This is the perfect time. The whole town is at the Waverlys', preoccupied with Beatrice's death. It's a good thing for you to pull out of the public eye for a while, after your business with Elliot. I knew there wouldn't be a better time, so I made arrangements for this. There are two rooms booked for us, Philipa. But we can decide after dinner whether or not we want to stay."

Philipa was immediately ashamed of herself for having suspected him of a less than honorable design. She gripped the arms of the rocker tightly, unable to relax her fingers. He leaned forward in his chair, reaching across the narrow gulf separating them to place his hand upon her own. She had not realized how cold her hand was until his warm one covered it. She made herself meet his gaze, and she found him monitoring her steadily, with no hint of amusement.

"I'm sorry," she got out, compelled by his earnest, dark-eyed gaze. "I should have known that you—I do trust you, Terry, I do! Forgive me. I—it's very thoughtful of you to have arranged all of this for us. And I appreciate it. And I—I promise I'll try to relax and enjoy it."

She closed her mouth, sensing that there was nothing more to be added, although she felt a pressing need to continue talking. Terry seemed to perceive her confusion, and he smiled.

"Have I ever told you," he said softly, caressing the back

of her hand with a bold, lazy finger, "how extraordinarily lovely you are?"

Mrs. Minnick clattered out onto the porch, bearing a tray which she set upon the small table before them. The tray, containing a big pitcher of pale yellow liquid with a chunk of ice floating in it, blue checkered napkins, two tall, sapphire-colored glasses and a plate piled high with delicate wisps of some sort of pastry dusted with sugar, completely dwarfed the table upon which it was set. Philipa silently blessed the woman's timing even as Terry withdrew his hand.

"Thank you, Mrs. Minnick," Terry said to her, his smile becoming more cordial as he turned it to the older woman. "We may take a walk in a bit. What time is dinner?"

The woman issued a small but expressive shrug.

"Whenever you come back," she told him, then returned to the house.

The lemonade was cold, sweet and wonderful. Philipa gulped the first glass without a thought for her manners, and was abashed until she noticed that Terry had done the same. He looked up at her, then at each of the empty glasses. He chuckled, that gentle, rumbling sound that always seemed as intimate to her as a kiss.

"Our drawing-room manners are slipping," he declared, refilling both of their glasses from the pitcher. "The next thing you know, we'll be licking our fingers instead of using napkins."

Indeed, the accompanying pastries were crisp and flavorful and light as air, and soon the plate was empty. Philipa resisted the urge to fulfill Terry's teasing prediction, amazed at how quickly she felt so at ease with him.

"Walk with me, Philly," he invited her, rising. "Or Mrs. Minnick will bring out another plate of these things, and we'll have to finish them, too."

Refreshed, she got up from her chair and accepted his out-stretched hand without a second thought. His long, strong fingers loosely entwined with her own, and the gesture was warm and deliciously possessive. He led her along a sandy path into the pines, where the smell of the forest mingled pleasantly with the salty scent of the bay somewhere beyond it. The cicadas, high in the trees around them, provided an unceasing chatter that all but drowned out the sounds of the gulls.

"This is such a pretty place, don't you think?"

Terry's hand had tightened upon her own. She loved the feel of it.

"This whole area is beautiful," she observed with no small twinge of pride. "When I left Braedon's Beach to go to college in the city, I thought I'd never return to it. To live, anyway. The city, it seemed to me then, was so alive with people, and culture, and possibilities. And I liked living among people who had so many different views of the world. But in the end, I missed the sea. With my mother gone, and after my father died, I found I wanted to come home. To maintain that connection with my family. If I were a man, I might have been a sailor. As it is, I must content myself with—"

She stopped herself, choking on her imprudence. Emma Hunt had very nearly stepped between them, and she had only caught her in time.

"With what?" Terry's voice was gently prompting.

"With my 'scholarly pursuits,' as Essie so disparagingly puts it," she managed, brushing a light band of perspiration off her brow.

For an awful moment, she thought Terry might challenge her remark, for it did not quite sound natural, even to her. But when he spoke again, it was on another matter entirely.

"I have always wanted to sail," was what he said, with an unmistakable note of wistfulness in his voice. "Many of my classmates at Princeton used to talk about yachting off Newport and Long Island."

"You would love it," she assured him, warming to his enthusiasm. "My father taught me the rudiments when I was very young. We had a small skiff that he would allow me to take out on the bay. My mother used to worry, but I was a good swimmer, and I only sailed in good weather. I shall have to teach you sometime."

"And I should love to learn. It must be a thrilling experience, to pit one's skill and strength against the whims of the elements in such a manner," Terry mused, sounding envious.

"I was once invited to summer with a fellow out on Long Island, but after I was dismissed, of course, it never materialized. The irony of it is that the fellow had done exactly the same thing as I had only the week before, but had not gotten caught."

Terry's tone had gone bitter, like dark coffee left too long on a hot stove. Philipa was aware of a stab of pity for him, although he did not seem to want it, nor, she was sure, would he have accepted it, had she offered any.

"What happened at Princeton, Terry?" she ventured softly, stopping before him. "Why did you not complete your studies?"

Terry's countenance was, if not grim, then certainly impassive as marble. She watched him draw in a long breath and expel it quickly as he looked over her shoulder at some unknown phenomenon beyond her.

"Surely you heard the gossip," he began in a hard voice which, she knew, was not directed at her. "I was dismissed for a fraternity prank. I don't want to go into details, because it involved—a young lady. If lady she can be called. Suffice it to say that I was robbed of my degree by my own stupidity."

"You are very hard on yourself," she told him, tugging on his sleeves. "Do you know that?"

He looked down at her, and the stony look in his mahogany eyes softened. His mouth, which he had drawn into a tight grimace, relaxed as he considered her.

"And you," he replied, pulling her close in a gentle embrace as he grinned, "would spoil me if I allowed it. I shall have to watch myself very carefully, I think."

"You are quite spoiled already, I fear," she teased him, unable to resist the urge to touch the dimple in his left cheek with the tip of her finger.

"I am," he agreed, kissing that finger lightly. "And I think it only fair to warn you that I intend to spoil you, as well. At every opportunity. You are a most delightful challenge to me, Miss Braedon. And I have never backed down from a challenge."

His smile vanished. In its place was a rapt expression. *Kiss me*, she had begged him, what seemed so long ago. As though responding to her sweet memory, he lifted her on her toes and took her mouth with his own. The fire he kindled raged through her body with breakneck speed and a thoroughness that left her will in ashes. He had robbed her of her reason again, and she thrilled to his mastery in awakening her most potent desires. If she was, as he had said, a challenge, then he had already overcome her, completely. Her mouth responded as if it had been created for the very pleasures his offered.

His kiss was many things at once. It was gentle. It was fierce. It was both teasing and inviting, and his tongue was unbearably adventurous. A small cry broke loose from her throat as his hand cradled her jaw and his fingers toyed with her earlobe. She wished suddenly, desperately, that they were alone in one of Mrs. Minnick's rooms . . .

Her cheeks burned at the very thought of it, and she pushed him away with one hand, weakly. Before her, Terry swallowed hard. His hot breath seared her neck.

"If you teach me to sail," he began in a throaty whisper that rooted itself somewhere deep in her loins, "what shall I teach you in return?"

She opened her eyes and found him, inches away, absorbing her with his unyielding gaze. There was but one answer to his question.

"Instruct me in your love," she whispered, holding on to his lapels because she knew she would fall if she released him. "And you will find me to be a most eager student."

His grin sent a ripple of anticipation down to the base of her spine.

"I think it only fair to warn you," he replied, still speaking in a hushed tone, "that I give rigorous examinations."

A shuddering sigh took her by surprise, and his magnificent arms tightened around her.

"Oh, I do hope so, Mr. Gavilan," she was able to murmur just before he plundered her mouth once again.

It was different, this time. She sensed a tension like the silent building of a great storm around them; inside of them. His kiss grew more demanding, and his fingers played upon her throat, tugging with astonishing expertise at the tiny buttons of her high black collar. Her hand was on his, and her sense told her to stop him while her desire began to assist him in his urgent mission. Within moments her throat was exposed, and he slipped his fingers impatiently inside, touching her collarbone. As he slid his hand downward, the buttons reluctantly gave way to his insistence. Her breath came in hard little gasps as his progress was halted just above her left breast.

Had he paused, or had the obstinate buttons thwarted him at last? Before she could speculate, the distant sound of children's voices approaching them reached her ears, and she tore away from him in alarm. His eyes were wide, and his face pale. Obviously, he had heard the sound too. It was as if a bucket of cold water had been thrown upon them from above.

Quickly she turned away from the sound. Her fingers shook maddeningly as she fumbled with the buttons on her bodice. She had barely completed the task when two boys and two girls, the oldest perhaps twelve and the youngest seven or eight, came out of the woods a mere five feet in front of her and Terry. They were breathless and laughing in their wet underclothing, their hair clinging to their heads and their eyes bright with exercise. They stopped dead as they beheld, as one, the spectacle of the two adult figures in black. What must we look like to them? Philipa wondered, aghast at her own behavior and at the fear in their young faces. Terry, too, seemed overcome, for he offered no comment to the children.

A tranquil male voice filtered out of the woods in a language Philipa could neither identify nor comprehend. She perceived at once that it must be Mr. Minnick, the children's father, calling for them. Sure enough, a moment later a middle-aged man appeared, not very tall, but slender, wearing a greatcoat that barely concealed his swimming costume. His hair was completely white, but his face was unlined. His European features fell into a warm smile.

"Dober Dan, Mr. Gavilan!" he exclaimed, in the same accented tones as his wife. "Zlatka! Srechko! Remember Mr. Gavilan? Say hello!"

Gavilan was shaking. Moments ago a thunderous display

of fireworks had been waiting to go off inside him, and he'd been obliged, at the very last second, to cut the fuse. He risked a glance at Philipa. She had righted herself quickly but was undeniably pale, except for the circle of crimson upon each cheek. He sensed that she could not look at him.

Remembering to speak, he greeted Mr. Minnick and the children, whose florid Slavic names he'd forgotten. His voice, he noticed with some satisfaction, was robust and cordial in spite of his reeling senses.

Philipa could not be drawn into any conversation during dinner, and she would only steal furtive glances at him, then quickly look away when she realized she had caught his eye. He guessed she was flustered, not to say mortified, by what had happened, although he could not help but wonder whether her embarrassment was due to the interruption, or to the activity which had been interrupted.

She had wanted him, as surely as he had wanted her. Of that he had no doubt. Her teasing words and the invitation of her eyes had been unmistakable. In fact, he admitted to himself, watching her stare fixedly at the half-eaten plate of food before her, her words had practically done more, or at least as much, to titillate him as her physical willingness. There had been something inspired about the poetry they had shared. Something that had aroused to memory a strong hint of one of Emma Hunt's innocently sensual heroines . . .

"I'm afraid I am not very hungry. Please excuse me, and offer my apologies to Mrs. Minnick. It's quite good. I just can't—"

Her soft words splintered his musings, and he hastily rose from the table as she did. His gesture seemed to fluster her into meeting his gaze. She hesitated, then quickly left the table.

He followed her outside to the porch, where she stood with her back toward him, framed against the sunset like a fragile young willow tree. Looking at her, he wished for the eloquence of one of Mrs. Hunt's heros.

"I feel so foolish," he heard her say in a muffled voice before he could speak. "I can't begin to understand what has gotten into me. I love you, Terry, you must know that. And I—I want you, too. But there is something—terribly wrong here. If the expressions of four children can make me feel like a criminal, or a—a—I can't begin to imagine how I'd feel facing my friends and neighbors every day, knowing that I—that we—''

He felt her pain and her confusion as keenly as if they were his own, deep in his gut. His hands were upon her shoulders suddenly, although he did not recall having crossed the porch to where she stood.

''You have very rigid and exacting standards for yourself which you don't apply to anyone else.'' He was, he knew, gently rebuking, and he could not resist pressing his cheek against her soft, fragrant hair. ''And I love you so much that I can't even find the words to express it, except for these: would you do me the very great honor of becoming my wife?''

Her body leaned back against his slightly, and he thought she might faint. But instead she turned to him, wearing a look that made him want to crush her in his embrace.

''Terry, you're sure?''

Her voice was as soft as a caress. His heart wanted to explode with joy.

''My darling Philipa.'' He breathed, his arms finding their way around her even as he searched her tender gaze. ''I have never been more sure of anything in my entire reprobate life. Will you have me, or are you trying to decide how best to mock me, this time?''

He could sense rather than see her blush in the fading light, and he smiled, knowing her answer.

Chapter Twenty-seven

Gavilan came in to the office late, and he was whistling. Owen Parrish looked up from his work, adjusting his ink-stained sleeve guards as the annoyingly tall and handsomely groomed entrepreneur passed by his desk. Gavilan, to his dismay, was swaggering like a carefree schoolboy.

Had he discovered Emma Hunt? Had he breached the citadel that was Philipa Braedon? Owen discovered that he himself was sweating profusely at both thoughts. And it looked as though Gavilan was not about to volunteer the reason for his uncommonly good mood. Damn him.

"You're looking pretty chipper for a man who spent the day at a funeral yesterday," he greeted his employer, barely able to control his hostility.

Gavilan, to his surprise, looked him right in the eye, still smiling broadly.

"I'm getting married, Owe," he announced, looking, the secretary thought, for all the world as though he credited himself for the invention of the institution.

Parrish restrained his urge to break his blotter over Gavilan's head.

"Really?" He managed a congenially derisive tone. "This is an unexpected development. Who's the unlucky bride-to-be?"

Gavilan laughed, tossing his skimmer to the peg on the wall. He missed, and did not so much as mutter an oath as he stooped to retrieve it.

"Come now, Owen, not even you could be *that* dense," his boss mocked him. "Philipa Braedon, of course."

Parrish digested this, sitting perfectly still. One wedding, he thought, watching the smile broaden upon Gavilan's boyish features, which will never take place.

"Does Elliot Waverly know of this change in his plans?" was what he asked Gavilan finally, looking back down at his work while affecting what he hoped was a bored tone. It would not do to allow Gavilan to guess at his dismay. Not, at least, until he had divined the extent of Gavilan's knowledge of and adventures with the said Miss Braedon. And Gavilan, he knew from experience, possessed an uncanny ability to anticipate people's thoughts. Which might, he ruminated further, account in part for the man's legendary success in his business.

Gavilan did not respond to his admittedly rude question immediately, and Parrish could tell he was standing before him, in front of the desk.

"Congratulations?"

Gavilan's baritone was a snide imitation of the mocking tone Parrish recognized at once. It was the same one he himself had employed on the morning when Elliot Waverly had made a similar announcement to a roomful of men at the Town Hall. Parrish considered his response. Gavilan was smart, he knew. Too smart. But the secretary suspected his boss's judgment might be impaired this time by this improbable, almost laughable, infatuation with that chilly, straitlaced pretender to innocence, Philipa Braedon.

But had she confided her secret to him? Parrish was burning to know. He wanted desperately to look at Gavilan, to peer into the man's very soul, if he had to, to learn the truth of it. Then he had a most pleasant revelation.

If Terence Gavilan had indeed learned the secret of Emma

Hunt, he would certainly want to boast of it to his secretary.
Parrish allowed himself a small sigh of relief. As long as
Emma Hunt clung to her secret, he was certain this otherwise
unlikely union would fall apart of its own accord. Nevertheless, he could not afford to leave anything to chance. Not
where both Terence Gavilan and Emma Hunt were concerned.
Feigning indifference, he shrugged, still not looking up at his
employer.

"Congratulations, I guess," he said, keeping his hands
steady as he guided the pen across the page before him. "Or
perhaps an expression of condolence would be more in order?"

He looked up, not in the least surprised, or concerned, to
see that Brownie was scowling at him.

"Damn it, Owen, for once in your miserable life, can't you
be happy for somebody else?"

Parrish allowed himself to invent a note of despair in Gavilan's self-assured voice. He held the younger man's grimace.

"Since when do you look for my approbation for your
activities?" Parrish countered, placing his pen down deliberately before folding his hands on the desk before him. "It
used to be you never asked my opinion unless you hadn't
really made up your mind about something."

That was not quite what Brownie had asked him, he knew.
But perhaps he could redirect the conversation. Perhaps he
could plant a small but fertile seed of doubt . . .

"Damn it, I'm not asking for your approbation, you presumptuous ass!" was the crackling retort he heard as Gavilan
paced away from him. "But as you pointed out to me several
weeks ago, it is customary to offer some sort of acknowledgment of such an announcement. And aren't you even a little
curious about it?"

Parrish yawned.

"I might be if I thought it would last," he said at the end
of it. "But I know you too well, Brownie. That Braedon
woman has gotten under your skin like some kind of an itch.
You wanted her right off, because you knew you couldn't
have her. She belonged to that Waverly sap. You remind me
of a dog I had as a kid. He'd try like hell to catch the pigeons

in the park. Must have thought they were the tastiest things
in the world. Then one day the poor bastard caught one, and
all he got was a damn mouthful of bones and feathers. Sorriest
looking mess you ever saw.''

Gavilan looked pained.

''Is there a point to this rather unflattering comparison?''

Parrish shrugged, pleased with the way his impromptu
monologue was playing out.

''Only that the dog wanted that damned pigeon so badly,
then hadn't the first idea in the world of what to do with his
unexpected mouthful once he got her. Am I going too fast
for you, or do you see the analogy?''

Gavilan had begun staring at him in a most unsettling way,
and he started to think that perhaps he had overstepped his
admittedly broad bounds. He held his tongue, hoping Gavilan
would speak next.

''You know, this is really funny, Owe,'' Gavilan mused,
not blinking as he considered the secretary. ''I don't think she
cares very much for you, either. Do you really dislike her all
that much, or are you just jealous to think that somebody
might be closer to me than you are?''

Parrish had to restrain himself from laughing. Jealous!
Him! Of Philipa Braedon? He stared back at his boss, almost
pitying him. If you only knew, Brownie, he thought, shaking
his head as he smiled. If you only knew that your prim and
correct little Miss Braedon was actually the literarily lusty
Emma Hunt!

By God, that was it!

Parrish got up from his work, stretching a little. This was
going to be fun, he thought.

''Maybe you'll understand this parable.'' Parrish affected
a patient tone, glancing at Gavilan once to be sure he had his
attention. ''My cousin Harriman fell in love with a girl who
reminded me a lot of your Miss Braedon. She had gone to
Radcliffe. Smart, like her. Pretty enough, too, if you over-
looked the spectacles. Harriman courted that girl forever,
waiting on her rationed kisses and genteel protests of chastity,
certain he was going to unleash all of her hidden passions on

their wedding night. Do you know what happened to poor old Harriman?''

''What?'' Gavilan's voice was hard, but he had taken the bait.

''Nothing,'' Parrish laughed, sensing a measure of success. ''Absolutely nothing. Old Harriman discovered the hard way that there wasn't anything more to the woman after all, in spite of himself. He found that beneath that cool exterior was an even cooler interior. Harriman stuck it out though, poor bastard. Of course, I doubt Harriman ever had one-tenth the women you've had, so he probably never really knew what he was missing. And knowing you, you'd rather chew off your own leg than admit to a mistake like that, so you'll be just like him. Only you *will* know. And that's the real tragedy of it.''

Tragedy. Gavilan stared hard at Parrish, hating him for reminding him of Oscar Wilde's cynical pronouncement. Parrish was a crude and mean little bastard, and he wanted to choke him. Cousin Harriman, indeed! Trust Parrish to spin some wild tale just to try and spoil his good mood.

''You don't know what you're talking about,'' he muttered, but could not deny the spark of doubt the story inspired.

Suppose, after all, Philipa's ardor *was* feigned? Suppose—just suppose—he was to discover on their wedding night that all of her coy reticence had been a facade for a passionless, even frigid, personality. He shuddered, then immediately felt ashamed at such a demonstration before his secretary, and at his disloyalty to his betrothed.

''I don't give a damn about your dog, or your cousin, or you. And the next time I want your opinion on any of those topics, I'll be certain to ask for it. I'm marrying Philipa Braedon, Owen, so you may as well get used to the idea.''

Owen merely shrugged.

''I can if you can, boss,'' he replied, settling back in his chair to return to his work. ''After all, I won't be wearing the yoke. Excuse me. I meant to say 'ring.' ''

Gavilan did not trouble himself to reply. He stood by the window behind his own desk, thinking about Philipa in the woods at Mrs. Minnick's.

*   *   *

"Philipa, what can you have been thinking of?"

It was a warm morning, but Philipa was certain the temperature had nothing whatever to do with Charles Tavistock's ruby complexion. The banker had been announced moments earlier, and he greeted her standing in the middle of her parlor rug, clenching and unclenching his gloved fists.

"Good morning, Charles."

She had a theory as to Charles's unusual early morning visit without his wife, but she had decided to allow him to speak. It was always more amusing when Charles was permitted to make a complete ass of himself without any interference.

"I see nothing good about it!" he huffed, glaring at her. "Elliot is devastated, Philipa. He has lost his mother and his fiancé! And for what? For the sake of a—a libertine rogue who ruins young women the same way he ruins communities! Look, for example, at what he did to Jessamyn Flaherty. Why, the poor girl can't even walk down a respectable street anymore."

"Jessamyn Flaherty could not have done that long before Terence Gavilan came to Braedon's Beach."

"That is completely beside the point, Philipa, and you know it!" Charles retorted, pacing in a small, tight circle as he wagged a finger at her.

"Kindly keep your voice down, Charles. Remember, the girl's sister works in my home."

Philipa knew she should invite him to sit down, but her real inclination was to invite him to leave. Still, he was her best friend's husband, even if he was a pompous ass. She would, she decided, grant him the courtesy of listening to his tirade. For a few minutes anyway.

"What exactly is the point, Charles?" she inquired patiently, crossing her arms in front of her. "That you are attempting to interfere in something that does not concern you? Or does this outburst of yours reflect the more personal matter of the recent falling out you and Terry have had?"

Charles reddened still further.

"What—what has he told you about that?" he demanded,

his round jaw slack and his eyes wide.

"Nothing at all," she assured him. But I shall certainly ask him at the very next opportunity, she thought, still watching him.

"That's just as well," Charles hissed, averting his stare to the rug. "The man is a known liar. Has he told you what his plans are for Braedon's Beach?"

Philipa felt a tiny shudder of foreboding.

"No, he hasn't," she admitted before she had intended to speak. An arcade, an amusement pier, and possibly a casino. Those were the items mentioned in Terry's original proposal, the one scrutinized and ultimately approved by the Advisory Board, she recalled.

"Of course he hasn't!" Charles exclaimed, waving his hands as though practicing semaphore signals. "Because he knows you would protest! He plans to turn Somers House into a lavish casino and—and fancy house, Philipa. I have it on the very best of authority. And if he marries you, his plans are assured. As a wife, you would not be in a position to stand in his way, legally. Don't you see, Philipa? He has been using you in the most atrocious, most despicable of ways, just to get what he wants!"

Philipa heard him, but he had begun to sound as if he were very far away. For a brief, horrifying moment, she thought she was going to faint, right in front of Charles Tavistock. She mastered herself. That must not happen.

"Charles." She trained her voice to a calm tone she was far from feeling. "Do you realize what you're saying? According to you, Terence Gavilan would no doubt have had to marry several women along the way, for no better reason than to ensure his plans. Come now, Charles. Not even you could believe such a far-fetched fantasy!"

It was Charles's turn to cross his arms before him, regarding her with a satisfied, even triumphant, expression.

"And how do you know he has not?"

For the first time, Philipa was sorry she had not invited Charles to sit down. She felt as though her own legs would not support her much longer.

"What proof have you that he has?"

Charles's expression changed. Philipa had seen him look at his own wife in that way. It was a patronizing expression, and she detested it. He took two steps toward her and she wanted to back away from him, but she could not.

"My dear Philipa," he said in a gentler tone, holding out his hands in supplication. "You are my wife's best friend. You will, in all likelihood, be my son's godmother. I have come here today to beg you—to plead with you—to see reason. Terence Gavilan is using you. He means to have his way in Braedon's Beach, Philipa, and if that means deceiving and ruining you in the process, he won't hesitate to do that, either. Please, Philipa. You must believe me. Ask yourself this: what reason would I have to lie?"

Philipa considered him. A great, crushing weight pressed inside of her. She loved Terry. Love meant trusting. At least, she had always thought it did. Didn't all of Emma Hunt's heroines, without exception, trust unfailingly in their heros? And had their heros ever failed them? A broken sigh caught her off guard. Real-life héros, as she had learned all too well at Bryn Mawr, often had feet of clay. And what of Terry? Terry, whose tender caress she could still feel upon her cheek? Terry, whose dark, adoring eyes made her want to yield her very soul to him?

" 'The wicked are like chaff which the wind blows away,' Philipa." Charles's tone was restrained and quiet. For once, Philipa noted, his biblical metaphor was not mixed. "For Elliot it is too late. As his dearest friend, I can tell you that his pride has been utterly crushed. He could never take you back, I fear. But it is not yet too late to preserve your good name, Philipa, and the name of your family. Terence Gavilan has laid waste to more than his fair share of communities, and, sadly, of women. Ladies. But you may yet salvage your reputation among your friends and acquaintances by renouncing him. The choice is yours. Go forward with this folly, and risk ridicule and ruin. Or end it, here and now, and keep your family's honor intact."

She had behaved foolishly. In a totally irrational fashion, she had abandoned all the ideals and precepts in which she had been so carefully schooled all of her life. She had only acted this way at one other time in her life, and it was not a time she enjoyed calling to mind. She stared at Charles, unable to guess at her expression. She only knew that she felt as though the floor beneath her had given way, and that she stood suspended by a hair over a great chasm. She fought an urge to turn and run and try to claw her way back to safety.

This was horribly unfair to Terry, she realized, ashamed. She straightened her spine and forced herself to return Charles's stare with a chilly one of her own which befitted a Braedon.

"Thank you for your interest in my well-being, Charles," she said gravely. "However, I must ask you to leave my house. It is my intention to marry Terence Gavilan, and it would require far more proof than you have been able to substantiate in order for me to change my mind. For the sake of my friendship with Essie, I hope I have heard the last of these baseless accusations."

There, she thought, breathing an inward sigh of relief. Even Charles must be persuaded that I am resolute.

Why, then, am I having these terrible, terrible doubts?

Charles's mouth tightened to a hairline, and his nostrils flared.

"You are a silly, foolish woman, Philipa Braedon!" he declared. "After Terence Gavilan has made you a complete laughingstock, you'll remember my advice and wish you had heeded it while you might have. I wash my hands of this affair! And I will tell you right here and now that I don't ever want that man to set foot in my home, for any reason! Do I make myself clear?"

A favorite expression of Charles's, Philipa reflected dispassionately, returning his stare with far more equanimity than she felt.

"I have never known you not to, Charles." She managed to maintain a civil tone in spite of the challenge to her breeding. "Good morning."

She left Charles Tavistock alone in her parlor, neither knowing nor caring how he found his way out of her house. So long as he left it, that was enough for her.

But the damage, she knew with an awful sense of foreboding, was done. The seeds of distrust had not been cast upon stone, after all. She retreated to her study and sat at her desk before her typewriter for five full minutes before she noticed the new paper in the platen.

Chapter Twenty-eight

"I know your secrets Emma Hunt"

Philipa stared at the page before her. She was still shaking from her confrontation with Charles, and still reeling from the implications of their discourse. Now this brazen white banner from her nocturnal visitor, who apparently was incapable of punctuating even the simplest of statements!

It was too ridiculous for words. Her response began as a giggle, deep in her chest, and quickly crescendoed to a laugh which bordered on hysteria. You claim to know my secrets, do you? she thought disdainfully, staring at the page. And Charles professes to know what is best for me. What more could a woman ask of this absurd life?

Suddenly she was angry. This intruder, whoever he was, apparently meant to hold her hostage in her own home. So he knew—or suspected—her secret identity. So what? Did that give him the right to terrorize her with it? She played her fingers rapidly against her thumbs, her thoughts racing. What would the intruder do, she wondered, feeling reckless, if she confronted him? On paper, of course. The idea was intoxicating. In a surge of euphoric energy, she began typing a response, so quickly that she did not even watch the page before her.

"Sir:

You are a coward. Your tactics are contemptible, and I challenge you to reveal your identity to me."

She examined the page when she was finished, and made a startling discovery.

The note composed by the intruder had not been typed on her typewriter, but on another machine altogether. The ribbon was not even the same shade of black, and the typeface was subtly different from her own Smith Corona. Amazed by this fact, she liberated the sheet from the platen and examined it more closely.

Even the paper was different, she noticed, rubbing the vellum between her thumb and forefinger. She held the sheet up to the light. It bore a Philadelphia watermark and was of remarkably fine quality. Too fine for an ordinary person to use for everyday correspondence. In fact, she seldom saw paper of that quality on any but the most professional of communications, usually from her attorneys or other businesses. Her own paper came from Hammonton and was of good enough stock for her manuscripts, but nowhere near the texture of the sheet she held in her hand. Why, it had a weight to it.

The question then plagued her: Who in Braedon's Beach possessed, and used, paper of such remarkable quality on a regular basis? Quickly she made a mental list of candidates. The first person she thought of was Charles Tavistock. The idea seemed so ludicrous that she nearly dismissed it out of hand. But he was a banker. He certainly had access both to the paper and the machinery required for such messages. Father Michaels? She rejected that idea at once, ashamed of herself for even thinking of him. There was, however, Terence Gavilan . . .

She shook her shoulders, hard. No, she thought firmly. This is precisely what this craven terrorist wants me to do, and I will not yield to his vile whims. Resolutely she set the paper aside in a drawer, making a mental note to return it to the platen of her typewriter that very evening before she retired. She always locked her study at night, so there was virtually no chance that Mrs. Grant or Arliss would stumble upon it before she opened it the following morning. We shall shortly see, she thought, what sort of man we are dealing with. And he shall shortly find out what sort of woman he has undertaken to harass.

By late afternoon, Philipa was applying the finishing touches to Mrs. Hunt's last book, *The Tender Trap*. It was with a combination of relief and regret that she closed the final chapter, reflecting soberly on the implications of the act as they related to her personal life. Emma Hunt was dead, but she was leaving behind a final monument to the triumph of pure, true love over the temptations of a weary and decadent world. Philipa sighed heavily, rereading the final passage:

> *"You have taught me so much, my sweet Sarah," Jack whispered, clasping his hands firmly about Sarah's waspish waist. "What shall I teach you, in return?"*
> *"Instruct me in your love," was what Sarah replied simply, allowing the flaming Rocky Mountain sunset to take the credit for her blush.*

Would Terry, she wondered, if she ever revealed herself to him, be flattered or insulted by the plagiarism? She smiled to herself, thinking of Terry. He would probably be amused by it. In fact, she thought, encouraged by her musings, he would probably be greatly entertained by the fact that she had written as Emma Hunt.

If he wasn't utterly furious with her for keeping such a secret, that is.

She placed a fresh paper in the platen and began a letter to Royal Godfrey which would accompany the manuscript. She intended for it to be a brief note, but was halfway through page two when she heard the knock upon the study door.

"It's open, Mrs. Grant," she called, not wanting to disturb her train of thought.

The knocking ceased, and a gentle breeze alerted her that the door had been opened. In a moment, to her astonishment, there were gentle hands upon her shoulders and a pair of warm, tickling lips teasing her neck.

"Oh, dear God!"

She leaped from her chair and Terry jumped back a good six feet, laughing.

"I'm sorry I startled you, Philly," he told her, his eyes merry. "But when no one answered my knock and I found your front door open, I came in looking for you myself. I hope you aren't disappointed that it's me instead of Mrs. Grant. Were you expecting your tea?"

Philipa could only stare at Terry for a minute, uncertain whether she was terrified or furious at his unexpected appearance.

"T-Terry," she said, feeling incredibly stupid as she sidled in between him and her typewriter. "What—what are you doing here?"

He looked mildly offended.

"Visiting my fiancée, I thought." He straightened his jacket as he narrowed the distance between them. "Have you been working?"

She backed into the desk, desperately trying to compose herself.

"No. Yes," she stammered, gripping the edge of the desk. "I am. I mean, I was. Just some correspondence. I—I can't imagine why no one answered the door. Shall we go into the parlor?"

"No, I like it here," he replied easily, not seeming to notice her discomfiture. "It reminds me of how very much I have to learn about you. I see, for example, that I'll probably have to furnish the study at Somers House with two sets of everything."

His remark stunned her into silence. Somers House? But of course. Where else would he have expected to live after they were married? Somers House was, after all, far larger, and a far more grand place than her own home. And she hadn't expected to remain in her home on the beach for the rest of her life.

Terry placed his hands on her arms and rested his gaze on her face. She watched as his handsome, angular features clouded with concern.

"Is anything wrong, Philipa? You're not still upset by my abrupt appearance, are you?"

She took in a hard, shuddering breath, hugging her arms to her chest. She fixed her stare upon his pumpkin-colored silk tie.

"I—No. Yes. I—I'm sorry, Terry. I was just—I was concentrating on my work, and I—I never expected—"

She could not go on. She was trapped, with Terence Gavilan in front of her and Royal Godfrey and Emma Hunt behind her. Terry chuckled, reaching for her with one hand and pulling her recklessly into his arms.

"I'm sorry, sweetheart," he murmured, nuzzling her ear in a way that made her shiver. "My God, you are frightened! You're trembling! Here, let me—"

He clasped his hands together behind her back, holding her firmly before him as he sought her lips. She allowed his kiss, fleetingly. When it deepened, however, she broke away from it, looking over his shoulder to the open door of the study.

"Terry!" she scolded him in a whisper. "Someone might come in!"

She felt his hand on her chin, and he directed her gaze to his own. He was not smiling, as he had been.

"We're engaged, Philly. There's no harm in it, even if someone sees us. I've been shut in my office all day with Owen Parrish, thinking about kissing you. If you think I'm going to wait until we're married to—"

Impulsively, she sprang forward in his arms and stopped his mouth with her own. She had intended only to mollify him with a brief kiss, but soon discovered that he had no intention of letting her go so quickly. Against her will, she allowed herself to enjoy his kiss before she remembered that Terry was facing her typewriter, along with the letter to Royal Godfrey containing references she did not want to explain. She wriggled to free herself from his embrace.

He held her back by the shoulders. His dark eyes narrowed like slivers of dark, shiny metal.

"Philipa, what's wrong with you today?" he demanded, shaking her once, gently. "You're fighting me! Why?"

Philipa could not sustain that gaze. *Tell him!* some part of her urged. *Tell him about Emma Hunt and her secret tormentor! Father Michaels even said it was the best thing to do! No*, she told herself, seeing the anger in his eyes. *I'll tell him sometime when we are both calm, and alone together.*

But you were calm, and alone together at Mrs. Minnick's, yesterday, her inner voice argued with her. *You are procrastinating, Philipa. And it will only lead to trouble.*

She hung her head, trying to collect herself.

"I'll tell you," she managed in a quiet, shaking voice. "But in the parlor. Please. I—I feel more at ease there."

"I knew there must be something troubling you," he scolded her as she led him from the study by the hand, closing and locking the doors behind them. "Philipa, surely you know there isn't anything you can't tell me. I want to share your burdens, but I can't do that unless I know what they are."

She tried to compose her thoughts, but the five steps from the back of the hall to the doors of the front parlor offered not nearly enough time or space for her to accomplish that feat. She drew back the doors and admitted him to the darkened room.

She realized at once the error of bringing Terry in there. He did not like the room, she knew. Its furnishings he had described as dreary and cumbersome. The darkness of the room only enhanced the effect. The room was kept shielded by shutters against the heat of the afternoon, but it was still noticeably warmer there than it had been in her study. And she was already warm, owing to her dread of revealing her secret to him. She invited him to sit down, and he chose the settee, leaving ample room for her to join him.

She did not. A trickle of sweat edged down her spine, untouched by her stays. The sensation reminded her of how very hot, and how very confined, she felt.

"Now, what's this all about?"

Terry's words were stern, but his voice was as gentle as a caress. She sighed, forcing herself to face him.

"Terry, there are things I haven't told you," she began. The words clung to her, begging her to keep them inside. "About me. Things . . . I hardly know where to begin . . ."

"Are you quite sure you want to tell me?"

He was sitting very still, and his dark eyes were sober and unblinking. She caught her breath, and nodded.

"You don't have to tell me, you know, Philipa," he went on, almost, she thought suddenly, as if he might not want to hear them. "We'll have no secrets from one another as husband and wife, but I think we're both mature enough to understand that each of us may have done some foolish things in the past. Things better forgotten rather than brought up for the sole purpose of starting with a clean slate. As long as our slates are clean with one another, we needn't allow the mistakes of the past to mar the future, need we?"

My God, Gavilan thought. That was all he needed! To be forced, by Philipa's integrity, to recount every disgraceful act in his own past, just because she felt compelled to confess to him her indiscretion with that Bryn Mawr professor! Gavilan could not recall the half of his own transgressions, much less did he have any desire to share them with her. His mouth went dry as he witnessed her struggle for words. It was too painful to watch.

"But Terry, this is—you must understand that I—that I am—"

He could not bear it any longer. Quickly, so quickly that he nearly upset one of the garishly ornate end tables, he went to her. He touched her shoulder lightly, determined not to allow her to put herself, or him, through this futile, possibly treacherous and certainly unwise exercise.

"I know, Philipa," he whispered in swift interruption, gazing into her eyes as he held her face in his two hands. "Please don't do this to yourself." *Or to me*, he thought, feeling only a little guilty for his selfish motivation. "I know all about it, and it doesn't matter to me at all."

Philipa returned his look with an expression of utter amazement on her lovely, shadowed features.

"You—you knew?" She sounded as though she could scarcely breathe. "How?"

"I—" He hesitated, damning himself for not having anticipated the incriminating question before admitting to the knowledge.

Philipa stared at him in undisguised wonder, and his tongue

momentarily cleaved to his mouth. He felt as though he had unknowingly disrobed in a glass room. He moistened his lips and swallowed the lump in his throat, not allowing himself to look away from her.

He could not lie. But he could color the truth a little. He drew in a sharp breath.

"You intrigued me from the very first," he began, wondering how the room had become so stifling in so short a time. "And as a businessman, I have a habit of thoroughly investigating people who interest me, or with whom I intend to do business."

Philipa could not seem to sustain his gaze any longer.

"I—I had thought I was so very careful," she murmured, sounding disappointed. "How long—how long have you known?"

Gavilan, sensing her capitulation, allowed his arms to encircle her.

"Almost from the very beginning, sweetheart," he told her, noticing with no small relief that she was no longer stiff and uncompliant in his embrace. "I sent Owen off to—"

"Owen!" She appeared dismayed, and drew back from him. "Owen Parrish? He knows, too?"

Instantly he was on the alert again. He had forgotten about her dislike for his secretary. Ruing his oversight, he nodded.

"Yes, he does," Gavilan admitted. "But he is sworn to confidence. And anyway, my darling, it all happened so very long ago. Why must we allow it to create trouble between us now?"

Philipa appeared confused, meeting his gaze again.

"Long ago?"

He forced himself to smile, wanting to set her mind at ease.

"You graduated in '98, did you not?" he reminded her, seeking to smooth her puckered brow with the back of his index finger. "And the professor had been fired in '97. I assume, therefore, that the incident occurred prior to that. And even if it didn't, what's the difference? It changes nothing. Nothing, Philipa. Not the way I feel about you, nor, I hope, your feelings for me?"

Philipa stared at him in a most peculiar and somewhat unsettling manner. As though she suddenly did not recognize him. Her stare continued, and he grew uneasy. What had he said? What would she, in turn, ask him?

"The—the professor?"

Her voice sounded weak. He thought she might faint.

"Philipa," he ventured, taking hold of her arms. "Sit down. Please."

"N-no," she said hesitantly, her own hands in turn grasping his arms. "I'm all right. I—just a little stunned, I think. I—I'm still trying to understand . . ."

She looked so fragile that he could not restrain himself from enfolding her to his breast again, gently but firmly.

"Oh, my sweet, sweet love," he breathed, pressing his lips against her temple. "How could you think that my feelings would be so ambivalent as to be swayed by so trivial a thing? It isn't"—he managed a laugh, wanting to lighten her humor—"as if you had confessed to being Lizzie Borden!"

In his embrace, Philipa trembled. No, she agreed silently. But to some, the name of Emma Hunt might be equally, if not surpassingly, unpalatable. She allowed herself to be comforted by his closeness, unwilling to think beyond the enticements of his arms.

"It doesn't matter," he whispered, and she felt his hand in her hair. "It means nothing. I love you, Philipa. Nothing can alter that fact. I hope you feel the same for me. I would hope there could be nothing that would turn you against me."

You would not be in a position to stand in his way, was how Charles had put it earlier. She shuddered again, in spite of Terry's embrace. Oh, Charles, she thought. What serpents have you unleashed? She drew in a deep breath.

"Nothing," she repeated, "except betrayal."

His arms fell away from her. He stood perfectly erect, two feet in front of her, staring at her without a trace of amusement on his handsome, concerned features.

"Betrayal!" he ejaculated in a disbelieving whisper. "Philipa, what—what can you mean?"

She maintained his gaze, hoping to pierce the mask of deceit, if one existed. But how would she know?

"Somers House," she said quietly, her stomach in so many

knots that she wondered how she was able to stand upright. "A Long Branch casino, right here in Braedon's Beach. Was it to have been a surprise, Terry? Or were you planning to tell me about it before the wedding?"

His arms hung limp at his sides. His dark eyes widened, and his wide mouth went slack. He moistened his lips with the tip of his tongue. He did not look away from her.

"Where did you hear about that?"

Philipa felt the crush of a deadly weight press upon her breast. So it was true, after all. She could no longer bear to look at him.

"Charles Tavistock was here earlier," she replied, staring at the tiny diamond pin in his necktie. "I didn't believe him at first."

"But you believe him now?"

Terry's voice had gone hard as ground glass.

"It was something you said to me a minute ago. Please don't lie to me, Terry," she got out, preventing a sob from following it. "I can tolerate anything from you but a lie. Are you planning to turn Somers House into a gambling hall?"

The room was silent, and dark as death. The sun must have disappeared behind a cloud, creating a ghastly mosaic of shadows upon his angular face.

"Would you recognize the truth if you heard it?"

His words pierced the gloom like shafts of fire.

"If you tell me it isn't true, I'll believe you," she got out in a small voice, still unable to look at him.

"That isn't what you said a moment ago, Philipa," he reminded her, placing his hands at his waist. "Do you think I would lie to you? Look at me!"

Her heart shuddered, and she glanced once at his face, long enough to see that his dark eyebrows met uncompromisingly over the bridge of his nose.

"Look at me, Philipa!" he said again, louder. "Look at me and make your hearsay accusations. Charles Tavistock! Good Lord, Philipa, the man despises me! He would have told you anything to turn you against me!"

Philipa said nothing. Her throat had constricted, as if Charles Tavistock had fastened his hands around her neck and choked her. She swallowed hard, but that did not lessen her distress.

"And why is that? For a while it seemed that you two were the best of friends."

Gavilan felt a pain low down in his gut, as though he'd been kicked hard enough for his attacker to have left an impression. And as if that were not bad enough, someone had then come along to pour hot acid into the void. Philipa suddenly seemed to be on the other side of a narrow but unbreachable chasm.

"That isn't really important, is it?" he said. "What is important is that you believe me to have lied to you, and to be capable of lying to you again. I had planned to convert Somers House into a casino, originally. But something happened to me on the Fourth of July which altered not only the course of my plans for Somers House, but for my very life, as well. You were a part of that, Philipa. A large part, it's true, but only a part of it nonetheless. You see, I met myself that day. And I saw an opportunity to do something, for once, of which I could be truly proud. Do you believe me?"

Philipa looked stricken. He longed to gather her into his arms again, but that chasm between them prevented him from doing so. He wondered, looking at her, if that chasm, quarried by doubt and distrust and Charles Tavistock, would ever close again.

"I do," Philipa answered him, sounding wounded. "But that doesn't matter anymore, does it?"

So she realized. The damage had been done. Gavilan took in a hard, broken sigh, and released it all at once.

"No," he replied, more weary than angry. "No, it doesn't."

He closed the door behind him, and it was a long while before he could rid himself of the image of her, standing in that dark, monstrous parlor.

Chapter Twenty-nine

Philipa spent a warm and restless night in her room. Not a breath of air stirred the curtains, even a hot one. She felt as though she might have perished and gone to hell, a dark, inhospitable place where pitiless demons pounded upon her skull with hammers. She was unwilling to go downstairs because of her fear of encountering her phantom visitor, and unable to sleep for recalling her ugly confrontation with Terry.

She knew she had hurt him by her indictment. She could tell by the expression on his face when she had uttered it. It had seemed as though she had struck him, hard. But accusations, like spilled cream, were impossible to reclaim.

How could she make it up to him? she wondered all that night. For make it up she would. She must. Somehow. She could not bear to think it had ended. She could not bear to think that Charles's horrid accusations, and her own distrust, would have led them to an irrevocable parting. She could not bear to believe she had destroyed his love with her incautious, not to say foolish, misgivings.

She dozed off just before dawn, fitfully. When Mrs. Grant

307

called for her, she opened her eyes, stunned to discover that gray daylight filled her bedroom.

"Miss Braedon?"

Mrs. Grant's voice sounded incredulous. And no wonder, thought Philipa, rolling clumsily to a sitting position on the bed. It must be quite late. Ordinarily she was an early riser.

"I'm here, Mrs. Grant." She suppressed a yawn. "What is it?"

"You have a caller."

Instantly Philipa was on her feet, yanking her nightgown over her head.

"Is it Ter—Mr. Gavilan?" she asked, imbued with energy. "Tell him I'll be—"

"No, miss, it's Father Michaels."

Philipa's disappointment was painful.

"Oh," she murmured, sitting down on the bed again. "Please ask him if I may call upon him later. I—I'm afraid I overslept."

And I feel as though I might have died sometime during the night, she thought miserably.

"He says it's rather important, Miss Braedon, and he'll wait."

Philipa sighed, rubbing her eyes with the heels of her hands.

"Very well, Mrs. Grant. Tell him he may have to."

It took her nearly twenty minutes to wash and dress, and to secure her hair into a hasty bun at the back of her neck. She glanced at herself in the mirror, and was dismayed to see that she looked as though she had been crying. Her eyes were puffy and somewhat red, and the pale skin around them was mottled with red blotches. Well, there was no help for it. She disdained rouges and cosmetics of any kind, so there was no way to camouflage herself. He will take one look at me and know something is wrong, she predicted gloomily, looking away from her reflection in disgust.

But something was wrong or he would not have visited so early, or have expressed the desire to wait for her. Her heart stopped: Terry! Could something have happened to him? Could he have met with an accident after their argument yesterday? Had Father Michaels come to tell her that he had been injured—or worse? Flooded with terror, she fairly flew down the stairs and ran into the parlor. There she found Father Michaels seated on the divan, quietly enjoying a cup of coffee and a cinnamon roll. He did not look as though he had come to impart some dire news. She clutched the door frame, breathing hard, unable to compose herself in the face of his unabashed stare.

Father Michaels put down his cup and roll and stood up.

"Philipa!" he exclaimed, taking several steps toward her with his hands outstretched. "Whatever is the matter? I had no wish to alarm you. I hope you are not distraught on my account?"

Philipa promptly disgraced herself in her own estimation by erupting into an uncontrollable wash of tears. Appalled by her outburst, yet incapable of suppressing it, she pressed her hands to her eyes. Her fingers and her face were quickly wet, and her body shook with convulsive sobs.

"Philipa!" the priest said again, the creak of the floorboards telling her that he was approaching her quickly. "Merciful heaven, what has made you—Come here, sit down! What event has brought this on?"

She allowed the big man to lead her to the credenza, and she sat down trying to regain her poise as he hastily closed the parlor doors.

"Has this something to do with Emma Hunt? Or perhaps with Terence Gavilan?"

Father Michaels's ordinarily robust voice was reduced to a reedy whisper. Philipa's relief that the cleric's visit did not correspond with some disaster involving Terry was tempered by her despair in recalling to mind the quarrel she'd had with her fiancé the day before.

"I have driven him away, Father Michaels," she said in a choked whisper, still trembling with erratic sobs. "I meant only to tell him about Emma Hunt, but I never even got that far. I—I charged him with lying to me, based on something that had been told to me as rumor. I don't think he'll ever f-forgive me for it. And I don't know that he sh-should!"

She sobbed harder, wishing she could stop herself. Crying

never helped her, she had learned long ago. On the few occasions in her life when she permitted herself a thorough cry, she always felt worse afterward. But this cry was completely unauthorized, unscheduled and unwelcome, especially in the presence of an acquaintance. Still, if one was going to burst into tears, she reflected, she could think of no one more appropriate than the parish priest to witness them.

"Philipa, I think you underestimate Mr. Gavilan and his regard for you," Father Michaels admonished her mildly. "We are but human beings, remember. We are all prone to the failing of saying things we don't mean, or harboring ugly doubts and suspicions which have no foundation in truth. Human love is imperfect at best. But it is the nearest thing to the constant love of God that we may find on this earth. And along with its hazards, we must not discount its power, and its strength."

Philipa allowed herself to be consoled. Father Michaels's words, as well as his temperate manner, had wrought their spiritual mastery. She drew several deep breaths, rejoicing that her body was, once again, under her command.

"I have been guilty," she said when she was able to speak, "of the sin of despair, among my other offenses. And you have helped me to regain my perspective. The Lord truly does move in mysterious ways. He knew I needed you this morning."

Brushing the last tears from her cheek with the back of her hand, Philipa finally looked at the priest. Father Michaels smiled at her.

"You needed Him," he corrected her gently. "And I am thankful that I was here to help you find Him when you thought He was lost."

Father Michaels got up from his seat, straightening his jacket.

"Will you be all right now?" he asked, his voice regaining some of its customary vigor.

Philipa nodded as the last of her sobs wore itself out, like a wave spent upon a sandy beach.

"Yes," she replied, feeling much better than she would

have expected. "But we have digressed. What was the reason for your call?"

Father Michaels shook his finger in self-remonstrance.

"Thank you for reminding me. In all of the excitement, I had forgotten. Daniel Orsy, the telegraph operator, reported this morning that a ship was lost a hundred miles off Cape Hatteras late last evening. Apparently a hurricane is on its way. Norfolk also reported high winds and heavy rains, so it's only a matter of time before the effects are felt here. It's rather early in the season, but in view of what happened two years ago, I believe it wise that the mayor and the council wish to take no chances. The church and the parish hall, being on the highest ground on the island, will be the safest place for residents of low areas and the beach, like yourself."

A hurricane! Philipa shivered once again, still staring at Father Michaels's calm countenance. She had not forgotten the storm of two years before, nor, she was sure, had anyone else in Braedon's Beach. Lives had been disrupted and forfeited in that assault of natural forces, and homes and businesses destroyed. Families had moved away, never to return.

"John Brewster, Roger and others are already quietly organizing evacuations and relief supplies," Father Michaels continued. "We don't wish to alarm the public unduly. St. Gabriel's is opening its doors to families, as well. I wanted to come 'round to tell you personally, in case you might have some more discreet arrangements to make regarding, uh, Mrs. Hunt."

Philipa nodded quickly.

"I appreciate your thoughtfulness," she replied, fully recovered from her earlier collapse. "I will assign Arliss and Mrs. Grant to begin collecting blankets and such at once. Has Orsy any information on when the storm is expected to hit?"

Father Michaels shook his head, biting his lower lip.

"I'm afraid not," he lamented on a small sigh. "The best he can tell is that Hatteras reported last night, and Norfolk early this morning. On the conservative side, I hope to be accepting evacuees as early as this evening. Shall I put you on Roger's list?"

Philipa considered this. Roger's carriage would have been

put to use running refugees and supplies throughout the day. But the church was not far. If she sent the supplies along in the carriage, she could surely walk to the church, even if it was raining by that time. Assuming, of course, that she would choose to leave her home.

Briefly she envisioned Emma Hunt's tomes and manuscripts being swept along Ocean Avenue by a storm surge. She stood up.

"That won't be necessary, Father Michaels," she said. "His services will be needed elsewhere. I can manage, myself."

Philipa saw the priest on his way and began forming a mental list of preparations. She had much work to do before joining the others at the church.

Mayor Brewster's unannounced visit to Terence Gavilan's office surprised the latter out of his wooden humor. A hurricane was coming. A real one. Gavilan had been sullenly going through the motions of this dark and dreary day, finding the slate gray sky to be a fitting accompaniment to his foul disposition. The idea that a hurricane might be on its way to Braedon's Beach did not trouble him overmuch. In fact, it was something of a curiosity to him. He had never experienced so violent a force of nature. He rather looked forward to the event.

His confrontation with Philipa stayed with him like an attack of gout throughout the day. It pained him whenever he thought about it, which was constantly. He took advantage of John Brewster's warning and escaped both his office and the unapologetic stares of his secretary, under the guise of inspecting the hurricane preparations effected by the staff at the arcade and the amusement court. A stiff wind was blowing off of the ocean by early afternoon, and the sky resembled boiled porridge. The waves, he noticed as he strode boldly along the deserted Promenade, were high, and would probably reach its deck by high tide.

Fred Hanover paused in his labors for a moment to wave to him. The young man was helping Mr. Jarrett secure lengths of board across the large, multipaned windows of the arcade.

Further down the Promenade, the construction crews were securing tarps and scaffolds on the completed amusements by means of ropes. They were having trouble with the canvas covering over the carousel. Gavilan joined their efforts, wondering if the puny attempts by Man would prevail against the mindless, immeasurable forces of Nature.

He chuckled, thinking of himself and Philipa Braedon in that context. It certainly had not worked in his case, he was forced to admit.

The exercise felt good, though, and he devoted the remainder of his afternoon to assisting in the evacuation. He sent his workers home at three o'clock to tend to their own preparations, judging that the storm would take its due on his own properties with or without further measures of prevention. By that time, the trees along Ocean Avenue were bowing and swaying to the wind as if in some primitive ritual dance. Gavilan continued his shuttling of refugees to Holy Innocents and St. Gabriel's, glad of any labor that would not permit him to dwell on Philipa. Perhaps, he thought, determinedly staying away from the vicinity of her house, he might soften toward her by this evening, when they would be thrown together at the church by more powerful forces. Perhaps he might allow himself then, after this unending day of mind and body wracking labor, to forget and forgive her stinging accusations.

But not yet.

By half past five the sky over Braedon's Beach was dark as scalded coffee, and every bit as ugly. The streets were dark and deserted, except for the occasional rattle of a cart driven at breakneck speed. It had not yet begun to rain, but there was a stiff and gusty breeze blowing that made it difficult for Philipa to complete her work. Her arm and shoulder ached from pounding ten-penny nails into the shutters of every window of her house for the better part of the afternoon. Despite the use of gardening gloves, her hand was blistered in two places, and her fingers were still and crooked from clutching the heavy hammer. Her left thumb was sore and bruised, having endured the penalty of her inexperience as a carpenter. As she surveyed the job she had done securing her windows, she felt the first large drops of rain begin to fall. Nearly all of the other homes in the neighborhood were dark, their owners having abandoned them some hours earlier for the safety of higher ground. Casting a last glance at the threatening sky, Philipa hurried inside, hoping she had done enough.

It was even darker inside the house. Philipa had dispatched Mrs. Grant on to the church along with the blankets and other goods hours ago, and Arliss had been sent home earlier in the afternoon to be with her mother. The Flaherty home was on higher ground on the bayside, and not in much danger of tide damage. In any case, there had been no one in the house to light the lamps, and now the interior seemed very forbidding indeed. Her rigid fingers fumbling with the matches on the etagere, Philipa struck one and lit the small fixture.

A gust of wind through the open door nearly blew it out before she could replace the glass globe. With some effort, Philipa leaned her weight against the door and bolted it. Outside, the wind howled and hammered at it like an angry notions salesman deprived of a commission.

Philipa removed her hat and allowed a sigh, massaging her right hand with the fingers of her left. Her work was not finished yet.

She carried the lamp with her to her study. The room was still locked from the night before. She had been so busy since Father Michaels's visit earlier that day that she had not even had time to think about her writing, or about the reckless challenge she had left for her nocturnal visitor. The light from the lamp was laughably small, casting a weird pattern of dim shadows about her. This was ridiculous.

Resolutely ignoring the ceaseless rattle of the nailed shutters, Philipa lit another lamp, and another, and another, until all of the lamps were lit, all about the room. The light was quite gay, and she was encouraged by it. She dusted her hands off with satisfaction and looked about the study.

The first thing she noticed was that the typewriter platen was barren. *So my personal terrorist is a coward after all*, she thought, too weary to be either angry or afraid. Well, whoever he was, he was no doubt safe within the walls of St. Gabriel's or Holy Innocents, or in his own little rat hole, wherever that might be. She could not bring herself to dwell upon him. She slid open the drawers of the desk containing the final work of Emma Hunt, pleased to see that her papers had been undisturbed.

I can't leave this, she thought, quivering. The very idea of remaining alone in the house had not occurred to her prior to that moment. It had been her intention to secure *The Tender Trap* and her printed volumes in a locked armoire upstairs, but suddenly the notion seemed like abandoning one's children. It seemed a cowardly, not to say incautious, way to respond to the danger of the imminent storm.

A sudden gust of wind seemed to shake the house to its very foundation. Philipa cried out aloud. The sound of her own voice startled her. She laughed, feeling foolish for her behavior.

"I'm as bad as an old spinster," she said aloud.

It might not be so bad, she thought, her gaze scanning the molding around the ceiling and the windows. The house had weathered the last storm without much damage, with her in it. And hurricanes did tend to move rather quickly. Why, by this time tomorrow, it might all be over. Anyway, judging by the sound of the wind outside, it would likely be more dangerous to attempt the walk on darkened, deserted streets than it would be to remain right where she was.

She was hungry.

Setting aside her plans to protect Emma Hunt's archives for the moment, she retreated to the kitchen, carrying a lamp with her. She lit another lamp in that room, too. She was pleased that the place was still warm from the stove. Mrs. Grant had, unfortunately, extinguished it before she had left, and there seemed no point in relighting it. Sighing, Philipa found a biscuit in the bread bin. Dinner would be cold. There was a green apple and a piece of crumbly New York cheddar cheese in the icebox. She took all three and sat at the kitchen table between two lamps to partake of a meal fit for church mice.

Church. She nibbled pensively on the sharp cheese, cradling the apple in her other hand. It must be quite a noisy and anxious atmosphere at Holy Innocents. She wondered if,

in the confusion, anyone might be giving a thought as to her
whereabouts during this storm. Anyone. She laughed once,
aloud, and it was not a happy sound. "Anyone," to her,
meant Terry. She felt a queer, stabbing pain in her breast, just
thinking his name. All day she had managed not to think
about him. All day she had been able to avoid brooding over
their quarrel, and over the very real possibility that she had
driven him away for good with her accusations. Oh, why had
she listened to Charles? Why had she allowed his cruelty and
vindictiveness to tarnish the luster of her love for Terence
Gavilan?

A roar shook the house suddenly, as if a speeding train had
taken a path directly through her front hall. Philipa leapt to
her feet, uttering an involuntary cry. She ran to the kitchen
window, and realized at once that it had been shuttered. She
could not have seen out even had it not been as dark as the
devil himself outside. Abandoning her meager repast on the
table, she seized a lamp and hurried into the front hall. Her
inspection yielded nothing but a seam of moisture surrounding
the front door. The wind was blowing so hard, she guessed,
shivering, that the rain was being driven directly against the
door, despite the porch roof.

It was going to be a long night, she thought with no small
trepidation.

She was about to return to the kitchen when she was startled by a series of poundings on her door. She thought she
heard a voice accompany the noise as well, but it was impossible to tell, what with the rattling of every shutter in the
house. Someone, she deduced, had gotten caught in the storm,
and no doubt hers had been the only lights in the neighborhood. Praying that she could close the door again once she
had opened it, she set her lamp down upon the etagere and
threw the bolt with her two trembling hands.

A large figure, almost reptilian in a wet, black So'wester
and cap, fell into her foyer and splayed itself flat against the
floor. Forcing the weight of her entire body against the door,
she was able to persuade it to close again, even managing to
secure the bolts.

The figure on the floor had not moved. Numb with terror,

Philipa knelt beside the lump of well-disguised humanity and pulled the cap from its head. She gasped at the sight of a steady stream of blood issuing from an ugly, fresh wound above Terence Gavilan's left eye.

Chapter Thirty

"Terry!" Philipa exclaimed, seizing his wet coat by the shoulders, shaking him. "Terry! You must get up! Please! God . . ."

She rolled him with great difficulty onto his back. He lay there like a great fallen statue, his eyes closed and his lips parted slightly. Frantically, she worked the fastenings of the So'wester. His clothing was wet as well, as though the wind had blown the rain right through the fibers of his outer protection. Fearful, she pressed her head against his chest. His heart was beating a steady, if rapid, pace. He was breathing.

Her relief in discovering that he was still very much alive was tempered by her horror at the monstrous gash in his forehead. She left him alone and ran to the kitchen, where she retrieved several clean towels and a basin of water. When she returned, she was startled to find him attempting to sit up.

"Lie down," she ordered him, pushing him back gently after she had divested herself of her nursing implements. "Don't move."

He shook her off groggily, like a bear disturbed prematurely from its hibernative state.

318

"Help me to a chair," he mumbled, his eyes squeezed shut. "Oh, Terry—"

He leaned on her heavily as he struggled to his feet. She thought she might collapse under his weight. As she guided him back to the study, though, he seemed to recover somewhat from his dependence on her support. He shrugged himself out of the soaked So'wester and collapsed again, this time onto the comparative comfort of the divan.

"What's that noise?" he muttered, still not opening his eyes.

Fearing he might be delirious, Philipa felt his cheek and neck with a tentative hand.

"It's the wind rattling the shutters," she told him. "Please, Terry, you mustn't talk. Lie still, now. I must take care of your—of this."

She hated leaving him alone, even if only to fetch the basin and the towels from the foyer. This time, however, he had not moved when she returned. She knelt beside him and wrung out one of the tea towels with the tepid water. She began first to clean the blood from his cheek and temple. He started at the touch of the cool, wet cloth.

"Lie still," she urged him, just above a whisper.

The strain and tension in his features eased as she gently cleansed the wound. It did not look nearly so bad afterward, but it was still a respectable gash. She wondered how he had come by it, but she did not ask. She did not want him to tire himself with answering questions. She found a brown bottle of carbolic solution in the pantry and applied some to the wound, hoping to stave off an infection. By that time, she was relieved to note, Terry was breathing easier. She could not resist cupping his cheek in her hand.

"That feels good," the patient murmured, and she did not know whether he referred to her nursing or to her caress.

"Shh," she whispered automatically, mopping his brow with a clean towel. "Don't ta—"

Terry batted her hand away, his features contorting with annoyance as he looked at her for the first time.

"Damn it, Philipa, stop saying that!" he exclaimed irritably, struggling to sit up. "You're making me feel like an invalid!"

Philipa backed off in surprise.

"You *are* an invalid!" she retorted. "Or aren't you aware of that gaping hole in your forehead?"

Terry grimaced, reaching one hand up to his head. Gingerly he touched the area near the cut.

"Damn!" he swore softly, closing his eyes again. "This is your fault, you know. If you had come to the church like you were supposed to—"

"It was a voluntary evacuation," she reminded him testily, shifting her weight on her knees. "And besides, no one told you to come out after me, I'm sure!"

"Well, what in hell did you expect me to do?" he exploded, taking his hand away from his face and glaring at her darkly. "Let you ride this out alone? In your house on the *beach*? Honestly, Philipa! Have you no sense at all?"

She was stung by his words. Her face grew hot under his sullen scrutiny.

"I have sense enough to know when the weather is too rough for heroic expeditions!" she snapped, wanting to strike him for his insults. "Of the two of us, I am the one with dry clothing and an unscarred face! Or need you be reminded of that fact?"

"The only thing I need to be reminded of at this moment is why I bothered to come all the way out here after you in the first place!" Terry retorted, not moving from his repose on the pillows of the divan.

He was staring hard at her, but she could tell the effort hurt him. His wide, sensuous mouth was drawn into a thin, tight line, and his temples pulsed as he clenched his angular jaw. His admonishments no longer stung. They became as transparent to her as the glass globes of the many lamps in the room.

"You were worried about me." She watched him.

He lowered his severe glare for a fleeting moment, then resumed it at once. But it was too late. He had revealed himself to her. Had she blinked, she would have missed the signal altogether.

"Of course I was worried about you!" he got out roughly, to mask his emotions, she guessed. He closed his eyes again as if trying to squeeze the pain from between his compressed eyelids.

"Oh, Terry," she murmured, overcome by an unexpected swell of tenderness for him which she translated into caressing his furrowed brow lightly with her fingers. "You poor, dear, sweet, foolish man!"

His hand was upon her wrist with a surprisingly strong grip, holding her to her caress.

"Foolish?" he echoed with a slight laugh, still sounding weak. "No more foolish than a certain woman I could name, who's sitting in a dark, drafty house that makes more noise than my motorcar."

He opened his eyes again. He was teasing her, she knew, and yet something about his tone made her feel like crying. She was not surprised, therefore, to feel a cool tear work its way down her warm cheek. She could not speak for a moment for the choking lump in her throat. He did not release her arm, but she did not want him to. She laid her head upon his damp breast, unwilling to let him see her cry.

"What happened to you?" she managed to whisper, for she did not trust herself to give body to her speech. "How did you hurt your head?"

Terry's grip tightened on her wrist, and she felt his other hand in her hair. His gestures brought a sob to her throat, but not out of it.

"The Hurricane turned over."

His words rumbled in his chest. She knew he was referring not to the weather, but to his motorcar.

"You were probably driving too fast," she admonished him, trying to control the tremor in her voice. "You're lucky you weren't killed. And—and so am I."

Her throat caught at last, betraying her. She could no longer govern her tears, any more than she had been able to that morning with Father Michaels. She was sobbing freely, clutching his wet shirt front with her free hand, her face still buried in his breast.

"Oh, Terry, I'm so s-sorry," she got out between sobs. "I

treated you so abominably yesterday. Can you ever forgive me?"

His arms tightened around her wonderfully.

"My love, I can't help but forgive you," he said in that familiar, caressing baritone she had come to love so well.

She held him tighter, loving the feel of him all around her, a sensation she had thought she might never know again. She was quickly reminded of something else. She pushed herself up, disentangling herself from his arms.

"Terry, you are soaking wet!"

His grin was sheepish and adoring.

"Why, so I am," he murmured with a brief shake of his head. "What do you recommend?"

Stunned, she stared back at him. He could not sit there for the next several days, or even hours, in wet clothing. But she had nothing in the house that would come close to fitting him.

"Do you think you could make it upstairs to the bedroom?" she asked, eyeing his wound with no small doubt.

Terry shook his head, wearing a thoughtful expression.

"We're probably better off on the first floor, Philly," he replied. "If the wind gets any stronger, it's liable to blow the roof off the house. Unless it floods, it's safer down here."

Philipa bit her lip. He was right.

"I'll go up and get some blankets and things," she told him, unable to look at his eyes. "You get undressed in here and leave your wet clothing in the hall. I'll have to relight the stove to cook something for you anyway, and your clothes can dry in the kitchen. Can you manage on your own?"

He grinned at her.

"If I can't, will you help me?"

To her annoyance, she blushed profusely.

"I suppose I'll have to, won't I?" she mumbled, closing the study door on his insouciant face.

Philipa's first mission was to relight the stove. There was plenty of wood in the woodbin, and despite lack of practice, she was able to accomplish the feat in relatively short order. She passed by the study again on her way upstairs and noticed that Terry had not left his clothing out yet. Tentatively, she knocked.

"Are you all right?" she called to him through the door.

"I'm still breathing, if that's what you mean," was his saucy retort.

"I'm going upstairs now for the bedding."

"I'll be waiting."

It took Philipa some time to pull the feather mattress, pillows and comforter from her bed and throw them down the stairs into the hallway by the light of one lamp. The darkness and unceasing racket of the wind testing the shutters played upon her nerves. She had thought the house chilly before, but her exercise made her feel quite warm. She paused in her labors to unbutton her high collar and pat her handkerchief to her lightly perspiring neck. When next she stood beside the study door, her arms laden with bedding, Terry's clothing was piled in a wet heap on the hall floor.

She found herself, to her embarrassment, picturing him unclothed, with nothing but two inches of oak between them. For a moment, she could think of nothing else.

"The bedding is out here." She collected herself finally, dropping the things beside the door. "I'm going to hang your clothes in the kitchen. Are you all right?"

"Still fine."

The kitchen was unbearably warm when she entered with Terry's wet things. Still, she managed to arrange his clothing on the furnishings of the room so they might dry to some usable form. She turned her attention to foraging in the pantry and the icebox. It took some time, but she was able to effect a passable meal and a pot of steeping tea out of the contents of the larder. The tray was heavy, and she had to set it down before opening the study door. Self-consciously, she knocked first.

"Who is it?"

She laughed in spite of herself, and opened the door.

She could not immediately perceive his location in the room. She carried the tray into the room and set it upon the low table away from the desk, where she and Essie had enjoyed afternoon tea so very long ago.

"Excuse me for not getting up."

Philipa felt a surge of heat swell along her spine to the very

base of her neck. Terry was behind her, not far away. His
baritone was lazy, and warm as honey butter on a July
afternoon. She composed herself and turned to confront him.

He had spread her feather mattress upon the floor before
the unused fireplace, and piled it with pillows. He lay in the
midst of them like some indolent heathen pasha, her hand-
quilted comforter pulled up to his collarbone, just barely concealing his chest and the rest of him. One muscular arm was
crooked above his head, and the other rested on the coverlet
over his stomach. His face was turned toward her, and his
wide smile was winsome in spite of the abrasion above his
eye.

"It seems, Miss Braedon," he addressed her in a throaty
whisper, "that you have me completely at your mercy."

He was only teasing her, she knew, but nevertheless she
swallowed hard. Looking at him, she forgot about the tray
she had lately brought into the room. The emptiness in her
stomach was replaced by a hunger of quite a different sort.
The rest of the room became mysteriously blurred. He was
the only aspect within it that remained completely, starkly, in
focus. She could not move.

"Come here," he invited her, sliding over a bit. He patted
the spot he had vacated, smiling at her in a way that told her
she would be a different person when she got up again.

"Terry, you're hurt," she reminded him. Somehow, looking at him, she knew he would not allow so trifling an im-
pairment as a possible concussion stand between them now.

He sighed melodramatically.

"I know," he lamented, an impish twinkle in his warm,
mahogany eyes. "You will be gentle with me, won't you,
Philipa?"

Outside, hurricane wind roared through Braedon's Beach.
That place beside him on the floor looked like paradise to her.

"You," she heard her own voice say in a tone spread thick
with desire as she slipped into the place beside him, "are
incorrigible."

He welcomed her beside him and she touched him, running
her hands delightedly along the well-defined contours of his
arms and shoulders. The very feel of him, his nearness and

his strength, rendered her weak with longing. She had no thought of refusing him. Indeed, she encouraged him. She began to tear at her buttons with trembling, maddeningly weak fingers.

"Let me," he urged her, placing a still, strong hand over her own as his gaze gently penetrated her nervousness. "Please."

For a man with a possible brain injury, Terry suffered no deterioration of his motor coordination. With astonishingly deft articulation, he solved the buttons of her shirtwaist even as his warm lips nibbled at the soft part of her neck below her right ear. The activity of his mouth and hands coaxed the very breath out of her through the base of her trunk. It was a wondrous sensation.

She heard a soft cry, and knew it was her own wordless murmur. It sounded small and far away.

"My sweet love." Terry punctuated each word with the tip of his tongue on her earlobe. "My honeysuckle . . ."

His hand found its way inside her bodice, sliding easily between her yielding flesh and the fine lawn of her loosened stays. How had he done that? she marveled, but had little time to wonder. His hot, gentle touch upon her hardened nipple engendered a rush deep within her, like the bursting of a dam. The sensation frightened and excited her, and made her keenly aware that she wanted something more from him. Much more.

He continued to massage that most sensitive portion of her being, and amazingly, that rush swelled forth again, and again, until she thought she might faint, or die, of delight. Her hands were in his hair, and she wanted his mouth upon hers. She demanded it. He was happy to oblige her, welcoming her tongue, daring her to investigate him. When she heard his low moan, she felt a ripple of triumph.

She wanted, more than anything, to hear him moan with delight again. To compel him do it. Feeling deliciously emboldened both by his caresses and his responses, she probed deeper still with her tongue, and allowed her hands to outline the lean muscles of his back. She pushed aside the shield of the comforter and found his narrow hips, exulting in his groan of fresh bliss. He lifted his head from her, his drowsy, sensuous smile a breath above her attendant lips.

"My love," he murmured with a ring of joy in his voice. "You never cease to astonish me!"

"It is my most fervent hope," she replied in a breathless whisper, "that I never shall."

Where before he had been deliberate, Terry now grew more intense in his passion. The material of Philipa's skirt capitulated to his impetus with a delicate tearing sound, and her body enthusiastically anticipated its liberation from layers of tiresome Victoriana to join with his. Suddenly he was around her, and within her, and she was around him. She did not know which cries were hers or which were his, or which belonged to the mighty tempest outside. She knew only that she was, at last, exactly where she belonged. And her senses gloried in the knowledge.

The air in the study was still, and filled with the musky scent of satisfied love. Philipa felt a gentle tug on her arm. It was Terry, pulling her arm over his chest. He was warm, and the steel of his muscles beneath his surprisingly soft skin made her quiver with delight. She felt his lips brush against her forehead and she, in turn, kissed the hard mass at his throat. Outside, the rain continued to hammer the house, although the wind, judging by the quiet shutters, had abated somewhat. She realized, smiling, that she might not have heard it anyway. The very sound of Terry's breathing, slow, regular and deep, held her in thrall.

"You are the sweetest thing I've ever known, Philipa Braedon," Terry whispered.

He chuckled, a low, rumbling sound that shook his considerable chest. The sound imprinted itself on her heart and overwhelmed her with love for him.

"I used to think your name harsh," he told her in a confidential way that warmed her to her core as he stroked her forearm with gentle fingers. "I liked to think of you as . . ."

He stopped.

"What?" she urged him.

"You'll laugh," he warned, and she could sense a trace of chagrin in his soft voice.

"Probably."

He kissed her forehead again, as if to buffer her from some impending shock.

"Honeysuckle," he murmured, and she could hear the sheepish grin accompanying his reply.

She giggled, more at his titillating caress than at his absurdly cute epithet.

"Not 'Bluestocking?'!" she teased him, propping her chin on her hand atop his broad, bare chest in order to see his face.

His dark eyes were unabashedly adoring.

"Now, where did you hear that?" he scolded, gently brushing her cheek with the backs of his fingers.

"My best friend," she answered ruefully, staring at the mouth that had lately given her such delight. "Essie felt it her duty to inform me as to the reputation my education and interests had earned me on the island. I'm sure she didn't mean it to be cruel, but I must confess—although you're the only person I would ever tell—it hurt me. Deeply."

She drew in a shuddering breath, remembering just how deeply. He tilted her chin upward with one finger until she was compelled to look into his eyes.

"I'm honored that you would share that with me," Terry told her, his dark eyes serious. "But I'm sorry you suffered so at their hands, alone. How hard it must have been for you, my sweet, sweet Philipa . . ."

She had to have his mouth again. She inched closer to him and he gave it to her willingly. She had meant just to enjoy a taste, but the taste became a savor, and the savor a craving, and soon she found herself wanting to explore him all over again. He allowed her adventure and invited her to seek more. He seemed to want her to hunger for him, and she was happy to accommodate him. Indeed, she could not help but accommodate him. The bold design of his hands, strong yet gentle, as they glided along her sides to her hips and her buttocks encouraged her desire.

"I want you," she breathed in amazement.

His gaze was compelling.

"Take me," he urged in a whisper.

He did not need to tell her how. She straddled his loins and guided his rock-hard manhood with her hand into the soft, swollen, throbbing place it had found before. Her hips began to rock and thrust against his own with a smooth, undulating motion which seemed entirely involuntary, as though she could not have stopped if she wanted to.

But she did not want to.

Beneath her, Terry groaned softly.

"My God, Philly," he fairly sobbed. "You are so good, so good . . ."

The combination of her movement and his moans of delight carried her to the very brink of climax and held her there, a captive of her own desire. As his body shuddered and his breath caught in his throat, he pulled her down on top of him and her climax broke like the tumultuous storm outside. How, she wondered, as the tide slowly, slowly receded inside her, had she ever lived without him?

"I think I'm going to die right here." He echoed her thoughts after a time, still holding her in a desperate grip she had no desire to break.

She laughed, giddy with sated desire.

"Please don't." She gasped. "However will I explain the naked body of Terence Gavilan in my study to the coroner?"

"I have it! You can tell him we were married in secret."

That sounded a little like one of Mrs. Emma Hunt's fanciful plot twists. She smiled.

"You are incorrigible," she chided him, caressing the stark line of his jaw, dark with the faint growth of beard.

"And you," he rejoined, touching the tip of her nose with a lazy, accusing finger, "are adorable. Insatiable, but adorable. Now. Shall I tell you my secret?"

She stared at him, drawing her eyebrows together.

"Secret?"

He shrugged, coloring a little.

"I have one to confess, too, my darling."

My darling. How wonderful those words sounded in his rich, quiet baritone! How incredible that she had no fear of his secret. No fear at all.

"Only one?" she teased him again, hoping to make him blush. "I believe, Mr. Gavilan, that you are full of secrets, and that it will take me a very, very long time to unravel them all."

He did not blush, but he did smile languidly, like slow, golden honey dripping.

"Believe it if it pleases your romantic soul, my sweet Philipa. But this is my most important secret."

Dutifully she sat up, pulling the comforter about her shoulders to shield her nakedness. It would not do to distract him from a sober confession.

"I'm ready."

He gazed at her for a full minute, as if trying to gauge the most effective way of imparting his news to her. He reached for her hand and massaged it lightly.

"Are you familiar with the novelist Emma Hunt?"

Chapter Thirty-one

Philipa resisted an impulse to pull her hand away from his. She was glad of the dim light from the lamps, for she felt as though she had paled visibly.

"Who?"

Was her voice really shaking, or was it merely the sudden constriction of her throat that made it seem so? His quicksilver grin gave her no clue. She remembered, suddenly, that she had left him alone in her study for over half an hour.

"I thought not," he replied with an unmistakable note of triumph.

Her relief that she had not been found out was tempered by her curiosity at what Emma Hunt could possibly have to do with his secret. The activity of his hand on hers was most distracting. She tried to ignore it, and she tried to remember to breathe, uneasy over what he might be about to reveal.

"Emma Hunt," he was going on with the hypnotic lilt of a practiced raconteur, "was the 'secret woman' in my life for the last four years. She writes—wrote—the most enchantingly erotic tales of love and desire. They were like an opiate to me. I could never have enough of them. For four years, my

330

hobby has been to look for Emma Hunt, whoever she might be, and to make her mystery my own. It was my mission. My quest, if you will. I confess, I thought myself in love with her. Until I met you.

"Emma Hunt is still a mystery, but now she may remain so. She is no longer important. The reality of Philipa Braedon is far more intriguing to me."

Philipa could not move. The roaring sound in her ears, she knew, had nothing to do with the hurricane outside. Staring at Terry, she tried to assimilate the fact that she had been competing against herself, and that she had not even been aware of it.

"You were—you were in love with her?"

Her question came out as a choked whisper. How could she explain it to him, now? Should she even try? He tugged on her hand, pulling her toward him again. She resisted only slightly, stiffened by the import of his revelation.

"What's wrong, Philly?"

He sounded surprised, and perhaps a little hurt. He had, she knew, perceived her reaction. She made herself relax in his possessive embrace, but she was nevertheless filled with a profound and bewildering sadness. She was two women to him, and he was not even aware of it. One was a demure, sheltered and most proper lady. The other was an erotic, sensual creature of fleshly pleasures.

How, she wondered with a tightening in her breast like a tested knot, would Terence Gavilan reconcile the two if she confessed the truth to him now?

"Nothing is wrong." She remembered, finally, to answer him. "I—I'm only wondering what I must do to compete with my—my rival for your affection."

His arms tightened around her and his lips sought hers urgently. Tenderly. She wished she could abandon herself to the glorious sensation, as she had before.

"You have no rivals, my love," he murmured, tasting her mouth, rendering her weak with desire once again, against her will. "You never shall. I simply needed for you to know that, while to others I appeared to be chasing women, in my heart I was pursuing an elusive fancy. I suppose I am, as Father

Michaels so adroitly observed only recently, a romantic.''

"Father Michaels?" Philipa echoed, feeling hopelessly stupid. Had the priest let slip some morsel of her confession to him?

Terry was smiling at her in that lazy, adoring way of his that reduced her to warm pudding.

"Father Michaels," Terry repeated firmly, touching his finger to her lips. "Which reminds me. There are to be no further delays, my love. I want to marry you immediately. I won't tolerate any blemish upon your reputation, and you know what the talk will be, after this."

Through her apprehension, Philipa could not restrain a smile. She nestled her head in the hollow between his neck and his shoulder, inhaling deeply of his intoxicating male scent.

"You once told me that reputations counted for little."

"I was wrong," he declared, his hand covering her shoulder. "Or I was ignorant. Reputations are more important than money in Braedon's Beach, and I intend that my family shall have the best of both."

Philipa shuddered inwardly. Emma Hunt, she knew, was certainly no party to a sterling reputation. It was beginning to look as though she might have to preserve her secret indefinitely. Perhaps forever.

Or at least as long as Thomas Goliard, whoever he really was, would allow her to.

But Emma Hunt, she remembered with a swell of hope, was dead. And whoever this Thomas Goliard was, she was certain he had no hard proof of his theories. Still, she thought, clinging tightly to Terry's arms as she closed her eyes, if Terry himself confronted her with the truth, could she deny it?

They slept. When Philipa awoke, she was damp. She opened her eyes with a start, and for a few sleepy moments she had no idea of where she was. Beside her, Terry stirred, pulled her close with a protective arm, and settled back into sleep. Philipa lay still for a moment and sniffed the air, frowning. What was that smell?

The sea!

She disengaged herself from Terry's embrace and sat up on the pile of bedclothes. They were wet. The lamps offered their pale golden illumination, but she could tell it was still dark outside. And the entire floor of the study was wet too! Beneath her, under the floorboards, she detected the sound of water slapping against the underbelly of the house.

Terry made a sound she took for annoyance and rolled over, rubbing his eyes with his balled fists.

"What is it, Philly?" he murmured groggily. "What—"

Abruptly he sat up as well, frowning. He met her stare with one of confusion.

"Flood?" He uttered the single word in a half-whisper.

To Philipa, it was as if he had pronounced the death sentence upon her home. Suddenly, to her astonishment, he began to laugh. It was a joyous sound, complemented by the involvement of his entire face. She stared at him for a time, trying to comprehend his amusement.

"The heavens themselves are compelling us, my love," he declared, spreading his arms wide as if to illustrate his point. "We'll have to live at Somers House for certain now, won't we?"

"Terry, this isn't funny!" Philipa reproached him. "The foundation might give way! The whole house could come down on us! And heaven only knows if this is the worst of it!"

Completely disregarding her unclothed state, she stood up and ran from the room. Already an inch of briny water coated the floor in the hallway, and there was no way to tell how much worse it might get. The place reeked of seawater. Some detached part of her was thankful that the rugs had been taken up and stored in the cedar closet in the attic back in June. But of what use would rugs be on a rotted pine floor? Assuming the house itself could endure the deluge. Seized by panic, Philipa ran up the dark staircase to escape the flood.

Gavilan leaped up after her, disregarding the sudden throbbing of his head that reminded him of his injury. He took the stairs two at a time, his head pounding with each step.

"Philipa!" he called into the darkness of the second floor. "Philly, wait! There might be—"

He was cut off by the sound of her scream, coming from the direction of the bedroom in the back of the house. Above his head, the rafters groaned as if stressed by the weight of a careless, heavy hand. He broke into a run, cursing in the darkness as he stubbed his toe on some unseen piece of furniture.

Philipa stood in the doorway of her own bedroom, her naked form silhouetted by the eerie gray light shining unnaturally through the east wall. Gavilan perceived at once that the hurricane had taken, as part of its toll, Philipa's bastion of innocence and privacy. The shutters had not held; indeed, the wall had not. Wind, rain and sea mist were flowing unchecked through the gaping wound in the side of the house. It was a ghastly and sobering sight. He could not bear it. Enfolding her to his breast, feeling her tremble against him, he wondered how she could.

"There's nothing for us to do here, Philly," he shouted to be heard over the roar of the elements. "Let's go back down. It's safer. Come on, sweetheart."

She did not speak or resist as he guided her out of the doorway. He released her only long enough to close the door behind them, then led the way back down the stairs.

The water was already ankle-deep in the foyer. Gavilan was fascinated by the poetry of it. The forces of nature had confined him with Philipa from the very beginning, first in Braedon's Beach, and now in her very home, which was about to come down around them. He wondered, watching her pause at the bottom step, why he was not frightened by this possibility. He stopped behind her, placing his hands gently upon the tender flesh of her narrow shoulders, and pressed his cheek to her damp hair. He wanted to say something to her. He wanted to console her for the inevitable loss about to befall her. But he could think of only one gentle phrase to offer.

"I love you, Philipa."

Philipa, watching the foamy sea water swirl over the floor, said nothing. In a moment, however, her hand closed, as softly as an alighting sandpiper, upon his own.

Owen Parrish was more curious than he was concerned about Gavilan's disappearance from Holy Innocents. He knew, of course, where the entrepreneur must have gone, but he was annoyed at himself for having allowed the man to slip away unnoticed. The commotion at the church was such that no one had seen Gavilan leave. In fact, few remembered seeing him at all, except for those whom he had brought to safety in his Hurricane.

Owen himself wished, very early on, that he had remained at Gavilan's office, or that he had made for the comparative comfort of Somers House. As if the ceaseless racket of whining children, howling babies and scolding mothers was not enough, he was being called upon incessantly to perform a variety of menial tasks, from fetching water to dumping slops.

He had even considered paying a call upon Emma Hunt, whose absence he had noticed immediately. But he had rejected that idea at once. Her recent response to his nocturnal invasions had unnerved and annoyed him, and he had not yet charted his response to her. She was trying her wings with him, as it were. And he wanted to clip them, neatly and effectively. He wanted to keep that most rare and elusive of birds in her gilded cage a while longer before feasting upon her.

After a hot, dismal, restless night, the wind outside abated. The long hours of their confinement, he thought with no small relief, might at last be at an end. Hurricanes, he had learned, were powerful and deadly, but at least they were quick. The gray light of morning shone through the thin slits of the shuttered windows of the church, and Owen was helping to pass tins of crackers among the refugees when the church shook with the sound of hammering upon the door. All heads turned in that direction.

"Open up!"

The voice outside belonged to Terence Gavilan. Owen tried to will his feet to move, but he could not.

John Brewster, coatless and in his shirt sleeves, was nearest to the door. He put down his pitcher of water to answer the summons. Not one but two figures in black So'westers blew into the apse in the fore of a gust of wind. Gavilan swept his rain hat from his head, revealing a wide, beaming smile beneath a brutal gash.

"I'm glad to see you're here, John," Owen heard him say in a hearty, if breathless, tone. "You can make out the license. Is Father Michaels about?"

License?

"Here, Mr. Gavilan." Father Michaels had been right behind Parrish, and the priest went forward through the curious refugees even as Mayor Brewster closed the door behind the two newest additions. "What happened to you? Is Miss Braedon—"

Father Michaels had not even the chance to complete his question before the second figure removed the obscuring hat. It was Miss Philipa Braedon, and her smile was unmistakable.

To Parrish, anyway.

If the clamor before had been deafening, it was now unbearable. Everyone in the small building clustered about the new arrivals—the Tavistocks and Mosses, the Brewsters, Mrs. Grant, Miss Stoner and even lone Roger Waverly, whose son had outraced the hurricane back to his Philadelphia seminary. Only Owen could not persuade his feet to move forward. Something was happening, he perceived. Something terrible and irrevocable. And he could only stare stupidly and watch. Holy Innocents, he thought, was about to be a party to an event which had not been brought about wholly by innocence.

"We would like you to marry us, Father Michaels." Gavilan spoke again, his baritone cutting through the barrage of questions and remarks by the others. "Right now. Will you do it?"

Parrish wondered, in a detached fashion, if Philipa Braedon had inflicted that head wound on Brownie. Perhaps that was the basis for Gavilan's lunatic request.

Father Michaels seemed only a little taken aback.

"Right now?" he echoed, looking uncertainly about the crowded church. "I don't know if—"

"Oh, yes, Father Michaels!"

That was Essie Tavistock, squealing in a delighted whine. She squeezed through the crowd, beaming a radiant smile, as though she herself might be the prospective bride.

"You must! You must!" she was going on, taking Philipa's arm firmly, despite the other woman's wet outer garment. "It would be perfect. All of Philly's friends are here, and I can be her matron, and—oh, what a perfect way to end such a wretched, wretched night!''

Parrish doubted, analyzing the rapturous expression on Miss Braedon's face, that her own night had been quite as wretched as anyone's in that hot, miserable little church.

''That cut should be treated, Mr. Gavilan.'' Roger Waverly's admonishment sounded sincere.

Parrish glanced at the older man, wondering how genuine was the sentiment behind it. Much of the gossip through the night, what little of it he was able to hear over the roar of the wind and the racket of children, had centered on speculation over the recent broken engagement and the reasons therefor. Roger Waverly was generally believed to be heartbroken over it. If he was, thought Parrish, the doctor gave no outward sign of it on this occasion.

''The wound to my heart will be much greater unless we can marry at once.'' Gavilan dismissed the doctor's concern with his usual elan as he helped Miss Braedon out of her drenched overcoat. ''John: a license? Father Michaels?''

It was, without a doubt, the most preposterous wedding Parrish had ever witnessed. The bride, ordinarily so excessively proper, resembled a half-drowned kitten. The bridegroom, on most days a picture, if not a paragon, of sartorial brilliance, looked like a rumpled prizefighter, and not a very good one, at that. Still, their outward appearance served but to charm their witnesses, and before very long the entire assemblage was toasting the new Mr. and Mrs. Terence Gavilan with tepid water and stale, soggy crackers.

Parrish, unnoticed, was sickened by the demonstration.

Chapter Thirty-two

By midafternoon the wind had died and the rain had all but stopped. The men went forth first, like Noah's dove, to be sure there was no danger from storm damage and that they still had homes where they could bring their loved ones.

The news was mostly good. Families began, little by little, to filter from the haven of Holy Innocents back to their homes, to wade through the receding waters and salvage what remained of their worldly goods. Braedon's Beach, or most of it, would survive.

Somers House had suffered only superficial damage, but Terry asked Philipa to remain at the church while he went to inspect his interests on the Promenade. They would make a complete reconnaissance of the Braedon house on the beach the following day, he promised. Philipa agreed to his plan, not being anxious to see her home in its ruined state. Surely, she thought, her final manuscript was safe in its locked drawer of her desk in the study, even from the attentions of her nightly visitor. *The Tender Trap* was ready to go to the publisher, a trifling detail that would require but an hour of privacy to accomplish. And afterward, Mrs. Hunt would depart

Braedon's Beach, and the mortal world, forever.

Aside from Philipa herself, Essie was the last to leave the church. The Tavistock home had escaped serious damage and was deemed fit for habitation. Philipa hugged Essie before helping her into the carriage Charles had sent around for her.

"Mrs. Terence Gavilan!" Essie exclaimed, beaming her fondest smile at Philipa. "I knew that it must be. I have always known that I possessed a degree of clairvoyance. We shall have a party in your honor as soon as things return to normal, Philly. Don't worry about Charles. He refuses me nothing, now that I am about to present him with an heir. We shall work things out. Oh, I think it was the most romantic wedding I've ever attended! You lucky, lucky girl, to have such a gallant and forthright cavalier. That's what he is. A—"

"Essie, go home!" Philipa interrupted her friend, embarrassed by her exhibition. It was one thing to believe such qualities about the man one loved, but quite another to hear someone else extol those virtues aloud for the whole world, or at least Father Michaels, to hear. Essie merely giggled in a coquettish fashion.

"I shall! I am. I'm on my way. I shall call upon you later in the week, Philly. We must give the newlyweds a chance to settle in, after all!"

She waved, and the carriage lurched off. Philipa watched her go, wondering, with a little shiver of memory, when Terry would return so they could begin some of this "settling in."

"It was a lovely wedding," Father Michaels agreed. "And it was certainly the most unusual one I've yet had the pleasure of performing."

Philipa blushed, although she tried to subdue it before she turned her attention to the rector.

"I must apologize, Father Michaels," she said, meeting his merry eyes soberly. "We bullied you into it, I think."

The rector laughed, mopping at the perspiration on his high forehead with his handkerchief.

"I thought so too, at first," he confessed, adjusting his collar. "But then I decided there must have been a reason why the Lord put us all in one place at one time. I can think of no happier result to a terrible storm such as this one than two people in love making their vows to one another. Can you?''

''No,'' she admitted, looking down the road to see if Terry might be on his way at last.

''I assume this means your problem of yesterday reached a happy result?''

For a moment, she could not recall to what he might be referring.

''Yes,'' she said at last, remembering. ''Oh, yes. I was so foolish, Father Michaels. I hope you will forgive my—''

''Nonsense, Philipa,'' the priest scolded her gently. ''You were upset. Rightfully so. But you have made your peace with your husband. And of course he knows now, about Emma Hunt?''

Philipa's reply stuck in her throat. Father Michaels arched an eyebrow.

''Philipa?''

She could not lie, nor could she bring herself to confess the truth aloud to him. She shook her head, swallowing hard.

''I started to tell him,'' she said in a small voice, aware that she was no longer looking him in the face. ''But then he told me something that stopped me cold.''

''Which was—?''

There was a small, frosty pain in her chest, as if she'd been stabbed by an icicle, as she remembered Terry's innocent confession on the study floor.

''He was in love with her, Father Michaels,'' she all but whispered to the breeze. ''He was obsessed by her. He says he has given her up, and that he wants a respectable life with me. But Emma Hunt is hardly a respectable entity. I have been thinking it might be best, after all, to leave Emma Hunt to history, as Terry has done with all of his past involvements. Am I rationalizing?''

She looked up at him again. Father Michaels was considering her with a thoughtful expression on his pleasant features.

''You are,'' he assured her. ''But you might be doing the right thing for the wrong reasons. 'The truth shall set you free,' it says in the Book. But it also says to 'let the dead bury the dead.' I recommend prayer, Philipa. God will give you the answers you seek. Perhaps He has in fact given them to you already, but you have not allowed yourself to listen to Him. Take a space during this joyous time in your life to nurture your spirit, as well. Is that your husband coming now?''

Philipa followed the direction of Father Michaels's stare. It was not Terry in the buggy that was still over a block away, but Roger Waverly. He was driving fast toward them, as if pressed by some crisis. In moments he was upon them, his features grim.

"Philipa, I must speak with Father Michaels privately." Roger made no attempt at a polite salutation. He was breathless, and his gloved hands held the reins in a tense grip. Philipa did not move.

"If it's an emergency, perhaps I can help," she argued, approaching him.

He eyed her uncertainly.

"N-no, Philipa," he said in a gentler tone. "It's a rather—delicate matter. Father Michaels, can you come with me now? Will you be all right here alone until Gavilan gets back, Philly?"

Philipa stared at the doctor. Was it her imagination, or had Roger hesitated before speaking Terry's name, as if the effort might have cost him?

"It's getting dark," she observed. "May I just ride with you? I can wait in the buggy, if I would be in the way. Or perhaps I could be of some help."

Roger returned her stare, apparently weighing her offer. He nodded quickly.

"But hurry," he admonished as both Philipa and Father Michaels climbed into the buggy. "Time is precious!"

Something was very wrong. Roger spoke not a word as he drove the horse hard, although Philipa suspected that had she not been present, he and Father Michaels would have conversed freely. Sandwiched between the two men, she felt as though she were a barricade. Unable to think of anything to say that might relieve the tension, she remained silent, watching as Roger drove the buggy to the north side of the bay, one of the poorer sections of town. He braked to an abrupt halt before a small bungalow. The porch roof was partially caved in, thanks to a tree branch which had been brought down by the storm, and several of the shutters were gone. Inside, there was a small light.

"Wait out here, Philly," Roger told her without looking at her. "Under no circumstances are you to come inside. Do you understand?"

Ordinarily she might have taken umbrage at such a peremptory command, but something about Roger's tone stopped her. She merely nodded and folded her hands in her lap as Roger and Father Michaels hastened into the small, ramshackle cottage.

For a time, there was no sound except the mournful cry of gulls returning to their homes, no doubt discovering the devastation wrought by the hurricane. Presently Philipa heard, from within the house, the faint but unmistakable cry of a woman in pain. A young mother-to-be in labor, she guessed, stealing a glance at the front door of the cottage. But why had Roger needed Father Michaels? And why had he forbade her to come inside?

Philipa had a terrible thought: suppose the young mother's life was in danger. Women died in childbirth, she knew. Not often, but it did happen. And sometimes complications threatened the life of the newborn. As happy as she had been, she could not help but feel a pang of sorrow for the woman who travailed inside the dilapidated hut. Roger, of course, would do the best he could, but he was not a worker of miracles. That was Father Michaels's department. Perhaps with the two of them working together, that poor woman might have a hope of seeing a happy conclusion to her suffering.

Philipa breathed a quick prayer for the woman, and for her child. She tried not to listen to the cries anymore. They had become more plaintive, and more difficult to ignore. It was as though the woman was calling to her in warning, like a withered spirit of the underworld. A Jacob Marley to her Ebenezer Scrooge. "You may yet have a chance of escaping my fate . . ."

She shook herself. She was being foolish. She began to wish, shivering with the chill of the evening, that she had not insisted on accompanying the men. She wished she had stayed behind at Holy Innocents and waited for Terry. He must have returned there by now, she thought, shifting restlessly on the uncomfortable buggy seat. He must be wondering what had happened to her. He must be as eager as she to get home, and to get on with their wedding night . . .

"Miss Braedon! Wh-what are *you* doing out here?"

Philipa was jolted out of her meditation by the familiar, kittenish voice of Arliss Flaherty, who sounded every bit as surprised to see her there as she herself was to see Arliss. Staring at the girl, who stood by the broken-down gate in front of the cottage, Philipa saw that she had been crying. But surely those cries of pain she heard could not have been Arliss's!

"I—that isn't important right now, Arliss," she told the girl, aware that her voice sounded faint. "What is happening in there? Is your mother ill?"

Arliss's pale blue eyes filled up again, and her thin lower lip quivered.

"No, it's my sister," she replied, obviously trying hard not to cry again, but only partially succeeding. "She—she's hurt. She's bleeding, and she won't stop. Dr. Waverly is trying to help her, but she looks bad, Miss Braedon. Ma's beside herself with worry, and Dr. Waverly says there isn't anything more we can do . . ."

She was going on, but Philipa scarcely heard her. All she could hear was the sound of her own heart pounding in her ears. Before she quite knew what she was doing, she had climbed down from the buggy. She stood before Arliss and squared the girl's narrow shoulders with her own two hands.

"Get hold of yourself, Arliss," she commanded the girl, surprised by the stern quality of her voice. "What is wrong with Jessamyn?"

Arliss shook her head, shrugging helplessly.

"I—I don't know," she admitted feebly. "She came home yesterday, before the storm. She was acting sick then, and Ma put her in bed straightaway. Dr. Waverly won't tell me. I think Ma knows what's wrong with her, though. I think Ma knows she's dyin', but she's afraid to tell me."

Philipa curbed her impatience, and her growing apprehension.

"Arliss, your sister is a healthy young woman," she admonished the girl, glancing past her at the house. "Healthy young women don't just die, not without a very good reason. Please take me inside. We'll see what this is all about."

Philipa could not justify her action with any excuse save curiosity, but she followed anyway as Arliss wordlessly led her into the run-down house. The first thing Philipa noticed was the smell. The place reeked of rancid cooking fat and a metallic odor. Iron. Frowning, Philipa followed Arliss through the tiny, cluttered sitting room and into a cavelike hallway leading, Philipa guessed, to the back bedrooms. A light shone from a small doorway beyond Arliss, and from inside Philipa heard the hushed, pastoral tones of Father Michaels reciting the Twenty-third Psalm.

Jessamyn's cries seemed to be quieter now. The fight had gone out of her. Arliss stood aside at the doorway averting her eyes, and she turned to Philipa with a slight inclination of her hand.

Philipa suddenly did not want to go inside, but her feet would not stop their forward progress. In a moment, she was in the doorway. She perceived at once why she had smelled iron.

Roger had removed his coat and rolled up his sleeves. His arms were covered in blood to his elbows. His shirt front was stained crimson, and a pool of blood soiled the sheets upon which the lovely, dying Miss Jessamyn Flaherty lay. There seemed to be not an object in the room untouched by blood. Even the small silver cross dangling from a chain about Father Michaels's neck glistened red from the reflection. Jessamyn's pale mouth moved in a soundless supplication with the priest's, and her eyes were closed. An older woman, who could only have been Mrs. Flaherty, bathed Jessamyn's pale brow with a damp cloth in a loving way that was painful to behold.

Dear God, thought Philipa, horrified by the scene before her eyes.

"What—what is wrong with her?" Philipa got out in a gasp.

Roger and Father Michaels looked up at her as one.

"Get out of here, Philipa!" Roger ordered her harshly, his eyes hard. "You'll do no good in here."

"I'm not a child, Roger!" she retorted coldly, meeting his stare without flinching. "What is wrong with her? Arliss wants to know. It isn't right not to tell her! She is Jessamyn's sister, after all!"

"She has had an abortion, Philipa," Roger informed her woodenly. "She has been butchered. There is nothing to be done."

Philipa tore her gaze away from the dying girl and stared in horror at the doctor, whose face was a study of anguish.

"Why did you come in here?" he demanded in a rough whisper. "There was nothing you could do! I wanted you to be spared knowing!"

Philipa shook her head slowly, numbed by the awful sight.

"Arliss, take Miss Braedon away from here! Now! I must—"

Another sharp cry from Jessamyn abbreviated whatever Roger had been about to say. Philipa was shuttled quickly along the corridor again. She felt faint. She steadied herself, not wanting to swoon before strangers, or to give Roger a reason to abandon Jessamyn. She needed to sit down, but she could not bear to remain in that house a moment longer. She escaped outside and drew in a sharp breath, so deeply that it hurt. There was death in that house, and not merely one death. She paused at the gate, for suddenly the earth was shaking beneath her and the sky above was spinning. She leaned over the gate and vomited, although there was nothing in her stomach to bring up.

She made it to the buggy somehow and pressed her head against its lacquered side panel. It was cool against her heated brow, but its comfort could not ease the ache in her breast. Jessamyn Flaherty had been with child. Jessamyn Flaherty, who had flaunted her estimable figure in dresses of red and blue. Jessamyn Flaherty, whose scandalous reputation had earned her the scorn of every decent woman in Braedon's Beach.

Jessamyn Flaherty, who, up until less than a month ago, had consorted openly with Terence Gavilan.

The evening air was heavy with the stench of bayside salt marshes and of dead, rotting things. Philipa choked on her own bile as her stomach heaved once again. Logic told her that Terry couldn't have been the only man to have enjoyed Jessamyn's charms in the last few months. But her heart was not persuaded by reason. Besides, even if that were true, it merely lessened the possibility that the aborted child had been his. It did not eliminate it completely. There was no power on earth that could offer her that consolation.

A sob choked her as she thought of the child who would never see the ocean, and of the mother who would never walk beside him on the beach. She thought of the helpless mother at the bedside who was watching her daughter's life ebb from her as inexorably as the blood seeping from the girl's ravaged womb.

Philipa was shaking. She was hot, and cold. She had no strength to climb back into the buggy. She wished desperately that she had not ventured into the house, and that she had not witnessed the awful sight of Jessamyn Flaherty bleeding out her young life in that cramped and noxious place.

From inside the cottage, there came another small cry, like the faraway sound of one of the gulls. Then everything was silent. Trying to keep her stomach at bay this time, Philipa knew that Jessamyn was dead.

She knew, with an awful conviction, that something within herself had died, as well.

Chapter Thirty-three

Gavilan ached. From his shoulders, through his back, and down into his legs, he ached with such a profound hurt that he yearned to collapse on the ground where he was, and sleep. His head hurt, too, where he had banged it during his accident. It throbbed mockingly with every step he took.

The Promenade was a disaster. The arcade had been razed from beneath by the flood like some flimsy paper model. The bathhouse had survived serious damage somehow, but the half-finished amusement court had been reduced to rubble. Painted wood and twisted metal littered the beach. Even the horses from the carousel, what were left of them, lay haphazardly among the devastation, giving the area the aspect of some medieval battleground where noble steeds had been senselessly slaughtered.

There was nothing to do but start from the beginning, or to abandon Braedon's Beach completely and start afresh elsewhere. Gavilan had seen to it that his interests had been well insured, so money was not the problem. But summer was already half gone. There was virtually no chance, in the time remaining in this season, that he could effect the kind of regeneration the area would need in order to appreciate financial success.

He could, he reflected moodily as he made his way along the deserted avenue, like the hurricane, simply strike and move on.

He thought of Philipa.

His heart warmed, and his aching muscles were soothed at once. His wife was waiting for him at Holy Innocents. A smile tugged at the corners of his mouth, and he quickened his pace in spite of himself. Philipa, he knew, would want to stay here. It was her home. And he himself, he realized with some chagrin, had come to feel at home as well in this place called Braedon's Beach. Somehow he had begun to take root; a phenomenon he had, until now, managed to avoid. He had made a commitment. Several, in fact. One of those commitments reminded him of the feel of soft, gentle hands in his hair, soothing him. His aches disappeared, replaced by the overpowering need to feel those hands caressing his brow again.

It was dusk by the time he reached the church, and there was no one about. He wasted no time waiting, assuming that Philipa had gone on ahead to Somers House without him, possibly having accepted a ride from a neighbor. He smiled to himself again, ruefully. She was not known for her diligence in following instructions.

He did experience some alarm, however, when, upon returning home, he discovered that the place was completely dark. He took the steps to the porch two at a time, wincing at the throbbing in his head.

"Philipa!" he called out loud as he gained the top step. "Philly! Are you here?"

The door was open. He had not locked it. He went inside and lit a lamp. He called her again, but heard only his own voice echoing in the dark, empty rooms.

At the other end of the hallway he saw a thin seam of light showing under the kitchen door.

"Philipa?" he said again, half to himself, as he made his way back.

She was in there, seated at the oak table with her back to the door. Her arms were folded upon the table top, and her head lay on them. She did not move when he entered. Across from her, on a blue and white checkered napkin, was a single place set for dinner. The kitchen was warm and smelled of fresh coffee.

His heart swelled with affection for her and he touched the spilled honey of her hair, falling softly from its severe pinnings.

"Are you all right, sweetheart?" he whispered, allowing his hand to rest, finally, upon her head.

To his surprise, she sat bolt upright, although she did not appear to have been startled.

"*I* am fine," she replied in a quiet voice. Slowly she got up. He watched her rise, his arms anticipating a sweet embrace.

Philipa did not look at him. She made for the warm stove and set an iron skillet on it with a clang. Confused by her action, he set aside his disappointment.

"The only thing in the icebox was half a dozen eggs," he heard her say in a cool, indifferent tone that struck him like a splash of cold water in the face. "Do you like them fried?"

"Philipa, you don't have to—"

"Very well. I shall fry them, since you have no preference."

What had gotten into her?

He stared at her back, unable to think or speak. She had begun methodically cracking eggs into the pan, which hissed and crackled like a greedy lizard. Damn it, what was going on? His anger rose swiftly at the sight of her hurried gestures and stiff back. In three steps he was beside her. He took hold of her arm with more force than he had intended and turned her toward him with a shake. Her eyes were very green, and they were wide, but not frightened. She wore, to his dismay, an expression he had never seen in them before, and it scared him a little. It was remote. Cold. Stunned, he released her arm, but did not retreat from his position.

"Everything's gone but the bathhouse, Philipa," he said, trying mightily to keep the edge from his voice. "The arcade. The Ferris Wheel. The carousel was all over the beach in so many pieces I don't think an army could reassemble it. I didn't even bother to go to my office. I've had a terrible day, and I don't intend to—''

"Jessamyn Flaherty is dead," Philipa said, staring squarely at him.

He backed up, mentally.

"What?"

She looked away again, to the stove and the bubbling eggs.

"I believe you heard me."

"*What did you say*?" he repeated, his ears filled with a sudden roaring. He had taken hold of her arm again.

Philipa turned to him once more. This time her eyes were full of tears. The sight wrenched his gut.

"Jessamyn," she repeated in a quivering whisper, "is dead. She bled to death in her mother's arms. She'd had an ab—"

She stopped, and Gavilan knew she could not go on. He knew, with a sickening certainty, what Philipa had been about to tell him. He wanted to enfold her to his breast, and to quiet her shuddering sobs in his arms. He allowed his hand to relax its grip and to slide down her arm to her fingers, hoping to comfort her. She pulled them away from his touch, and an arctic chill went through him.

Staring at Philipa, who had turned away from him again, he thought of Jess. He thought of the times when he had taken her to Long Branch, and the silly things he'd bought her. He thought of her nestled in his arms in bed like some soft, spoiled kitten. He was shocked that he could barely remember her face.

Jess was dead. Of an abortion. And the child . . . *his* child? Owen's? Elliot's? Or who knew who else's?

"She didn't deserve to die." He thought it, and was surprised to hear the words spill forth from his lips.

"No, she didn't," Philipa agreed in a tight voice that betrayed the fact that she was still trying to govern her tears. "And neither did the baby. And neither did Mrs. Flaherty deserve to lose a daughter in so appalling a fashion. But there it is, Terry. There it is, for anyone to draw whatever conclusions they may from the tragic event."

He watched her back, considering his next words carefully.

"And what conclusions have you drawn?"

She whirled about, her eyes hard and dry.

"What conclusions would *you* have drawn if our positions had been reversed?" she hissed at him. "A young woman has died for a life she never wanted! A mother and a sister grieve! And somewhere a man walks away from it all, with no more care than a—than a base, rutting creature! This is a terrible injustice, Terry. A vile and unspeakable crime. It isn't right that it should go unpunished—"

"And so it is your intention to punish *me* for the crime?"

His hurt, he knew, sounded like anger. He could not help it. Of course he felt badly for Jess, and for her family. How could he not? But he had only known the woman for three months. It was possible—his heart leaped at the thought—it was possible that she had been pregnant even before he had arrived in town. He opened his mouth to say as much to Philipa, but looking at her, he shut it again. She had not, after all, accused him of having slept with the girl. Why admit to it now, and remove all doubt from her mind?

"Philipa," he began again, feeling slightly ill, "this is a terrible tragedy, certainly. I would feel badly about it even had I not known Jess. But there is nothing to be done about it, is there? Jess is gone. And we are here. We are husband and wife now, and we have our entire lives to look forward to. We were to have forgotten the past, and—"

"Your idea, not mine!" Philipa retorted, clenching her small fists in the folds of her rumpled shirtwaist. "Besides, Jessamyn's death is now, Terry! Right now! I saw her—I watched her die, only an hour ago. I watched the life seep out of her. I saw the anguish in her mother's face. I won't ever forget it. Ever!"

Gavilan could control his helpless rage no longer.

"What were you doing there in the first place?" he exploded, aware that he wanted to throw something. "Was it Roger Waverly's idea to take you? If it was, by God—"

"Roger tried in every way possible to prevent me from coming along," Philipa interrupted him coldly, her eyes glittering and hard. "I wish to God that he had succeeded. Oh, you have no idea how I wish he had succeeded!"

Gavilan was alone, suddenly. The smell of burning eggs stung his nostrils, and his head was throbbing wildly. He wanted to sit down. He held on to the high back of an oak chair for a moment, to steady himself. This was not the time to faint, or to retreat. His very future might depend upon what he did in the next few minutes.

Philipa was in the parlor in the dark, sitting in a wing chair which she had turned toward a window. Gavilan elected not to light a lamp. He felt weak, and he knew he must be pale. He would not use his infirmity as a device against her. He sank gratefully into a chair offering him a view of her stolid profile in the failing light while not revealing his own condition to her. He thought for a moment that there were fireflies loose in the room, but he realized it was merely his overtaxed mind playing a cruel joke upon him.

"What now, Philipa?" he asked.

For a long while, Philipa did not reply. Gavilan thought that he had lost consciousness. His head was swimming, and he felt worse than when he had been standing up. He closed his eyes, hoping to clear his vision, and his brain.

"I don't know, Terry," she answered on a broken sigh. Her voice sounded small, and very far away. It was as if she were speaking to him through a long, dark shaft. He listened hard for her next words, but all he could hear was the sound of the ocean.

"I was so happy this afternoon," Philipa said, not wanting to speak but unable to prevent the words from coming forth. "I thought nothing could mar that joy. I only wanted to be your wife, Terry, nothing more. And now all I can think of is Jessamyn. It seems so unfair that we should be here, and that she is gone. I can't forget, Terry. I won't ever forget. I need time to see if I can put it behind me, behind us. And if I can't, we may have to consider an annulment. Right now, I can't live with the fact that you may have fathered her child, and that she died because of it. I simply can't."

"A stirring oratory, Miss Braedon."

Philipa jolted in her seat as if she'd been struck by lightning. It was the voice of Owen Parrish somewhere behind her in the darkened room, and it grated like steel on stone. She stood up quickly, backing against the window. Night had fallen, and she could scarcely see at all into the room. What had happened to Terry?

"Mr. Parrish," she managed, her voice only shaking a little. "You should have made your presence known."

There was a moment of bitter, amused silence.

"I believe I did, just now," he replied, and she still could not see where he was in the big, dark room. "I take it, from what you said, that Jess Flaherty is dead?"

Philipa hugged her arms to her chest, shivering. She did not like Parrish. Nothing had changed that. Her face burned at the thought that he had eavesdropped, and that he had heard her entire discourse, meant for Terry's ears alone.

"Terry, where are you?" Philipa ignored the secretary's question, peering into the gloom at the spot from which she had last heard Terry speak. She was frightened, for Terry and for herself, but she did not want to alert Parrish to the fact.

"He's passed out, or dead, I guess," Parrish's mocking voice assured her from deep within the dark recesses of the room. "I noticed him in the chair. That head wound probably got the better of him at last. I thought he was a little touched when you two tied the knot earlier. Brownie never was one to let an injury stop him. I guess one finally did."

Swallowing a cry, Philipa edged in the direction of the last words she'd heard Terry speak. It was obvious to her that Owen Parrish, for some unknown reason, had no intention of assisting his boss.

"Please go and get Dr. Waverly." Philipa tried to exert a commanding tone, and was pleased by the result as she edged closer to her goal. "We must have help."

Suddenly something seized her wrist, hard. She cried out in shock and pain.

"Must we?" Parrish's tone at her ear was faintly mimicking. "I think not, Mrs. Gavilan. Or perhaps I should say, Mrs. Hunt?"

Philipa felt as if the breath had been knocked from her body, and she choked in a gasp. She pulled her arm away, but he held it fast in his rough grip. Thomas Goliard, she thought, feeling oddly detached. Owen Parrish was Thomas

Goliard! Why hadn't she seen it before?

"Your work," she managed in a cold tone, "is the work of a coward, Mr. Parrish. Release me at once!"

The sound of his laughter was as ugly as it was disturbing.

"So you told me, Emma Hunt!" He sounded positively gay. "I must admit, you've got a lot more sand than I expected. And even more vinegar! So Jess Flaherty killed herself with a botched abortion. And you're ready to throw the baby out with the bathwater, if you'll excuse a rather crude metaphor, and set aside your marriage to Brownie because of it. What a good joke! Will we see that plot in Mrs. Hunt's upcoming novel?"

He did not let her arm go, nor did he make any further move to either restrain or release her. Her heart hammered painfully against her chest.

"This is absurd, Mr. Parrish, and very, very dangerous!" she insisted, unable, this time, to keep a tremor from her voice. "Now relea—"

"Oh, I must agree, my dear Mrs. Hunt!" he interrupted her, his tone low and menacing. "It is quite absurd. And more than a little dangerous. For you. You see, I have been planning for just such an event as this, to find you alone, defenseless, and completely under my governance, with no chance of interference from outside forces. And now, here you are."

Philipa twisted her arm and yanked it away with a quick jerk, freeing herself from his grip.

"You are completely mad!" she breathed, backing toward the window, still unable to see her adversary. "This has gone quite far enough, Mr. Parrish! I must insist that you—"

She was interrupted by his hearty and most distressing laughter, which echoed coldly in the room.

"My dear Mrs. Gavilan," Parrish said in a patronizing tone. "I regret to inform you that this hasn't gone anywhere near as far as it's going to go."

His words struck a note of real terror in her. Terry was there, in the darkness, unconscious. He needed help. And the only people who were there to render assistance were herself and this miserable excuse for a secretary, who was making the most hideous threats imaginable. She rallied, stiffening her spine. Owen Parrish was merely a man. A mad one, perhaps. But a man, nonetheless. She must gain the upper hand with him. But how?

"Mr. Parrish," she began, trying with reason to keep her terror at bay. "Surely there must be a better time for this discussion! Terry—Mr. Gavilan—needs our help, at once! Have you no sense of duty to him? After all, you are his trusted secretary—"

"Trusted secretary!" Parrish spat. "Secretary, yes. Trusted? Hah! Not even Brownie is that naive, I doubt. We have far too much history between us for that, my dear. You see, it was I who set Brownie up with the dean's niece back in our Princeton days. And it was I who alerted the dean to the liaison, although Brownie, of course, doesn't know that. It was him or me then, and I wasn't willing to sacrifice my future, my degree, for the sake of a spoiled rich boy who'd already had more than his fair share of good looks and good luck in this life. He still thinks I'm the one who talked the dean out of having him prosecuted, and saving his bacon from prison for the escapade. That's why he tows me along like some faithful mutt. But I've been a good secretary, for the most part. Even better than he thought. I found Emma Hunt, after all, although I never told him about it."

Philipa thought quickly, her heart pounding. Parrish was obviously proud of his dubious accomplishments. Perhaps if she could keep him talking . . . what? Someone might come? To rescue her? She bit her lip, peering hard into the darkness. She realized that if there were to be a rescue, she would probably have to effect it herself. She had to use her head.

"That is something which has been troubling me, Mr. Parrish," she said, wanting to sound coldly curious. She was pleased by the result. "How did you manage to uncover Mrs. Hunt's secret?"

Parrish, in the dark, chuckled.

"Please, call me Owen," he said in an exaggerated tone of politeness. "Because I promise you, we are going to be very close, Emma. Very close indeed."

Chapter Thirty-four

"If you insist upon calling me Emma, should I not then return the favor and call you Thomas?"

Philipa edged slowly along in the darkness in the direction from which Terry's last sound had come. Owen Parrish seemed pleased by her interest, and she hoped he would continue in his vain recitation at least long enough for her to ascertain Terry's condition.

Parrish laughed again. He was either bordering on hysteria, Philipa thought, or else supremely confident of his ultimate triumph in the situation. She mastered her urge to run from the room, sure that she would not get very far.

"I never could see until now just what Brownie found in you that was so appealing," he told her, hoping, she was sure, to be insulting. "You have a most delightful wit, Mrs. Hunt. It surprises me that I had not deduced from that fact alone that you were actually the creator of those clever passages."

"You were about to tell me how you reached the conclusion that I was," she reminded him, bumping into the chair where Terry sat, unconscious or dead.

"I wasn't," he remarked, and his voice grew nearer to her.

"But I believe I will, after all. Your publisher very obligingly furnished me with the name of Royal Godfrey. And Godfrey's miserable pet parrot quite innocently revealed the connection to me. You no doubt recall the occasion upon which we chanced to meet in New York?"

Philipa scarcely heard him. She felt Terry's face with her hand. It was cool and moist. She felt his faint breath against her fingers. He was alive. The discovery buoyed her.

"I congratulate you," she said, withdrawing her hand from Terry's face, "on being the most completely amoral individual I've ever had the dubious pleasure of encountering."

In the shadows, her eyes having finally adjusted to the darkness, she saw his outline. He stood but half a dozen feet away from her, and he bowed slightly.

"I accept the compliment," he mocked her. "But I must confess: in a very real sense, it is you, Emma Hunt, who have created me in this image. I have patterned my behavior upon one of your own characters."

Philipa shuddered. Owen Parrish was mad. There could be no other explanation for such a bizarre confession.

"Which one?" she could not help wondering aloud.

"Let us," he said in a light, ominous tone, "repair to the bedchamber, my dear. And perhaps, from my behavior there, you will be able to guess."

She recalled the wonderful, intimate things she and Terry had shared only the night before, then pictured Owen Parrish in his place. Everything within her screamed "No!" For Terry's sake, however, she mastered herself, summoning her haughtiest tone.

"And if I refuse?"

He was before her, like a potent, dark spirit.

"You've toyed with me enough, Emma Hunt!" He seized her arms in a painful, bruising grip, and she cried out before she could prevent herself. "I have nothing to gain by releasing you, and you have everything to lose, no matter which way the cards fall: your honor, your reputation, and your life. Even your husband's life, if it comes to that. Yes, Mrs. Gavilan, I am that resolute. Emma Hunt has preyed upon my mind for far too long. I consider murder to be a negligible wage to pay for this opportunity. Shall I prove that to you before we begin?''

Philipa thought quickly. She could faint, but then he would only carry her, or else have his way with her where she lay. She could scream, but it was likely that no one would hear her. She could protest further, but Terry might pay the penalty.

Or she could play along. Not too willingly; that would surely make him suspicious. He was mad, she knew, but Parrish was no fool. He knew she despised him. An opportunity might present itself upstairs, or along the way . . .

''That—that will not be necessary,'' she replied in a faint tone. ''I know when I've been bested.''

The Willing Slave.

The title came to her as if a voice had spoken it aloud. Parrish, fiend that he was, had obviously cast himself in the role of the evil slave trader, and her in the role of Diana. One of Mrs. Hunt's earlier, somewhat more risqué plots, involving the submission of the heroine to the lust of the villain in order to preserve the life of the hero. She shuddered. The metaphor struck too close to the bone for her liking. She swallowed hard, although her mouth was dry as sand.

''I hope,'' she said in a small voice, echoing Terry's sentiment from the previous evening, ''that you will be gentle with me.''

Parrish sucked in a gasping breath of triumph, although it sounded more like a drowning man coming up for the final time.

''Mrs. Hunt,'' he replied in a breathy tone that shook with anticipation. ''I shall be anything but!''

He wanted her to struggle against him!

He seized her arm, and she fought her natural inclination to pull away from him as he dragged her through the darkness toward the stairs. That he even wanted to perform the rape in a bedroom intrigued that part of her which remained detached from these ghastly proceedings. He was mad, and probably not thinking clearly. She quickly decided it would be to her advantage to precede him up the stairs. After all, did not generals always prefer to command the high ground? She maintained a steady, lachrymose pace, like a condemned prisoner climbing to the gallows. Counting each step in the darkness, she tried to order her thoughts.

As far as she could tell, Owen Parrish possessed no weapon of any kind, save for his ugly threats. He was not a tall man, but he was rather bulky, no doubt too burly for her to consider overpowering by force alone. The stairs were a perfect opportunity for her to attempt to thwart him—if, and only if, she could keep her wits about her.

"I hope you're not thinking of trying anything stupid, Emma." Parrish's reedy voice sounded bored as they neared the landing. "I would hate to have to hurt you—before our little event, that is."

His voice was at her ear. She blessed her good fortune that he had spoken, and given her a clue as to his position on the stair.

"Stupidity," she murmured, grasping the railing beside her firmly with both hands, "is not a trait of which I have ever been accused."

Before the last lilting word had escaped her lips, she cleared her trailing foot from the hem of her dress. On the last syllable, she thrust her foot backward with all her strength. She felt the pointed heel sink deep into soft flesh—whether Parrish's groin or midsection, she did not know. He let out a sharp groan of pain and surprise. His hand grasped her ankle and she screamed, filling the dark house with the terrible, lusty noise.

Unable to keep his balance, Parrish fell, and he pulled her part way down with him. She clung to the railing with both hands, saving herself from tumbling with him through the darkness. His bulk thudded hard on every step as he cascaded to the bottom like so much dirty linen, and he made a sound each time, like the whimpering of a beaten animal. The awful noise stopped, and everything was still. Her breathing came in hard, painful gasps, and she could not pry her fingers loose from the railing to which they desperately clung. She uttered a quick prayer that the man was either dead or unconscious, for if he was not, there was no telling what the consequences of her action might be.

Philipa became aware of noises outside on the porch. She thought she might be imagining them, but they were followed by an insistent pounding upon the front door.

"Philipa!"

The voice, she realized with relief, belonged to Father Michaels. She swallowed a painful gasp of air and tried to answer him, but her throat would not yield a sound. The handle rattled, and the door swung open on protesting hinges.

"Philipa!" he called again, louder. "Mr. Gavilan! Is everything—"

"Terry's in the parlor." She conquered her recalcitrant throat at last, still trying to command the hammering in her chest. "He's unconscious, Father Michaels! We must—we must get Roger—"

"At once, Fred!" Father Michaels's most forceful tone addressed another party, whose footsteps immediately scuttered off into the misty night.

"Philipa, what has happened here? Why are you in the dark?" the priest demanded, moving into the hall. "And what is this . . ."

Philipa maneuvered herself to a sitting position at the top of the stairs, finding some shred of composure. The rector had, no doubt, found Owen Parrish.

"Please find a lamp and light it, Father Michaels," she begged him, shaking from relief and sudden exhaustion. "I think if I have to stay here in the darkness for another moment, I'll scream again. There isn't time for explanations just now. We must get Terry to bed. He is—I'm afraid he—" She broke off, unable to persuade her throat to continue. A small golden light grew in the hall downstairs, and Philipa could barely see it through the tears in her eyes.

Philipa and Father Michaels managed to get Terry into bed after stretching Owen Parrish out on the hall floor under the stairs. The secretary was dead. Philipa offered no explanation to the priest, being far more concerned about Terry. His color was not good, and his breathing was shallow and irregular.

His condition reminded Philipa, chillingly, of Beatrice Waverly on her deathbed. She got his clothes off him, with

Father Michaels's assistance, and bathed his brow with a washcloth wrung in a basin of cool water. He did not seem feverish, but she could think of nothing more to do for him. She wanted to cry, seeing him in this comatose state, but the tears, for better or for worse, would not come. Instead, they translated into action, and to prayer. For she was praying, although not with words. Every act she performed became a prayer for Terry's recovery. When at last there was nothing more to be done but to wait for Roger, Father Michaels pulled two chairs close by Terry's bedside and made her sit in one, while he occupied the other.

"How did all of this come about, Philipa?" the rector asked her in a gentle voice that radiated patience. "I don't like to press you, under the circumstances. But there will be inquiries. Perhaps it would be easier for you if you sorted it out now."

Philipa sighed. In halting words, she told Father Michaels of Owen Parrish's appearance, and of his revelation that he was Thomas Goliard. She recounted, as best she could, their dialogue that resulted in her sending the unfaithful secretary down the stairs to his death. She fell silent, staring at Terry's handsome, slack features, which looked in the pale light as though they might have been carved from ivory, or from the white granite of a cemetery monument.

"There is a piece of this puzzle missing, I think," the priest prompted her quietly. "The house was completely dark. Mr. Gavilan was seated alone in the parlor. Is there anything else you wish to tell me, Philipa?"

She had no secrets from Father Michaels, it seemed. The rector knew her all too well. She swallowed hard several times, blinking back more tears as she kept her gaze on Terry's immobile features.

"I reproached him over Jessamyn," she admitted, filled with remorse over her behavior. "I told him that—that I was considering an annulment, that I couldn't bear the thought that he might have been responsible for her death. He must have been failing even then, for he never uttered another word to me. Oh, Father Michaels, what if those were the very last words he was ever to hear me say?"

Father Michaels said nothing. For a time, the only sound in the room was that of three people breathing.

"Did you really mean them?"

She nodded, slowly.

"Yes," she all but whispered. "I love him, Father. I'll always love him. But I can't bear what's happened to Jessamyn, and to her family. I can't bear to think that Terry may have played a part in it, however small."

"Jessamyn Flaherty," Father Michaels said thoughtfully after a minute, "is in the company of the saints. She has already forgiven him, if there was any forgiveness necessary. As has our Heavenly Father. Can you as his wife, Philipa, do anything less?"

Philipa tore her gaze away from Terry's distressingly peaceful features and stared at the priest in wonder. He was regarding her with a blank look, although there was rebuke in his eyes. She knew at once that he was right. Filled suddenly with shame, she could not form an answer for him.

Fred Hanover escorted a weary Dr. Waverly into Terry's bedroom, and Roger immediately fell to tending the stricken entrepreneur. Father Michaels dispatched Fred to the police to attend to the matter of Owen Parrish. And Philipa, her heart in her mouth, watched as Roger conducted his examination of her husband. The doctor looked into his patient's eyes, whose lids he lifted with his thumbs. He listened to his chest with his stethoscope, and took his pulse. He examined the wound, now clotted over and actually quite small, although the area around it bore a respectable purple bruise. Philipa monitored his activity hopefully, watching as he straightened from his examination.

When he turned to face her, his features were grim.

"This isn't good, Philipa," he said tersely, shaking his head once. "It's very unusual for a patient with this kind of an injury to behave in a perfectly normal fashion one minute and to be completely unconscious the next, especially after the passage of a day or more. When it does happen, it's often a sign of internal bleeding, or swelling of the brain. If that is, as I suspect, the case here, there is nothing we can do for him except to watch and wait."

"Wait?" Philipa was trembling. "Wait for what?"

Roger Waverly sighed. He looked exhausted. She dreaded his answer.

"I'm afraid it's—it's very much like Beatrice's situation, Philly," he breathed, pulling the stethoscope from around his neck with a resigned gesture. "It's a matter of time. He will either come back to himself within a day or so, or—" The doctor stopped, looking away from her again.

Philipa's legs evaporated beneath her. She took hold of Roger's rumpled lapels, desperately looking for solace in his eyes.

"You—you can't mean that, Dr. Waverly!" she argued in a whisper, stunned. "Terry's a young man! He can't d—"

The word refused to come forth from her throat. Roger regarded her with a look of profound weariness, as though he had taken the burden of all of these lives upon himself, like some distressed Prometheus.

"Younger men than him have died," the doctor muttered, glancing over his shoulder at the patient once again. "And women, too. I'm sorry, Philipa. But I know you would want the truth."

She released him, as if by so doing she could disassociate herself from the tidings he had imparted.

"Then," she said slowly, finding the back of the chair to hold on to, "there is nothing . . . ?"

She could not finish her question. A heavy mass swelled in her throat, pressing tears into her eyes and making it difficult for her to breathe.

Roger shook his head once again, although the movement was barely perceptible.

"Nothing," the doctor replied evenly. "Except for your husband's own will to continue living. But you mustn't give up hope, Philly. It is altogether possible that his love for you may be strong enough to pull him back from the edge. Time alone will tell."

Philipa swallowed, trying to relieve the obstruction in her throat. Her action had exactly the opposite effect. Rather than finding comfort in Roger's words, she grew more desolate. Had she already sealed her husband's doom with her self-righteous pronouncements? She abandoned Roger and sat down on the edge of the bed.

Terry's handsome, angular features were loose and expressionless, and he did not move. His lips were slightly parted, but his mouth, which she could so vividly recall widening with a grin, seemed smaller than usual. She thought of Beatrice Waverly, and how her death had changed her features into a strange and unfamiliar aspect. Could this change in Terry mean that he was beginning to die, already?

She took up Terry's heavy, lifeless hand, holding it tightly in both of hers. An awful weight pressed in on her, the weight of tears struggling to stay hidden away inside her. *Please don't die, Terry,* she thought, pressing her face against his cool hand. *Please don't leave me now, before I have the chance to tell you . . .* There were droplets of salty water on his fingers as well as on her own. Her chest ached so badly that she thought, even hoped, that she might die, herself.

Chapter Thirty-five

Life, it became apparent to Philipa sometime during that long night, was going to go on, whether or not Terry survived his affliction. She was acutely reminded of this fact by the gnawing pain in her stomach the following morning reminding her that she had not eaten since noon the day before. Terry had not moved, as far as she could tell, and although she was reluctant to leave him alone, she finally succumbed to her various needs and abandoned him, resolving to return shortly.

While she puttered awkwardly in the unfamiliar, decimated kitchen, she was interrupted by a knock on the back door. She frowned, wiping her hands on the dish towel affixed as an apron about her waist. Who could it be? she wondered. The police had seemed satisfied the previous evening when they had removed Owen Parrish's body from the hallway. Perhaps it was Father Michaels?

She was surprised to find Mrs. Grant standing outside, her grandmotherly features placid but unsmiling, bearing two large canvas sacks brimming with groceries. Relieved and grateful, Philipa hurriedly ushered her into the kitchen.

"Mrs. Grant, you have no idea how happy I am to see

you," she murmured to her housekeeper, closing the door behind the woman. "Have you seen the house? Have you heard about—"

Mrs. Grant, having unburdened herself of her parcels upon the kitchen table, put up a broad, gloved hand.

"I have seen the house," she said in a resigned tone, shaking her head sadly. "And I have heard about everything. I didn't know what sort of a state you might be finding yourself in here, so I thought I'd take it upon myself to find out. And besides"—she fished into the bottom of one of the brimming sacks—"there's something in here I got from the house. I thought you might need it."

To Philipa's astonishment, Mrs. Grant lifted out the stack of white pages which was *The Tender Trap.* The housekeeper unceremoniously dropped the bundle onto the table with a resounding slap.

"I wouldn't expect looting in Braedon's Beach," Mrs. Grant remarked matter-of-factly. "But you never can tell. I didn't think you'd want that left about."

Philipa stared from the unscarred manuscript to the unsmiling features of her housekeeper, who met her gaze evenly. She could not speak. Mrs. Grant waited.

"How did you—" Philipa muttered on a breath, aware that her shock must be etched on her features.

Mrs. Grant allowed a half-smile, her watery blue eyes wrinkling at the corners.

"Oh, I've known for quite some time," she replied, looking pleased. "Two years, at least. You were very careful, miss. But I'm a thorough housekeeper. Naturally, I never said anything to you. It wasn't my place. Anyway, I've been a fan of Emma Hunt's, myself. It tickled me that you wrote those stories. Many's the time I wanted to boast to my friends, but I've held my tongue. It got so I enjoyed the secret, too. Then when I read that bit in the paper, about Emma Hunt's dying, I thought: now, why would she want to go and do a thing like that? Then all the business with Mr. Gavilan started, and it became clear to me."

Philipa stared at the woman, who returned her gaze as if she might be the cat that ate the proverbial canary.

"Well?" Mrs. Grant demanded, smiling a little more. "Say something!"

"Mrs. Grant," Philipa obeyed with a shake her head, "you are even more amazing than I ever suspected. Thank you. Thank you. I—you can't know what a relief it is, after all these years, to talk with someone about this. There were times when I thought I'd go mad, or that I was mad already. This, you realize, is Emma Hunt's last tome. Her requiem, as it were. I was going to post it on the day of the hurricane."

Mrs. Grant nodded quickly, seeming to be embarrassed to propriety by Philipa's impulsive revelation. She emptied the bags of their contents, which proved to be grocery staples.

"I'd be pleased to take care of it for you," the woman mumbled in a gruff tone. "After I see to things in here, that is. This place is in a state! What became of Mr. Gavilan's housekeeper?"

Philipa sighed heavily, reminded of Terry.

"I don't know," she admitted, looking about at the topsy-turvy room. "I haven't had much time to think about it. Arliss's sister has died, Mrs. Grant, and Ter—Mr. Gavilan is—is—"

Philipa's eyes filled with tears again. Quickly she looked away from her housekeeper, blinking them back. She wondered, after the last 24 hours, how it was that she had any tears remaining.

"Yes, I know," Mrs. Grant told her. "Now get on with you, miss. I told you, I'll take care of these things. You have your hands full right now, and your heart as well, I'm sure."

Mrs. Grant abandoned her domestic occupations and guided Philipa toward the kitchen door with gentle but firm hands upon her shoulders.

"I'll bring up breakfast in a bit, as soon as I get this stove going. And I'll go back to the house later and collect such of your things as I may. That's one more worry you don't need right now, I'll warrant. So just you go and look after your Mr. Gavilan. Tell him I asked after him. He thinks I don't like him."

Philipa could not help but smile wryly. Terry had said the very same thing to her, not long ago. Mrs. Grant was wiser than even she, Philipa, had given her credit for being.

"I'll tell him," she promised the housekeeper, who appeared satisfied by her words. *And I'll pray that he hears me*, she thought wearily as she left Mrs. Grant alone in the kitchen.

Philipa was away from Terry only long enough to bathe and change, once her things had been fetched from her house. By supper time, she was discouraged to note that his condition had not altered. She was about to consider sending for Dr. Waverly for no better reason than to hear the sound of his voice when Mrs. Grant ushered Roger into the room. Philipa rose from her chair beside Terry's bed to greet him, and the older man embraced her tenderly, as the daughter she would now never be to him.

"I'm so glad you've come, Roger," she said simply, aware of an overwhelming weariness. She so wanted this to be over, to know whether Terry was going to live or die. The waiting was taking its toll on her.

"I had to come, child," he whispered, pressing her against his breast. "I couldn't leave you alone with this. I couldn't continue to allow you to think . . ."

His voice trailed off. Frowning, Philipa pushed him back, but remained in his embrace.

"What do you mean, Roger?" she urged him. "Have you something more to tell me about Terry? About his condition? What is it? Tell me!"

She held on to his lapels, shaking them. Roger, looking as fragile as he had upon his own wife's death, covered her hands with his own, his gray eyes infinitely sad. Philipa saw a shadow pass before her eyes, and she thought she might faint.

"What is it, Roger?" she forced herself to ask again, although she dreaded his answer.

He swallowed hard, his eyes veiled.

"It isn't about Terry," he assured her. "Not directly, anyway. Sit down, please, Philly. This will not be easy for me to say, or, I am sure, for you to hear."

Philipa sat down in the chair beside Terry's bed where she

had passed most of the day. Roger sat beside her, covering her hand with his. She could not bring herself to look at him as he spoke.

"I paid a call this morning upon Jessamyn Flaherty's . . . abortionist." He spoke in a low, quivering tone that made Philipa blanch. "I don't know the woman's real name, but she is well known in darker circles for her butchery. The law, for some reason, cannot touch her. She told me something I think you should know."

Philipa wanted to stop her ears. She wanted to plead with Roger to hold his peace. Having disobeyed enough requests in the last day to make her regret her impetuousness for the remainder of her life, she wanted nothing more than to forget that there had ever been a Jessamyn Flaherty, much less that she had died in such a fashion. Her throat, however, remained mutinously silent.

"It seems," Roger went on in a faint tone, "Jessamyn was well along in this pregnancy. Four or five months, at least. In view of the fact that Terence Gavilan only came to Braedon's Beach in mid May, it is medically impossible that he could have fathered the child."

Before her, on the bed, Terry continued to breathe in his shallow, regular manner, not moving. She watched him, allowing the import of Roger's statement to penetrate her consciousness. Terry, Roger was saying, had not been the instrument of that tragedy. He was, as far as the senseless death, blameless. Whatever else he may at one time have been to Jessamyn Flaherty, he had not been the cause of her last desperate act. Relief blended with profound remorse within Philipa as she continued to gaze upon the motionless face of the man whom she loved more than life itself.

"Thank you, Roger." She found her voice at last, although only a small portion of it ventured forth.

The room was quiet. Roger did not move from his place, or take his hand from hers.

"There is—there is something else which honor constrains me to say, Philipa."

Philipa closed her eyes. Whatever Roger had to say could not, she was certain, cause her any more relief, or pain, than

what he had just revealed to her. She inhaled deeply and released a broken sigh.

"Some months ago," Roger was going on quietly without
prompting, "I had a rather ugly confrontation with my son. I
won't belabor the details, Philipa, but—and it pains me to tell
you this—he confessed to me that he—that he himself had
been seeing Jess Flaherty on a regular basis for some time.
My own son. My own son may have been—"

Roger stopped. Philipa thought she had imagined the entire
monologue. Slowly she turned toward the doctor, who sat
utterly still beside her. His gray face was a study of anguish.

"Elliot?"

She could only conjure that one word, trying to comprehend the import of this revelation, and its interwoven meaning
in the fabric of the recent months of her life. In light of Roger's confession, it appeared that Terry had saved her from
far more than a loveless marriage.

"I am sorry, Philipa," Roger breathed, like a deflating balloon. "I'm sorry I tried to keep pushing the two of you together, even after I had been made to see what my son—had
been doing. I have never been more glad than I am right now
that you had the wisdom to break off your engagement to
him. I find myself wondering now if—if I will ever be able
to forgive him for this tragedy, myself."

Philipa was silent. She returned her gaze to her husband,
and reached for his pale cheek. It felt warm; or were her hands
so cold? She could not tell which. She stared at him hard:
had his facial muscles twitched, or had she imagined it? She
watched, but he did not move again. She remembered that
Roger still sat beside her, waiting.

"Jessamyn has already forgiven him, if he is responsible."
She echoed Father Michaels's own earlier words to her. "And
so has God. He is your son, Roger. He loves you. You love
him. Hasn't there been more than enough tragedy in our lives
during these last few weeks without useless recriminations?"

"You have a loving heart, my dear, dear, girl," Roger said,
his voice husky. "God bless you. Yes, we have, haven't we?
And it isn't over yet, I fear. Take heart, though: I can't believe
that the Lord would have given you this long-awaited love,

only to strip it from you. Don't let him go, Philly. You must fight for him. We must both fight for him, for he is too weak to fight for himself, now.''

When Roger had gone, Mrs. Grant came into the room in her dressing gown, carrying a lamp and a paper portfolio. She asked after Terry, glancing at him on the bed, nodding curtly when Philipa told her there was no change in his condition.

"Perhaps it would be best if you slept in a bed tonight, miss," Mrs. Grant suggested, eying her critically. "You can't keep this up. You'll wear yourself to a thread."

Too late for that, Philipa thought wearily, but she found a brief smile for her housekeeper.

"I'll stay here for the night, Mrs. Grant," she replied, arching her stiff back. "Dr. Waverly thinks that the change— whatever it might be—will happen very soon. I must be here. In either case, I feel it will all be over—soon."

Her voice trembled, but there were no tears remaining. She did not feel as though she could ever cry again.

Mrs. Grant nodded again, and Philipa looked away from her shrewd, knowing gaze.

"I never got to the post office today," she said, handing Philipa the portfolio. "I will tomorrow. I thought you might like *The Tender Trap* for a little company tonight while you sit up with him."

Philipa took the offering from her, nodding her thanks, and bade the woman good night. Noticing an ache of weariness in the side of her neck, she made her way back to her chair at Terry's side.

Terry's condition had not changed. Sighing, Philipa adjusted the covers about his chest and bent to kiss his forehead. How long, Terry? she wondered, allowing her fingers to smooth back his sable locks. She resumed her vigil in the chair, setting the portfolio containing the manuscript on the nightstand beside a small, well-worn book. With weary curiosity, she picked up the book and examined its spine.

Fire Beach, it said, by Mrs. Emma Hunt.

She smiled to herself. She would have been shocked, she realized, glancing at Terry, had he not told her of his secret obsession already. She thumbed the pages, and the book fell

open to a spot as though the starch had long since been ironed
out of it at that place.

Gavilan floated down gently through a spacious, dark tun-
nel onto a soft, fragrant, cotton mat. He did not want to move,
although he knew he should try. He examined himself from
the inside out, cherishing the darkness that enveloped him.
There was no pain; no weariness. Only a warmth radiating
from his hand, as if the source of this heat had attached itself
firmly to his fingers and palm. A small sound issued from his
throat after a breath, and he knew he was alive. He opened
his eyes.

There was a line of rosy golden light across the ceiling of
his room. The dawn was creeping uninvited through the window. Outside, noisy starlings argued over territorial rights.
The gulls broke up the arguments, moving in by force. Looking down, Gavilan saw that Philipa's hand had been the
source of warmth, holding his firmly even as she slept with
her head upon his coverlet. He wanted to touch her hair, but
could not will himself to accomplish so complex a gesture as
yet.

Philipa, he thought, although his mind could not yet bring
into focus the events leading to this circumstance. All he
could remember was darkness.

A short time later, the sun was higher. The room was
brighter. Still Philipa slept at his side, leaning over from a
chair beside the bed. Her hold on his hand had not loosened.
In fact, he felt as though he had gained strength from its firm,
warm grip. He drew in a deep breath, feeling as though the
greater capacity of his lungs had lain dormant for an unknown
span of time.

The fingers of his left hand moved. He exercised them,
enjoying the sensation. This, he thought, is what it must be
like to be a baby just coming into the world.

God, he felt wonderful!

For a moment he considered awakening Philipa. She looked
so peaceful beside him, though, that he decided against it.
There would be time enough, he thought, remembering the

night of the hurricane with no small satisfaction. They had all of their lives ahead of them.

He turned his head and saw an unfamiliar bundle on his nightstand. Gently, stealthily, so as not to disturb Philipa, he drew his hand from hers. Surprised by his strength and co-ordination, he reached for the portfolio, wondering at its contents.

Chapter Thirty-six

"Slow down!" Philipa admonished Terry, pulling back upon his arm. "You are taking far too brisk a pace for a man recovering from a head wound."

Terry made a sound of impatience. He turned toward her, squinting against the July sunshine. A gust of ocean breeze nearly took his skimmer, but he saved it just in time.

"I have married a general, I think," he declared, but his smile belied his annoyance. "Or at least a most bossy woman."

But he did, thereafter, reduce his speed. It was a beautiful day for a stroll on the Promenade. Repairs from the hurricane the week before had already begun. Merchants had even made shift to continue doing business, except for Terry's own concerns. Philipa had not allowed him to resume work, not until he had proved to her that he could walk the whole length of the Promenade and back without tiring. He had argued with her most persuasively, pointing out that it had taken him hardly any time at all to resume his husbandly duties, but she persevered. Today, three days after he had emerged from his unconscious state, was the test of that feat.

"From the look of the arcade, I might as well rebuild as repair," Terry remarked, pausing in the trek to survey the wreckage of the place. "But the first order of business must be to hire a new secretary, I suppose. Owen used to put out for bids. I'll miss his expertise. Although I must admit, I won't miss him. Don't tell Father Michaels I said that. It's a rather un-Christian thing to think, isn't it?"

"It so happens," Philipa replied, looking straight ahead, "that I agree with you. Moreover, I don't think our opinions mattered much to Mr. Parrish, anyway."

Terry stared for a time at the ruined arcade.

"Will I ever know what passed between you two that night?" he wondered aloud.

Philipa did not answer him right away. She had not revealed the whole story of Owen Parrish's untimely demise, except to say that the man had tried to rape her. Terry, when he had awakened, had not pressed her for more details. She suspected, however, that her husband knew there was more to the story.

"Will it make you feel better if I tell you?" she countered his question softly.

She felt his hand on her own, and the gesture impelled her to meet his gaze.

"I think it would make you feel better, Philipa," he said simply, his dark-eyed gaze penetrating her soul. "When you're ready. It's been a difficult time for you, too, I know."

Philipa did not answer. They began to walk again, slowly. Since Terry had awakened, she had told him much. Roger's disclosure had been, to her, a revelation which had liberated her from all guilt surrounding her dealings with Elliot, and from any misgiving about her future with Terry. Terry had not reproached her for her feelings after Jessamyn's death, even saying that he understood how she felt. But there remained, she knew, one last barricade between them that she had not yet been able to breach.

Emma Hunt.

Until she did that, she could not divulge the whole of the Owen Parrish business. And until she did *that*, she knew, watching the surf tug playfully at the beach, she would not be free to love Terry with her whole heart.

She prayed daily, as Father Michaels had suggested, for courage. For a sign. She had tried, in the last few days, to broach the subject with Terry in every way she knew. It amazed her that, for all the clever words she had conjured during Emma Hunt's rather scandalous career, she could not seem to piece together a monologue which would reveal her secret to the man she loved so desperately that at times she thought her heart would burst.

"We'll order a new carousel at once." Terry looked sadly at the ruins of the amusement court. "Although I've been thinking: perhaps a pier out over the ocean might be a better venue. Think of the attraction, Philipa!" His enthusiasm was apparent in his voice. "Think of the wonder of it! Think of our children on that carousel, with the sea breeze in their faces."

His words made her think of something else.

"Do you mean," she ventured, her fingers tightening about his elbow, "that you plan for us to live here in Braedon's Beach? Permanently?"

He pulled his arm from her grasp and faced her again, taking hold of her arms with his two strong hands.

"Where else," he intoned, his sable eyes absorbing her with that intense, adoring look she so loved, "would Henry and Julia Braedon's grandchildren live?"

"Oh, Terry." She breathed, feeling lightheaded at his closeness. "I haven't dared to hope you would want to stay, but—do you mean it? Truly?"

His angular features softened with a smile that was as intimate as if they were alone together in their bedroom.

"As truly as I stand here," he said, just above a whisper. "And as truly as I love you, Philipa Braedon Gavilan."

If the other strollers on the Promenade that morning were offended by the public demonstration of affection that followed, none of them gave notice of it. Perhaps, Philipa thought later, the residents of Braedon's Beach were by now accustomed to Terence Gavilan's eccentricities, as well as her own.

*   *   *

Charles Tavistock behaved that evening in a fashion that was almost human. Essie had been true to her word, orchestrating a lovely, lavish dinner party in honor of the newlyweds in spite of the animosities between her and Philipa's husbands. Indeed, to all appearances, Charles and Terry reconciled, or at least temporarily set aside their differences for the evening. The men, Mayor Brewster, Father Michaels and others, were intensely interested in Terry's embryonic plans for the Promenade. Even Charles crowed his approval, offering the bank's support of Terry's proposals.

Philipa's heart swelled with pride as she beheld the acceptance the community had extended to him. She could not help but recall a time not very long before when Terence Gavilan's motives had been suspect, and his plans held up for scrutiny in minute detail. She had to drag him away from the party near midnight, insisting he needed his rest before his workday, which the walk earlier had earned him.

It was a warm night. The sky was clear, and a three-quarter moon afforded a pale glow to the town. Philipa felt wonderful. The night needed but one element to render it perfect.

"Shall we walk down to the beach, Terry?" she asked, slipping her arm into his. "I would like to see the house. It probably won't look as bad in the moonlight. Perhaps it will be easier to face in the day, after I've seen it at night."

Beside her, Terry chuckled.

"Are you sure there isn't some other reason why you want to walk on the beach?" he teased her tenderly.

Against her will, Philipa trembled. Arianna, she thought. And Philip. The lovers of *Fire Beach*. What better guise under which to reveal her secret to him? She quickened her pace, and Terry's chuckle became a laugh.

"What's your hurry?" he asked. "The beach isn't going anywhere."

But he quickened his step with her, as though anticipating something wondrous himself.

The moon afforded just enough light upon the beach, but not too much. Philipa could barely keep herself from skipping on the warm sand. For so long, she had tried to find a way to tell him. Now, suddenly, she could barely keep the words inside of her.

It was low tide. There would be no undertow, she thought with relief. Just the warm waters of the North Atlantic on a July night.

"There, just beyond those lights," Terry offered in a conversational tone. "That dark, ominous-looking building. Isn't that your house?"

It was. It didn't look so very bad, Philipa thought, pleased. If the interior had not sustained much damage, it would probably not take much to fix it up. It would certainly be an attractive rental prospect to a summer family, with its private beach . . .

It was as if some unearthly spirit possessed her suddenly. She unhooked her arm from Terry's and began to trot, then to run, up the dark beach, toward the waves. Terry called her name, but there was no panic in his voice, merely wonder. There was no light from the Braedon house, so the beach was even darker than it might have been, except for the pale, seductive light of the moon. Before she quite knew what she was doing, Philipa began unbuttoning her shirtwaist. A feeling of peace enveloped her. She realized, smiling to herself, that she had been a fool to worry.

"Philipa, what are you—"

Somewhere behind her, Terry stopped. She did not answer him. She continued undressing slowly, enjoying every new liberation of her body from its rigid confinement. It was a matter of minutes before she stood completely unclothed in the darkness, gazing upon the rushing sea.

"Philipa!"

There was awe in his quiet baritone. She turned toward him, a slow smile spreading across her mouth. The moon was high and she knew, standing five feet away from him, that he could see her face in its glow. She could see his, as well. His eyes were wide with amazement.

"Philipa!" he said again, only this time it came forth as a whisper.

"Swim with me," she invited him, and he stared at her for only an instant before his jacket came off.

Philipa did not wait for him to disrobe. She stepped into the ocean, thrilling to the feel of the tepid salt water teasing her ankles as it rushed past. The water became deep very quickly in low tide, and soon she was bobbing in the waves.

"It's cold!"

That was Terry. Marveling at the speed with which he had undressed, she faced him in the water. He was beside her, his expression at once amazed and triumphant.

"I've been trying to find a way to tell you," she said as he pulled her close to him. "Then I saw *Fire Beach* on your nightstand. I nearly laughed when I saw the page to which it opened."

His intense, adoring gaze drew a warm blush to her cheeks, even in the cool surf.

"Emma Hunt," he intoned with a broad smile, wrapping his bare arms about her. "This explains Owen. And a few other things."

Philipa felt deliciously weak in his embrace.

"Are you terribly disappointed in me, my love?" she whispered, settling her arms about his neck as she continued to monitor his gaze.

A wave nearly tumbled them over their heads. Philipa cried out and clung more tightly to Terry's neck.

He did not let her go, and she did not try to escape. It felt too good, being this near to him, being free at last of her terrible burden. In a very real sense, they had never been closer to one another than they were in that moment.

"Disappointed," he replied softly in her ear as the wave broke on the shoreline, "is hardly how I would put it."

His warm breath sent a familiar ripple along her spine, as if a playful sea creature had tickled her.

"And how would you put it, Mr. Gavilan?" she inquired breathlessly, wishing his eyes would always burn into her so brightly.

"As we did at Mrs. Minnick's," he replied, a faint smile playing upon his wide mouth and in his eyes. "And as Jack and Sarah did in *The Tender Trap*."

Philipa swallowed a mouthful of salt water and coughed.

"Where—how—" she sputtered, stunned by his revelation.

He stopped her words with a gentle kiss that quieted her heart as well.

"Books left on a nightstand are fair game to both of us, my sweet," he murmured, punctuating his declaration with another kiss, and another. "I awoke sooner than you thought. Although I did not have a chance to read the full manuscript."

The water became very warm. It seemed to press them together. Philipa closed her eyes, smiling.

"Would you like me to tell you how it ends?" she offered, rubbing her cheek against his.

"You are a consummate storyteller, my darling; I would be the first to admit," he assured her with a smile in his voice that stirred her. "But I think I would rather that you showed me, instead."

"Incorrigible," she murmured, finding his mouth with her own. "Delightful man . . ."

The moon obligingly found a cloud behind which to hide for a time.

SPECIAL SNEAK PREVIEW FOLLOWS!

Madeline Baker writing as Amanda Ashley

Cursed by the darkness, he searches through the ages for the redeeming light, the one woman who can save him. An angel of purity and light, she fears the handsome stranger whose eyes promise endless ecstasy even while his mouth whispers dark secrets. They are two people longing for fulfillment, yearning for a love like no other. Alone, they will face a desolate destiny. Together, they will share undying passion, defy eternity, and embrace the night.

**Don't miss *Embrace The Night!*
Available now at bookstores
and newsstands everywhere.**

He walked the streets for hours after he left the orphanage, his thoughts filled with Sara, her fragile beauty, her sweet innocence, her unwavering trust. She had accepted him into her life without question, and the knowledge cut him to the quick. He did not like deceiving her, hiding the dark secret of what he was, nor did he like to think about how badly she would be hurt when his nighttime visits ceased, as they surely must.

He had loved her from the moment he first saw her, but always from a distance, worshiping her as the moon might worship the sun, basking in her heat, her light, but wisely staying away lest he be burned.

And foolishly, he had strayed too close. He had soothed her tears, held her in his arms, and now he was paying the price. He was burning, like a moth drawn to a flame. Burning with need. With desire. With an unholy lust, not for her body, but for the very essence of her life.

It sickened him that he should want her that way, that he could even consider such a despicable thing. And yet he could think of little else. Ah, to hold her in his arms, to feel his body become one with hers as he drank of her sweetness. . . .

For a moment, he closed his eyes and let himself imagine it, and then he swore a long vile oath filled with pain and longing.

Hands clenched, he turned down a dark street, his self-anger turning to loathing, and the loathing to rage. He felt the need to kill, to strike out, to make someone else suffer as he was suffering.

Pity the poor mortal who next crossed his path, he thought. Then he gave himself over to the hunger pounding through him.

She woke covered with perspiration, Gabriel's name on her lips. Shivering, she drew the covers up to her chin.

It had only been a dream. Only a dream.

She spoke the words aloud, finding comfort in the sound of her own voice. A distant bell chimed the hour. Four o'clock.

Gradually, her breathing returned to normal. Only a dream, she said again, but it had been so real. She had felt the cold breath of the night, smelled the rank odor of fear rising from the body of the faceless man cowering in the shadows. She had sensed a deep anger, a wild uncontrollable evil personified by a being in a flowing black cloak. Even now, she could feel his anguish, his loneliness, the alienation that cut him off from the rest of humanity.

It had all been so clear in the dream, but now it made no sense. No sense at all.

With a slight shake of her head, she snuggled deeper under the covers and closed her eyes.

It was just a dream, nothing more.

Sunk in the depths of despair, Gabriel prowled the deserted abbey. What had happened to his self-control? Not for centuries had he taken enough blood to kill, only enough to assuage the pain of the hunger, to ease his unholy thirst.

A low groan rose in his throat. Sara had happened. He wanted her and he couldn't have her. Somehow, his desire and his frustration had gotten tangled up with his lust for blood.

It couldn't happen again. It had taken him centuries to learn to control the hunger, to give himself the illusion that he was more man than monster.

Had he been able, he would have prayed for forgiveness, but he had forfeited the right to divine intervention long ago.

"Where will we go tonight?"

Gabriel stared at her. She'd been waiting for him again, clothed in her new dress, her eyes bright with anticipation. Her goodness drew him, soothed him, calmed his dark side even as her beauty, her innocence, teased his desire.

He stared at the pulse throbbing in her throat. "Go?"

Sara nodded.

With an effort, he lifted his gaze to her face. "Where would you like to go?"

"I don't suppose you have a horse?"

"A horse?"

"I've always wanted to ride."

He bowed from the waist. "Whatever you wish, milady," he said. "I'll not be gone long."

It was like having found a magic wand, Sara mused as she waited for him to return. She had only to voice her desire, and he produced it.

Twenty minutes later, she was seated before him on a prancing black stallion. It was a beautiful animal, tall and muscular, with a flowing mane and tail.

She leaned forward to stroke the stallion's neck. His coat felt like velvet beneath her hand. "What's his name?"

"Necromancer," Gabriel replied, pride and affection evident in his tone.

"Necromancer? What does it mean?"

"One who communicates with the spirits of the dead."

Sara glanced at him over her shoulder. "That seems an odd name for a horse."

"Odd, perhaps," Gabriel replied cryptically, "but fitting."

"Fitting? In what way?"

"Do you want to ride, Sara, or spend the night asking foolish questions?"

She pouted prettily for a moment and then grinned at him. "Ride!"

A word from Gabriel and they were cantering through the dark night, heading into the countryside.

"Faster," Sara urged.

"You're not afraid?"

"Not with you."

"You should be afraid, Sara Jayne," he muttered under his breath, "especially with me."

He squeezed the stallion's flanks with his knees and the horse shot forward, his powerful hooves skimming across the ground.

Sara shrieked with delight as they raced through the darkness. This was power, she thought, the surging body of the horse, the man's strong arm wrapped securely around her waist. The wind whipped through her hair, stinging her cheeks and making her eyes water, but she only threw back her head and laughed.

"Faster!" she cried, reveling in the sense of freedom that surged within her.

Hedges and trees and sleeping farmhouses passed by in a blur. Once, they jumped a four-foot hedge, and she felt as if she were flying. Sounds and scents blended together: the chirping of crickets, the bark of a dog, the smell of damp earth and lathered horseflesh, and over all the touch of Gabriel's breath upon her cheek, the steadying strength of his arm around her waist.

Gabriel let the horse run until the animal's sides were heaving and covered with foamy lather, and then he drew back on the reins, gently but firmly, and the stallion slowed, then stopped.

"That was wonderful!" Sara exclaimed.

She turned to face him, and in the bright light of the moon, he saw that her cheeks were flushed, her lips parted, her eyes shining like the sun.

How beautiful she was! His Sara, so full of life. What cruel fate had decreed that she should be bound to a wheelchair?

She was a vivacious girl on the brink of womanhood. She should be clothed in silks and satins, surrounded by gallant young men.

Dismounting, he lifted her from the back of the horse. Carrying her across the damp grass, he sat down on a large boulder, settling her in his lap.

"Thank you, Gabriel," she murmured.

"It was my pleasure, milady."

"Hardly that," she replied with a saucy grin. "I'm sure ladies don't ride pell-mell through the dark astride a big black devil horse."

"No," he said, his gray eyes glinting with amusement, "they don't."

"Have you known many ladies?"

"A few." He stroked her cheek with his forefinger, his touch as light as thistledown.

"And were they accomplished and beautiful?"

Gabriel nodded. "But none so beautiful as you."

She basked in his words, in the silent affirmation she read in his eyes.

"Who are you, Gabriel?" she asked, her voice soft and dreamy. "Are you man or magician?"

"Neither."

"But still my angel?"

"Always, *cara*."

With a sigh, she rested her head against his shoulder and closed her eyes. How wonderful, to sit here in the dark of night with his arms around her. She could almost forget that she was crippled. Almost.

She lost all track of time as she sat there, secure in his arms. She heard the chirp of crickets, the sighing of the wind through the trees, the pounding of Gabriel's heart beneath her cheek.

Her breath caught in her throat as she felt the touch of his hand in her hair and then the brush of his lips.

Abruptly, he stood up. Before she quite knew what was happening, she was on the horse's back and Gabriel was swinging up behind her. He moved with the lithe grace of a cat vaulting a fence.

She sensed a change in him, a tension she didn't understand. A moment later, his arm was locked around her waist and they were riding through the night.

She leaned back against him, braced against the solid wall of his chest. She felt his arm tighten around her, felt his breath on her cheek.

Pleasure surged through her at his touch and she placed her hand over his forearm, drawing his arm more securely around her, tacitly telling him that she enjoyed his nearness.

She thought she heard a gasp, as if he was in pain, but she shook the notion aside, telling herself it was probably just the wind crying through the trees.

Too soon, they were back at the orphanage.

"You'll come tomorrow?" she asked as he settled her in her bed, covering her as if she were a child.

"Tomorrow," he promised. "Sleep well, *cara.*"

"Dream of me," she murmured.

With a nod, he turned away. Dream of her, he thought. If only he could!

"Where would you like to go tonight?" Gabriel asked the following evening.

"I don't care, so long as it's with you."

Moments later, he was carrying her along a pathway in the park across from the orphanage.

Sara marveled that he held her so effortlessly, that it felt so right to be carried in his arms. She rested her head on his shoulder, content. A faint breeze played hide and seek with the leaves of the trees. A lover's moon hung low in the sky. The air was fragrant with night-blooming flowers, but it was Gabriel's scent that rose all around her—warm and musky, reminiscent of aged wine and expensive cologne.

He moved lightly along the pathway, his footsteps making hardly a sound. When they came to a stone bench near a quiet pool, he sat down, placing her on the bench beside him.

It was a lovely place, a fairy place. Elegant ferns, tall and lacy, grew in wild profusion near the pool. In the distance, she heard the questioning hoot of an owl.

"What did you do all day?" she asked, turning to look at him.

Gabriel shrugged. "Nothing to speak of. And you?"

"I read to the children. Sister Mary Josepha has been giving me more and more responsibility."

"And does that make you happy?"

"Yes. I've grown very fond of my little charges. They so need to be loved. To be touched. I had never realized how important it was, to be held, until—" A faint flush stained her cheeks. "Until you held me. There's such comfort in the touch of a human hand."

Gabriel grunted softly. Human, indeed, he thought bleakly.

Sara smiled. "They seem to like me, the children. I don't know why."

But he knew why. She had so much love to give, and no outlet for it.

"I hate to think of all the time I wasted wallowing in self-pity," Sara remarked. "I spent so much time sitting in my room, sulking because I couldn't walk, when I could have been helping the children, loving them." She glanced up at Gabriel. "They're so easy to love."

"So are you." He had not meant to speak the words aloud, but they slipped out. "I mean, it must be easy for the children to love you. You have so much to give."

She smiled, but it was a sad kind of smile. "Perhaps that's because no one else wants it."

"Sara—"

"It's all right. Maybe that's why I was put here, to comfort the little lost lambs that no one else wants."

I want you. The words thundered in his mind, in his heart, in his soul.

Abruptly, he stood up and moved away from the bench. He couldn't sit beside her, feel her warmth, hear the blood humming in her veins, sense the sadness dragging at her heart, and not touch her, take her.

He stared into the depths of the dark pool, the water as black as the emptiness of his soul. He'd been alone for so long, yearning for someone who would share his life, needing someone to see him for what he was and love him anyway.

A low groan rose in his throat as the centuries of loneliness wrapped around him.

"Gabriel?" Her voice called out to him, soft, warm, caring.

With a cry, he whirled around and knelt at her feet. Hesitantly, he took her hands in his.

"Sara, can you pretend I'm one of the children? Can you hold me, and comfort me, just for tonight?"

"I don't understand."

"Don't ask questions, *cara*. Please just hold me. Touch me."

She gazed down at him, into the fathomless depths of his dark gray eyes, and the loneliness she saw there pierced her heart. Tears stung her eyes as she reached for him.

He buried his face in her lap, ashamed of the need that he could no longer deny. And then he felt her hand stroke his hair, light as a summer breeze. Ah, the touch of a human hand, warm, fragile, pulsing with life.

Time ceased to have meaning as he knelt there, his head cradled in her lap, her hand moving in his hair, caressing his nape, feathering across his cheek. No wonder the children loved her. There was tranquility in her touch, serenity in her hand. A sense of peace settled over him, stilling his hunger. He felt the tension drain out of him, to be replaced with a nearly forgotten sense of calm. It was a feeling as close to forgiveness as he would ever know.

After a time, he lifted his head. Slightly embarrassed, he gazed up at her, but there was no censure in her eyes, no disdain, only a wealth of understanding.

"Why are you so alone, my angel?" she asked quietly.

"I have always been alone," he replied, and even now, when he was nearer to peace of spirit than he had been for centuries, he was aware of the vast gulf that separated him, not only from Sara, but from all of humanity as well.

Gently, she cupped his cheek with her hand. "Is there no one to love you then?"

"No one."

"I would love you, Gabriel."

"No!"

Stricken by the force of his denial, she let her hand fall

into her lap. "Is the thought of my love so revolting?"

"No, don't ever think that." He sat back on his heels, wishing that he could sit at her feet forever, that he could spend the rest of his existence worshiping her beauty, the generosity of her spirit. "I'm not worthy of you, *cara*. I would not have you waste your love on me."

"Why, Gabriel? What have you done that you feel unworthy of love?"

Filled with the guilt of a thousand lifetimes, he closed his eyes and his mind filled with an image of blood. Rivers of blood. Oceans of death. Centuries of killing, of bloodletting. Damned. The Dark Gift had given him eternal life—and eternal damnation.

Thinking to frighten her away, he let her look deep into his eyes, knowing that what she saw within his soul would speak more eloquently than words.

He clenched his hands, waiting for the compassion in her eyes to turn to revulsion. But it didn't happen.

She gazed down at his upturned face for an endless moment, and then he felt the touch of her hand in his hair.

"My poor angel," she whispered. "Can't you tell me what it is that haunts you so?"

He shook his head, unable to speak past the lump in his throat.

"Gabriel." His name, nothing more, and then she leaned forward and kissed him.

It was no more than a feathering of her lips across his, but it exploded through him like concentrated sunlight. Hotter than a midsummer day, brighter than lightning, it burned through him and for a moment he felt whole again. Clean again.

Humbled to the core of his being, he bowed his head so she couldn't see his tears.

"I will love you, Gabriel," she said, still stroking his hair. "I can't help myself."

"Sara—"

"You don't have to love me back," she said quickly. "I just wanted you to know that you're not alone anymore."

A long shuddering sigh coursed through him, and then he

took her hands in his, holding them tightly, feeling the heat of her blood, the pulse of her heart. Gently, he kissed her fingertips, and then, gaining his feet, he swung her into his arms.

"It's late," he said, his voice thick with the tide of emotions roiling within him. "We should go before you catch a chill."

"You're not angry?"

"No, *cara*."

How could he be angry with her? She was light and life, hope and innocence. He was tempted to fall to his knees and beg her forgiveness for his whole miserable existence.

But he couldn't burden her with the knowledge of what he was. He couldn't tarnish her love with the truth.

It was near dawn when they reached the orphanage. Once he had her settled in bed, he knelt beside her. "Thank you, Sara."

She turned on her side, a slight smile lifting the corners of her mouth as she took his hand in hers. "For what?"

"For your sweetness. For your words of love. I'll treasure them always."

"Gabriel." The smile faded from her lips. "You're not trying to tell me good-bye, are you?"

He stared down at their joined hands: hers small and pale and fragile, pulsing with the energy of life; his large and cold, indelibly stained with blood and death.

If he had a shred of honor left, he would tell her good-bye and never see her again.

But then, even when he had been a mortal man, he'd always had trouble doing the honorable thing when it conflicted with something he wanted. And he wanted—no, needed—Sara. Needed her as he'd never needed anything else in his accursed life. And perhaps, in a way, she needed him. And even if it wasn't so, it eased his conscience to think it true.

"Gabriel?"

"No, *cara*, I'm not planning to tell you good-bye. Not now. Not ever."

The sweet relief in her eyes stabbed him to the heart. And

he, cold, selfish monster that he was, was glad of it. Right or wrong, he couldn't let her go.

"Till tomorrow then?" she said, smiling once more.

"Till tomorrow, *cara mia*," he murmured. And for all the tomorrows of your life.

An Angel's Touch

Longer Than Forever
BRONWYN WOLFE

"A wonderful, magical love story that transcends
time and space. Definitely a keeper!"
—Madeline Baker

Patrick is in trouble, alone in turn-of-the-century Chicago,
and unjustly jailed with little hope for survival. Then the
honey-haired beauty comes to him, as if she has heard his
prayers.

Lauren has all but given up on finding true love when she
feels the green-eyed stranger's call—summoning her across
boundaries of time and space to join him in a struggle against
all odds; uniting them in a love that will last longer than
forever.

__52042-7 $5.99 US/$7.99 CAN

An Angel's Touch

Time Heals
SUSAN COLLIER

Tired of her nagging relatives, Maeve Fredrickson asks for the impossible: to be a thousand miles and a hundred years away from them. Then a heavenly being grants her wish, and she awakes in frontier Montana.

Saved from the wilderness by a handsome widower, Maeve loses her heart to her rescuer—and her temper over the antics of his three less-than-angelic children. As her angel prods her to fight for Seth, Maeve can only pray for the strength to claim a love made in paradise.

_52030-3 $4.99 US/$5.99 CAN

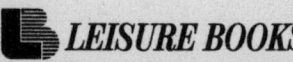